CLOSE ENCOUNTERS OF
THE ALIEN KIND. . . .

Have you ever wondered if other intelligent life-forms exist in the universe? Have you ever wished you could meet them? Well, now you can in such powerful and thought-provoking tales as:

"Fit to Print"—Frank had been coming to Bonner Bay ever since he was a small child. An isolated little hamlet by the sea, he thought it was the perfect haven—and it was until something else decided to get away to there, too. . . .

"Earth Surrenders"—They hadn't even been able to put a dent in the alien ships, and these invaders had effortlessly wiped out the Mars colony on their way to Earth. It looked like surrender was the only option—but there are all kinds of ways to surrender. . . .

"Random Acts"—His plane inexplicably late and haunted by dreams of an alien encounter, he was determined to uncover the truth—but nothing he'd ever imagined could have prepared him for the truth he discovered. . . .

"If Pigs Could Fly"—It was the scoop every reporter dreamed of, his very own first contact, he'd gotten it down on tape, and the aliens had given him an amazing gift. Now even his uncle would have to believe him—wouldn't he?

FIRST CONTACT

S0-BMR-805

FIRST CONTACT

edited by Martin H. Greenberg and Larry Segriff

DAW BOOKS, INC.

DONALD A. WOLLHEIM, FOUNDER

375 Hudson Street, New York, NY 10014

ELIZABETH R. WOLLHEIM
SHEILA E. GILBERT
PUBLISHERS

First Printing, July 1997
1   2   3   4   5   6   7   8   9

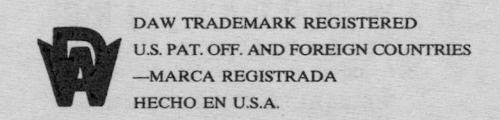

ACKNOWLEDGMENTS

Introduction © 1997 by Larry Segriff.
Fit to Print © 1997 by Kristine Kathryn Rusch.
A Game of Mehen © 1997 by Josepha Sherman.
Small Heroes © 1997 by Jane Lindskold.
Heavenly Host © 1997 by Nina Kiriki Hoffman.
We Have Met the Enemy © 1997 by Rosemary Edghill.
The Xaxrkling of J. Arnold Boysenberry © 1997 by David
   Bischoff.
Earth Surrenders © 1997 by Barbara Paul.
Objects Unidentified (Flying) © 1997 by Gordon Eklund.
Random Acts © 1997 by Marc Bilgrey.
If Pigs Could Fly © 1997 by Jack C. Haldeman II.
Kite People © 1997 by Gary A. Braunbeck.
Ambassador to the Promised Land © 1997 by
   Dean Wesley Smith.
Black Ops © 1997 by Barbara Delaplace.
Absolution © 1997 by Paul Dellinger.
Take Me to Your Leader © 1997 by Jody Lynn Nye.
The Seepage Factor © 1997 by John DeChancie.
The Allure of Bone and Ice © 1997 by Linda P. Baker.
First Contact, Inc. © 1997 by Julie E. Czerneda.
Palindromic © 1997 by Peter Crowther.

CONTENTS

INTRODUCTION

Twinkle, twinkle, little star . . .

Space has been called everything from the final frontier to the last, best hope for mankind. It promises wealth and wonder, treasure and mysteries, new worlds and new challenges. Perhaps most of all, it offers companionship and an answer to that age-old question: Are we alone?

The truth is out there. All we have to do is go out there and find it. But some of us don't want to wait that long, so we've asked today's top writers to show us their versions of what First Contact might be like. When we do finally meet our first aliens, will they be friendly, or will they materialize over Washington, D.C., and destroy our nation's capital? For that matter, will they even be truly alien at all?

First Contact. The words themselves are filled with hope and promise. And yet—and yet, they are also ominous and filled with threat. What lies out there, out among the stars, waiting for us? A galaxy-wide union of peace-loving races and planets? Extraterrestrial big brothers and sisters? Psychotic killers who want our planet and our resources? Or something so totally alien that they won't fit any of our expectations?

Turn the lights on bright, put out the welcome mat, and come with us now as we find out.

FIT TO PRINT
by Kristine Kathryn Rusch

Kristine Kathryn Rusch has worked as an editor at such places as Pulphouse publishing and most recently *The Magazine of Fantasy & Science Fiction,* though she is currently a full-time writer once again. Forthcoming novels include *Hitler's Angel* and *The Fey: The Rival.* Her short fiction appears in *Mystery Fairy Tales* and *Wizard Fantastic.* A winner of the Hugo, Locus, and World Fantasy Award, she lives in Oregon with her husband, author and editor Dean Wesley Smith.

First, let me give you the story as I reported it. From the Sunday edition of *The New York Times,* June 29, 1997:

MYSTERIOUS FIRE DESTROYS OREGON TOWN
FRANK BUTLER
SPECIAL CORRESPONDENT

PORTLAND, OR. June 27, 1997. Fifteen people died as fire destroyed the sleepy hamlet of Bonner Bay on the Central Oregon Coast. The fire, which began in a hotel north of town just after midnight yesterday, quickly became an inferno that raced down the town's main road, leaping from roof to roof.

Residents sought shelter in caves on the town's north end. The caves, accessible only on the beach in low tide, provided a safe haven for nearly 3,500 people.

"We're lucky the tide was out," Mayor Ruth Anderson said. "We're lucky the fire burned out before the tide came in."

Experts believe Bonner Bay's location contributed to the fire's quick spread and its quick end. Bonner

Bay was built on a four-mile-long rock ledge between two cliffs. With the ocean to the west, and the Coast Mountain Range to the east, Bonner Bay was isolated. Until 1950, Bonner Bay was inaccessible by land.

"By the time we learned of the fire, the entire bay was aflame," said Joe Roth of the Central Coast Fire District. "We couldn't get into the area, except by boat. I'm amazed anyone survived."

The fire burned out in a matter of hours, Roth said, "because it ran out of fuel."

The fifteen people who died were in the hotel where the fire started. Their names have not yet been released.

Four column inches. Four column inches to describe the experience of a lifetime.

My grandmother was born in Bonner Bay, and she retained a home there until she died. The home then became my family's West Coast vacation house. We rented it out most of the year for the additional income, and used it ourselves two weeks every summer. When my parents died, they bequeathed the home to my two siblings and me, and we decided to maintain the arrangement: vacation rental much of the year, with six weeks carved out for individual family time. During my marriage, my wife and I only went to Bonner Bay once. She was a native New Yorker, and the isolation terrified her.

I returned every summer after the divorce.

My two weeks in Bonner Bay ran from June 16 to June 30. This year, conveniently, the two-week period began on a Monday. I have three weeks of vacation at the *Times*—I've been on staff since 1970—and I usually used two of them in Bonner Bay.

A man could no get farther away from New York.

Bonner Bay was an old fishing community built around the turn of the last century. In the affluent twenties, Portland residents discovered it, and an enterprising businessman built a natatorium on the rock ledge overlooking the beach. Hundreds of homes were built in the small space, and almost all of them were abandoned in the 1930s. It wasn't until the fifties that the tourists redis-covered Bonner Bay.

I wrote it up in the mid-seventies for the *Times* travel section as a place that time forgot. And, indeed, it looked like a European fishing village. The nearby mountains had been deforested; the trees used to build the homes crammed side-by-side on the ledge. Because there was no main road, and no need of one, there were no streets. Only houses, packed together like an audi-ence in a concert hall.

Television hadn't touched the community. No broad-cast signals could come over the mountains. A local radio station tried to fill the gaps, but its performance barely rated above that of a community college station. Until the highway was carved through the cliffs, the food was either locally grown in the thin topsoil or brought in by ship. I remember childhood summers surviving only on the fish we caught because the local stores had run out of produce and basics before the weekly supply ships had come in.

The Bonner Bay of my adulthood had amenities cour-tesy of the highway: tiny shops that appealed to tourists; restaurants that specialized in seafood; and two grocery stores, one on either end of town. The town had cable and access to the more powerful coastal radio stations. The culture had finally invaded Bonner Bay.

Sort of.

Every time I drove in, I, too, noted the isolation. I spent my first nights in the upstairs bedroom still crammed with my great-grandparents' handmade furni-ture listening to the ocean and nothing else. I missed the sirens and the honks, the shouts and the bustle of the city that never sleeps. My Manhattan apartment with its constant noise comforted me, and it took days of ad-justing before Bonner Bay's silence gave me the peace I craved.

On my first full day, to orient myself, I always walked to the caves.

But on June 17th, as I followed 101's curves through Bonner Bay, I noted the town no longer had the peace I remembered.

Everyone was worried—everyone was talking—about the strangers.

The first hint that something was different were the pictures taped to so many windows. The pictures were usually hand-drawn on 8½"×11" paper. I had to see the image several times before I realized what it was: a tiny person in a circle that appeared to be floating on the crest of a wave. Even though I figured out the image, I didn't know what it was for. I decided to go to the center of Bonner Bay's universe to find out what was going on.

The hub of all local activity was the Bonner Bay Café. The café took up two lots in the exact center of town. The original café was a shack that still stood even though it had been remodeled several times. It reflected the locals' need to sit and converse in a public place, even in the days when maintaining a restaurant seemed to be a foolhardy idea. Since then, the restaurant had expanded several times, each time absorbing a building instead of adding on. The result was a labyrinthine maze that most tourists never figured out.

Mayor Ruth Anderson usually held court in the café, since Bonner Bay had never gotten around to building a town hall. The council met in the café on Tuesday nights, and most other local meetings were held there as well. In grand Bonner Bay tradition, each meeting had its own room of the restaurant, and none of the other meetings ventured into it. Mayor Anderson used the original shack which had no windows. That way, the town felt that her meetings were entirely private.

I went in the shack door, struck, as I always was, by the uneven wood flooring and the baked-in smell of coffee. The wood on the walls was so ancient that it was gray and flaking. The tables in this area were 1950s Formica, also gray. If it weren't for the plastic faux Tiffany lamps with Coke™ painted on them, the entire place would be dark and gloomy.

"Well, if it isn't the big shot," Ruth said when she saw me. She came and put her arms around me. She was a large woman who was probably in her eighties now. She had been mayor since the early seventies, and remembered my grandmother as well as my parents. Ever since I had gotten work at the *Times* I had been "the big shot." "How're you, son?"

No one had called me "son" since I turned fifty. "Fine, Ruthie," I said. "Mind if I have a cuppa?"

"Naw," she said. "Slow business day anyway. Not much happening in this town." And, as if to prove it, she went and poured me coffee herself. The shack truly was her domain. A waitress I didn't recognize stuck her head in the door, but Ruth waved her away.

I took the coffee and sat at Ruth's table. It had been the same one for years: the only wooden table in the place, pushed up against the back corner, a desk lamp on one side, and vinyl chairs on the others.

"What're all the signs, Ruthie?"

She laughed, a sound of great gusto that reverberated through the place. "Leave it to you, kiddo, to notice that right out. When'd you get here—last night?"

"Last night," I agreed, marveling at her prodigious memory. Bonner Bay may have been small, but it was Ruth's domain, the way that New York City had once been Fiorello La Guardia's.

"You were born to ask questions," she said, and for a moment I thought she wasn't going to answer me. "Guess I knew that when your father brought you in here with him after the war. 'How come is this place so dark?' you asked. 'Ain't they got money for lights?' And you just a little thing."

I'd heard that story so many times that I could ignore it with ease. "The pictures, Ruthie."

"You won't like this, Frank. And you won't print it in your rag."

"It's not mine, Ruth," I said, smiling. "And I usually don't print anything about Bonner Bay in the *Times*. I'm on vacation."

"Sure as spit,' she said. "You'll go on vacation when you die. If a good story comes up in Bonner Bay, you'll write about it. You done that when we opened the new hotel. You wrote that whole travel article. And you wrote another thing when James bought the Sea Eagle."

"The travel article was nearly thirty years ago," I said,

"And James buying the Sea Eagle was news to New Yorkers. He was one of Manhattan's premier chefs."

"The whole summer we had people trying to helicopter in here to sample his cuisine." She pronounced it "qwe-zine."

"Ruthie, that was fifteen years ago. James is dead now."

"Still," she said.

"You're not getting off that easy," I said.

"You won't like this."

"Since when did you care about what I think?"

She grinned. "On this one, I care what everybody thinks. I'm getting old enough that folks might start considering me dotty."

"No one would consider you dotty."

"Not even if I told you we have a colony of space aliens living in the Sea Nest?"

I laughed. "Not even then." I sipped my coffee, and noticed she hadn't joined me in my mirth. "Ruthie? You can tell me."

"I just did," she said. "We have a colony of space aliens living in the Sea Nest."

I slowly set my cup down, not quite sure if her words were a test or not. I decided to treat her like any other difficult interview, and play along. "So what are the signs?"

"Support."

"As in political support?" I asked, trying to imagine Bonner Bay divided enough to need rallying cries. The locals here kept their political opinions to themselves because they knew better than to start that kind of squabbling. The town was simply too small.

"Physical support," she said, not quite looking at me. "They're different from us."

"Didn't they bring their own life support?"

"Sure," she said. "But they don't like to use it if they don't have to. So they use our homes as way stations."

"Way stations," I repeated. If she was testing me, this was a good one. "And they're staying at the Sea Nest?"

"Doris let 'em modify the ground floor."

"Does it still flood out?"

"Only in the rainy season," Ruth said. "Besides, it don't matter. They like mold."

"They sound like mighty accommodating aliens. What are they doing here, Ruthie?"

She sighed and sat down. Her chair groaned beneath her weight. "I knew you wouldn't believe me. Don't know why I even tried."

"I believe a lot of things, Ruthie. I haven't said I doubted you."

"Don't have to," she said. "You're playing them big city games on me. Humor the idiot."

"I would never consider you an idiot."

"Nope," she said. "But you might consider me a narrow-minded, small-town yokel."

"Only on a bad day," I said.

"I'm not sure I want to keep talking to you, Frank," she said.

"Sure you do," I said. "You've got my curiosity piqued. I'd like to meet those aliens."

"If you promise me you won't write about them."

"How can I promise that, Ruthie? If they're space aliens, they're news."

"That's why they're here, Frank. They don't want no media attention."

"Those sound like mighty savvy space aliens."

"You'd be surprised,' she said.

The Sea Nest was a gorgeous five-story hotel built against one cliff face on the site of the old natatorium. In fact, the hotel had used the natatorium's floor plan and foundation. The result was a Gothic building with real character: stonework, masonry, and gargoyles hanging off the roof. Its completion had sparked the now-infamous travel article. Ruthie never quite forgave me for that article because it had brought the first wave of out-of-state tourists into Bonner Bay. Once they'd discovered the quaint little hamlet, they had told all their friends.

Bonner Bay had never been the same.

I didn't entirely regret that. I never took full responsibility for it either. I believed that the responsibility truly

lay with the owners of the Sea Nest. They wouldn't have
built such a large, inviting structure without wanting
guests to inhabit it. Too many large hotels in out-of-the-
way places went out of business in Oregon. The state
had a (deserved) reputation for driving away outsiders.

I found that irony delicious as Ruth and I walked
through the Sea Nest's parking lot.

Since it was summer, the lot was full of Lexus, Jaguars, BMWs—as well as the occasional Geo Metro. The
hotel's four-star restaurant and its award-winning wine
list had upgraded the clientele from the adventurous of
the early days to the wealthy of today. I often thought—
privately, because I didn't dare say anything to Ruthie—
that the adventurous of those days had turned into the
wealthy and that someday the clientele of the Sea Nest
would simply die off.

I guess it doesn't matter now.

We bypassed the main entrance and went to one of
the lower-level doors. Ruthie stopped me before we
entered.

"Okay," she said. "I'm going to prepare you for this,
even though you'll think it strange."

"I think it's stranger that you worry about what I
think."

She sighed. "Humor me," she said.

I nodded, waiting. Ruth glanced toward the sea. That
morning it was a navy blue with patches of green. It was
as calm as it gets which, by most standards, wasn't calm
at all.

"I don't know the technical scientific terms for what
they are. But they're like sea lions. They can be in the
ocean and they can be on land. Only they need to do
both. They crave something in the salt water. If they
don't get it, they shrivel up and start flaking."

"Flaking?"

"Frank," she said in that warning tone all women
learn by the age of eighteen.

"All right," I said. "Keep going."

"The flaking's the reason for the signs. Those of us
with signs have saltwater baths ready in our houses in
case the aliens need it."

I think that was when I truly assumed she was batty. At this point, she was the only one I had talked to about the aliens. I hadn't seen them yet, and I couldn't quite comprehend houses with saltwater baths. Humans didn't do such nice things for each other. We didn't have cigarettes around in case someone needed a fix or additional oxygen in case someone went into arrest. Hell, most of us didn't even have extra soap, and I'll bet we all knew someone who needed that.

"I'm going to take you in," she said. "Remember your promise. No reporting."

"No reporting," I repeated.

She pulled open the door. It was a heavy metal door, rusted on the corners from exposure to the sea air. The Sea Nest never rented out its basement. The old foundation and the rough conditions had led to serious flooding in some stormy seasons, and the owners just felt it prudent to leave the basement alone. I had only been in there once, just after the building was finished. Even then the basement rooms had an old, musty air.

I stepped inside, expecting that musty smell. Instead, I nearly choked from the fetid odor of spoiled sea water and wet animal fur. It flashed across my mind that Ruthie was setting me up. Me and all the other reporters, the ones who had done travel articles on Bonner Bay and ruined its splendid isolation.

The lighting was thin and seventies: thick fixtures done in steel and dark wood that, no matter what the expense, still looked cheap. There was no carpet, only a gray concrete floor, with ancient white watermarks. The walls had once been paneled. Some of the paneling remained, peeled and ragged, as if it had been broken off by high water.

The smell got worse the farther inside we went.

"What've you got in here?" I asked. "A hundred and one soggy Dalmations?"

"You know, Frank, the one gift you never had was an effective sense of humor." Ruth led me through the wide corridor. It felt like night in there, even though it was the middle of the day.

Finally we reached the west side of the basement. Another door had been left open, letting in a thin trickle of sunlight. Through the door, I could see the edge of the rock ledge, and stone steps leading down to the boulder-strewn beach.

"I don't see any modifications," I said.

"Shush," Ruth said. She went to one of the side doors, and knocked.

There was some strange rustling and cooing inside. Then the door opened. I could see no one.

"I brought an old friend of mine," Ruth said to the empty air. "His name is Frank Butler. He owns a house here, and his grandmother was born here."

I heard some chittering, rather like a high-pitched voice speaking too fast to understand. Then Ruthie added, "Yes, I know he works for *The New York Times,* but he's promised me he won't write about you."

"Folks," I said, wanting this charade over with, "if you're as real as Ruthie says, *The New York Times* will want nothing to do with you."

There was a bit more chittering. Ruthie stood with her hands clasped behind her back, waiting more patiently than I had ever seen her do. Then it ended, and she turned to me.

"They said it'll be okay."

I wasn't sure if I was relieved or annoyed. I usually did well with new things: I was a reporter who traveled endlessly, interviewed people I had never met about topics I had only recently heard of, and yet this new thing was filling me with a sort of silent dread. Maybe it was because I expected to revise my opinion of Ruth afterward. Maybe it was because I was afraid I would discover I was gullible.

And maybe it was because I had never had an opinion about extraterrestrials, and I didn't really want one.

I followed Ruthie inside the room.

The room had been modified. The windowpanes had been replaced with blue-green stained glass, and the light fixtures had blue-green bulbs. The effect was to make the room look as if it were part of bad sixties movie— or if you squinted, an underwater dump.

The smell was stronger in here, wet fur and stagnant

water, so strong that I had to fight to keep my hand from my face.

In the blue-green light, I could see dozens of small furry creatures. They looked like electric shoe polishers, the kind you could order from an elite catalog. They were oblong, about a foot high, and covered with a thin layer of curly wool. Rather like a shrunken sheep without eyes, ears, or nose.

"Good heavens, Frank," Ruth said. "Look up."

"But—" I indicated the ground.

She snorted. "You've seen too many bad movies."

She had rounded a corner. I followed and ran into more than a dozen naked people. Then I paused and revised my first impression. They weren't people, at least, not completely. They all appeared young. They had two arms, two legs, a torso, a head and genitalia. They also had fins rising from their spines. Their eyes and mouths were completely round instead of oval-shaped, and they had little suckers on the ends of their fingers.

'What's in the other room?" I hissed.

"Their pelts," Ruth hissed back. Then she said in a normal tone: "This is Frank."

The strangers rose as a unit. Then I realized they had all been sitting in small tubs filled with half an inch of sea water. The water was particularly pungent. It was green with algae, like an overgrown, dying tidal pool that the sea hadn't reached in weeks.

One stranger came toward me. He was shorter than the rest, with hair the color of sea foam. He extended his hand, and I was about to take it when I heard a whoosh behind me. One of the shoe polishers zoomed through the air past me, connected with the stranger's hand, and covered him from his chin to his ankles. It looked like he was wearing an oddly sewn sweater that covered his entire body.

It also relieved me. I was too much a product of my culture to appreciate nakedness in anything vaguely human.

"You are the reporter," he said in a high squeaky voice. His lips moved like fish kisses as he spoke, and his eyes blinked in unison with the lip movement. I was amazed I could understand him.

"Well, I'm not just a reporter," I said. "I am also a person in my own right."

"Remains to be seen," he said. "Didn't think reporters were persons."

"What else would they be?" I asked.

"Unscrupulous money grubbers," he said with a primness that clashed with his kissing lips.

"Unscrupulous money grubbers are people, too," I said, glancing at Ruth. She was watching me nervously, as if she had just introduced me to the Pope and was waiting for me to declare that I was an atheist.

"You will report us, no?"

I was confused and uncertain for the first time since I was a cub reporter. I hadn't felt this far over my head since I met John Gotti on his own turf.

"I promised Ruth I wouldn't," I said.

"And you will hold to such a promise?"

"Of course," I said.

"Then we have no more need of you." He waved his wool-covered hand. "Let us absorb in peace."

"All right." I backed out of the room and walked gingerly through the pelts until I reached the hallway. I had to blink to get my eyes used to the light again. When Ruth didn't follow me immediately, I went outside the open door and stood at the top of the stairs.

The air was brisk with a bit of mid-morning chill. The sea smell was strong and refreshing after the fetid odors of the inner rooms. I checked my feelings like an old man who'd tripped would check for broken bones:

Unsettled? Yes.

Frightened? No.

Curious? Yes.

Frightened? No.

Worried? Yes.

Frightened? *No!*

All right, I was frightened, and that worried me even more. I almost never got frightened any more. I had lived in New York City too long. I swore at potential muggers and shook hands with mobsters. I had insulted one of the biggest serial killers of the century once, and had shared a urinal with the President and a squadron of Secret Service guys. I'd been shot at, knifed, and my car'd been firebombed.

Nothing should have bothered me. Especially nothing as mundane as a dirty hotel basement and a lot of creepy looking people.

"What did you do?" Ruth asked. She was behind me. I hadn't heard her coming.

"What did *I* do?"

"I'd never seen them act so rude before."

"That wasn't a them. That was a him, and he didn't strike me as rude."

"He's their spokesman. I doubt the others can speak English."

"How did he learn it?" I asked.

"I don't know," she said. "Apparently they've been studying us for a long time."

"Or maybe they're just as human as we are."

"Frank." That tone again.

I sat on the top step and patted the space next to me so that she could join me. I wasn't really worried that the creatures would come outside, even though I wasn't sure why.

She went back, put a rock between the door and its jamb, then sat down beside me.

"Have you ever seen them outside that room?"

"Of course," she said. "I told you they wander through town. With their pelts on."

"How come they weren't wandering this morning?"

"It's too warm for them. Imagine how you'd feel under all that fur."

"That room was warm."

"They weren't wearing their pelts."

I sighed. The ocean spread before me, now half green and gold, an endless vista of water. "All right, Ruth," I said, "Suppose I grant that these are aliens. Suppose I give you that."

"Generous," she murmured.

"If they are, what are they doing here? If they know

so much about us, how come they didn't appear at the White House or the Kremlin or something?"

"The White House isn't by the sea."

She said that so matter-of-factly that at first I wasn't sure if I had heard her correctly.

"What does the sea have to do with it?"

"They came out of the sea."

I turned to look at her. She was staring at the ocean, her nose and cheeks red with wind, her gray hair mussed.

"Their ships can't land on our ground," she said. "Something about pressure and movement and density and stuff I didn't understand. Their ships are like bubbles. They float on the sea's surface."

"And these guys swam ashore?"

She shook her head. "The bubbles dropped them off and then went out to sea. They'll call the ships when they need to go back."

"So they chose Bonner Bay specifically," I said. "Why?"

"I told you," she said. "Because it's isolated. They don't want coverage. They just want to learn about us."

"And you believe that?"

"Why shouldn't I?" she asked. "Why is it more normal to doubt them? Is mistrust so common in your life now that you can't accept a miracle when you see it?"

"You think they're miracles?" I asked.

"Hell," she said. "I think a sunset is a miracle. What do I know?"

"I don't know," I said. "It bothers me."

"Take them for what they are, Frank."

That surprised me more than anything. "What are they, Ruthie?"

"A gift," she said. "A gift from the sea."

"I hate anonymous gifts," I said. "They always have strings."

The next few days were weird. Beyond weird, really. Different and difficult for reasons hard to pinpoint.

I liked Bonner Bay for its clear blue summer skies, its cool breezes, and its lack of pretentiousness. In a way, my visits to the town were attempts to return to my boyhood—not my actual boyhood which was as confused and difficult as anyone else's—but those perfect boyhood moments when the air was warm, school was out, and the day felt full of possibilities. Possibilities and Tom Sawyer freedoms. Bonner Bay had that for me, with the ocean and the isolation, and those blissful moments when I would realize that the town would always remain the same, no matter how many personal computers people owned, or how many channels they could receive.

Bonner Bay would remain Bonner Bay.

Until this year. In those days, the aliens—which I took to calling them, like everyone else—appeared all over town. They walked every square inch of Bonner Bay, heads up, pelts on, greeting locals as they passed. Tourists stayed away from them, treating them like Bigfoot's cousins—something to cross the street to avoid. But the locals were intrigued and proud that these creatures had chosen Bonner Bay as a refuge, and they did all they could to accommodate the creatures' needs.

I ran into a number of the aliens. And, unlike the tourists, I didn't cross the street to avoid them. I went out of my way to say hello.

No alien ever answered me. They acted as if they couldn't see me.

And nothing I could do changed that.

They didn't spoil my vacation—Bonner Bay was still as calm and peaceful as ever—but they did ruin the possibilities of it: the Tom Sawyer/glimpse into my boyhood part. They constantly reminded me it was 1997, and that I was a man closer to dying than to his boyhood.

They also kept me from relaxing. The reporter part of my brain, the part that had enabled me to write several award-winning series on managed care, New York politics, and the mob's control of garbage service wouldn't shut off. I couldn't believe these guys showed up to enjoy Bonner Bay's isolation. I was certain that there were more isolated places in the world. I knew of at least two in North America: one in the Idaho Mountains which, granted, had no ocean, and one in Alaska that had no roads. It bothered me that they didn't go to

Seattle or San Francisco or Miami, some large city on the ocean, where they could be even more anonymous than they were here.

The fact that they could speak the language, even though they had just arrived, bothered me, too. I had seen enough sf flicks to be suspicious of that. If they learned quickly, well, that frightened me, too.

It also bothered me that I spent so much time thinking about them. After all, I couldn't write about them. **Aliens Arrive in Bonner Bay!** would never be a headline in the *Times,* no matter how accurate the story.

So I tried to ignore the aliens, as they ignored me.

And that worked.

For a while.

Until the night they woke me up.

My bedroom in my grandmother's house was at the top of the stairs, on the right, facing the ocean. The room was large by most standards and could fit two double beds and a cot easily. As children, my siblings and I shared that room. After my parents died, my siblings usually used the master bedroom on the first floor when they visited. I, however, could not break the old habit, and returned to my old room to sleep with the ghosts.

That room was alive. It creaked and moaned and moved ever so slightly in any wind. The constant roar of the ocean filled it, and always, on the first night of my arrival, I couldn't sleep, listening to the quiet sounds, letting them greet me after too many months away.

But by the middle of my visit, I would sleep sounder than I had in years. So when I awoke to a bright light and a chorus of voices, I at first thought it a dream.

The light had the intensity of a train's headlight on a moonless night. The voices were eerie, the whispered memories of an erased cassette. And the smell of wet fur was thick and pungent, a live thing that encased and enveloped me.

I never had odors in my dreams.

I sat up. A dozen aliens filled the room. One held the light—or seemed to hold the light—directly on me.

I held a hand over my face, blocking my eyes. "It's

considered rude in our culture to invade a man's home and wake him up."

"You are Frank Butler?" The voice was androgynous and yet high-pitched.

"Last I checked."

"The reporter?"

"State your business," I said, bringing my arm down, "and get the hell out."

The speaker came toward me. Its pelt was dark black, so dark that it absorbed the light. "I am—" the name sounded like a sneeze "—and I, too, am a reporter. I wonder if we could 'let's make a deal'?"

"You learned our language through television transmissions," I said, finally realizing, with a bit of relief, how they had learned to speak English.

"Is that not what the transmissions were for?"

I shook my head. "Get the damn light out of my face. Then we'll negotiate."

I couldn't imagine them wanting to negotiate with me. They hadn't wanted to speak to me all week.

The light lowered. The full dozen wore pelts of different colors. They glistened in the brightness. This room hadn't seen so much light since the turn of the century. Cobwebs graced the corners, and the flowered wallpaper, which I had thought unchanged in all the decades I'd seen it, was peeling near the top of the window.

"We wish to 'let's make a deal,' Frank Butler."

"I got that. What kind of deal-making do you want with me?"

The alien tilted its head and its entire pelt moved. "We also report. We believe information the center of all things. We will trade information with you."

This was a switch in attitude. But my reporter's instincts, never fully off, knew something was up. I wasn't going to give any information until I knew exactly what was going on.

"Trade information?"

The spokesalien nodded gravely. "We will let you be our contact to the Earth. You will have our 'Breaking News Exclusive!' We will subject three of our number to your scientists. We will give interviews, meet your leaders, and allow you and people of your choice to visit our crafts."

Complete flip-flop. Despite the warmth in the room, I was cold. "What do I have to do in return?"

"Take us to the illegals."

I rubbed a hand over my face. It felt sleep grimy. I resisted the urge to pinch myself. "The 'illegals'?"

"Yes. You are the reporter. You will know where they are. We have located their crafts in your sea. Their beacons led us here. You are the reporter. You will know where they are."

My brain was slowly kicking in. "And that's what you base your assumption of knowledge on? My profession?"

"And your passion for knowledge. This story will earn you great—moneys—will it not?"

Maybe. If I fought it through the *Times* editorial staff. If I was willing to risk my reputation to do so. If I was willing to run to a less reputable news agency if the *Times* changed its mind.

"How come you can't find them?" I asked, stalling. "You found me."

"We have studied this town. Your presence here has been a comfort and a distraction. We did not know when we chose this pueblo that it would have an information gatherer in its midst, however irregularly."

"And that's bad?"

"It adds an element of living dangerous," the alien said.

"Oh." I frowned. "What are illegals?"

"You have met them," the spokesalien said. "You have seen them."

"How do you know?" I asked, not sure if that question gave me away or not.

"Because you are not shocked to see us."

Ooops. Had me there. I grinned. "It's the middle of the night. You're a dream. I expect anything in my dreams."

"You are awake," the spokesalien said.

"I'm not sure of that," I said. "How can you be?"

It turned and conferred with an alien near it. Their

language sounded like sneezes, coughs, and hiccups. Somehow, in the midst of all that hacking, I came to believe in them.

Aliens.

Weird creatures from outer space.

And I wanted nothing to do with them. I wanted them out of my grandmother's house.

The alien turned toward me. "Will you help us?" it asked, apparently deciding to ignore my dream discussion.

"What are illegals?" I asked. "Drugs?"

The alien tilted its head the other way. It's pelt shone blue. "You have them," it said. "We have heard on your news transmissions. Illegals. Those who cross the wrong border."

"Illegal aliens," I said. "But they're illegal in the country they *arrive* in, not in the country they have left."

"So, if our people land here, then they are illegals, no?"

I had never thought of that, but I suppose it was true. I had been culturally conditioned to think that any visitors from outer space would be treated differently than Mexicans trying to cross the Rio Grande. I suppose it depended on what numbers they arrived in, and whether or not the government believed they could be of use to the country.

"I thought you wanted them because they were outlaws in your country," I said.

"No." The creature and others sneezed as well. I hoped it was a gesture of disgust and not some alien virus. "We want them because they have broken the great taboo."

"The great taboo?"

"They have left the blind."

It took me a minute to realize that analogy came courtesy of the *Discovery* Channel. "You're observing us, and they ruined the experiment?"

"Yes," the alien said. "They have decided to take the experiment a stage farther than mandated."

"Seems you have, too," I said, not believing them. "Especially considering the offer you just made me."

The alien's pelt fur rose and fell. I guessed it to be an alien shrug. But I might have been wrong. It could have been annoyance. Or an itch.

"This experiment has already been contaminated," it said. "More will not hurt."

"Then I don't understand why you need them."

"We do not need them," the alien said. "We must charge them. Interfering with information is punishable by death."

"Serious charge," I said. "Here information is free, and anyone can tamper with it."

"So you believe," the alien said, sounding as if it did not.

I was a bit rattled. Not by its skepticism, although that surprised me, too. But by the charge of death. We never took information that seriously here. In fact, as I got older, I found myself getting disgusted with my own business. No one cared about the facts, only the facts, ma'am. They cared about the scoop, only the scoop, sorry if it's wrong, folks. At the *Times* we tried not to fall into that, but we did, more and more, in a stuffy, snobby, elitist sort of way.

So if I gave those smelly, pathetic creatures up to these smelly, seemingly more powerful creatures, I would sign the first group's death warrant.

I'd be lying if I didn't say I considered it. After all, I was a practicing journalist. I had to make my money.

But I loved my job at the *Times*. And, as an editor there said to me just the week before as we casually discussed the possibility of reporting creatures from outer space: "Frank, aliens could bomb the White House, and we'd report it as 'Unidentified bomb destroys U.S. Capitol.' We can't publish anything that smacks of tabloids until we've got five years of documentation from national science centers and confirmation of the flight path from NASA. And maybe we couldn't publish it then."

These creatures would have been better off if Bonner Bay's resident reporter worked for the *Enquirer*.

"Sorry," I said. "I can't help you."

"Can't?" the alien asked. "Or won't?"

I fluffed my pillow, preparing to go back to sleep. "Can't," I said. "You're a dream, and I've never seen creatures like you before. If the aliens have taken over Bonner Bay, no one has told me about it. Better go invade someone else's sleep."

"You do not wish for the fame we offer?"

"Nope," I said. "I'm surprised I'm even dreaming of it."

"You are a fool, Frank Butler," the alien said. "You do not know what you have done."

Well, I know now.

Two nights later, I woke up to find myself in the sea caves, along with the rest of Bonner Bay. Some were nude, some weren't, but we were all wet, and we were, horror of horrors, smashing tide pools. The tide was out, and the caves were empty, and we were all confused. To add to the mess, all the house pets from town were in the caves as well. Dogs, cats, iguanas, houseplants, aquariums filled with fish. If it lived in a house, it was in the cave.

Unless it was an alien creature.

None of them were inside.

I hate thinking of this: The noise, the screams, the confusion. Waking up in the dark and the cold and the noise, not knowing how we got there, or why. Only Ruth seemed serene.

She said the aliens did it.

But she didn't know which ones.

She also organized us. Climbed onto a rock and shouted until she had our attention. She said there had to be a reason they hid us in here, and she said we would proceed slowly, in an orderly fashion, to the mouth of the cave.

It took five volunteer firefighters and a local bouncer to enforce order. But we went, lemminglike, to the mouth. I was with Ruthie at the head of the group. Fortunately, the two of us had chosen to wear pajamas that night. I'm not sure I wanted to see Ruthie nude.

When we got to the opening, we saw a bubblecraft,

hovering low. It released several small bubbles of light, and when they landed, they turned into fireballs.

I cannot describe this in any more detail. I refuse to look any closer than this.

It was ugly.

The balls engulfed the city in a matter of moments. Ruthie and I, as well as several members of the volunteer fire department, had to restrain others who were trying to get to their homes. The entire town went up as if it were gasoline-soaked kindling.

And the aliens went up with it.

Fifteen dead.

I had killed them anyway, along with the town.

And I didn't even get my story.

The last few months, I've been thinking about retiring. My editor says it's a grief reaction, triggered by losing my childhood home. But I think it's more than that.

I think I've lost my edge. I'm just not interested any more. That little spark, the one that made me investigate things, is completely gone. I could work a desk or even get promoted, assigning stories, making others do the running. But I don't want to.

Two ideas keep going through my mind:

One of them is the spokesalien's.

One of them is mine.

Information, in this society, is not free, no matter how much we like to pretend it is. It is paid for by corporate sponsors, from the ads on the TV News to the ads up front in the *Times*. It has rules and prejudices and traditions that defy the pure pursuit of knowledge.

And anyone can taint it.

Anyone.

Including a reporter, unwilling to stake his reputation on a difficult story.

I erred. I know I did. And the only reason I know it is because of the lost property as well as the lost lives. I didn't care about the lives. They were smelly, dirty, and alien. And, shameful as that is, it's my truth.

But I could have saved them. Or at least tried. If I had agreed to that Faustian bargain with the spokesalien,

I could have gotten those pathetic creatures out of that basement, told the *Enquirer*—*The American Journal*—anyone who would listen that these creatures were about to be murdered.

It might not have saved them.

But it might have.

And it certainly would have saved Bonner Bay.

I cannot even return there now. No one can. Geologists have ruled the site unsafe for building. Too unstable. They claim to be glad the town is gone.

I'm not. A bit of heaven disappeared with it. Heaven I thought tainted by a few pelts, by a few signs. Heaven I hadn't realized I would miss.

Until now.

And with it went a bit of my soul. The part that liked to reveal facts, to search for truth. My truth.

I found my truth.

And I hate what it revealed.

A GAME OF *MEHEN*
by Josepha Sherman

Josepha Sherman is a fantasy writer and folklorist whose latest novels are the historical fantasies *The Shattered Oath* and *Forging the Runes*. Her latest folklore book is entitled *Trickster Tales*.

Foreword: Imhotep was a real man, one of those amazing multitalented geniuses who occasionally appear in the human race. In the mid-third millennium B.C. *he served Pharaoh Djoser as Grand Vizier and Chief Architect— he designed the step pyramid and temple complex at Saqqara—but was also an astronomer and physician, as well as a scholar and writer.* Mehen *was a board game popular in his day.*

Egypt, Saqqara, Year 2659 B.C.

He was Imhotep, Grand Vizier to Pharaoh Djoser, as well as the god-king's Chief Architect, a lean, sharp-eyed, thoroughly competent man who was responsible for the smooth running of all the affairs of Egypt.

He was also, just now, a thoroughly frustrated man pacing impatiently in the desert, alone in the silence, having already waved away solicitous aides and guards so that he could think. One generally could think out here in the quiet, empty places, but now, now . . . Imhotep paused, bending to sketch a few lines in the sand, only to scuff them out again with an angry sigh.

The design! Why could he not find the right design?

That the pharaoh should wish a funerary monument prepared long before his death was understandable; such monuments took years to design and erect. That he should wish it more splendid, more original, than any

34

that had come before was understandable as well. And that he should turn to Imhotep for this new, original, splendid design—that, too, was quite understandable.

After all, I have never failed him before. And I have no intention of failing him now.

It wasn't that he was afraid of the pharaoh; god-king or no, Djoser was far too aware of his vizier's abilities and honesty to ever threaten him; Imhotep, common-born though he was, stood just below Djoser in status.

But a man did have his reputation to uphold! Imhotep, who was also, in his brief free time, a physician and student of astronomy, as well as a part-time writer collecting wise sayings, knew perfectly well that he intimidated people, those who could not keep pace with a mind that was always reaching for new challenges, new information. He was not particularly vain, but if one could not be popular, one could at least be effective.

But what in the name of all the gods is wrong? There should be a properly grand enclosure, something new, original. . . .

Ah, nothing. For once, his mind was empty of ideas. All there was to do was pace restlessly about and pray that whichever deity sent him inspiration would help yet again.

Space, Domain Year 154, Dynasty of the Dar

He was Azarak, a sometimes trader, sometimes scout, sometimes rather more than that, depending on the Domain's need. His specialty, and he performed it very well, with only the smallest, smallest exceptions (Wa'arin, he would not think of Wa'arin), was to land without detection on a primitive world, adapt to the local customs, blend in, and begin to subtly undermine the status quo till the population was prepared to accept salvation. As it were.

That he was expendable was something he didn't consider; it was as the Domain wished. That the Domain might be saving on precious resources by sending only one scout per planet and thereby might be showing a *need* for frugality—that idea was a treasonous, downright dangerous line of thought.

I am a loyal servant, an honored warrior.

But right now, Azarak thought, he was nothing more than an ordinary *meratik* struggling with his ship's recalcitrant controls as it streaked down through this world's atmosphere, trying to avoid the rough landing—no, more like a controlled crash—that seemed inevitable, and battling to properly set the humanoid mask he was assuming.

You would think that those whose job it is to oversee these ships would actually bother *to oversee them properly! I will see heads and skins hanging from the walls when I return.*

Azarak had done a quick scan of this new planet, the lone one of the nine to bear sentient life, and found much of it water, but some of it properly dry land. Some of that land was so densely covered with vegetation that he ruled out a landing at once. The sentients upon the more open areas, though, these humanoids, seemed for the most part suitably primitive, not the type to put up a dangerous fight or be perilously hostile to "holy visitors."

He was coming down in a singularly empty stretch of desert, though a quick glance out of the rapidly clouding viewscreen had shown a river to the east, signs of buildings.

No matter. Desert was most desirable. Primitives tended to have their best visions in deserts, their best religious enlightenments. They were most receptive to properly worded messages in deserts. All ready to pave their own way for their . . . ah, well, enforced integration would be the nice way to say it.

The Domain could always use more . . . helpers. Willing or not.

But first he had to survive the landing.

Imhotep looked up with a start to see a bright *something* streaking across the sky. A star? Some fiery sign from the gods? Yet falling stars always trailed a line of flame behind them. They were not made of solid matter.

A . . . vehicle? Some deity's chariot?

Whatever, it was landing behind that ridge and, judging from the sound, landing with considerable force. A pigeon leaped frantically into the sky, flapping wildly away, and for an instant, Imhotep was tempted to echo its panic and hurry back to the rest of humanity.

None of whom were coming to investigate. Had they not seen? Probably not; the . . . thing had come in from the west. They might not have heard either, since the wind was from the east. He really should leave, though, rejoin the others.

But . . . what *had* landed there? No divine chariot would have crashed so inelegantly!

You fool. It could well be a trap, some enemy of Djoser longing to get his hands on the Grand Vizier. You should have listened to the guards, not come out here alone.

And yet, and yet, the thought of seeing something no one else had seen, learning something no one else had known . . . Warily, Imhotep started forward, climbing the ridge, then flattening, peering over the crest.

Gods! What *was* that thing? A vehicle, clearly, but of some strange, dull metal (was that metal?), battered and scarred by the rough landing, though it seemed still mostly of a piece. The lines of the vehicle, even with the marring, were pleasingly sleek, austerely elegant, and Imhotep hastily stored them away in his mind for future use.

But whose is it? What nation has a—a flying craft? And of such a foreign metal that—

He stiffened as someone crawled out of the vehicle, a man (being? deity?) in gleaming gold robes that would have been more impressive if they hadn't been wrinkled and stained with .. what? Some of the vehicle's life-blood? The man smoothed the robes as best he could, then started resolutely up the ridge. Imhotep scrambled back, but there was no time to hide. With a sigh, he got to his feet.

And found himself face-to-face with the stranger. They both froze, staring. Almost exactly his height, the stranger looked *almost* right, as though he had only recently designed his appearance. The undisguised surprise on his face was at odds with the richness of those robes, stained though they were.

"Bow down," the stranger said without preamble.

Imhotep frowned. This was hardly a proper greeting! "I will not!" he said indignantly.

"Am I not speaking the language correctly?"

"You most certainly are. And I am most certainly not about to bow to one who has yet to name himself."

"Bow down, I say, before the Great God Azarak!"

"I would," Imhotep countered boldly, "were such a deity present. But I find it highly unlikely that any deity would appear as bedraggled as though he had staggered from a chariot wreck, or be so surprised to see me when surely an omnipotent being would have already known of my presence. If I am mistaken, my apologies. But I doubt that I am. Now, kindly tell me who you are. And, for that matter, why you are here."

Wonderful, just wonderful, Azarak thought. He had managed to land with only minor damage, had found the nice, glittery, primitive-impressing robes only slightly soiled and the translator undamaged—and now the first local he faced turned out to be both regrettably cool-headed and amazingly quick-witted. This was *not* the way matters were supposed to go! He had already lost the advantage of landing undetected, and he was hardly going to be able to blend in with the locals with *this* local blocking him.

Should I kill him? He's alone; no weapons, no witnesses, wilderness all around us . . . yes. Remove the intelligent one and hope that the rest of the primitives are more amenable.

Imhotep was not at all as calm as he pretended, well aware of his almost weaponless state and all that emptiness around him. Yes, he could shout, and the sound would carry well in the clear desert air, but he had been quite insistent about being left alone, and by the time anyone came to investigate—

Gods, what was that? The stranger, this Azarak, was drawing a sleek, metallic *something* from his robes, a thing that, judging from the way it was being pointed at him, was some manner of weapon.

What kind? I see no dart, no obvious projectile. A pellet weapon of some sort? Pellets projected by . . . by what? Some gas forced through that narrow—

How it worked was hardly the question! Mehen, Imhotep thought suddenly, *play this as a game of* Mehen, *just as one does with diplomacy: all strategy and maneuvering.* Forcing his voice to imperious calm, he said, "Ah, so you are nothing but an assassin. What a disappointment!"

"What—"

Keep him off-balance, get him talking. "Come, who sent you? Someone from court? Or are you a foreign agent?" *But what foreign nation has such weaponry? Not bronze . . . what is that metal?* "Who did send you?"

"I come," Azarak said haughtily, "in the name of the Domain."

"Ah? Which is . . . ?"

The stranger hesitated, as though trying to find words that would properly impress Imhotep, and the weapon wavered slightly. "The Domain is the mightiest of empires!" Azarak said at last. "An empire so mighty that it stretches from world to world!"

Imhotep disregarded that "world to world" as mere political hyperbole. *An empire so mighty that, while it has such wondrous inventions as a flying vehicle, it can afford to send only one representative? One who hides in empty desert like a thief?*

"Perhaps I know this Domain under a different name," he said, testing delicately. "Might I ask where it is located? Not to the East, surely." Trading routes to the East would have long ago revealed any such empire—and any such metallurgy. "To the West, perhaps? Beyond that distant sea?"

Azarak gave a sharp, contemptuous laugh. "Beyond the sea of stars!"

Hardly likely. The stars had been set in their constant patterns by the gods; Imhotep's observations had satisfied him that they were not worlds on which a mortal man could live, but balls of ever-burning fire. *And yet . . . it's true that I have wondered. If they are, indeed, like this divine Sun . . . The gods are infinite: more than one sun? More than one world? An empire that stretches from world to world?*

Unprovable. Frustrated, knowing there was no device keener than a man's eye, Imhotep said only a very careful, "Interesting."

The stranger started to speak, stopped, clearly puzzled by this lack of emotion, clearly having expected shock or fierce denial. *You are not,* Imhotep told him silently, *a vizier used to hiding your emotions from ambassadors.*

Pressing the advantage, Imhotep continued aloud, "The location of the Domain is not really the issue. Why, I wonder, could a mighty empire afford to send only one representative, and that to empty desert?"

He saw the stranger flinch; a sensitive point, that. *Careful, careful. One can win at* mehen *if one angers the opponent—but not if he's so angry he destroys the board.* "I cannot be vain enough to think that you've been hunting me." *Have you? So far you seem not to know who I am, but . . .* "What, if I may ask, does this Domain wish of us?"

"Integration," Azarak said after the slightest of hesitations.

"Ah." *A euphemism for "conquest." Predictable.*

"We mean only well! We wish to bring your people up to our level of . . . of . . ." Whatever word the stranger sought was obviously not in the language. "Of inventions," he finished lamely.

"That is very kind of your Domain," Imhotep said in his smoothest Grand Vizier voice. "We shall consider the offer. Now, if you will come with me, perhaps we can—"

"No." His hand tightened on the weapon.

Delicately, now. "I must warn you that if you slay me, the others will hear."

"This weapon is soundless."

"Is it? Then I was correct: it *is* a projectile device, and presumably powered by some gaseous release. Assuming, of course," Imhotep added very carefully, "that it actually does perform as you say. Not that I question your veracity! But still . . ."

*   *   *

Azarak bit back a hiss. This was *not* going the way he had planned. Not only had the local identified the *shrak* as a weapon, he had even speculated on its operation. A primitive wasn't supposed to do that! And he had shown not the slightest alarm at learning of an interstellar empire.

Have I made a mistake? Are these not primitives at all? Arr-ahk, *they must be! The sensors would have picked up any signs of a higher technology. So stop hesitating. Kill him and get on with your job.*

Unless he . . .

Oh, no, that's too fantastic.

But what if he, too, is an agent?

What if I have underestimated him and his people?

"Watch," the stranger said curtly, and aimed his weapon at a small rock. A slight depression of a finger—and a flash of white-hot light blazed forth and . . . the rock was no more.

Gods!

But years of court training came into play, and though it took every bit of will, Imhotep's start was only the slightest of reactions. *Ra, Isis, all of you, offerings to the lot of you if you let me win this game!* Quickly, gambling all on a throw of the *mehen* dice, he said, as though greatly disappointed, "Is *that* all? I expected something far grander!"

"Far grander! You have no such . . . such inventions!"

"Of course not." Imhotep took a breath, then said, marveling at his calm and the strength of his lie, "We abandoned such toys long years ago."

"*What?* Are you—you have no—are you—"

"The mind," Imhotep added, not sure where he was going with this, "is a wonderous thing. Far greater than any mere physical inventions. It would be such a simple, simple matter to control an object. A mind."

"*Psionics!*" The word meant nothing to Imhotep, and after an instant of blank staring at each other, Azarak added, "The power of the mind, the . . . ah . . . are you trying to tell me your people—"

It's working! By all the gods, it's working! "My dear

Azarak," Imhotep said with a world-weary smile, "what do you think brought down your vehicle?"

Azarak stared at this too self-possessed, too tranquil primitive—no, no, *not* primitive—for a panic-stricken moment. No wonder the local hadn't shown any signs of high-tech! No wonder he was so infernally serene! If any of the Domain overlords discovered he had been tampering with a psionic world—that was strictly forbidden after the sad affair of Wa'arin. Wa'arin, the nicely low-tech, helpless world thought securely part of the Domain till those cursed priests had all concentrated and blown apart every last Domain outpost on the planet—

And the only reason the Domain was there at all was because I was the one who said it was safe, that the natives were all nicely pacified— They'll kill me! Another Wa'arin—the overlords will have my skin!

Babbling something, he wasn't sure what, to the calm-faced native (*like those calm-faced priests, just like those calm-faced, deadly priests!*), Azarak turned and not-quite ran back to his ship. Was the native following? No, he hadn't moved. Waiting.

Waiting to blow me up, too?

The ship started up without much trouble, went through its cycling without more than a groan and a hiss. It would launch . . . launch . . . please, please, let it launch. . . .

It did. Praying to all the deities he had never believed existed, Azarak rode his whining, hissing ship back up into safe, safe space.

It never happened. I was never there.
There is no such planet.

The roar had been nearly deafening. The earth had shaken, almost as though glad to have this foreigner off its soil, and in a short time others would—must—come running to investigate. Imhotep stood, trying not to tremble, in these few moments of remaining solitude, watching the eerie vehicle rise up into the heavens like a fiery chariot till its noise had faded and he could see it no more.

Where is he going? To a foreign land? Or a foreign . . . world?

Ah, to know the truth!

No. Best not to know that much. Best to accept only that the stranger was gone, leaving no trace behind but some torn, scorched earth.

"I won," Imhotep said aloud, not quite believing it. "The game of *mehen* is complete, and I have won. *Psionics,*" he added, repeating the alien word warily. Magic. It could only mean magic. His bluff had worked. "He thought I was a mighty magician, just as I prayed. Isis, Mistress of Magic and Mother of the Gods, I owe you much for this!"

What of that mysterious Domain, though? Was Egypt safe? Would the Domain send more emissaries? Warriors?

Unlikely. Azarak had clearly been terrified that he'd committed some great misdeed—terrified, as well, of his superiors learning about his visit to this land and about this land itself.

Besides, Imhotep thought, experienced in politics as he was, though the trappings of alien tools, alien metals, had been impressive (gods, yes!) any empire could overreach its bounds, stretch itself too thin—as the evidence of Azarak, a single scout sent alone and poorly prepared, and his ship, so incredible in design, so weak in repair, had shown. The Domain, Imhotep mused, wherever it might lie, would not be an empire for much longer.

And I . . . dare tell no one of this. They would think me mad or touched by the gods.

Have I been?

Or have I truly been speaking with someone from another world? If so, if there are indeed other worlds . . . lands beyond all fathoming . . . He shook his head in wonder. *Then someday, who but the gods know when, we and . . . others may communicate, may meet, may share yet unknown wonders. . . .*

No. He would not worry about what could not be proved, nor spend too much time in wondering what might someday be. What had happened was done. Dreams of the future were well and good, a scope for one's imagination. But what was here and now was all that must, all that could, concern a man.

That ship, though . . . its sleek, deceptively simple lines . . . something about those lines . . .

Imhotep knelt, began sketching in the sand. What if he extended this line, like this, yes . . . straightened it, like this . . . ? Yes! Gods, yes!

Kneeling there, the Grand Vizier of all Egypt, the first in human history to meet one from another world, began to laugh. All that drama, all that tense game of *mehen* and bluff, to come down to *this:*

Pharaoh Djoser would have his funerary monument, and it would, indeed, be like none other. For it would be based not on what had come before—at least not in Egypt, nor in any of the known lands.

The design of that funerary monument would be based truly and literally on something out of this world!

SMALL HEROES
by Jane M. Lindskold

Jane Lindskold resides in Albuquerque, New Mexico with six cats, all named after figures in British mythology. To support them (and her four guinea pigs and many fish) she writes full-time. Her published works include the novels *Brother to Dragons, Companion to Owls, Marks of Our Brothers, The Pipes of Orpheus,* and *Smoke and Mirrors,* Her short fiction has appeared in a variety of collections, including *Heaven Sent, Return to Avalon,* and *Wheel of Fortune.* Currently, she is under contract to complete the two novels left unfinished by Roger Zelazny as well as several novels of her own. Her latest novel, *When the Gods Are Silent,* will be published in 1997.

"I tell you, I'm certain that they're holding something back!" protested Carmelita Margarita Ortiz.

"Of course they are," answered her senior, Diplomatic Expeditionary Leader Percy Tremand. He chuckled indulgently. "Who wouldn't in a situation like this? Our party is the first extra-system group to be invited to Bismarck. Do you expect the kazsatorezs to tell every little detail of their civilization to five visiting humans?"

He pronounced the aliens' race name "kazsssator-ezsss," handling the drawn out hisses with irritating perfection.

"No. But it's not a little detail they're withholding. I'm sure . . ."

Percy Tremand cut her off with an indulgent clucking noise that was as infuriating as it was effective. A tall, slender man, his brilliant blue eyes and silver hair seemed accessories to his perfect tailoring and instinctive *savoir faire.*

Ortiz lowered her chocolate-brown eyes, staring at the

floor, trying hard not to glower. It was difficult. She knew that Tremand thought little of her. When, during a layover on the colony world La Tigre, Tremand's handpicked cultural anthropologist had fallen ill with an attack of food poisoning, Carmelita Margarita Ortiz had been the only available person even vaguely qualified to take the man's place.

Now here she was, certain to be immortalized as one of the first five humans to set foot on the kazsatorezs' world, and equally certain to be dismissed as mere baggage by the other four members of the expedition.

The remaining three members, Doctors Li, Van Meek, and Raunga, looked uncomfortable with Tremand's behavior, but none of them spoke up. In the three weeks the *Tallyrand* had taken to get from Ortiz's home world to the kazsatorezs' Bismarck, she had learned that DEL Percy Tremand completely dominated his associates.

During the first few weeks of their acquaintance, she had wondered how a man so insensitive to his colleagues had been the only diplomat to win enough of the kazsatorezs' trust to garner an invitation to their isolated home planet. Now, having studied the kazsatorezs' own social structure, she thought she understood.

Tremand and the kazsatorezs had a great deal in common: belief in a strict hierarchy, use of ritual to replace substantial communication when necessary, and employment of underlying threats to enforce the rest.

The threat Percy Tremand proffered to his subordinates was that of not being given a favorable mention in his Expeditionary Report. Although a tour of the capital city and a few xenology journal articles were hardly enough to base conjecture upon, from what Ortiz had seen, the kazsatorezs relied on forces far less subtle to maintain their social hierarchy.

"Certainly they wouldn't have shown us what we saw today," added Kero Van Meek, the party's botanist, "if they had much to hide. I thought I'd be sick when we were taken by the reformatory. The conditions they kept prisoners in were inhumane!"

"But apparently not un-kazsatorezs," Ortiz muttered. She didn't bother trying to offer other explanations.

In what Percy and his cronies saw as the beginnings of
an unrestricted, hands-on tour of a new world, she saw
a host of potentially dangerous implications.

The kazsatorezs had visited human colonies. In fact,
the two races had first encountered each other in a system colonized by humans. They should have known that
the conditions in the reformatory (and the tenements)
past which the humans had been driven earlier today
would be considered rather uncivilized. That the humans
had been permitted to see them suggested several possible motivations, none of which Ortiz particularly cared
for:

One: The kazsatorezs simply didn't care what the hu-
    mans thought.
Two: The kazatorezs cared, but only after the fashion
    of a veiled threat. "We do this kind of thing to
    members of our own race. Just think what we could
    do to you."
Three: The kazsatorezs had worse things to hide and,
    in contrast to those (presumptive) discoveries, what
    they had let the humans see of their society's less
    civilized aspects seemed moderate.

This last had been the theory Ortiz had been attempting to get Percy Tremand to acknowledge. His
stubborn refusal had more to do—she liked to think—
with his own belief that he and the kazsatorezs had
achieved a perfect understanding than with a flaw in
her theorizing.

Ortiz forced herself to remain in the public areas of
the suite long enough to not seem to be stomping off in
a huff. The expedition's zoologist and medical officer,
Doctor Chang Li, shared her passion for Go and they
played through several rounds before Ortiz departed for
her room, pleading exhaustion.

"I still think they're hiding something," she said as
she undressed. "I just wish I knew what."

When their kazsatorezs escort came for them the next

morning, Ortiz was again struck by how alien an alien could be. Since she had been added to the expedition at effectively the last moment (Percy Tremand had been told that he could bring five humans planetside and five he was going to bring), she had not had the careful indoctrination the other four had undergone before leaving Terra. This might account for her gut feeling of difference—or it might simply be that the kazsatorezs *were* different.

She hadn't needed Chang Li's thoughtful lecture to tell her that the kazsatorezs were most likely descended from some sort of carnivore. Her own impression had been of lanky dinosaurs—long-legged, long-armed, with whiplike tails that were prehensile for their last six inches, and mouths filled with lots of sharp teeth.

Despite their obviously predatory nature, the kazsatorezs were rather beautiful. Their tightly scaled coats were patterned in brightly colored stripes; red and orange, brown and gold, yellow and tan, green and blue were just some of the patterns the humans had observed. The scales of the upper class (Ortiz wasn't certain if the term was accurate, but chose to leave it stand for now) reflected the light with such brilliant iridescence that Doctor Li hypothesized a dietary additive.

Their guide for today was a slender six-footer with jagged green and yellow stripes. Baring his needle-sharp teeth in what was the kazsatorezs imitation of a smile (their equivalent gesture involved the release of pheromones which humans could not detect), he asked them to call him "Jack."

Idly, Ortiz wondered if the kazsatorezs had indeed learned to "smile" in an effort to cross the species gap (as Tremand said) or because they suspected that the sight of all those teeth scared the shit out of their human associates.

"This way," Jack said, his words coming from a voder set as a pendant in the elaborate necklace hung around his long neck.

Subconsciously, Ortiz expected him to hiss, but the words were in clear standard Trade. Both humans and kazsatorezs needed to use a translation unit to "speak" in the other's language—tongues and teeth were just too different. Kazsatorezs languages minimalized the use of inflection and tone so important to human languages, employing scent cues in their place.

The difficulty of programming translation units had kept linguists of both races busy for the first five years after contact and the devices were still inadequate for subtleties. Pressing keys to indicate "authoritative scent" or, on the kazsatorezs' side, "stern inflection" was a poor substitute for the real thing.

One of Ortiz's jobs on this expedition was to collect audio, visual, and olfactory recordings of kazsatorezs conversations to expand the linguists' archives. She rather despaired of having the opportunity to acquire the latter since, thus far, all their encounters with the kazsatorezs had been in groups too large for the olfactory recorder to isolate individual scents.

Today, for example, Jack was accompanied by a "specialist group" of six other kazsatorezs and a vehicle driver. Ortiz rather suspected that at least some of the "specialist group" were guards, rather than scientists, but she felt that was only fair. In their own party, Doctor Maurice Raunga was indeed a technologies specialist, but he was also a security officer, charged both with checking their quarters for eavesdropping devices and for protecting the party from physical harm. His job was made easier in that kazsatorezs technology was largely less sophisticated than human technology—although their work in some areas made them promising trade partners.

The planet the humans called Bismarck (and the kazsatorezs called by a word in one of their dominant languages that roughly translated as "Here") was enough like Terra that the humans could visit with minimal biomodifications. Doctor Li had inserted microfilters into their nostrils and windpipes to make certain that they didn't breathe in anything inimical. He had also coated their exposed skin with a light, protein-based shield against molds and spores.

Human colony expeditions to seven extraterrestrial worlds had made such cautions routine, but although humans had settled on worlds with native life, never before had they come to a world with an advanced civilization in place. Eager to make as much as they could out of this opportunity, the diplomatic party members each subvocalized notes into recorders while DEL Tremand chatted casually with Jack.

"Tell me, Jack." Tremand tapped with the fingers of one hand into his translator, his blue eyes wide and frank as he kept his gaze on Jack's face. "What treats do you have in store for us today?"

The fin ridges above Jack's eyes fanned slightly as the translator spoke. Ortiz swallowed a chuckle, suspecting that Tremand's idiomatic word choice had flustered the device. Tremand had been warned, but from time to time, he forgot—or perhaps he didn't care.

Jack answered, the inflection of his words cordial. "First, we are going to inspect a game preserve and botanical garden for the edification of Doctors Li and Van Meek. Then, after a lunch break, we will visit one of our spacecraft design facilities. This evening, we will socialize with important government personalities."

Again Ortiz suppressed a chuckle. Early kazsatorezs/human relations had discovered that shared meals—a social tradition in both cultures—did nothing to enhance relations. The kazsatorezs' teeth were designed for shredding large chunks of meat, their gullets for handling smaller items swallowed whole. For them, a banquet involved merry dismemberment of enormous, elegant roasts, crunching unshucked shellfish, and swallowing live sea creatures that rather resembled eels.

Humanity's comparatively delicate table customs, relying as they did on an array of specialized tools, simply did not harmonize. Both parties were made uncomfortable by the contrasts. A colonial anthropologist present at a few of the early banquets had suggested that the kazsatorezs viewed the human customs with something like contempt. His reflections had been dismissed as humanocentric, but Ortiz could not help but recall them as she watched Jack.

As the day progressed, many of her doubts and worries eased—Bismarck was simply fascinating.

The region which they were touring was roughly tropical (although Jack reminded them that Bismarck had its temperate zones as well). The planet lacked Terra's vast oceans, but in the low, heavily vegetated regions, there were hints that oceans had once existed in sufficient quantities to provide the primordial soup biologists believed was essential to spark life.

On this continent, animal life was largely oviparous (as were the kazsatorez themselves), but Jack informed them that there were regions where marsupial life was strongly represented. Bismarck apparently possessed nothing equivalent to mammals and many of the kazsatorez specialists' questions had to do with mammalian life cycles and family bonding rituals.

Although the specialists used the "courteous" inflection on their translators when the kazsatorez scientists spoke to the humans, Ortiz thought that the flicking of tail tips, and rising and falling of crests and brow fins when they spoke to each other indicated a great deal of debate and conjecture among themselves.

During the morning's tour her opportunities to observe the culture in action were limited. The sites Jack had chosen were devoid of villages or towns. Still, watching their escorts interacting among themselves and with those locals they encountered, she gathered further evidence of a rigid hierarchy with an upper or ruling class firmly in place.

DEL Tremand clearly believed himself accepted within that ruling class. She wondered if he was correct, but with the stinging contempt of the previous evening's confrontation still vivid in her memory, she kept her suppositions to herself.

That evening, after a reception with the shimmering, jewelry-bedecked government "personalities," Ortiz retired to her room to organize her notes. The evening's social events had given her plenty of data, but as of yet, she had only the vaguest notion of its significance.

Tomorrow their agenda included a visit to a kazsatorez incubator and créchè, a religious ceremony of some sort (or was it something else? The translator kept wobbling between the terms religious/political/philosophical), and another meeting, this time with cadets at the Space Academy.

This last was very important to the kazsatorezs. Even their best space-going craft were far less sophisticated than those used by humans (as Ortiz had nervously observed during the shuttle ride in from the *Tallyrand*) and clearly they wanted to impress the humans with their desire to join in space exploration as equal partners.

Ortiz sighed and stared at her screen, fingers automatically tagging and cataloguing images for later analysis. The nagging suspicion that she was still missing something crucial haunted her, along with the equally persuasive suggestion that whatever it was didn't really matter—DEL Tremand would choose someone else for the follow-up expeditions, someone else would unravel the puzzle, and she would be back on La Tigre continuing her dissertation. Somehow, the cultural implications of physically adapting the evolving colonial population to its new environment didn't seem as compelling a topic as it once had.

She sighed again, making an inventory of the jewelry styles worn by tonight's government representatives: size, style, elements, shape, craftsmanship. "Star" gems (sapphires, rubies) seemed to be more valued than faceted gems. Tiger-eye opals were included in most badges of honor. But were they symbolic or merely fashionable? Who could she ask? Jack? One of the kazsatorezs mineralogists?

"I still think there's something going on that they're not telling us about," she muttered.

"You're right, you know," said a high voice from behind her. It rolled the "r's" as it spoke.

Ortiz swung around in her chair. She was certain that she had left the window tightly locked. Indeed, she couldn't have opened it if she had wanted to, given the number of microminiaturized security devices that Raunga had set up. Now, however, the window stood open and crouched on the sill, staring at her from large golden eyes with slit pupils like a cat's, was a small, slender furry creature.

Her mind raced to categorize it: bilaterally symmetrical, covered with short fur, possessing a long tail. Perhaps a meter—maybe a meter and a half in height—or should that be length? The creature on her windowsill looked as if it might move easily on all fours. Eerie facial features, something like a cross between a cat and a human: cat's ears, almost human mouth and nose, but set in a face covered in fur and sprouting whiskers.

All this her mind filed as she swiveled her chair and stared. In the same amount of time, the little creature had leaped from the windowsill and taken a seat on a chair—one out of the line of sight from both the window and the door, she noted, but close enough that it could jump to the window again if it needed to do so.

"What did you say?" she asked, too stunned to manage anything memorable.

"I said," the creature repeated in the same, burred Trade, "that you're right, you know. The kazsatorezs are hiding something. Us."

"Us?" Ortiz's skin prickled with excitement. "You? You're native to this planet?"

"That's right," said the creature. "We're rovag. We live here, too."

It wrapped its tail around its toes, apparently relaxing a bit since she hadn't called for help or fled in panic.

"Rrrovag," she said, attempting to imitate the burr.

" 'Rovag' will do," her odd visitor said, rolling the "r" only slightly.

"Why haven't we met any of you?" Ortiz asked, already suspecting the answer.

The rovag blinked its golden eyes. "Because the kazsatorezs consider us a slave race: a race not as intelligent or useful as their own. They know that you humans might not agree, so they're keeping us a secret until the basic diplomatic provisions are in place—and you can bet that those provisions will include something about leaving planets independent in matters of internal governance."

"We'd insist on the same," Ortiz said, then swallowed hard, her excitement nearly choking her. "But how do you know all of this? How do you speak our language?

How did you come here, and why are you talking to me?"

The rovag squeaked something that might have been a laugh.

"I learned your language from the kazsatorezs' archives. Some of our people were trained to speak the language—our mouths, throats, and lips are not greatly dissimilar from your own."

Ortiz nodded. "I can see that. Still, your fluency amazes me."

The rovag shrugged, a gesture clearly imitated from the human. "It shouldn't. The idea was to have us act as spies on your people. What good would a spy who couldn't follow the subtleties be?"

"Spies?"

"Sure. We're small, agile, easily overlooked. Most human body-mass scanners are set below a certain size." The rovag trilled a shrill laugh. "The kazsatorezs' observers noted this first, but I found it was true when I was working through your security alarms. They simply did not see me."

"Oh." Taking refuge in the familiar, Ortiz turned and flipped on her recorder. "May I take some notes?"

"Sure," the rovag said, "but I want to warn you that you shouldn't show what you record without due consideration of the consequences."

"What consequences?"

The rovag squeaked again. Its golden eyes shifted restlessly from place to place, constantly on guard.

"For one," it said, "you'd probably have an accident before you could leave Bismarck with them—maybe your entire group would be executed. And if you make your recordings public after you leave, you will very likely trigger genocide."

"Genocide?"

"I do have the word right, don't I?" The rovag frowned, its whiskers curling down. "Extermination of a race. The kazsatorezs have too much to gain from interaction with a human culture. They've been subjugating the rovag for about a century, wiping out those who won't cooperate. They don't need much prompting to decide that we're a nuisance species."

"No!"

"Why not?" The rovag's eyes widened—perhaps indicating surprise. "It's the pattern of things. The stronger dominate the weaker. Rovag could compete when . . ."

The rovag stopped speaking, ears twitching alertly. Carmelita froze in her seat, instinctively holding her breath.

"This isn't a great place for us to chat," the rovag said at last. "Can you come out with me?"

Carmelita didn't even pause to think. "Yes."

"We'll go out as I came in," the rovag said. "Can you climb?"

"Not well," Carmelita admitted, looking at the retractable claws that tipped each of the rovag's three-fingered, two-thumbed hands. "At least not without assistance."

"I've brought a rope, and I can haul you up," the rovag said. "We're going to the top of the building, then across and down. No acrophobia?"

"None." Carmelita swallowed hard. The diplomatic party was housed on the fifth floor of a hotellike building. The lower floors contained dining facilities, food storage, and other areas they had politely not asked about.

"Good." The rovag leaped onto the windowsill and crouched, listening and sniffing the air. "I'll drop the rope down in a moment."

Carmelita checked to see that her door was locked, clipped her recording unit to her belt, and turned out the lights. She resisted a childish urge to lump her pillows under her bedclothes. In all the weeks she had traveled with Tremand and his cronies, not even friendly Chang Li had ever visited her after she had retired for the evening. Why would anyone bother her now?

When she climbed onto the windowsill, she felt very exposed. What would she say if someone saw her? "I'm just going out for a stroll"?

The rovag didn't give her much time to worry. Almost as soon as she was in place, a rope with a loop on the end dropped in front of her. Putting her foot into the loop, Ortiz stepped out into the air.

Swinging there, wondering how the little rovag could possibly pull her up even one story, she felt herself rising.

"Grab the edge of the roof," came a high-pitched whisper, "and swing yourself over."

She did so, grasping a wall about fifteen centimeters wide, and (as she discovered when she landed on the other side) forty-five centimeters high, then thudding to the other side. At the sound of her landing, the rovag looked up from winding the rope around a spool which it dropped into a pouch. Carmelita could have sworn it grinned.

"This way," was all it said before it scurried off on all fours into the shadows. Then it stopped and, going back on its haunches, looked at her. "How well do you see in the dark?"

"Fifty percent better than human norm," she responded.

The rovag flicked its tail once—perhaps a gesture corresponding to a nod. "Well, I guess you won't need the goggles I rigged for you." It seemed vaguely disappointed but continued off across the rooftop without further comment.

Ortiz hurried after, grateful for the biomodifications standard to La Tigre colonists. Mentally, she made a note for her dissertation about the usefulness of those modifications outside of their intended environment.

Although the goggles had not been needed, her rovag guide had ample opportunity to show off its technical brilliance. Various devices interrupted optic beams, redirected sonic scans, masked scent cues, and otherwise disabled security systems wherever they passed. Others made it possible for the much clumsier human to follow where the rovag climbed with claws and natural grace.

In this way, Carmelita crossed rooftops, ducked through doors, crept around walls, and climbed up and down ropes. Eventually she was led into the attic of what she took for an abandoned factory.

Only then did the audacity of this thing she had done

catch up to her. At the best, she could be said to have
acted with initiative, but at the worst (and she was certain that "worst" was how Tremand would judge her
actions) she had been insubordinate, reckless, impru-
dent, and just plain foolish.

Whatever. Sitting on the dusty floor of a structure that
smelled faintly of motor oil and nutmeg, Carmelita Margarita Ortiz of La Tigre looked at her rovag guide (cap-
tor?) and managed a brave smile.

"Now can you tell me what is going on?"

"I hope so," the rovag said. "My name is K'denree,
by the way. Yours is Ortiz?"

"Carmelita Margarita Ortiz," she answered. "My
friends call me Carmelita."

" 'K'armelita,' " the rovag repeated, rolling the "r" in
the first syllable delightfully. "I hope indeed that we
shall be friends."

"You need my help," Carmelita prompted, hoping she
seemed decisive rather than nervous.

"Yes, we do," K'denree said simply. "To understand
the rovag's troubles, you must understand something of
our history—and how that history relates to the
kazsatorezs."

"I'm listening," Carmelita said, switching on her
recorder.

K'denree stroked its whiskers with one claw-tipped
finger. "According to studies done by kazsatorezs scientists, the rovag and the kazsatorezs may have evolved
within overlapping ecosystems. Some of their theories
even argue that rovag and kazsatorezs may have involuntarily assisted in the selection for intelligence within
each of our ancestral groups."

Carmelita nodded. "Did the kazsatores prey on your
ancestors?"

"The kazsatorezs prey on anything that moves,"
K'denree said bitterly. "They are carnivores. My own
people are omnivorous, although some traits suggest that
we were originally arboreal hunters."

"The claws," Carmelita suggested, "and the teeth."

"Yes. Rovag may have once been prominent in all
forested regions. However, the spread of the kazsatorezs

eventually restricted rovag groups to those forests that possessed damp footing—swamps and marshes. The primitive kazsatorezs, who relied on strength and tremendous running speed for their hunting, did not like the places and mostly left us be. There we flourished.

"Millennia passed. Rovag and kazsatorezs societies took different turns. The kazsataorezs' competition among themselves escalated their technological developments, especially in weapons and fortifications. Our people had no such need. Our family structure argues against intraspecies warfare and we had the kazsatorezs to fear—while they did not much need to fear us."

"Your family structure?" Carmelita asked, anthropological curiosity piqued.

"We are," K'denree paused, as if reviewing its vocabulary to make certain that the terms were correct, "marsupial hermaphrodites."

"Huh?" Carmelita blurted, then blushed at her rudeness.

"Our breeders," K'denree said patiently, "mutually impregnate each other—each functions as male and female. In most cases, one young is born to each of the pair. In about one quarter of births, twins are born. In this instance, one of the twins will be sterile. This sterile twin will grow larger than the breeders and possesses a strong protective urge toward the group as a whole. I am one such twin."

Carmelita's mind was whirling at the implications of such a society. "An entire subset of the population that cannot breed, but is inclined to protect the whole. Fascinating! Doesn't this lead to severe competition between protector groups?"

"It might," K'denree said, "but for the fact that we have many natural enemies. The kazsarorezs are the most intelligent, but Bismarck possesses many other large carnivores. It is as much as the protectors can do to defend the breeders. Although our young are 'born' when very tiny, still they must be carried in a pouch for a long while. Even after pouch emergence, they are vulnerable."

"Go on," Carmelita prompted.

"One of the first things that the kazsatorezs warred over was their own unhatched eggs. These are a valuable resource to any kazsatorezs group, since they are generated at the expense of their parent group, but can be reared to revere their hatching group."

"The kazsatorezs imprint—like ducks or geese?"

"I fear I do not understand the reference," K'denree said.

"Terran avians," Carmelita said. "When they hatch, they adopt the first moving thing they see as their parent. Since most of the time this is their mother, this isn't a problem, but orphans have been known to imprint on humans or other animals."

K'denree flipped the tip of its tail. "The kazsatorezs' reaction is not as extreme as this one you describe, but it is similar. The servant class in kazsatorezs society comes largely from imprinted captured eggs."

"The kazsatorezs still do this today?" Carmelita asked, rather appalled.

"Some isolated groups do," K'denree said, "but between the larger nations the consequences of raiding now include war with weapons of mass destruction. Instead, many servant eggs are the descendants of servant parents. The kazsatorezs have come to believe strongly in the superiority of certain family strains."

"How do they differentiate these strains?"

"Through pedigree, tradition and, lately, genetic coding. Once there might have been physical characteristics as well, but these have been lost with time," K'denree replied. "One of the most prevalent 'fairy tales' among the servant classes has to do with a servant egg smuggled into the aristocratic hatchery and raised as a leader."

"Does this leader then return to free the servants?" Carmelita asked.

"Only rarely. Usually the pride of having engendered one who cannot be distinguished from their betters is considered reward enough." K'denree shook an admonishing finger. "Remember, the imprintation factor is a real imperative, not merely a matter of upbringing."

Carmelita nodded. "I think I understand, but it's an odd concept for a human."

"Or for a rovag," K'denree agreed. "Even though as a protector I am aware of the power of a biological imperative, I do not feel that my imperative keeps me blindly obedient to anyone else."

Carmelita mused that while the rovag might not like to accept the idea, their race could be as blindly directed by its biological imperatives as the kazsatorezs. What a topic that would make for a dissertation! "The Role of Biological Imperatives in the Social Development of the Sentient Species of Bismarck." She could almost see the square gilded letters against a black binding.

She shook herself out of fantasy. "So you and the kazsatorezs lived in different ecological niches long enough to evolve separate societies. What happened to imbalance this?"

"Technology," K'denree said simply. "The kazsatorezs surpassed us again and again. The first improvements were weapons that enabled them to kill at a distance. Then there were vehicles that enabled them to navigate our swamps and marshes or merely to fly over them. They developed chemicals to denude our trees of leaves and so force us into the open."

Carmelita shuddered. "They certainly didn't need you for food, did they?"

"No," K'denree said. "Although there are always rumors. What they need us for is labor. We are small and agile—traits they do not possess. Over the centuries, we have been useful for jobs ranging from the washing of exterior windows to the weaving of textiles. Today our labor has become essential to the manufacture of microtechnological devices."

Remembering historical reports of children being used for similar tasks in Terran civilizations, Carmelita swallowed her own automatic protest that a modern, technological society would not need to do such things.

"So as their technology advanced," she said, "the jobs that they trained you to perform changed."

"Yes. Until now, we have been useful. Now, however, human methods of doing the same jobs may make us less necessary."

"So you mentioned earlier," Carmelita frowned, "when you mentioned the possibility of genocide."

"Precisely." K'denree looked sad. "Like the kazsatorezs, rovag are not tied to the peculiar 'nuclear family' system that you humans advocate."

"It works for us," Carmelita interrupted, "and despite efforts to argue otherwise, we keep coming back to it."

"I don't doubt it," K'denree said, "but imagine rovag society as a large family in which almost everyone is a mother and a father both, where there are protective 'cousins' to help with raising the children. Given how we view our relationship to each other, entire rovag tribes have succumbed to slavery rather than see kinfolk suffer. Recently . . ."

K'denree paused, whiskers twitching in what Carmelita guessed was agitation.

"Recently?" she said gently.

"Recently, the kazsatorezs have found an even more effective way to use that mutually protective tendency against us."

K'denree rose from where it had crouched on the floor and began to pace on all fours, tail lashing.

"They have created a biomechanical device that can be implanted into a rovag's brain. It is little more than a bomb and a receiver. At its lowest setting, it causes immense pain. At its final setting, it kills."

"No!"

"Yes. At first they implanted these into the protectors, since we were the greatest source of trouble to them. Later, they realized that we were willing to die for our clans—for any of our race. Now the devices are systematically implanted into the brains of each enslaved breeder rovag when the rovag reaches full growth. Our enslaved people have become hostage against our race's cooperation."

Carmelita felt nauseated, but even that reaction couldn't keep her from seeing the implications.

"Then when you spoke of genocide . . ."

"I meant something that could occur swiftly. Within a few hours, most captive rovag of breeding age could be killed. Protectors are sterile. Even if we fled, we could not breed more of our people."

"Are all rovag enslaved?" Carmelita asked hesitantly.

"There are stories of free communities," K'denree said, "but they may only be legends. In any case, they might not provide a sufficient genetic base to rebound from the slaughter, and, if they did, what would await them? Further slaughter or eventual enslavement."

Carmelita rubbed her hands across her temples, unable to draw her gaze from the small, slim figure pacing restlessly across the dusty floor.

"What do you want me to do?" she asked.

"Smuggle me off-planet," K'denree said promptly. "Let me testify before your leaders to my people's existence and to our need."

"That tactic just might work," Carmelita mused, "but the *Tallyrand* is out-system, not here in orbit. We were shuttled in by a kazsatorezs vessel, and when we leave, we're being shuttled back. I expect that our luggage will be searched."

K'denree's ears drooped. It stopped pacing, and its tail dragged on the floor.

"Then there is nothing you can do?"

Carmelita suddenly wanted to pat the valiant little protector. "I don't know how to do it, but certainly I can think of something. We're being permitted to take out samples, trade goods. Perhaps . . ."

"Perhaps," K'denree said, tail perking, "is far better than 'no.' Now I must sneak you back to your quarters before you are missed."

Over the next several days, Carmelita Margarita Ortiz met with K'denree almost every night. The rovag introduced her to others of its kind. She found the children irresistibly cute; the breeder adults (who seemed especially tiny to her after meeting the larger K'denree first) awoke a fierce protectiveness in her. It was probably unfair, but she didn't find the mass of the kazsatorezs nearly as appealing.

At great risk, she visited the barracks in which the kazsatorezs kept their enslaved rovag, carefully recording the details K'denree would need to support its case.

She even grew accustomed to the concept of a society structured around breeding status. The rovag's naming system helped with this. Very young were designated with an "M" prefix to their names. Adults who had not yet borne a child were designated with an "R." Breeders' names were prefixed with an "L" and the elderly, post-breeders (there were few of these in the slave quarters) with a "V." Protectors, of course, were designated with a "K."

Ironically, she found that, because of the hard "C" sound that began her own name, most of the rovag viewed her as a protector—a human protector, capable of defeating the kazsatorezs as the rovag alone could not.

During one visit, K'denree introduced Carmelita to a black-and-white striped rovag who was, like her, a cultural anthropologist. V'sarth explained that the prefixes had once varied slightly between rovag populations (for example, "V" in one area had been replaced by "F"), but under the kazsatorezs' domination such cultural differences were gradually dying out.

"We are becoming something other than rovag," V'sarth said. "We are becoming what the kazsatorezs make us—a people who exist for their convenience. Someday we shall cease to be useful. Then we shall cease to exist at all."

"Not if I can help it!" Carmelita promised passionately.

K'denree, she learned, was something of a legend among his own people—a daring rebel against the doom that overshadowed their race, a heroic freedom fighter. The idea of a ferocious freedom fighter not much over a meter long—small enough to stuff into a travel bag—gave her the giggles at first, but reasonably she knew heroism had nothing to do with size. Indeed, the more she learned of the risks K'denree took for its people, the more she grew to accept their view of it as a fierce and terrible figure worthy of legend.

Sometimes, hazy despite the stimulants she was taking

to remain alert, Carmelita would indulge in fantasies in which she was revered as the discoverer and savior of a new sentient species. Headlines marched through her imagination:

"Anthropologist Discovers New Race!"

"Daring Escape From Bismarck!"

"Another Alien Among Us!"

"La Tigre Native Awarded Doctorate for Contributions to Interstellar Accord."

"Ortiz Named Head of Diplomatic Mission."

Other times she toyed with scenarios in which, once the *Tallyrand* was safely in human space, she revealed K'denree and her records to her astonished crew members. The thought of arrogant Percy Tremand heartily shaking her hand and telling her how valuable a crew member she had proved to be was sweet, but Ortiz knew full well that only her exhaustion made it seem at all likely.

After exploring several possible ways to smuggle K'denree off-planet and finding problems with each of them, Carmelita came to an unpleasant conclusion.

No matter how much she wanted to deny it, she couldn't do this alone. Not only were the logistic problems formidable, but the consequences of failure—not only for herself and K'denree, but for the rest of the diplomatic expedition and possibly for the entire rovag race—were simply too terrible to gamble.

"I've got to tell Percy Tremand," she told K'denree as they conferred one night in the factory attic. "I simply don't have a choice."

"Why Tremand?" K'denree asked, wrinkling up its nose in a gesture of distaste. "I thought you didn't like him."

"I don't."

"Why not ask a few of the others to help you—perhaps Doctor Li or Doctor Raunga?"

"They would be my first choices," Carmelita admitted, "but I can't take the risk that they would choose to report me to Tremand rather than simply assist. If they do so, I lose any chance I have because Tremand will take my going to them as a tacit admission that I don't trust him."

"You don't." K'denree grinned, reminding Carmelita of the Cheshire cat.

"Yes, but once he knows that, he is certain to balk at anything I would ask him." Carmelita sighed. "And I'm not certain I would blame him. This expedition is his baby—his chance at immortality—and I would effectively be telling him that the kazsatorezs had been manipulating him."

K'denree flicked the tip of his tail. "Can you enlist Tremand without telling him that?"

"I think so," Carmelita said. "I simply will need to hope that his vanity is greater than his arrogance."

"I hope you're right," K'denree said uncertainly.

Carmelita drew in a deep breath of the spicy air. "I had better be."

"DEL Tremand?" Carmelita said, knocking on the door of the room Tremand had appropriated as his office. "May I have a private word with you?"

In preparation for this meeting, she had made certain to get a solid night's sleep. Then she had waited for the time when the three physical scientists usually worked on packing their samples for shipment. This left the residential suite clear.

Tremand himself opened his office door. "What can I do for you, Ortiz?"

He looked and sounded impatient. Whatever Carmelita thought of his attitudes, she couldn't deny that he had been working as hard or harder than any member of his team (her own nocturnal exploits excepted).

"I need a word with you in private," she said, stepping into his office as if he had invited her, flicking on the static field as she closed the door.

"Yes?" Tremand's impatience was tempered with some puzzlement. No wonder. She had avoided any personal contact with him pretty much since their arrival on Bismarck.

"I have a problem," she said, appealing to him as

chief in their hierarchy, "and I can't handle it alone. I need your help."

Before he could make a belittling comment and ruin her resolve, Carmelita set her recorder atop his desk.

"I have evidence of a conspiracy that will make anything in history seem like nothing," she said, making her voice breathless, "but I can't deal with it alone."

For a moment, she was terrified that Tremand would reject her approach, dismiss her concerns as he had before, but there must have been something new in her demeanor—perhaps a bit of the intensity she had learned from little K'denree—that made him take her seriously.

"Tell me," he said, motioning her to a chair. "I'll listen."

When she had finished her account, including a brief, specially edited version of the recordings she had made during her tours with K'denree, Tremand sat in thoughtful silence before turning his stern gaze on her.

"Why didn't those rovag come to me themselves?" Tremand said sharply.

Carmelita was ready to deal with DEL Tremand's piqued pride. "They couldn't get close to you, sir. The kazsatorezs have been watching you carefully. They know who among us has the power."

Tremand relaxed slightly. "And why did the rovag come to you rather than to a more senior member of the expedition?"

"They learned I was the anthropologist," Carmelita said. "They hoped that a student of our own cultures would be more receptive to a meeting an entirely new one."

A small smile quirked the corner of Tremand's mouth. "Well, they were right enough there. Now we need to find a way to get their representative off-planet without the kazsatorezs discovering what we plan. I can't be responsible for setting off a genocidal attack on an entire species."

Carmelita nodded respectfully, trying not to let too much relief flood her face. She hadn't been at all certain that Tremand would agree.

"Eventually, we'll need to let the kazsatorezs know we are aware of the existence of the rovag, of course," Tremand mused. "It's the only way to keep the rovag safe in the long run. And when the kazsatorezs learn that they cannot continue simultaneously to trade for human technologies and to exploit their planetary coresidents, I believe we will find that they will opt for access to human technologies."

"Are you sure, sir?" Carmelita said anxiously, this last not at all feigned.

"Of course I am," Tremand said in his most fatherly tones. "The rovag cannot give the kazsatorezs everything they want—the better stardrives, the growing space that new planets offer. Technology can, and since we hold the technology, we can name our terms."

Privately, Carmelita wondered if the kazsatorezs, with their taste for conquest, would remain controllable once they had access to human technology. However, that was a problem for later. Tremand seemed willing both to dupe the kazsatorezs and to help the rovag. Once K'denree was off-planet, she was going to make certain that she was in a position to advise on the course of human/kazsatorezs policy.

She wondered at her sudden surge of confidence. Tremand was still in charge, but she no longer felt that his approval or disapproval controlled her destiny. Odd. Realistically, she was still nothing more than a doctoral student from a colony world, but her awareness of what she could achieve had been altered.

Maybe knowing a meter-long hero could do this to a person.

"Hsst, K'armelita!" K'denree jumped lightly down from the windowsill.

"Good! You're here!" she said, almost patting the rovag lightly on one furry shoulder. "I'll get Doctor Li and DEL Tremand."

After some thought, Tremand had decided that the biologist must be let in on their plans. Carmelita had been less than happy, knowing the risk the rovag were taking was accentuated with every person who was in

on their secret, but she was forced to admit that Trem-
and had thought more about the details of K'denree's
escape than she had.

Chang Li did an admirable job of maintaining his
poise when she led him up to the rovag.

"Holograms did not do you justice, K'denree," he
muttered, setting his med kit on the floor next to the
rovag.

"I felt the same way about humans," K'denree said.
"I thought I was prepared for the tufts of hair and naked
skin, but I was relieved that my first meeting with K'armelita was in partial darkness."

"Thanks, bud," Carmelita said.

She stood nervous watch while Doctor Li outfitted
K'denree with breathing filters. While the biologist was
working, Percy Tremand entered the room. He still gave
the impression of silver tailored elegance, but today that
elegance was edged with excitement.

"Raunga and I have explained to the kazsatorezs security that we cannot have our samples torn through without undoing our scientist's careful work. I think we've
pulled it off. They've agreed to do their security checks
through remotes."

"Great," Carmelita said.

K'denree, wriggling its nose around the jury-rigged
filters, flipped its tail in agreement.

"Now, K'denree," Doctor Li said, holding open a
transparent vac-bag partially packed with labeled plant
samples, "get in. The bag will keep you safe in case
we're accidentally decompressed and the other contents
should help disguise you against a scan."

"I'll look like a prepackaged meal!" K'denree said, its
dignity wounded.

"Better packaged than not," Doctor Li insisted, "especially if the kazsatorezs get suspicious. The vac-seal
will keep them from locating you by scent and protect
you until I can make certain that you aren't susceptible
to anything in the *Tallyrand*'s environment. The filters
are backup."

DEL Tremand hunkered down so that his blue eyes

could meet the rovag's gold. "This is important, K'denree. If we are detected now . . ."

"You're right," K'denree admitted. "I know you're right, but if my people ever learned of this!"

With a single, woeful glance at Carmelita, K'denree walked into the bag, then crouched down as Doctor Li sealed it and hooked in a compressed air cylinder. Then Doctor Li and DEL Tremand departed to finish preparations.

"In my dreams," K'denree said, before the bag sealed, "I never imagined my escape from our people's enemies would be so undignified, but for now I will pretend to be a biological sample and you . . . What will you pretend to be?"

"Nothing," Carmelita said firmly. "I'm going to be what meeting you has made me—the first advocate of rovag independence, a prying nuisance with no respect for anyone else's terrestrial boundaries."

K'denree squeaked cheerfully. "The kazsatorezs will be terrified of the possibility that the humans will attack them!"

"I wish our approach could be so obvious," Carmelita replied, "but I suspect that we will need to work quietly and subtly through diplomatic channels for years to come. After all, if the kazsatorezs wipe out your people, we have nothing left to gain."

The slight hum of a lift generator announced Doctor Li's return. Without further ceremony, the two humans sealed the vac-bag and loaded K'denree in with the biologist's other samples. Lastly, they sealed the crate, adding a small alarm borrowed from K'denree's own kit that would warn them if the crate was opened without permission.

The trip on the kazsatorezs shuttle *Friendship* was not as uneventful as they could have wished. Midway between the planet and the waiting Tallyrand, the vessel began to yaw wildly.

"Keep to your seats," the kazsatorezs pilot's translated voice announced. "We have encountered unexpected turbulence."

"Turbulence?" Tremand said, cocking a doubting eyebrow. "Out here?"

"It is possible," Maurice Raunga said. "Their technology is not what we are used to. Perhaps this is meant to demonstrate their need to us."

"Perhaps . . ." Tremand said, but he looked thoughtful. "Ortiz, you have a young person's sense of balance. Why don't you step to the cargo bay and see that our samples were properly anchored."

The kazsatorezs flight attendant was clearly unwilling to challenge Tremand's order, so Ortiz unbuckled her restraints and, keeping at least one hand firmly on the seat back, walked toward the bay into the hold where their gear was stowed. Sealing the hood on her vac-suit, she entered the air lock, and, from there, the cargo bay.

A kazsatorezs cargo handler, also vac-suited, was lounging in a safety harness along one wall. None of the crates seemed to have been tampered with, but then he would have had plenty of opportunity to cover his actions. Having seen K'denree at work, Ortiz was well-aware that Bismarck's technology could be used to bypass the humans' security. Perhaps Raunga could tell if the security seals had been breached, but she had to be content with the knowledge that K'denree's alarm hadn't gone off.

She touched her vac-suit's comm link. "Everything seems fine for now, DEL, but I think I'll stay back here so I can help the cargo handler if there's trouble. There's a spare harness I can use."

"Very good," Percy Tremand said calmly. "I have advised our shuttle's captain that this is my wish."

He sounded as confidently arrogant as ever, but for now that arrogance was on her side. Waving casually at the kazsatorezs across the cargo bay, Ortiz strapped herself in.

Soon after, she noticed, the shuttle's yawing stopped.

Hours later, after the expedition had achieved the *Tallyrand* and the human ship was heading out of the Bismarck system, Carmelita took K'denree to a sterile room and let it out of the vac-bag. Then they went over to a window to catch a last glimpse of the starlike brightness that was the only world it had ever known.

When even that glitter had blended into the panorama of the stars, K'denree spoke.

"I hope that someday I will return—and not as a refugee."

"I'm planning on it," Carmelita promised.

"I anticipate the day," K'denree said thoughtfully, "when part of our world shall once again belong to free members of my people. When it does, I shall let them celebrate me properly."

The golden eyes gleamed, seeing honors she could only imagine. She thought of the papers she had dreamed about writing, of the headlines that might have proclaimed her. It was rather nice to know that K'denree, too, could hope for fame as well as success. The rovag seemed to guess the drift of her thoughts.

"When we are free," it said, "I shall make certain that there is a special place named for K'armelita M'argarita Ortiz."

Looking down at the rovag, Carmelita resisted yet again an impulse to pat it on the head. K'denree caught the motion and pointed to a spot behind one shoulder.

"I can't reach that," it said, trilling slightly. "Would you mind?"

HEAVENLY HOST
by Nina Kiriki Hoffman

Nina Kiriki Hoffman has been nominated for several awards for her fiction, the most recent being a Nebula nomination for her novel, *The Silent Strength of Stones*. She also has stories in *Tarot Fantastic, Enchanted Forests,* and *Wizard Fantastic.*

But then, I never said the Pledge of Allegiance when I was in grade school either. Just stood there with my hand over my heart, moving my lips, while the other kids said the words.

I'm not much of a joiner.

The aliens are like vampires. They don't come in without an invitation.

I'm not sure people knew what they were inviting in. I think they had completely other ideas at the time. Most of them opened the door, though.

The small town of Bethlehem, Oregon, has changed quite a bit in the past week.

But let's start at the beginning.

My name is Ira Silver. I live in a triplex the Lowells made out of an old Victorian two-story house on Maple Street. I've got half the upstairs and my own outside staircase.

When I look out my front window, I can see the First Christian Church a block and a half up the street. When I look in the other direction, I see Shook's Market and the Laundry Queen. First Inland Bank is a little square block of a building all by itself in the parking lot outside of Shook's. There's also a Gas N Go, a video store, a feed store, a farm equipment rental place, other small businesses, and a hole-in-the-wall post office.

The public library, where I work, is one block over and out of view. It's another small building in a town full of small buildings.

Doc's Tavern is also out of sight of my apartment, I play darts there some evenings, and pool. I don't drink anymore. I just go there to be with people.

This is a small life I have here, rigid around the edges, but that's what I was looking for when I left Seattle. A little life, with stories written in wheat, snow, winter sunlight, something besides blood. I am content. For the most part.

On the other side of the wall from me in the upstairs of the Lowell house is Clyde Pressler, another bachelor and an extremely irritating person. He has execrable taste in music, and the habit of playing it too loud for the makeshift walls between us to muffle. When I ask him to turn down the volume, he turns it up instead.

Downstairs is Maudie Lowell, somewhere in her eighties, the last of a long line of Lowells, who lives with three cats and a couple of parrots. How she makes them all get along, I don't know. I admire her for it, though.

She has hearing aids she can turn down, so Clyde's music doesn't bother her. Something to think about, how sometimes there's a blessing side to a curse.

So it's the day of Christmas Eve, and most of the people in town have already made their long-distance pilgrimages for gifts to the mecca of malls and factory outlet stores in Bend, an hour's drive west of us, but there are a few last-minute desperadoes prowling Shook's, the pharmacy, the feed store, the Gas N Go in search of gifts. They are bundled up against the freezing air. Only their eyes show how hunted they feel.

I don't celebrate Christmas, and though I have many acquaintances in Bethlehem, I've been here a little less than a year, and I don't know anyone well enough to edge past my cultural boundaries and actually buy gifts for them.

So I'm sitting at the front window of the library, alternately leafing through today's magazines and watching these desperate souls, amused and a little sympathetic toward their plight. I'm glad that the library's heater is working well. Better to be in here and warm and comfortable than out there with a difficult mission.

There's a noise like a hundred thousand bees behind the library building, a scary summer sound in the dead of winter.

The only thing behind the library building is a parking lot and some trash cans. Maybe some kid has customized his engine to emit this bee sound, but it doesn't sound the way a kid would want his car to sound. Not a wall of power; more like a curtain of irritation. Surely an effect to be striven for, but too subtle for most of the local kids—louder is more sophisticated, to them.

So I go look out the back window.

Nothing to see.

Well. There's this globe of light with pale sparks shooting off it, but I figure it's just some kind of visual error. It's not in focus. More peripheral.

It's noisy. Disquieting, in more than one sense.

I'm not going out to look at it closer.

If it goes on doing whatever it is that it's doing, maybe I'll call the sheriff.

But half a minute later, it's gone, and so is the noise.

Easier to just think it's a daydream.

I mean, what did it hurt?

Right before closing, which is early because of its being Christmas Eve, my favorite reader, Sally Hardesty, dashes in. She's a freckled girl of fifteen, stocky, solid, and graceless, with reddish-blonde hair and nearly invisible eyebrows and eyelashes. "I need a book bad, Ira," she says with what breath she can muster.

"What kind?" I ask. Sally reads almost anything, which is only one of the things I really like about her.

"Something to read when you're locked in your room on Christmas Eve," she says in a squashed voice.

This sounds serious. Not that I know what most people do on Christmas Eve, but I can tell it means a lot. The media is choked with the whole Christmas shtick this time of year. Christmas movies eclipse sensible television. All the sitcoms have Christmas-themed episodes. Carols play everywhere—you can't turn on the radio without getting an earful. Clyde, my next-door neighbor, likes the ones about reindeer, snowmen, and that terrorist in red, Santa. Loud.

I load Sally's backpack with a selection: one science fiction, one fat romance, a couple of Calvin and Hobbes, a mystery, and just a straight fiction, all good reads. "You studying anything specific in school?" I ask her.

"School's out for Christmas break," she says. "What have you got?"

"Here's one on being a backyard naturalist," I say.

She takes it. "I may be spending a lot of time that close to the house. . . . Thanks, Ira. Gotta go," she says, peeking out the front window for suspicious parental-shaped objects in the vicinity. "I don't want them to know I got a stash, or they'll take it away. Merry Christmas, Ira."

"Thanks. Same to you." It's like a tide sweeping over everything. You can't stop it. I'm not much of a joiner, but I go with a few flows now and then.

"Oh, it won't happen this year," she says, zipping up her pack. "Not after what I did."

Then, after another reconnoiter, she's gone.

I sure hope she'll tell me what she did sometime to get into this kind of trouble. One of the other things I like about Sally is that she has Adventures, and she's willing to share them.

I close the library at three. I've got a day off tomorrow. What will I do with myself?

Later, at Doc's Tavern, Frank Shepherd asks me if I'm coming to the carol service tonight at the church.

"Uh, I wasn't thinking of it," I say. I've never been inside that church. It's a squat, ugly pink building with skinny windows. Nothing about it appeals to me.

"There's a lot of music," says Joe Patton, chalking his pool cue. "It's pretty."

"You guys are all going?" I ask. I've known these guys for nearly a year, and we've never talked about religion before. Not that we are now. But almost.

They shrug. "The wife wants to."

"Hell, it's just once a year."

"Makes you feel good."

"Huh," I say. "So, when?"

"Eleven tonight," says Frank.

"That's weird. Usually you people have church in the morning, don't you?"

"Tonight is Christmas Eve. It's special," Joe says, as though explaining to an idiot. Not far off, really.

"It's open to everybody," says Frank.

"Come on, Ira."

"Try it. You'll like it!"

"Hey, maybe if you learned how to pray, your pool game would improve."

Suddenly I'm looking around at these men I have known for almost a year and they look different. The group-mind thing. Scary. I don't ever want to be on the wrong end of a group-mind.

It's not overwhelming, but it's there, under the surface.

This is the first time they've really let me know they realize I'm different.

"Well, thanks for the invitation. I'll give it some thought." I really don't want to see a lot of people raving about the birth of some Jew they later plan to kill, but why offend them with an outright refusal?

We go back to our game.

The bar clears out about supper time. I head home myself. Shook's is closed and has a sign out front that says it won't open until after Christmas; and I forgot to buy groceries. It's going to be a Top Ramen holiday.

Maudie Lowell darts out onto her front porch before I start up my staircase. She is bundled in a variety of many-colored scarves and looks like a babushka. "Ira!" she says. "Are you going to the carol service tonight?"

"No," I say.

"Oh, please," she says.

"What? What? You *want* me to come?"

"I hate to go alone. The ground is so slippery, and my hips are brittle. Would you walk me?"

Maudie Lowell is over eighty. The streets are icy tonight, and going to get icier before eleven."

"Well, sure," I say. I can walk her to the church and come pick her up when it's over. I can't help wondering if Clyde couldn't do it. However, he is nowhere in evidence.

So this is how I end up going to church on Christmas Eve.

Maudie Lowell is thinner and lighter than I thought. I have my arm around her shoulders, and I'm practically carrying her. Which is good, because she does slip, but I stop her from falling over. She thanks me and tells me what a nice young man I am, and I appreciate that. I'm forty-five.

So we come to the door of this pink plaster building. People are pouring into the building—looks like everyone I know here in town, and some I don't know yet. They're full of cheer, greeting each other.

I help Maudie up the stairs, and before I can release her and escape, Frank is there, thumping me on the shoulder. "Good, you came. You won't regret it," he says.

I wonder if he has any idea just how offensive it is of him to be pushing his faith in my face. What kind of lack of respect is that? I thought Bethlehem wasn't like that. Nobody has bothered me about this since I came here—until now.

"You're all right now?" I asked Maudie. She has her feet planted under her and she's in the entrance hall with everybody else.

"Don't go," she mutters to me. She takes my hand. "Sit with me," she says.

What am I going to do? It's my landlady, whom I like. This singing won't kill me, I don't think. It'll tell me something about my neighbors. I'm pretty sure I won't like what my neighbors will think it says about me, but hey.

Here I am.

So that's how it is that I go into the church and see the rest of it.

As we pass through the entrance hall, Mary Culpepper hands us each a folded piece of paper with a photograph of snow-covered trees on it.

For a place that looks like a block of strawberry ice

cream with a roof on top, the church is kind of pretty inside. There are ranks of wooden benches to either side of a central aisle. The near ends of these benches are hung with evergreens, and there are shoulder-high candle holders lining the aisle. Flames dance above white candles all over the church. The air is full of the scents of bundled humanity and candle wax and pine, and the temperature is rising past lukewarm into comfortable.

Way up front is a raised dais with a railing in front of it, and on the dais a big table with a white, lace-edged tablecloth, and silver goblets and other paraphernalia atop that. Behind the table is a black cross hung on the back wall, big enough to crucify a giant on. An implement of torture and execution. Such a cheerful thing to study while you're worshiping.

Maudie leads me to about the middle of the church, and then pulls me into one of the pews until we're about in the middle of that, with people packed in on either side of us, and I know there is no escape.

I check out the piece of paper Mary gave me and find it is a program of the evening's entertainment, full of cryptic numbers and a few bits of dialogue. Apparently the service involves acting.

Somewhere a hidden organ strikes a loud chord, and all around me people rise to their feet and turn toward the back of the room. I stand too. Maudie and others pull books out of the backs of pews. She checks her program and opens the book to a song, then nudges me and shows me. "Oh, Little Town of Bethlehem."

Interesting. Ironic?

Boys in white robes come in, carrying big candlesticks. Father Paul enters after them, singing, and then along comes the choir, also robed in white and singing. All around me people are singing. Not particularly well, but pretty much all at the same time.

Since all this is technically foreign to me, I don't even move my mouth to the words. I just figure here I am, might as well see what it's like, and I look around at the townspeople, people I play pool with, people I've watched drink themselves into a stupor, people who check out books I wouldn't read, people whom I've seen in the market and at the video store, people who have, for the most part, been pretty nice to me.

There they all are, sharing a common experience.

I can almost feel how the song is settling them into a certain spirit. It brings them right here and into now.

Then I notice that all the flames in the room aren't above the candles. Some of them are just loose in the air.

And I hear words.

> *"How silently, how silently*
> *The wondrous gift is given*
> *So God imparts to human hearts*
> *The blessings of His heaven.*
> *No ear may hear His coming,*
> *But in this world of sin,*
> *Where meek souls will receive Him, still*
> *The dear Christ enters in . . ."*

Meek souls, I think. Well, I wouldn't call these people meek.

What I don't hear is that door, opening a crack. But it opens, just the same.

> *"O holy Child of Bethlehem!*
> *Descend to us, we pray;*
> *Cast out our sin, and enter in,*
> *Be born in us today . . ."*

The floating flames are descending now, one above each earnestly caroling head. The people sing on, inviting Other to join with them in this strange song, and I watch as one by one the tops of their heads catch fire; and then the flames wink out.

I wonder if I am sick, dizzy, hallucinating. No one else seems to notice. Maudie's blue-gray hair dazzles me and then the flame melts into her head, leaving me with retinal ghosts that darken her hair for a fleeting moment.

This can't—*can't* be what happens every time these people go to church—can it? In this movie or that movie, I would have seen this. Bing Crosby would have told me.

I'm looking everywhere. Finally I look up and see a little flame hanging above my own head, and it scares me. I swat at it with my hand.

And it shoots away.

God in heaven!

And so from there. There is singing, some readings, sermoning, prayers, more singing.

By this time Maudie has given me the secret decoder ring and showed me how I can figure out where in the ritual we are in the Book of Common Prayer by using my program.

No one faints. People carry on as if this is all going according to plan. Maudie had fire on her head and she still seems fine.

Then there is communioning.

Maudie pats my hand and tells me to just stay where I am while she goes up and gets fed a wafer and wine, that residual cannibal/vampire thing they do. "The Body of Christ, the bread of heaven. The Blood of Christ, the cup of salvation."

This, too, is a door. They're opening their mouths and saying come on in. I see a few more flames fall on people's heads during this part, fall, flame, and wink out. Maybe those were people who didn't get burned during the opening song.

I glance up. There is no flame waiting over my head this time.

But what *is* this? What can it be?

It can't be real.

More songs, and then people leave the church. Nobody mentions the flames. Maybe I was dreaming. Sure, that must be it. All the candle flames were using up the oxygen, and I had a brief blackout and dreamed the whole thing. Just another darned figment.

It takes me a couple days to figure out that something radical has changed.

Sally clues me in, though I'm already uneasy when she comes in to talk about it.

I've noticed my friends at the bar aren't drinking as much as they used to, and that nobody ever fights. That smiles break out far too often, and nobody watches sports on the TV in the corner, and they don't care if they win or lose at pool or darts. Frank has finally consented to learn chess from me—I've been looking for a match since I got here—but he has no killer instinct at all, which makes for frustrating play.

So when Sally bursts into the library and thumps some books down on the counter and says "Ira!" in thrilling tones, I look up and hope she knows something. She sounds more alive than anybody else I've talked to recently.

"Ira, what's happened to everybody?" she says.

"You've noticed, too?"

"My parents let me read as much as I want to! They're calm. They're reasonable. They're scary!"

"I was thinking maybe it's something in the water," I say, "except it didn't work on me. Do you feel different?"

"No!" She leans forward over the counter and drops her voice to a whisper. "They're pod people!"

"That's it. You're right!" We think about *Invasion of the Body Snatchers*.

"Do they try to make you sleep?" I ask her. I am not seriously entertaining this body-snatchers hypothesis, even though I don't have a better one.

"No. They don't seem to want to turn me into one of them. But they're just so insufferably good!"

"They never complain," I mutter.

"They just do whatever needs doing."

"And they're so nice to each other."

"It's sickening!" she cries.

"It's unnatural!" I say. "Let's have a fight just to clear the air."

She waves a fist in my face, and I smile.

Then I think, *Seriously, what makes me and Sally different from everyone else?*

"Did you really stay home Christmas Eve?" I ask Sally. I don't remember seeing her in the church.

She nods. "They apologized when they got home and said I'm not grounded anymore." For a moment she stares over my shoulder at the reserved book shelf. Her mouth draws into a frown. "I think—I think that was when everything changed."

I remember my dream of flames in the church.

I remember the ball of light-bees out behind the library Christmas Eve afternoon. In daylight they looked like sparks, but in the darkness of the church, lit only by candle flame, wouldn't they look like flames, too?

"I saw it," I say slowly. "I saw it."

"What?" demands Sally. She stares at me.

"I saw it happen." I stare into the past. I watch a flame melt into Maudie Lowell's head. *What was that?*

Sally grips my shoulder. "What happened?"

So I tell her.

She pulls up a chair and collapses into it. We sit there for a while without words, alone in our own heads.

Edith Archer comes into the library. "Hello, Ira, Sally," she says. "Ira, do you have any good books on the history of Europe?"

"Sure," I say, and lead her to the right shelf. Edith is the mother of six kids whose ages range from sixteen to nine. I can't remember ever seeing her in the library before, and I never wondered; I don't imagine she has a lot of spare time.

The bell above the door rings again and I turn to find Henry Lamott standing there, still in the coverall he wears when he pumps gas at the Gas N Go. "Say, Ira, you got a book on the world's great religions?"

"Sure," I say, unnerved, and find him one.

And in comes Joe Patton, asking for a cookbook.

By this time, Sally is hiding behind the checkout counter. She doesn't emerge until all three have made their selections, checked them out, and taken off. "What was *that*?" she asks.

"It's been like this ever since Christmas," I say. I look around at my library. So many books are checked out that the shelves look ragged and empty.

"Those flames did something," she says. "Burned their brains out, or something!"

"They think okay, or maybe better," I say slowly. "They're just acting differently." I look at Sally. "If you had been in the church that night, would you have been singing that song, too?"

"Sure," she says. "I love singing."

"I wonder if it would still work. If you sang it now, would the flame come?"

She shuddered. "I don't want that," she said. "It's not like it hurt any of them—as far as I can tell. . . . Everyone's kind of like themselves, only much nicer than they used to be. But I don't want a personality transplant."

I don't want Sally to get a personality transplant either. She's better than fine just the way she is.

"But what happened?" she asks again. This time she's whispering.

I'm not sure how to find out.

It turns out tea is the way to go.

I'm on my way through the snow in the driveway, heading for my staircase, when Maudie pops out onto her front porch. "Ira!" she says. "We're having tea! Want some?"

Who's "we"? "Sure," I say.

Go into her parlor, with the lace doilies everywhere and knickknacks no sane person would have ever invented. Mice dressed as people, cats walking dogs, dogs smoking pipes, a fox dressed up like a Musketeer, waving a sword. All ceramic, most posed in little groups. The room smells like lavender, cat boxes, and, faintly, mildew.

Cats wind around the legs of the tables and slip into other rooms. Two perches close to the space heater sport parrots. The birds are gnawing on sunflower seeds and scattering shells on the carpet below.

Sitting on the couch with a teacup and saucer balanced on his knee is Clyde Pressler, who smiles at me.

I have never seen this man to talk to. I used to resort to yells, but that just made him more obdurate. Since the Change, though, I haven't heard any music from his apartment at all. I thought maybe he went somewhere else for the holidays.

"Cream? Sugar?" Maudie asks me, after waving me

to a seat in an overstuffed armchair with a doily on the headrest.

"Sure," I say. I stare at Clyde. I've never gotten a good look at him before. He looks like a nice fellow, young and almost presentable. Who knew.

Maudie brings me a teacup on a saucer, and a small silver souvenir spoon—it has a little color picture of the Chicago World's Fair on the handle. Also a napkin.

I stir. I sip. Maudie settles in a flourish of skirts beside Clyde. "How *are* you?" she asks me, offering tea cakes on a flowered plate.

"I'm fine, just fine. How are you?"

"Why, I'm wonderful," she says. "You know Clyde, don't you? You boys have lived side by side for months."

"I don't know if I know Clyde," I say. If I did before, I'm not sure it's the same as knowing him now. Maudie, on the other hand, hasn't changed hardly at all that I can tell.

Then I decide. Sally wants to know. I want to know. I haven't figured out any other way to find out. Why don't I just ask them?

"What happened?"

"Excuse me?" Maudie says.

"Christmas Eve at the carol service, Maudie. What happened to everyone?"

She blinks a few times, then cocks her head and stares at me.

I glance at Clyde. I remember now: he was one of those guys whose flame hit his head during the communion. "What happened, Clyde? Do you know?"

His lips compress into a thoughtful frown. He sets his teacup on the table and leans back. "Well. I guess I do." He taps his finger on his lips. "The question is, if I tell you, what are you going to do about it?"

I shrug. "What could I possibly do about people having a religious experience?"

"I'll tell you if you promise this information won't leave the community."

"Meaning what? I'm not allowed to leave town for the rest of my natural life?"

"Meaning you don't call up newspapers and talk about it."

"Sure, that's me, I talk to reporters every day." Well, there was a time when that was true—when I worked on the paper in Seattle. When it seemed like there was a new dead kid every day, when every day challenged my belief that there were some things people wouldn't do to each other. I came to Bethlehem so I wouldn't have to talk to reporters or news sources anymore.

"I need your word, Ira," says Clyde. He's more solemn than he should be.

I put my hand over my heart, just like I used to when I didn't pledge allegiance. "I won't talk to anybody outside town about whatever it is you're going to tell me," I say. "What I want to know is, did it hurt? Do you wish it hadn't happened? Are you okay in there?" I stare at Maudie as I say this, because I don't know Clyde enough to care a whole lot about what happens to him.

"I'm fine," Maudie says.

"Is that you talking, or the thing that came over you?"

She walks across the room and holds a twisted hand out to an African gray parrot on a perch. It jumps onto her hand. "It's me," she says. She strokes the bird's head.

Well, that was fruitless. No way I can tell if she's lying. I look at Clyde.

"What happened on Christmas Eve was that we found friends," he says.

"A flame is a friend?"

"The flames are people," Maudie says, sitting next to Clyde. She is still stroking the parrot. "People from another world. They're joiners."

"Joiners . . ."

"When you open your heart to them, they come inside you and help you live as the best self you can possibly be," she says.

"Yikes!" I say.

She smiles, stops stroking the parrot long enough to pat my knee. "Well, of course that's scary to some," she says gently.

"Mind control!" I say.

"Not a bit."

"How could you possibly tell?"

"Young man, I'm eighty-four years old, and I think I know my own mind well enough to know if it's been tampered with."

She sounds like her old self. I guess there's no way to be sure. And not much I can do about it.

"So are the flame things waiting around to join those of us who weren't joined on Christmas Eve?" I ask.

"It won't happen involuntarily," Clyde says.

"But what if you sing that song? Then do they pop up and burn your hair?"

"No," says Maudie. "It only happens when you open to it."

"I, for one, would like to stay closed," I say.

"Are you sure?" Clyde asks.

"I'm sure."

Clyde shrugs. "No problem."

"They won't sneak into my dreams?"

"No."

"I just hum some song, they won't come along and pounce on me?"

"No," says Maudie. "You have to want it."

"It's hard for me to believe that all those people who went to the service the other night *wanted* to be, uh, 'joined.' I mean, how could they want something they never even knew could happen?"

"We yearned for it," says Clyde. "We longed for it and didn't believe it was possible."

I shake my head. People rage and storm and argue. They never all agree to the same thing at the same time. Well, excluding sports and The Wave.

It's hard for me to imagine angry young Clyde yearning to be joined to something that acts like a Jiminy Cricket conscience. I shake my head again.

Maudie sits up straighter. Her hands lower to her lap, where they lie side by side. Her pose strikes me as Egyptian: like someone in a tomb painting. And then a voice comes out of her; it is cleansed of everything I know as Maudie:

"On world after world, we have found forms of religion." This voice is calm and low and almost without tonal variation. "At the heart of most religions, there is an impulse toward perfectability, a reaching toward help from an outside source to become better. We can be a source. We help implement that impulse."

I think of AA meetings I have been to, talk about turning it over to a Higher Power, stories I have heard. "How long have you been coming to this planet?" I ask.

"This is our first expedition."

"So what next? You send for your relatives? You mount a full-scale invasion?"

Clyde shakes his head. He, too, rests his hands on his lap and talks like a robot. "There is no plan. We are seeds, blown by solar winds in all directions. We descend when we sense fertile soil below us. Maybe another cluster will arrive, and maybe none ever will. We have homes now, and that's all that matters to us."

I wonder if this will last, this, well, induced goodness in people. No one locks a door. Everyone returns anything they've borrowed, and everyone helps when someone has a big project. Clyde bought headphones for his stereo because he knew his noise bothered me.

Sally and I huddle in the library after hours and talk about what's happened to the others in town—besides us, only babies and kids too young to read seem to have escaped assimilation. It's possible we'll leave town in three years, when she hits eighteen. But in the meantime we feel safe walking the streets at night.

I'm becoming accustomed to this sense of safety. If this continues, and we acclimate, we'll undergo culture shock when we leave.

I'm teaching Sally chess.

Some nights when I listen to Clyde tapping his foot to unheard music, I think about open doors. How, when I was a boy, we would open a door during the Seder for the Prophet Elijah to come in.

Prayers sometimes have strange answers. I wonder who prayed for this. Maybe Clyde was right, and everybody did. Maybe even I did: a story written in hearthfire.

WE HAVE MET THE ENEMY

by Rosemary Edghill
(With India Edghill)

Rosemary Edghill is the author of *The Sword of Maiden's Tears*, *The Cup of Morning Shadows*, and *The Cloak of Night and Daggers*. Her short fiction has appeared in *Return to Avalon*, *Chicks in Chainmail*, and *Tarot Fantastic*. She is a full-time author who lives in Poughkeepsie.

It was amazing, Jordan Kendall thought as she lugged home two brown paper bags full of overpriced groceries, how little real difference the alien invasion of Earth had made in the average American's daily life.

True, the major channels ran what they optimistically called "news" twenty-four hours a day—an endless babble of guesses, allegations, theories, and special-interviews-with; world stock exchanges were in chaos; city streets were patrolled by grim-looking soldiers in uniforms foreign and domestic. But little else seemed to have changed.

At least, it hadn't changed yet—except that now everyone used the aliens as their excuse, rather than the computer. *"Sorry, lady—no milk today. The aliens loused up the shipments."* *"I'm sorry, but your call cannot be completed as dialed. All long-distance circuits have been preempted by alien channels. Please use surface mail instead."*

Maybe that excuse would work for her, too—although to date there'd been no indication that the IRS had even *noticed* Earth had been invaded—or at least orbited—

by aliens. The IRS's *soi-disant* help-line message stated firmly that normal tax rules and regulations—and especially filing dates—still applied, alien invasion or no—which meant Jordan was two weeks late on her quarterly payments, and no quarter given.

At least for the moment food shipments were still reaching Manhattan—hadn't James Burke said once that the city could only survive for about four days on its own resources? As it was, these days it took all day to shop for not much, half the time the subways weren't running—aliens again—and most of the D'Ags had closed.

It was their (Earthling's, that was) own damned fault that the incoming spaceship had first been sighted by Hubble close to midnight on December 31st. A number of people who couldn't count—plus the two-thirds of the world population for whom the Gregorian calendar was only a suggestion—had decided it was the end of the world and rioted accordingly. In the U.S., thirty years of a stalled American space program had left the current President without the ability to ensure certain reelection by engaging the enemy, and the ease with which the alien vessel had swept the sky clear of satellites in the twenty-four hours following its arrival made every talking head on television daringly predict that the aliens would probably be a serious military threat.

Jordan turned the corner onto West Houston, ignoring the street vendor who attempted to interest her in an "I Love Alien Visitors" T-shirt—for thirty dollars, yet. In the window of the Korean deli was a sign promising irradiated milk (at ten dollars the pint) with a "guaranteed one-year shelf life"; inflation was rampant, and economic opportunists roamed the streets like packs of immoral jackals.

Fortunately, as long as they still had McDonald's and cable TV, most people seemed willing to treat alien invaders as a new kind of media cvent. It was almost a month now since the alien spaceship had first appeared, and most of Jordan's East Village neighbors seemed to have almost forgotten Earth had been invaded (and theoretically conquered) by space aliens nobody'd yet seen—unless you counted the spaceship hovering a hundred miles above the planet like a timid latecomer to *Independence Day*.

That you could see any time you wanted; even the Home Shopping Channel had an inset of the feed from Palomar. And once the aliens had figured out what the Earthlings wanted, they'd helpfully begun broadcasting a much better quality image of their own ship. So everyone on Earth with access to a television set—which meant, at a conservative estimate, at least 99% of the planet's population—now knew exactly what an alien spaceship looked like.

Meanwhile, all attempts to negotiate with the newcomers had been met by serene, speech-synthesized assurance that whatever Earth government was making the attempt to communicate did not exist, and everything would be better soon. Not that the aliens were in the least reticent about their requirements; in fact, by now the aliens were broadcasting nearly as much telebabble as the Earth networks (now reduced once more to line-of-sight relay for transmissions), and anyone with a satellite dish could pick it up: an unnerving mix of captured television broadcasts, language lessons (alien), and a lengthy and rather muddled list of "compliance requirements" (English) that included requests for complete disarmament, world peace, and large gardens, prompting commentators to speculate that the space aliens might not have a very good grasp of Earth's primary language.

The invaders' "requirements" were accompanied by very simple diagrams that held as much real information content as the plaque in *Voyager* had—but no footage of aliens.

Jordan doubted Earth would get *that* any time soon; the aliens were probably at least intelligent enough to figure out that pictures of sentient slime molds, tentacled insects, or whatever other drooling horror they really looked like, wouldn't contribute much to interstellar amity and understanding.

And meanwhile, Life had to go on, even though a number of people were taking this conclusive proof of the existence of Other Intelligent Life in the Universe as a license to play hooky from all kinds of things. Like common sense.

If only the invaders would stop orbiting and *do* something, like invade. Even a senses-shattering apocalypse would at least be more interesting than being nagged twenty-four hours a day at umpty-yillion megahertz.

Jordan crossed the street, ignoring the kiosk set up to peddle scarves and "Aliens Go Home" buttons and keychains. *Who buys all this stuff, anyhow?* Jordan asked herself. *Now there's an X-File: The Consumers No One Sees, details at eleven.*

She shivered in her parka, thinking of her unheated fourth-floor apartment only a few blocks away. The alien invasion had been enough cause for El Alcalde to declare a rent freeze for the "Duration of the Emergency," which somehow translated at Jordan's level to a tenant freeze in January: no heat. She'd seen an alcohol stove on sale up at the Union Square flea market, but its price was a thousand in greenback dollars or three-hundred-fifty in gold (by the latest London fix, delivered via shortwave radio), so the stove might as well *be* in London, for all the good it did Jordan.

And all anybody'd wanted to talk about at the shops this morning was some new military beachhead established in Tompkins Square Park, of all the unlikely places. All *that* meant was more guys in leftover Desert Storm uniforms suspiciously prowling the increasingly-filthy streets, and still more places you couldn't go without a pass.

Some invasion. Maybe the aliens were just sitting around waiting for the Earthlings' infrastructure to break down, in which case they should be here no later than this Groundhog Day.

She turned the corner onto Clinton—in sight of home—and Jordan realized she'd made a serious mistake.

People had gathered in the street—like demonstrators, only nobody'd be demonstrating this far from the UN. Jordan couldn't imagine what would bring this many people out at the end of January—and in *her* neighborhood, too. If there was a speaker, she couldn't see him, her, or it.

The loiterers on the fringes of the crowd turned, sighting her, and Jordan became very aware of the bags of groceries she was carrying. *Never a cop around when you need one.* The *Times* and the *Post* both published skeleton editions daily, but you didn't need the paper of record to tell you that street crime and other forms of light anarchy were on the upswing. Jordan took a step backward, watching the crowd in front of her swirl and spread like the contents of a psychotic lava lamp.

Incredibly, the people looking at her didn't follow her retreat. But whatever had drawn the crowd here was still drawing more gawkers, and Jordan backed right into two of the newcomers.

New Yorkers abhor physical contact; Jordan felt a thrill of alarm when she banged into the bodies behind her, and more when she saw them clearly. Battered leather jackets and beady little eyes; Roaring Boys out on a tear. Her neighborhood had never been good even Before the Aliens—now, Jordan suddenly saw, it was untenable. One of the newcomers shoved her. The other grabbed the sack she didn't drop out of her arms as if it were a football. Eggs and milk went everywhere.

And finally the rest of the crowd, which had not been standing still while Jordan had problems of her own, erupted into violence.

For a moment.

Then, apparently, they all decided to go to sleep.

Jordan blinked, staring down at the ground, listening to the retreating footsteps of her erstwhile adversaries. Something had melted the ice on the unplowed street all the way down to the potholed asphalt. The pavement smoked slightly. The half-circle of melt stopped just short of her feet.

She looked up.

My God. The Ruritanian National Guard has finally sent troops.

The last man standing belonged on a January street in the East Village about as much as EuroDisney had in France. He was approximately six-foot-four, with a body that looked as if he'd escaped from a Chippendale's revue. He was wearing a close-fitting gold helmet with a red feathered crest that bobbed and swayed in the wind off the river, an amber velvet jacket, gold-encrusted black patent-leather gauntlets, the tightest white pants Jordan had ever seen outside of a superhero comic, thigh-high gold-heeled black patent leather boots with spurs and embossed toe caps, and a sky-blue velvet cape frogged in gold and lined in red satin.

"Oh," he said, looking at Jordan. "You're still standing up."

He was also holding something in his hand that might as well have had "Acme" printed on the barrel and a sign over it saying "Caution: Alien Death Ray (does not meet OSHA emission guidelines)." And he was pointing it at her.

"The new housing must have thrown off the range finder," he added severely, gazing down at the death ray. "You ought to be unconscious at this very moment, experiencing a culturally-indexed hallucination induced through ULF-irradiated deep mind triggers."

"Really?" Jordan said, enchanted. The Technicolor Vision sounded just like Ronald Colman—and talked like Marvin the Martian.

"Certainly," he said. "The Anthropology Unit assured me that it would be far less traumatic for you to believe you had seen events rooted in your own expectations than to see us."

Probably afraid we'd all die of jealousy, Jordan thought wisely to herself.

"And that's what they're doing?" she asked, looking at the people lying scattered in the street.

"Oh, yes. They'll awaken soon, convinced they've seen one of your UFOs and possibly even spoken to its inhabitants."

"And this seems like a good idea to you?" Jordan demanded.

"Well, the only other setting on this unit is 'kill,' " he said apologetically.

The mention of "kill" reminded Jordan that in addition to being out a morning's shopping she was also in phaser range of a dangerous (though colorful) nutcase who might—or might not—be one of the alien invaders.

"So," Jordan said nervously. "What are you going to do now that you've landed?" *Why, I'm going to Disney World . . . ! Yeah, right.* She could run, Jordan supposed, but she'd probably slip and fall on the ice, and his legs—alien or not—were a lot longer than hers.

"I'd wanted to do some sightseeing of the world-capital while your homeland is still in its native unspoiled state," the picturesque stranger said cheerfully. He pulled off his helmet and shook his hair out. "We can't figure out why it is you've chosen to live like this, though. It isn't—" he searched for a word "—appropriate."

Jordan stared in disbelief. *Michael Rennie, come back. All is forgiven.* The representative of the Alien Conqueror had shoulder-length wavy blond hair. His skin was the rich creamy color of a Kraft's caramel, he had piercing blue eyes, and overall, he looked like a Ralph Lauren print-media ad on a very good day. Jordan circled around the sleeping rioters to get a better look at him and stopped in the middle of the street.

These are the alien conquerors? Jordan thought. *We've been invaded by the editorial staff of GQ?* Like all the rest of the television audience that had been breathlessly watching events (not) unfold since New Year's Day, she'd been expecting something else—anything from green Jell-O to mouse-eating lizards—not people who looked like the better-than-human Gilbert and Sullivan Hussars from Outer Space.

Suddenly she heard a faint sound rather like somebody dropping a Mixmaster into the Jacuzzi, and a few moments later a long black limo—it looked like its mother'd had a heavy date with the Batmobile—came racing up the street toward Jordan and the alien conqueror. Fog belched luridly from the undercarriage, and as the vehicle drew closer, Jordan could see that it didn't have any wheels. *This would be a good time to leave,* she thought to herself, just before the alien invader grabbed her wrist.

The limousine slid to a stop. It gleamed velvet-glow bat-fuzz black and—hovering there on its cloud of steam—looked like the second cousin to an Art Deco jukebox.

A hatch in the limo's side slid open in all directions.

"*There* you are," said someone in a disgusted—and English-speaking—voice. "Get in, Your Highness, we have no time to spare."

His Highness—*a Prince? Now this* (Jordan told herself) *was more than any twentieth century COSMOS-watcher should be asked to believe*—surged into the vehicle, dragging Jordan with him before she could object. The door closed.

Despite the fact that it had looked like a licorice jellybean with chrome trim from the outside, from the inside the alien limo looked like velvet seats suspended within a transparent soap bubble.

"This is the Lord Commander Teris," His Highness said proudly, indicating the man in black-and-silver armor who was regarding them with a look of profound and resigned suspicion. "He's head of my Secret Police."

A silver helmet with a long black plume sat on the velvet seat beside the Lord Commander Teris. The Lord Commander was wearing a number of uniform adjuncts last seen in the nineteenth-century Polish cavalry, and like Richard Cory, he probably glittered when he walked.

Secret Police? They can't be very secret if you're telling me about them, Jordan thought, staring numbly at her alien captors.

"Your Highness will recall that Anthropology agreed the appropriate title would be 'Colonial Reclamation Officer,' " the Lord Commander Teris murmured gently. The Lord Commander's tone was that of one who has reminded His Highness of this fact at least 1,983 times, and who fully expects to have to remind His Highness of this fact at least 1,983 times more. "By Your Highness' grace, of course, and while we're on the subject, what is *this,* Nicco?" The Lord Commander asked, looking directly at Jordan for the first time. The Lord Commander's eyes were the true tiger-green and the Lord Commander's silky hair fell in dusky lovelocks around his face. Jordan fell instantly in love for the second time in fifteen minutes.

"It's an actual native," the Prince said excitedly (just as if she weren't sitting here beside him, Jordan reflected). "And do you know, Anthropology was quite right: the soothing Command Gold of my uniform melded with the indigenous cultural archetypes we've studied to produce a feeling of trust and soothing calm in the natives."

Command Gold? Cultural archetypes?

"He was standing in the middle of a riot when I came along," Jordan said helpfully. *And dressing like something out of STAR TREK: LA CAGE AUX FOLLES YEARS doesn't help anything. Don't you guys have any native advisers?*

"But the blaster works quite well, too," Prince Nicco added placatingly.

"I see," the Lord Commander said, not sounding as if he did.

"Look," Jordan said. Outside the limousine the wintery street whirled by. She wondered where they were going. "Just what is it you guys are trying to do here, really? You hang a ship up there in orbit and don't come out—and now that you do come out, it's in the East Village! And if you look just like everyone else—well, better, but that isn't important right now—why didn't you come out sooner?"

"Why shouldn't we look just like everyone else?" His Highness seemed genuinely bemused by the question. "Is it another of your quaint native taboos?" he asked hopefully.

Just as if he were a journalist visiting Disney World for the first time. . . .

"Well, you know, strange visitor from another world, conquerors from outer space, that sort of thing," Jordan said. "You're supposed to be *different*; unimaginable—not the centerfold next door."

Prince Nicco looked blank.

"She thinks we're aliens," Lord Commander Teris explained, smiling faintly. He looked like a tiger deciding on an appetizer. "We aren't aliens," the Lord Commander added, speaking directly to Jordan. "We're people of precisely the same species you are, though personally I'd put on full protective gear before taking a dip in *your* gene pool. What have you people *done* with this place?" By now they were heading uptown, straight up Second Avenue with a serene disregard for traffic signals and other vehicles—twelve feet above the roadbed.

"Don't ask me," Jordan muttered. "It was a fine place before you showed up. If you think it's so rotten, why are you people here?"

"We've come to accept transfer of power from the world government," Lord Commander Teris said. "At least, we're going to try to. Again," the Lord Commander added broodingly.

"But we don't have a world government," Jordan said. "And if we did have, it'd be in Washington, not here."

"No, it wouldn't," Lord Commander Teris said, correcting her with the exasperated patience of someone who has been dealing with this problem for longer than he cares to remember, "We have been monitoring your broadcasts very carefully: New York has the United Nations, New York is The Big Apple, New York is the largest English-speaking population center that is also a center of arts and commerce. Therefore, New York is your capital city, and we are going to accept transfer of power—*here, today*—if I have to crown the first person I see—even *you*—Queen of the planet first."

Jordan stared at him, mouth hanging open.

"But that's a wonderful idea, Teris," the Prince said. "You said it was only a formality so we can be in compliance with the Book. *You* said they'd never manage actual full compliance, but the forms *do* have to be followed. Why *not* her? We can meet with the other natives and then accept the transfer from *her*." The Prince smiled as if everything were settled.

"If we must," Lord Commander Teris said in resigned tones.

"Guys, I think there may be a few flaws in your plan," Jordan said. *Like, you left out the part where the miracle occurs and everyone else goes along with this idiocy.* It was impossible to be terrified when the specter of Earth invasion had suddenly been reduced to a few terminally-cute guys in comic-opera costumes. Jordan had always thought that The Beginning of a New Epoch in Human Understanding (as one CNN think piece had called it) would be a little more dramatic and clear-cut than two guys arguing in a flying limousine about whether or not to make the first person they saw Queen of Earth. As a scenario it lacked—well, explosions and a body count, for one thing.

Come on, *Jordan—do you actually want a great big war just to satisfy your sense of dramatic fitness?* If these alien strangers were willing to turn high drama into light opera, who was she to object? On the other hand. . . .

Something about this situation has got to make more sense than this situation is making right now, she thought wisely to herself. But it was going to have to do it later, because right now the floating limousine was sinking to ground level and heading across UN Plaza toward the doors of the United Nations Building. There the limo settled to the ground and its other hatches opened, disgorging still more Diet-Coke-commercial-quality hunks dressed in chrome and spandex.

The door to the Prince's own compartment opened. Jordan looked out and saw a selection of faces she recognized only because she watched television news. Lord Commander Teris stood up.

"Well, here goes one more useless foray into noncommunication," the Lord Commander said.

The Queen of Earth, affianced bride of Imperial Prince Nicco, Governor (*de facto* if not *de jure*) of Earth, stared at the ever-increasing pile of alien paperwork overflowing her new desk. She felt like the fairy-tale princess who'd been asked to spin straw into gold—only in this case, she had no idea what they wanted her to turn this paperwork into. Earth souvenirs, maybe? *"My parents went to Planet Earth and all I got was this lousy memo. . . ."*

Through the floor-to-ceiling window, Jordan could see the shining towers of the invaders' administration buildings rising in the South Bronx. There were more going in every day, here in the world capital.

Hah.

Lord Commander Teris had been right. The meeting at the UN hadn't gone at all well. The Lord Commander and Prince Nicco and all the rest of the space aliens she'd met in the week since then just didn't seem to understand that there *wasn't* a world government to surrender to them.

Or possibly they didn't care—so long as the letter, if not the spirit, of the rules was followed.

At least Jordan had managed to assimilate a few salient facts since last week's Close Encounter of the Couture Kind. The aliens weren't aliens. Prince Nicco was a prince. The head of the Secret Police was a Colonial Reclamation Officer. And Jordan Kendall had been crowned Queen of Earth because—because—

And new on our fall lineup, "Jordan in Wonderland," a wild-and-wacky sitcom in which a poor-but-hopeful starving artist becomes Queen of Earth in a zany mixup. . . .

"If somebody doesn't give me a full explanation right this minute," Jordan said dangerously to the Imperial paperwork, "I am going to fall down and have screaming, frothing hysterics *right here.*"

"You rang?" the Lord Commander Teris asked. The Lord Commander's grasp of Earth idiom—apparently culled primarily from *Nick at Nite* reruns—was getting better every day.

Jordan squeaked and spun around. Several piles of alien paper slid liquidly over each other and cascaded to the gleaming marble floor.

Lord Commander Teris winced. Queen Jordan didn't care. It was *his* paperwork, not hers.

"Why *this*? Why *that*? What's going on? And what do you want me to do about it?" Jordan demanded, suddenly on a roll. "Nobody but you and fifteen million other space aliens believes I'm Queen of Earth, you know. What's the *point*?"

"I've explained it often enough. Which part doesn't Your Terran Majesty understand?" the Lord Commander of the Imperial Secret Police of Earth—aka Chief Colonial Reclamation Officer—demanded crossly. The Lord Commander was wearing an especially elaborate uniform today, which meant he'd probably been attempting to explain Space Alien ideas to Earthlings again.

"I'm fine up to the part about Earth being a lost colony that the Empire is reassimilating," Jordan lied glibly. *And pray that they're making all this up or that they've got a wonky translator, because everybody knows there's no such things as galactic empires populated by studmuffins in spandex.*

But like the flight of the bumblebee—a creature which all right-thinking physical laws agree cannot possibly fly—the space aliens and their galactic empire refused to go away.

"But what I can't figure out is the need for this . . . charade," Jordan finished weakly.

"It is not a 'charade,' " Lord Commander Teris explained grimly. "It is a requirement." (That, of course, made it reasonable, Jordan thought to herself.) "I don't make the rules," the Lord Commander added, sounding like harassed policemen the world over. "You people petition for a license, you come here, you settle—and then you don't follow the regulations. Did you think you could get away with noncompliance forever?"

They kept coming back to that.

"Noncompliance?" Jordan asked with a sigh. "Noncompliance with *what*?" *And what am I supposed to do about it?*

"With the rules," the Lord Commander said with maddened forbearance. "According to Central Records, you people haven't bothered to file your last sixteen thousand quarterly reports—or make any of the scheduled payments. Did you think those lapses would be overlooked forever?"

Suddenly Jordan thought she might actually understand what the Lord Commander meant, and just as suddenly wished she didn't. Maybe she was wrong, Jordan thought hopefully. She'd been wrong before. Probably she was wrong now. Jordan took the plunge into what she had the awful suspicion would prove to be all-too-familiar—and too hot—waters.

"Lord Commander—I mean, Chief Colonial Reclamation Officer—tell me you aren't saying that the only certain things in the universe are death and. . . ."

"And taxes. Yes. Finally." Lord Commander Teris bent over and scooped up a handful of Jordan's fallen papers. He made a desultory attempt to put them back in order, then gave up and tossed the mess back onto the floor. Then the Lord Commander regarded Jordan sternly.

"And—Your Terran Majesty—your planet is four thousand years late filing its taxes. In addition, there will be a rather high amount of penalties and rate of interest accrued—"

The Lord Commander Chief Colonial Reclamation Officer Teris continued speaking, but Jordan Kendall stopped listening.

And then the Queen of Earth began to laugh. . . .

THE XAXRHLING OF J. ARNOLD BOYSENBERRY

by David Bischoff

David Bischoff is active in many areas of the science fiction field, whether it be writing his own novels such as *The UFO Conspiracy* trilogy, collaborations with authors such as Harry Harrison, writing three *Bill The Galactic Hero* novels, or writing excellent media tie-in novelizations, such as *Aliens* and *Star Trek* novels. He has previously worked as an associate editor of *Amazing* magazine and as a staff member of NBC. He lives in Eugene, Oregon.

He was in a basement lavatory of a San Francisco club called DIVE 69 when the alien first made contact.

"J. Arnold Boysenberry," said the alien, disguised as an American Indian medicine stick. "We have chosen you to spread the word."

Jack Boysenberry zipped up quickly and self-consciously and looked around at the sound of the gnarly, piping voice. The smart drugs had just kicked in, and he felt a little buzzing in his head, a razor's edge on his perceptions, but for the life of him he couldn't tell where the voice was coming from. The gritty men's toilet—black-and-white scuffed tile, naked fifteen-watt light bulbs dim, commodes overflowing, urinals caked with crud and pubic hairs—was empty, he thought, except for him.

Him and the medicine stick. He'd put it down on the solitary sink beside the urinal to use both hands to deal with his business. It was a long piece of driftwood with an eagle's talon on one end, covered with feathers down its shaft, and topped with what appeared to be the American Indian equivalent of a medieval harlequin, sequined eyes seeming to gleam of their own accord. Or had that been the effect of the Piracetam?

He shrugged and went to wash his hands.

As the cold water was trickling over his fingers (how interesting the sensation of *chill* was with his senses faintly stepped up and tingling) he wondered if there'd been something odd in the IQ Juice they'd been servicing at the bar. Whatever, he wanted to get out of this men's toilet—it smelled like the sewage and fungus and subterranean damp was winning its war with the disinfectant, and it was really time to get back to Ted's and Janet's pleasant townhouse apartment suite in Haight-Ashbury and away from this peculiar club scene.

"Jack! Jack? Aren't you listening to the cosmos, Jack? Aren't you properly plugged?"

"What . . . Who's that?"

He looked around, shivers seeming to wave over him with static echoes. When he saw no one, as before, the electric needles prodded again.

"Me, Jack Boysenberry. Look down!"

Jack looked down.

"Here I am." The dried gourd covered with khaki cloth moved. Actually, it was the rouged mouth that was moving—as though in mockery of speech rather than an actually properly synched statement.

"Jesus *Christ!*" said Jack, panicking. "I'm losing control. What'd they give me . . . acid?"

"Calm down, calm down, Jack—this is actually *realer* than your normal reality. A virtuous brand of virtuality. You're just able to perceive more than before. And don't worry . . . there was no LSD in the punch." The pronounced eyebrows of the Indian harlequin scrunched up and the glittery jewel eyes seemed to roll in their dry sockets. "Communication at this level is simply facilitated tremendously. Now lean closer, in case there are listening devices. We must talk very seriously about the fate of the Earth."

Jack looked down with astonishment at the medicine

stick. He found himself transfixed, unable to move. Could this be it? Could this be what he'd been looking for all of his life? That ineffable religious experience, that connection with the Universe, that Oneness?

The thing's eyes glowed hypnotically, seeming to reach up and grab him by the brain stem. He found himself reaching down and grasping the stick and raising it until he was almost nose to snout with it.

It smelled musky, like wet animal fur.

"That's right, Jack. Now let's get down to brass tacks."

Like a stainless steel tongue, a hypodermic needle flicked out from the mouth and jabbed him in his nose.

Jack Boysenberry was a writer/producer for the popular network space travel series, *Star Wagon*. He'd come up from Los Angeles to spend the long Memorial Day weekend with some friends in San Francisco. He'd read about the Smart Drug scene in *The Los Angeles Times Magazine*. It had intrigued him then, and so he'd decided that he should visit one of the special parties thrown by what his San Francisco friends called "smuggies"— flipped out young people, doing a cyberpunk kind of song, loading up on Energy Elicksures bubbling with choline and other odd vitamins and minerals aimed at boosting gray matter activity. These drinks—augmented by certain prescription drugs such as Hydergine, Piracetam, vasopressin, vincamine, and Dilantin—were supposed to increase intelligence, creativity, perception and make the cerebellum a hopping kind of place for ideas and other keen neuro-nuke stuff.

Just the sort of thing a soul searching for the meaning of life could probably use.

Just the sort of thing a television producer needed, especially if he worked on a show like *Star Wagon*.

Not that *Star Wagon* was particularly cutting edge in the creative science fiction department. In fact, it was pretty much 1950s *Astounding Magazine* stuff, decked out in contemporary techie jargon. It was more the crush of work, the crunch of egos, and the raging political intermeshes that demanded the extra juice. Jack took lots

of vitamins, he tried to fit in as much exercise as possible
three times a week and he didn't smoke. Nonetheless,
he'd been finding the stress such that he'd definitely felt
the need for something more than a vacation, something
that would boost him every day. Long ago he'd learned
that cocaine wasn't the answer, even before coke was
declared addictive. That had been before his television
career as well. So he couldn't turn to illegal things.

So why not try something perfectly legal? If it wasn't
necessarily scientifically sound, then it seemed experi-
mentally so. Lots of testimonial success. At the very
worst, maybe the placebo effect would carry him through
the season. Anything to get through this season, the Season Coughed up from Hades' Filthy Toenails, as Mary
Lou called it. And Mary Lou liked *Star Wagon* much
better than he ever had or ever would.

Once up in the Bay Area, his friend had nixed a trip
to the Dive 69. But a friend of a friend knew about the
scene and agreed to take Jack along. "Research trip"
was the phrase bandied about, but Jack had enough en-
thusiasm that it was clear he was really interested. The
"friend of a friend," a clothing designer who occasionally
did some work for Amoeba, dropped him off, did a little
business talk with a couple of people, and then took off
for Mad Dog in the Fog for a couple of beers, promising
to pick Jack up later.

That was okey-doke with Jack.

If nothing else, the scene here was good for a couple
of alien ideas to pitch back on the show.

Dive 69 was basement chic, blaring with synthesizer
beat from aurally correct audio speakers on the wall.
Computer nerds dressed up in ludicrous outfits mixed
with beatnik geeks, trying to be as sullenly obnoxious as
possible in the psychedelic spray of lights, pulsing
sounds, and jarring growls of the blenders at the bar.
There was a chemical smell to the air, but it wasn't the
comforting smoky smell of the sixties, nor the sedative
alcohol smell of the seventies, nor the exiting money
smell of the eighties. It was the smell of the nineties,
and it was neither classifiable nor particularly pleasant.

Jack, with his L.A.-trained casual manner and cool

ways, made friends immediately with the bartender, tipped the hairy wall-eyed fellow well and received an excellent introduction to the array of drugs available, along with, for a mere twenty dollars, the new updated paperback edition of *Smart Drugs and Nutrients* by John Morgenthaler and Ward Dean. Plus, of course, all the drinks and drugs that he could cram down his maw.

Somehow about two hours into the scene, when all the drugs had kicked into gear in their subtle ways, it all started to make sense. The lights, the sounds, the smells—

It was all just a bizarre excuse for a ritualistic party.

Jack wasn't sure how much all of this was going to help him on *Star Wagon*. In truth, a dose of choline might just make a tantrum by one of the executive producers or stars much harder to take. Maybe while he was writing a script, or developing an idea—maybe while he was brainstorming. He'd certainly give it a try . . . no harm, really, and anything might help. . . . But it was, he'd decided, hardly the revelation he'd been half-hoping for, the *catharsis* he'd been seeking.

Oh, well, a party was a party.

He'd hang out here a while, walk to a bar, have a beer, and then take a cab back to the house. Not a loss at all, but an *experience*. He liked San Francisco. It was a world away from L.A. with its affable natives and the rolling fog and the excellent food and night life. This was good for him, just getting away. Maybe he should try to get up here more often. He certainly had the money to now. Money, but not a whole lot of time to enjoy it, that was the problem. In the dim past, he'd had the crazy idea that writing for television was simply writing scripts. Which was like saying that marriage was simply making love.

That was when he went down to the toilet for his pee and his spiritual experience.

He fell back onto his butt on the filthy bathroom tile.

He lay there for a moment, disoriented. His nose felt like it had been stung by a bee. His head swirled as though in the vortex of a kaleidoscope. His nose stung, but it was overhelmed by a synethesia. Smell became sight and disjointed, cracked, dissipated into brackish, salty chemical taste.

Something hard was sitting in his hand. His head lolled sideways.

The medicine stick lay in his hand. Its far end was glowing. He lifted it and a beam of iridescence sprayed forth, bashing into a graffitied toilet stall door. It swung open, giving way into a rainbow splash of streamered, rotating light and tunneled back into the wall.

A form separated from the color.

It flopped along, a paramecium supported by stalks. Cilia flickered and whipped.

"J. Arnold Boysenberry," it said in an accent that sounded like a clam attempting to imitate a Frenchman's shot at the Queen's English. "You need not fear."

"No?" said Arnold. If there was any fear in him, he certainly couldn't feel it. His nerves felt lined with psychedelic silk. Muffled and slightly shuffled.

"You are a Chosen one."

"Oh?"

"Prepare to be Anointed."

"Anointed?"

"Xaxrkled, actually, it just doesn't translate very well, I'm afraid."

The alien crawled forward, the galaxies in the wobbling tunnel behind it gleaming and glazing.

If this wasn't precisely Saul-on-the-Road-to-Damascus, nonetheless it would certainly do! In any event, it was nice to know he might have a greater purpose in life than writing TV scripts.

The meeting was going badly.

"What's wrong with you people?" the executive producer moaned, flopping onto his couch. He picked up a paddle and started to bang the rubber ball attached to the length of rubber band as he chomped away on a wad of bubble gum. "All I'm asking is to come up with another good story line involving the Pelican People."

Arnie Boysenberry looked up wearily from his pile of notes. There was a list of about twenty story ideas he'd brainstormed before bed last night. None of them were quite up to snuff in William Minton's opinion. None of the other story editors or producers had any ideas that came up to snuff either. *Star Wagon* had been chewing up pitches for two solid months, with no sales, and there were only two scripts ready for production and five in various stages of preparation.

"Uh—can't we work with any you *sort* of liked, Bill?"

The executive producer blinked. He stopped the back and forth paddling of the rubber ball and stood up. "What? I can't believe you said that, Arnie! *Star Wagon* only has *quality* scripts. And only from *quality* ideas do quality scripts emerge." He shook his head sorrowfully. "Clearly I'm going to have to do a little thinking on my own—and I'm really going to resent it because it's not like I'm overflowing with time."

That certainly was true. The company already had other projects they wanted him to develop—and for more money as well. What this meant was that Bill Minton was going to be even more of a bitch to work with.

The others seemed totally defeated. They looked as though they just wanted to file out, get into their Ferraris and Jaguars, and start the long slog home. Sorrow was all over their faces—but nothing was forthcoming.

"Okay, okay . . . we'll talk about this tomorrow . . . first thing. Nine A.M. And I want some ideas, dammit!" Minton was grinning, but it was a nasty grin. An Or Else kind of grin.

Arnie Boysenberry got up, left the office, and moped down the steps to his office on the next floor. His assistant was already gone, and there was a stack of messages for him. He ignored them and went into his office.

He sat down in his chair, putting his head in his hands, and sighed. The ideas had been great ones, all twenty of them. He'd never had a brainstorming session like that one before—and it was all because of the drugs he'd been taking, because of the alien contact.

Inspired.

That was what he'd been—stone inspired.

"Inspire" of course meant to receive the breath of God. Well, it hadn't been God who'd given him mouth-to-mouth resuscitation—but it might as well have been for the way his brain had been blown out into a scattering of psychedelic cascading droplets.

He had hoped that Minton would see the genius of these plots, but clearly he hadn't. Which meant, unfortunately, that he'd have to go to Plan B.

After snorting a little of the brain-booster he'd brought back from San Francisco, he called Minton on his private line.

"Bill," he said, maintaining the rule of fake TV casualness. "I think I've got a couple more ideas you'll like."

"Shoot!"

"Can you stop by my office? They come with some things I did on my computer."

"Graphics?"

"Yes. Graphics."

"Good. I like graphics. I'll stop by on my way out."

"On the way out" was a good hour distant, but Boysenberry waited patiently. Just as well. The building would pretty much be empty by that time.

Finally, Minton showed, strolling in as he shrugged on a leather jacket.

"Just plain vanilla, please, Boysenberry." It was an old tired joke—but then, Minton was hardly in sitcom, was he? It meant: Get to it, guy.

"Something I want to show you, Bill. Something I brought back from San Francisco that really inspired me and I think you'll find it will work for you, too."

"Huh? You told me you had a couple of good ideas."

"I do, I do. Just come here for a moment. Five seconds. Five seconds of your time, that's all I ask."

Minton, clearly faintly intrigued, shrugged his leather epaulets and stuck his hands into his pockets. "Okey doke. You've got five seconds."

Boysenberry beckoned him back to the closet. He opened the door, reached in, and pulled out the medicine stick.

"What the hell is that?" asked Minton.

"The future," said Boysenberry.

Before the executive producer could do a thing, the hypodermic needle was buried in his neck.

*   *   *

"First things first," said Minton, beaming. "I want you all to congratulate Arnie here. He'll be our new co-executive producer."

The surprise registered immediately on the faces of the others. This was unprecedented. Nobody got promoted until the end of the work season when contracts were renegotiated.

And Arnie Boysenberry?

The buzz around the office—in fact, any office that Boysenberry worked in—was that he was a hell of writer, but a hellish producer. That he was the living embodiment of the Peter Principle—a man who had been elevated to a position just past his level of competence. Boysenberry could hack out the scripts, all right, and he could work with people okay—but when it came to actually doing the other kinds of stuff necessary to production sorts—backstabbing, political power plays, lying, casting—he just didn't have the chops.

And co-executive producer? He'd just leaped over the next rung past regular producer—supervising producer.

What the hell was going on? was what was in the staff's faces.

"You're probably asking yourself, what the hell is going on?" said Bill Minton, beaming. "I'll tell you what is going on. You guys know the problems we've been having with getting the quality ideas for *Wag,* right?"

Did they know? Of course they knew. But it wasn't a problem with *ideas,* so much as it was a problem with the executive producer's *attitude* toward ideas. That was to say, they were getting ideas all right, ideas that were perfectly workable, many of which would actually result in shows superior to the usual drone produced by *Star Wagon.* The problem was that one of the ways Bill Minton kept the show under his control was by staying in charge of every single facet—and by being so difficult.

Yes, was the silent reply from the staff to the previous question.

Minton stepped over and clapped a hand onto his new co-executive producer's shoulder.

"Well, my good friend Arnie here has broken through

that particular block. Just in the meeting we had yesterday we developed five solid story lines. Count 'em. Five. Copies are right on the desk over there."

The staff eyed the contents of the desk as though they were coiled rattlesnakes.

"Treatments, folks. Detailed treatments—beat by beat action, even dialogue. Each of you take one and do a first draft teleplay, keeping within the perimeters of the outline. Do you understand?"

The staff clearly hadn't gotten past the fact that Arnie was now co-freaking-executive producer. Having five detailed beat sheets was even more astonishing—perhaps even beyond their grasp.

"Good," said Bill Minton. He grabbed up the pile and distributed them to the rank and file. "Now get thee to thy offices and write thy tiny brains out!"

He grinned as the writers shuffled away, eyeing Arnie as though he were Judas Iscariot in a new suit flipping a silver coin.

When they were gone, Bill Minton turned to J. Arnold Boysenberry. He clapped him on the back. "Think they can handle it, Arnie?"

Arnie nodded. "There will doubtless be some rewriting necessary. But they can all do scripts. That's why they're here."

Bill Minton nodded. He went to a closet, opened it, and pulled out the medicine stick.

"Do you know how many people on Earth watch *Star Wagon,* Arnie?"

"Fifty million?"

"Closer to a hundred million, chum. A hundred million of the best and brightest." Minton touched the medicine stick. "What better way for communication from another planet, another race, eh?" The transcendence tunnel began to vortex open. "Not your flying saucer in front of the White House, but a slow preparation for contact by an intergalactic race. It makes you wonder— how long has this been going on? Has science fiction itself been the result of this kind of incredible medicine stick therapy?" He grinned and looked at the stick as though it was his new god.

Minton was high as a kite. Spaced out. On Beyond.
Arnie could tell because he was just as high.

"Think about it—what a brilliant master plan for the
gradual assimilation of truths about the universe. Preparation for a new age, Boysenberry. And to think that we
had something to do with it—we are bearers of the news.
Why, it's a grave and important thing, J. Arnold
Boysenberry."

Arnie could only nod, he was so fascinated with the
sparkling colors and the whirling spectromatics.

"And not just through story line, but a massive sub-
liminal hypnotic pattern transfusing each *Star Wagon*
presentation. These aliens—they certainly are brilliant."

"They certainly are, Bill."

They could see the creature coming through the tunnel now, crawling, undulating.

"Enlightened beings who have come to enlighten us,
Arnie. And at such a low, low cost." He gave Arnie a
significant look. "You *did* get what they asked for?"

"Yes. In the closet."

"From where?"

"South Central."

"Good. Get it."

Arnie went to the closet, opened it. In the closet was
a cloth gunney sack, and in the gunney sack was an
illegal Mexican immigrant, smuggled in last night, doped
to the gills, and still out. Arnie pulled the man from
the closet, unwrapped the sack and put him in front of
the tunnel.

Almost immediately, a set of tentacles unfurled,
wrapped around the man. Eyes opened just for a moment, horror flashing—and then the man was dragged
into the tunnel, and the sound of sucking and gnashing
and a muffled scream abruptly shut off was heard.

"Yes, Arnie. When things get underway and we can
operate a little more aboveboard, as it were, I know
some studio executives who will have meetings with our
tunnel friend here." He chuckled. "Ah, what a brave
new universe!" said Bill Minton, nodding.

"Yes," said J. Arnold Boysenberry.

Although it seemed pretty much like business as usual
to him.

EARTH SURRENDERS
by Barbara Paul

Barbara Paul has a Ph.D in Theater History and Criticism and taught at the University of Pittsburgh until the late '70s when she became a full-time writer. She has written five science fictions novels and sixteen mysteries, six of which are in the Marian Larch series. A new Marian Larch, entitled *Full Frontal Murder,* will be published in 1997.

We'd had little warning; a blip on a screen splintered into a thousand blips, so large a fleet for our one small planet. We assumed we weren't the only one, merely one of the last, perched out here in the galactic suburbs. Perhaps they needed a refueling station on their way to Andromeda. They'd destroyed our toehold colony on Mars, casually, in passing—like a slap on the wrist. There was no mistaking their intent.

We didn't even know who "they" were; our communication had all been us-to-them. Does a man introduce himself to a bug before he steps on it? Once the ships were in range, President Brigham didn't hesitate to launch every weapon we had, as did our counterparts in their own domains around the world. We didn't get one ship. The combined firepower of the entire world was insufficient to bring down *one* ship.

It took a while; this was no six-minute war. Most of us just watched while the military tried first this, then that. Long after the rest of the world had exhausted its resources, France finally got its act together and launched an attack. It made no difference. Their superweapons had no more effect than our superweapons.

President Brigham aged twenty years before my eyes as the reports came in; I think she understood before any of us that there was no stopping these invaders. She took a few minutes to marshal her thoughts and called us all together—her advisers, both civilian and military, as well as certain scientists who so far had been able to contribute nothing. Nor, indeed, had any of us.

"Since we don't know what the invaders are going to do next," President Brigham said, "we need to plan for every possibility we can think of. General Schumacher, are you ready with the Joint Chiefs' contingency plans?"

"I am, Madam President," Schumacher replied, looking unnaturally calm in the face of what was happening to us. "We've never seen the invaders, so we don't know what will work against them. But there are things we can do."

He started a show-and-tell with graphs, maps, computer simulations. What to do if the invaders don't destroy us but keep us alive for whatever purposes they have in mind. What to do if they kill most but not all of the people in the world in order to retain a manageable population. What to do if they have no need for the Earth but plan to destroy it simply because it is their nature to do so, like the scorpion in the story. The plans even took in the possibility that the invaders would never leave their ships . . . which meant we had no way of fighting back at all.

They were all survival plans, predicated on an assumption that we'd lost all our defenses and were at the mercy of whatever force had descended upon us. In every scenario, some form of the military was proposed as the authority that would bring a measure of order out of chaos. I made no mention of this; I knew the President had caught it. Besides, I had no official standing in the underground Command Center. But the role of First Husband did carry its perks, or I wouldn't have been there at all.

The President was frowning. "We can't have much time. What are they doing now?"

"Still circling," someone said.

The ships had entered the Earth's atmosphere, great silvery things that our telemetry said were loaded with armament. They had not returned our fire, other than blasting the Mars colony out of existence on their way here. The ships were positioning themselves . . . for what?

An hour later they were still circling, with no change in the orbital pattern of any of the ships. Round and round. We'd given up trying to contact them. They'd received our messages, we were assured; they just didn't bother to answer. Round and round.

"What are they waiting for?" the Secretary of the Interior finally cried out.

General Schumacher glared at the man. "They're trying to psych us out. Make us nervous so we'll do something stupid."

The Interior man accepted the reprimand and said no more. We all avoided looking at one another. So far there'd been no screaming or yelling, no top-of-the-voice arguing, no name-calling; we were all controlling our fear. So far.

The President was practically dead on her feet; she'd been awake for nearly forty hours. "Use this time," I said in her ear. "Sleep whenever you can."

She started to object but then changed her mind. We went into our quarters. "I sleep better when the First Lord is warming my back," she said. Our old joke.

We curled up together and drifted into a fitful sleep that lasted a couple of hours; then she was awake again and checking on the invaders' ships. No change in the circling patterns.

The public news channels brought us pictures of burning buildings, the inevitable looting, interviews with people who believed it was all a hoax. For those who didn't: hysteria, many suicides. The subways in New York had stopped running because the tunnels were packed with people seeking to get as far underground as they could, probably the smartest thing they could do.

It was our worst nightmare come true, the xenophobic buildup that began with the first venture into space now proving itself justified with a vengeance. The world reacted as it has always done to anything new and dangerous: with panic. The invaders were destroying us by letting us destroy ourselves.

She stood before one of the screens, sadly watching the terrified populace. "Time to run another reassurance speech, I think. Not that it'll do any good." She'd taped a number of them before we descended to the underground Command Center, all of them saying basically the same thing. *We're attempting to make contact, they haven't attacked the Earth yet, stay calm.*

I was watching a different channel. "Leila, listen to this."

A newsman (and self-appointed pundit) was speculating that the invaders hadn't attacked the Earth because they couldn't. The newsman's theory was that the invaders had the capacity to wipe out a colony of a couple of thousand people, but not enough to annihilate the entire population of the world. The destruction of the Mars colony had been a scare tactic, an act of intimidation.

"It's all a bluff?" She laughed shortly. "We should show him our telemetry readings. *One* of those ships could take out the Earth."

"Are they waiting for us to make a move?" I wondered.

Leila didn't answer, but said, "Interesting that all the contingency plans are strategic withdrawals."

Uh-oh. "You're not still looking for a way to fight back? All those contingency plans were based on an assumption of defeat."

"I know." She sighed. "General Schumacher is a realist. He knows when to attack, when to withdraw. His guns and rockets didn't do what they were supposed to do, so the next step in his rule book is to pull back and cut your losses. I can't argue with that."

I smiled. "But."

"But while I agree with Schumacher, on some level I feel we haven't done enough to resist."

"Resist how? After what they did to Mars?"

"They have some use for us, Peter," she argued, "or they would have done the same to Earth by now. We know nothing about those . . . people. What are they doing right now? For all we know, they might need to go into some sort of stasis periodically to recharge their batteries. And then when they wake up, they'll blow us to smithereens. Or not. We just don't know."

"Their ships are impregnable," I said, "but are they? The thing to do is get them to leave their ships. So we'll have a better shot at them."

"Won't work. We kill some of them, they'll use the ships to retaliate. No, we need to make them go away."

"But how?"

She tapped a fingernail against her teeth. "Our use of force failed. What if we do a complete turnabout? What if we ask them for help?"

We discarded the idea of presenting ourselves as a plague-ridden planet in desperate need of medical aid, since what was lethal to us might prove harmless to the invaders. Besides, the invaders would see right through that; it was too transparent a ploy.

The Secretary of the Treasury suggested we fake some readings that would make the invaders think our sun was about to go nova. The scientists quickly explained to her why that was not possible.

But that gave General Schumacher an idea. "How about faking readings that would suggest we're in for the biggest damn earthquake known to mankind? Some giant rift developing in the Earth, one that'll move continental plates, level cities . . . and just, in general, wreck the place?"

The President said, "And then ask the invaders to evacuate as many of us as possible? It might work."

The technicians and engineers and seismologists conferred and agreed they could produce fake readings that would fool *our* detectors. But since the invaders had already demonstrated superior technology, they couldn't promise that our unwanted visitors would be taken in.

Put that one on hold.

I cleared my throat. "Whatever we do, the invaders are going to be suspicious—because the first thing we tried to do was shoot them out of the sky. We lost our credibility with the first rocket we fired."

"Thank you, Peter," Schumacher said with a touch

of sarcasm. "We'll just have to be damned convincing, that's all."

That's all?

It was the President herself who finally made the suggestion that we ultimately adopted. "Let's invite them to dinner," she said.

First came the messages to the other heads of state requesting that they not attempt further contact with the invaders; we could only pray they would comply. That done, we turned back to the invaders themselves.

We surrendered. We acknowledged that the invaders occupied the dominant position and pledged to refrain from any further military action. Not that there was anything more we could have done along that line anyway. We asked the invaders what they wanted.

No response.

Then we offered to evacuate and leave the planet and all its riches to them. We were *giving* them our world. The only problem was that we did not have an interstellar drive. Did the invaders have any suggestions?

No response.

So we requested that the invaders assign us a few of their ships, so we could begin evacuating our people.

That brought a response. *Not acceptable.*

A gasping sort of cheer arose in the Command Center; the first words we'd had from them. And confirmation that they were indeed receiving our messages and were able to understand our language. Did they have translator machines? The pronunciation was a bit odd, but the two words were perfectly understandable. I wondered how many of Earth's languages the invaders (or their machines) had mastered. But we had established communication now; the first hurdle was over.

"Good," said the President. "Now we step it up."

We sent a three-part clarifying message. One: The requested ships would still be crewed and guarded by the owners of the ships. Two: We would go wherever they directed us to go. Three: If they needed a work force on Earth, we would leave part of our people behind.

There was a long silence. Then: *Not acceptable.*

"Still suspicious," Schumacher said, showing signs of nervousness for the first time. "I hope this isn't the stupid thing they're trying to psych us into doing."

"It's the reply we expected, General," said the President. "Send the next message."

The next message told the invaders to name their terms. We did not say please.

The next response finally told us what the invaders wanted. *Evacuate northern hemisphere. All those remaining north of equator after one lunar cycle will be destroyed.*

"Lebensraum?" a voice said unbelievingly. "They want living space for themselves?"

"Not necessarily," the President said. "They might want a way station where they don't have to worry about controlling the local population."

"Then why not just gas the planet? That would leave the structures intact."

Schumacher snorted. "It would also leave them with five billion corpses to dispose of. That's why they haven't attacked. The dead they left behind on Mars don't matter—they won't be using the colony. No, this is the best move, from their point of view. And you can bet that the equator is going to be the most heavily guarded boundary line we've ever seen."

"At least they seem willing to coexist," another voice suggested nervously.

"But we're not," the President replied firmly. "You're talking as if we've really surrendered." She frowned. "What would they expect us to reply?"

"More time," I said.

"Right. Let's ask for a year." The message was sent. *One lunar cycle.*

This time we did not respond.

The President turned to Schumacher. "I'd like film clips, news reports, still shots—everything visual that the military has on the fighting in Central America, Bosnia, Vietnam, anywhere, no matter how old." We hadn't had a real war on Earth for twenty-five years, so she had to dip into recent history. "And get it ready to transmit to the invaders."

Schumacher gave her a rueful smile and shook his head. "I don't think we're going to scare those creatures away."

"Not scare them, General. Make them think we're more trouble than we're worth. And we don't have much time."

He was dubious that even that would work, but he was in favor of trying almost anything. When Schumacher was ready, we requested visual contact with the invaders.

To our surprise, they agreed. There was a mutter of worried excitement in the Command Center; no one knew what to expect. A scientist named Pellegrino, of whom I'd never heard before the invaders arrived, was set up in a small soundproofed room so his instant analysis wouldn't be carried by our transmissions to the invaders. Miniature receivers in our ears would pick up his words.

But it seemed we were expected to go first. When the technicians had everything in place, the President stood alone before the camera and allowed her image to be transmitted to the invaders.

You are called what?

"My name is Leila Brigham. I am President of the United States of America. To whom am I speaking?"

A screen that had been showing a map of now-depleted missile sites flickered once, twice—and we had our first view of the invaders.

We were looking at a man. No question of that, he *was* a man. One head, two eyes, two arms. Very thick and squat, possibly shorter than we were—impossible to tell without a visual point of reference. Almost no neck. Flattened-out facial features.

From a heavy-gravity planet, Dr. Pellegrino's voice said in our ears.

The invader was black—not black like the Earth's black races, but a glittering black that was almost blue. No facial hair, not even eyebrows.

High melanin, said Dr. Pellegrino, *or their equivalent of melanin. Hot sun—hot enough to drive them away? Their home star might be an old one starting its final expansion. But they can't have a DNA radically different from ours.*

So the invaders weren't monsters, not even bugs or lizards. I wondered if they came in a variety of colors, the way we did. Somewhere else in the galaxy—perhaps in more than one place?—a life cycle like our own had begun. And produced an aggressive race that took what it wanted by force. Not too different from us.

The invader spoke. *Commander of the Broghoke.*

Ah, so that was their name . . . at least it sounded something like *Broghoke,* the second syllable more aspirated than spoken. This was not the voice we'd heard before; the Commander's tones were rougher, his accent thicker. He was waiting for the President to speak.

She said, "Commander, it's impossible for us to move half the Earth's population in only one month's time. Our best estimate is that it would take two or three months simply to launch a successful invasion of the southern hemisphere. Then the transportation problem alone would—" She broke off when the invader raised a hand abruptly in a commanding gesture.

Note the six fingers, said Dr. Pellegrino.

You do not understand well, said the Commander's rough tones. *You are not required to conquer. You are required only to vacate.*

"Vacating is impossible without conquering first. The entire southern hemisphere is in constant tumult, one war after another." That would come as a surprise to the inhabitants of Rio and Sydney. "Let me show you something. This is what's going on right now." She signaled for the transmission of our old war pictures to start.

There hadn't been enough time to do any sorting or organizing, so we watched Nicaragua and Sarajevo and Rommel's tanks in North Africa, all jumbled up together. We watched children armed with automatic weapons they could barely lift firing at soldiers. We saw emasculations and hangings. We watched explosions and bombings. People on fire ran from a burning building only to be shot down by the guerrillas waiting for them. We saw an entire Asian village lined up against a wall and shot; after the fusillade ended, only the sound of a crying baby could be heard. One more shot rang out, and then silence.

The Commander of the Broghoke had disappeared from the screen—watching elsewhere, we hoped. We finally stopped transmission when *we* couldn't take any more. Any invaders worth their salt ought to think twice about sharing a planet with that kind of turmoil. Even General Schumacher looked affected by what we'd seen, as did the other military bigwigs in the Command Center.

The invaders' Commander reappeared. *Is this fighting confined to the southern hemisphere?*

Schumacher shot to his feet and drew one finger across his throat. The technicians cut the transmission.

"What?" the President demanded.

"Let's think this through," the General said. "Is the fighting all in the south? Do we say yes or no? If we say yes, the Broghokers or whatever the hell they call themselves will just drive us down across the equator and that'll be the end of it—may the most vicious survive. They don't give a shit about us. All they want is a place for themselves, here, on half of our world, where they don't have to bother keeping an eye on us. And it's *our* half they want. We have to tell them the fighting is everywhere—it's the only weapon we've got."

"But if we say the fighting is worldwide," the Vice President said, "how will that stop them?"

"Isn't the point to make ourselves look like more trouble than the invaders care to handle?" Schumacher asked. "They just want us out of their way."

"One sure way of handling *that*," the Secretary of Defense said. "The fact that they haven't killed us all yet doesn't mean they won't still do it."

"Schumacher's right," said Admiral Somethingor-other. "It's the only weapon we've got. We'd be fools not to use it."

Then the loud arguing that had been absent earlier started in earnest. Everyone had an opinion which could evidently be expressed only at the top of one's lungs. I glanced at the screen; the Commander of the Broghoke had disappeared again. How long would they wait?

Leila put her hand on my arm and drew me aside. She kept licking her lips, a mannerism that appeared only when she had to make a decision she didn't want to make—and, until now, one that she indulged in only when we were alone. "Peter, what's your take?"

"It *is* the only weapon we have," I said. "If they try to kill us all, they'd have to tie up half their troops on permanent burial detail . . . or whatever it is they do with dead bodies. Burn them, perhaps. And it would be a tedious, time-eating process, since they seem not to want to destroy the cities."

She nodded. "Most of the industry is in the north, but the mining opportunities in the southern hemisphere— why don't they want those?"

"Perhaps they don't know about them. They can't have been monitoring our transmissions very long."

"So you agree with Schumacher?"

"I never thought I'd be saying this, but yes, I do. Confound the enemy and he is yours, as I think somebody once said."

She stopped being Leila and went back to being the President again, calling for quiet and getting it. "Are you agreed?"

General Schumacher looked around. "Most of us are, I think. The invaders will believe that we're quarrelsome, violent, unruly—because the first thing we did was try to shoot them out of the sky." He shot a self-satisfied glance in my direction. "Anything we can do to add to that impression can only help." There was a mutter of reservations expressed by a couple of the Cabinet members, but no one openly challenged the General's conclusions. "And Madam President," he went on, "maybe you don't have to be so polite?"

She nodded slowly. "Point taken. All right, let's restore transmission."

Another voice spoke up. "You're all taking a lot for granted." Dr. Pellegrino was standing in the doorway to his soundproofed cubicle. "Because they look like us doesn't mean they think like us. You might be provoking a reaction totally different from the one you're looking for."

"I'm sure that's already occurred to everyone here," the President answered with a touch of impatience. "But since there's no way of finding out, it's a risk we're forced to take, isn't it? Unless you have an alternate course of action in mind?"

The scientist looked at his feet. "No."

"Then we'll proceed." She stepped back in front of the camera. "Commander?"

He reappeared wordlessly.

"Sorry about the interruption. We're having technical difficulties down here, but it had *better* not happen again." She glanced angrily off camera at an empty chair, a little bit of theatrical byplay that may have been lost on the Broghoke. "You were asking a question about the fighting?"

Is the fighting confined to the southern hemisphere?

"The fighting is worse in the south," she said with stagy evasiveness.

Unacceptable answer.

"The fighting is worldwide, if you have to know." A nice touch of resentment there. "But it's more under control in the northern hemisphere. Still, we could use some help. If your ships' weapons could clear some space for us in the southern hemisphere, we could vacate a lot sooner. Can you help us?"

No response. The Commander's facial expression didn't even change.

The President plowed on. "Er, we made a little mistake when we transmitted those pictures of the fighting. That last series of scenes was from a European war. Northern hemisphere, not southern."

Our instruments detect no signs of warfare in either hemisphere.

The President made a *huh* sound. "Well, that's your doing, Commander. No one on Earth has ever fought an opponent like you before. None of our weapons work against you. Hostilities pretty much ground to a halt when we realized we have a common enemy now." She let a note of sarcasm creep into her voice. "I suppose I should thank you. You've brought us global peace."

Whether the Broghoke caught the nuance of her last two sentences or not, I couldn't tell. The Commander conducted a brief conversation with someone off camera; their language was muted and gutteral, and was even then being analyzed by our linguistic programs. Not much to work with, though.

The Commander turned back to the camera. *You have additional images of the fighting in both hemispheres?*

They wanted more? "Tons of it," the President said without batting an eye.

Resume transmission.

The old war pictures started again. The President ordered that this time transmission would continue until the Broghoke themselves called a halt. She instructed Schumacher to make sure they didn't run out of film, but one of his aides was already on the phone making the arrangements. The screen was showing two young boys throwing gasoline bombs at a convoy truck in a place that looked like Ireland.

Another problem had appeared. Other nations had picked up our transmissions to the invaders and were angrily demanding to know what was going on. Interestingly, none of them had been able to intercept the Broghoke's tight-beam transmissions to us. We couldn't risk the invaders monitoring any explanation we might give, so the White House Chief of Staff was given the dirty job of asking the rest of the world to be patient and trust us. Poor man.

Leila had a pinched look on her face that I recognized; I followed her into our quarters and found her taking her headache medicine. "You need something to eat," I said. "I'll be right back."

I went to the mess area and returned with two mugs of soup and a plate of cheese, crackers, and fruit. We took our time eating; the Broghoke were evidently fascinated by our moving picture show and sent no signal that they'd seen enough. We tried sleeping again; but

Leila was too restless and kept pacing back and forth in our small quarters.

"What else can we show them, Peter?" she said, more thinking out loud than actually asking. "Floods, other natural disasters? More problems for them to deal with. Volcanoes erupting?"

"Do you think you can perch for five minutes?" She sat down, and I started massaging her neck and shoulders. "He didn't answer you when you asked them to help invade the southern hemisphere."

"He probably didn't believe what he was hearing. I doubt that the Broghoke are used to being asked for help. Traffic accidents—we must have some footage of gory traffic accidents. Shuttle crashes."

"Schumacher is handling all that—leave it to him, Leila. There's nothing more you can do now."

"I know," she said tightly. "That's what scares me." She jumped up and started pacing again. "All that armament those ships are carrying. It would take us forever to outfit a war fleet like that, even if we had an interstellar drive. They must have been planning this excursion for years. And we're hoping to trick them with a few elderly newsreels?"

"You go with what you've got," I said inanely. It was a long shot; we all knew that. I stopped Leila in her pacing and wrapped my arms around her. We leaned against each other without speaking, both of us thinking the same thing: this could be our last night.

It was another three hours before the Broghoke had seen their fill. They'd asked for certain bits to be replayed; the invaders were interested not so much in big explosions and tell-all views of our weaponry as they were in close shots of the actual participants engaged in combat. Maybe they just enjoyed seeing blood spilled.

When the Commander appeared on the screen, the President took the initiative. "Well? Are you going to help us invade the southern hemisphere?"

Invasion is not necessary. You are no longer required to vacate the northern hemisphere.

Aha, a change in plans; something had gotten through

to them. "Well, that's a relief," said the President. "I don't know that we could have managed it anyway." A pause. "Does this mean you're leaving?"

We did not know what fearless warriors the people of Earth are. Even your children show courage and valor in battle. We have never before encountered a species of natural fighters such as you. Your soldiers are your greatest treasure.

Good God in heaven, they *liked* what they'd seen! All that carnage. . . . The President looked taken aback but tried to find an advantage in this unexpected response. "Yes, I'm afraid we're always quarreling about something. A number of our countries have gone bankrupt just from the cost of maintaining a war."

The Broghoke weren't interested in that. *We breed our warriors through controlled mating, but for you that is not necessary. You produce soldiers naturally without planning. The Earth is an even greater resource than we had thought.*

"Resource? For . . . ?"

For warriors. We always need brave warriors.

The temperature in the Command Center dropped twenty degrees.

"Let me understand this," the President said, shaken. "You want to *recruit* soldiers from the human race? From Earth?"

Your own wars must cease. Fighting among yourselves will not be tolerated. A force of Broghoke will be stationed permanently on Earth to protect the resource—this is a mandatory term of your surrender. The commander leaned toward the camera. *We don't want to lose you.*

The transmission ended.

We all stared at one another speechlessly. We'd just condemned humanity to an eternity of warfare? This was our destiny, to breed killers for a killer race? Warriors watching war, they'd seen what they wanted to see. They admired us for the very thing we'd been trying so hard all these years to suppress: human aggression. I went over to take Leila's hands, but she didn't look at me; she was staring beyond my shoulder at General Schumacher.

His eyes were gleaming.

"Look," said Dr. Pellegrino, pointing to the screen. We watched as shuttles began dropping from the warships, a dozen from each of fifty or so of the ships. Shining silver needles pointed straight at Earth.

They were coming.

OBJECT UNIDENTIFIED (FLYING)

by Gordon Eklund

Gordon Eklund lives in Seattle, Washington. He has been writing science fiction for the past twenty-five years. Notable novels of his include *The Eclipse of Dawn, Dance of the Apocalypse,* and *Find the Changeling,* co-authored with Gregory Benford. He has also written many excellent short stories. A winner of the Nebula Award, his most recent novel is *A Thunder on Neptune.*

CHAPTER ONE

In which the Nixon-for-Governor campaign train slashes through the star-crusted Central Valley night like a machete cutting through soft butter—

The Nixon-for-Governor campaign train slashed through the star-crusted Central Valley night like a machete cutting through soft butter.

Barney Runyon, ace political reporter for the L.A. *Dispatch,* choked hard like a sock had been jammed down his scrawny weaselly throat as he gulped his fourth bourbon-and-branch water of the night.

He wiped his mustache with the back of his hand.

Christ, but Runyon was in a mood black as a basket of dead kittens, sitting here looking out the train window at nothing but nothing, wiping his mustache with his hand, and thinking how his wife of only six months, a platinum-blonde sometimes TV actress, sometimes stewardess Normie McClain was, he was pretty fucking sure now, was biffing around with this creep who produced, directed, and starred in a totally different show on another network, Franklin Faraday, the so-called "Mystic to the Stars." How it worked was Faraday, a paunchy guy with a pink turban, would come on the show every Friday at 10:30 with some half-assed, half-forgotten star like Stuart Erwin or Edgar Buchanan and for half an hour they'd gaze into the crystal ball and rub palms and talk about what the signs of the zodiac meant for Stuart, meant for Edgar. It was pure raw crap.

For Runyon, the only lingering question now was should he kill him, kill her, kill both, or kill neither.

Or maybe he ought to just kill himself. For being so stupid as to fall in love when he was fifty damn years old.

Runyon had never killed anybody before in his life though. Not even in the war, where he'd written for *Stars and Stripes.*

But he had never fallen in love either.

What he adored most about Normie McClain was that she was the brightest, smartest, most intellectual woman he'd ever known. As dumb as she looked. It was the sheer dichotomy that got him so turned on. Christ-oh-Jesus, but she'd read all of *Anna Karenina* one weekend as he sat there just watching her. Hard as a stone. And then half of *War and Peace.* She even knew who Ivan Turgenev was. And could pronounce his name.

All of a sudden the train glowed bright as a candle, the cushioned seats throbbed and vibrated, the sky above flickered from night to day and back again.

Paying it no mind, Runyon poured himself another drink.

He choked.

Twenty minutes later, a boyish balding man with a white handkerchief sticking out of his blazer pocket entered the coach, glanced around at the various other reporters either dead asleep or getting there, and dropped into the seat next to Runyon.

"Christ, I've got to tell somebody," he said, hands shaking like a leaf on a tree.

"Tell them what?" said Runyon, drinking somberly.

"The old man," he said. "He's really flipped his goddamn wig this time."

CHAPTER TWO

In which the old man flips his goddamn wig—

The old man, Richard Milhous Nixon, who in that autumn of 1962 was still not yet fifty years of age, drew sharply on the long black Havana cigar clenched between his teeth.

He exhaled in a cloud of smoke like a storm in the wilderness.

Nixon was running for the office of Governor of California, having already served as a United States Congressman for six years, a United States Senator for two years, and for the eight eventful years from January 1953 to January 1961 as Vice President of the United States under the golfing general, Dwight D. Eisenhower. In 1960 Nixon had run for President on his own against John F. Kennedy. Kennedy had beaten him narrowly. There were many smart people in the business of politics who would tell you that election had been swiped out from under Nixon's long nose in Illinois and Texas by Lyndon Johnson and Dick Daley. One of those smart people was Nixon himself.

He'd shocked a lot of people by announcing he was running for California Governor. The incumbent Democrat, a genial if dull liberal named Edmund G. Brown seemed generally popular with his constituents. Moreover, Nixon himself hadn't really been that much of a political presence in California for nearly a decade and had barely edged out Kennedy there in 1960. But the conventional wisdom was that Nixon needed a base from which to launch his next presidential bid (presumably in 1964, presumably against Kennedy), and California was the only place he could anywhere near call home.

So he ran.

And now as October merrily hurtled toward November's election day and as his campaign train sliced a path beneath the star-spangled skies of the California Central Valley, Nixon continued to lag behind in the polls.

Plenty of people, Barney Runyon among them, were already mentally drafting his political obituary.

In his private coach at the back end of the campaign

train, cigar clenched in his teeth, Nixon placed both
hands in front of his chest and formed a big circle with
the fingers. Present in the car with Nixon were four
aides—including a balding, boyish, blazer-wearing young
man named Bert Murphy.

"It was this big," said Nixon. "And as bright as a
tiger's eye. And it never stopped, boys. Not once. I'm
telling you. It went from here to there—" Nixon made
a whooshing sound around his cigar "—and then it was
gone. Just like that."

There was silence.

Then one of the aides said: "Then it was a flying saucer, sir? It was—" he swallowed, "—like one of those
things from outer space?"

Nixon nodded. "As sure as I'm sitting here tonight."

"But, sir," said another aide, not Murphy, who still
had not found the words, "how can you be sure? It
might have been a . . ."

"An optical illusion," finished the other aide.

"Or a weather balloon," said the first, limply.

"Or shit from a tree," said Nixon. He plucked the
cigar out of his mouth and gazed at the moist wet tip.
"I know it wasn't any illusion. It talked to me. The people on board did. Bert—"

He waved a finger.

"Yes, sir," said Bert Murphy.

"Get me the President on the phone. Get me Jack
Kennedy."

CHAPTER THREE

Take me to your leader—!

Take me to your leader, Bert Murphy thought as his
pale plump fingers dialed the number. *Jesus Christ! Is
that what he thinks they said to him?*

"White House Operator," said a squeaky Southern
voice, across more than three thousand miles of telephone line.

Something Nixon didn't know, Bert Murphy was a gay
man, a practicing homosexual. In 1959, when he was a
senior at the University of California in Berkeley, he'd

been arrested on Turk Street in San Francisco for propositioning an undercover vice detective. He'd been given two years' probation by the judge and a lecture not to do it anymore. The probation he had served. The only other person outside his immediate family who knew about Murphy's arrest was Barney Runyon, the reporter for the L.A. *Dispatch*.

And Runyon had promised never to tell.

"My name is Bert Murphy," he said to the operator, "and I'm an assistant to Richard Nixon. Mr. Nixon would like to speak to President Kennedy. Would it be possible for you to put me through?"

Murphy glanced at his watch. It would be past two A.M. on the East Coast. The President was more than likely in bed.

With Jackie.

Murphy pictured the domestic scene.

There was a pause.

Then the White House operator came back on the line. "I can ensure that the President receives your message, Mr. Murphy. Is there a number at which Mr. Nixon may be reached?"

Murphy glanced over at the train's radio operator, who was staring back at him with a fixed, hollow-eyed expression that could not be read.

"And may I provide the President with a reason for Mr. Nixon's call?" the White House operator added.

"Just say . . ." said Murphy, "just say that he needs to talk to the President right away, immediately. On a matter of . . . of grave national significance."

"I will relay exactly that message, sir."

Then Murphy went off in search of Barney Runyon. *Christ, he had to tell somebody about this, didn't he?*

CHAPTER FOUR

In which Barney Runyon states the obvious—

"Jesus, I can't write that," Runyon said. "What the hell are you trying to pull, kid? Are you trying to make me look like a goddamn fool?"

Runyon was thinking about his wife again, about Normie. Suppose he snuck home early from this trip and kicked down the door and found her naked in the arms of her beloved Hollywood mystic. What was he supposed to do then? He'd surely have to kill them. Both of them.

And then blow out his own fucking brains all over the front porch.

There'd be no other real choice.

Except that he didn't happen to own a gun.

"But it's the truth," Murphy said, his voice struggling to keep to a whisper.

"So who gives a shit? Listen, chump. I, for one, do not. Truth is shit. What matters is what people want to hear, want to read. And what they don't want to read is that their favorite presidential candidate is a loony escaped from the bin. Now go back and get me something I can use."

"Just forget it then," said Murphy.

"I plan to. Now what's this about Nixon wanting to talk to Kennedy in the White House. What's that all about?"

"Just what I already told you," muttered Murphy.

"What you told me about what?"

"The thing he saw on the back platform. The spaceship."

"The flying saucer. He wants to tell Kennedy about the flying saucer?"

"I thought you said you didn't care."

"I don't. But if you take my advice, you'll find Nixon a good head doctor. Tomorrow. When we get into Frisco. It's full of head doctors. Now tell me about the Hughes loan. And no bullshit either."

CHAPTER FIVE

In which the President refuses to take a call—

The President of the United States, John Kennedy, sat bolt upright in the hardwood rocking chair that provided some slight semblance of relief from the spinal pain that accompanied him everywhere he went. Piled in front of him on top of an antique wood table lay a thick stack of high altitude black-and-white terrain photographs.

The terrain in question was the southern edge of Sierra del Rosario in west central Cuba.

The President rubbed at his eyes and then leaned back as far as the chair would accommodate him. "Then there's no further question?" he asked. "There's no doubt? There are missiles there."

"Offensive missiles," said his brother Robert Kennedy, the Attorney General. "At least sixteen that have been identified on the ground near the launch pads. Which are still under construction. SS4s. Not their best. But they can reach Miami, of course. New Orleans. Atlanta. A lot of our air bases. Maybe even Washington."

"It may be too early to write off the Southern vote entirely." The President, smiling, looked up. "So what do we do next?"

"We're still talking."

"And our options?"

"We could ignore them . . ."

"Which would be suicide. Politically and otherwise."

The Attorney General nodded. "Or we could take them out. An air strike. Before they know we know."

"Which might be suicide too," the President said. "The real kind. What about nuclear warheads?"

"They haven't found any yet. They're still looking. Helms says they're there, though. He says the Russians wouldn't put in missiles without them."

There was a gentle knock at the door. The Attorney General glanced at his brother, who was thumbing through the photographs again, and then crossed over to answer.

There was a soft murmur of voices.

The Attorney General looked over his shoulder. "It's Nixon. From California. He wants to talk to you."

"For Christ's sake, what about?"

"He won't say. Just that it's important."

"Ask him if he still wants this job."

"Don't worry. He does."

"Have them tell him I'll call later. Hell, if it's that important, Nixon would be the last to know anyway."

The Attorney General shut the door.

"You know," the President mused, glancing once

again at the photographs, "if you stare at these things long enough, they could be almost anything you want them to be. Like ink blot tests. Or an abstract painting. Like that New York fellow. Pollock. Jackson Pollock. Like one of his."

CHAPTER SIX

In which the campaign train grinds to a stop for the night—

The Nixon-for-Governor campaign train ground to a stop for the night.

The public always received the impression the campaign train ran all night and all day, never pausing, never stopping, never halting, always hurtling. But the truth was, there were scant few votes to be won between the hours of midnight and six A.M. With a rally in Sacramento set for nine the next morning and another in Oakland at ten and then across the Bay by limousine for a parade straight through the heart of San Francisco's financial district at noon, now was the time to grind to a halt and take a final snoutful of good clean sweet Central Valley air.

Or so Burt Murphy assumed. And he knew his candidate's itinerary as well as he knew his own mother's face.

Maybe better. He hadn't seen that much of Mom since his arrest and conviction (she provided bail) and then her own recent third marriage to a San Diego industrialist named Patton.

(Nobody ever talked much about the real father. He was somewhere off in Argentina, they said.)

Murphy stood outside in the brisk October breeze with Richard Nixon on the open rear platform of the candidate's private coach, both men gripping the hard iron railing, their knuckles white as paste. It was from this exact same spot that Nixon had today addressed rallies in Bakersfield, Fresno, Modesto, Merced, Stockton, Lodi. At each stop he spoke the same stirring words: *We're going to win this thing . . . we're going to do it for the people, blah, blah, blah.* At none of these rallies had Nixon dropped any reference to the unidentified flying object he claimed to have seen the night before. (From this exact same spot.)

But Murphy knew it was bearing on his mind. He could sense it in the tightness of his eyes.

Now, like an Indian scout indicating a landmark, Nixon pointed high into the dark star-stained sky. "It was right up there, Bert," he said, his voice sounding muffled somehow, as somber and deep as a base viol. "In the south-southeast quadrant, I'd say. The odd part was, at first I didn't even notice it there. Then it moved. *Whoosh!* All at once. You should have seen it, Bert. With your own eyes." He chuckled. "It raced like lightning through the sky."

"But you were alone then, sir." *Unlike now,* Murphy thought, peering obediently into the sky. But it was so fucking silly. There was nothing up there to see. Not a thing. Only the moon and the stars and the occasional puffy autumnal cloud dancing on high. But nothing else. No UFOs. No flying saucers. No lightning racing through the sky like seltzer from a bottle.

"Well, yes, I was alone," Nixon said. "As I am now. Except, of course, that you weren't there either, Bert." He chuckled. "The truth was, I'd stepped out for a smoke. A cigar. Mrs. Nixon does not approve of the habit, I'm afraid. You want to hear the amusing part? The cigars I've been smoking," His voice dropped. "They're Havana made. From Cuba. By Castro. Communist cigars. And do you know where I got them? From Jack Kennedy. Last year. As a post-election gift. Do you think he thought that was amusing, Bert? Giving me—Nixon—the man he stole the election from—a box of Cuban cigars?"

Murphy shook his head. He'd heard this story before. Many times. "I wouldn't know, sir. Maybe he was just trying to be friendly."

"Then you don't know the man. Not Jack Kennedy. Jack Kennedy doesn't have a friend in the world, Bert. Only that goddamn family of his. They're as tight as the skin on a drum, that crew. And twice as loyal. Then look at me. Look at my family, Nixon's family. My poor dumb brother Donald. That goddamn Hughes loan thing. They're all trying to make that out as something ugly, something crooked, something against me. All the newspapers. But I was only trying to help my own brother. Do you believe in signs, Bert?"

"Signs, sir?"

"You know—portents. From angels. Like this thing I saw the other night, last night." Nixon swung slightly away from the railing, edging closer. His hands formed a big circle in the air. "It was this big around, Bob. And gold. Glittering gold. Like light. But brilliant. Like a halo, you almost might say."

"And it was in the sky."

"Oh, it was, yes. For only a few seconds. At first I didn't even see it and then—*whoosh!*—just like that. It was gone forever."

"A flying saucer."

"Oh, no." Nixon reached out, clasping Murphy by the shoulder, squeezing hard. "Not a saucer, Bob. Not round. Not square either, but . . . spherical. I suppose that's what you'd have to call it. A spherical object."

Murphy wasn't altogether certain of the distinction between round and spherical.

"And you saw it, sir," he said.

Nixon formed another circle with his hands. "It was this big around, Bob. This big."

CHAPTER SEVEN

In which a message is given and received—

Murphy, fast asleep in his seat, dreamed his recurring Christmas dream, when he was a little boy and the gifts piled high under the shimmering tree glittered like a golden halo, and when he pried open the first box, ripped the gaily bright wrapping paper, snapped the green and red ribbon, a giant coiled snake, a cobra, leaped—

Somebody was shaking him awake.

Murphy glanced up, blinking.

The train was moving, hurtling like a burning spear.

He looked out the window. As bright as the middle of the day.

He stared up at the man who had shaken him awake, a USC intern by the name of Campbell.

"Are we in Sacramento yet?" Murphy asked.

The intern shook his big, round crewcut head. "You'd better come with me, sir."

He was whispering.

"Come? Come where?" Murphy always felt slightly askew whenever someone referred to him as sir. He was, after all, only twenty-six years old come next December 9. "It's Mr. Nixon, sir, the Vice President. He's saying . . . well, he wants to cancel his speech today."

"In Sacramento?"

"All of them, sir. San Francisco, too."

Murphy darted his eyes rapidly around the coach, but fortunately none of the press had slipped in during the night. Not even that goddamn blackmailing asshole Runyon.

He sprang to his feet. "You'd better take me to him right away," he said.

CHAPTER EIGHT

The Cuban Missile Crisis of October 1962, part 1—
How far back to go?

Hmmm.

Cuba lived for a long time under the really bad, mean, rotten Batista dictatorship. Many peasants were tortured, many killed. The secret police liked to thrust electric cattle prods up the anuses of suspected dissidents and then turn them on full blast, laughing all the while, laughing to beat holy fucking hell.

Then along came Fidel Castro, a medical student. There's a story told about Castro starting out to be a left-handed pitcher and hurling good enough to toss in the American major leagues. If you shut your eyes, you might as well picture him (albeit beardless) in the uniform of the Washington Senators. Like his hero, the great Cuban screwballer Camilio Pascual.

But he cared more about his own people, the buggered peasants of Cuba, than personal glory.

So in January 1959, Castro succeeded from his base

in the Lierra Maestra in overthrowing the rotting remnants of the brutal Batista regime.

Then he turned into a Communist, a goddamn Red. Castro said he'd been one all along, ya-ya-ya-ya-ya. In April 1961, a force of Cuban exiles sponsored by the American CIA landed at Bahia de Cochinos, a favorite fishing spot of Castro's. The invading brigade was soon encircled by more than 20,000 soldiers of the furious Cuban patriot forces. Many of the invaders were killed, the remainder, surrendering with their hands in the air like mad dogs with their testicles cut off, became prisoners. The defeat proved a vivid embarrassment for the United States and its newly elected President Kennedy. It was like going to work and forgetting to zip your pants.

Time passed like a clock whizzing on the wall. The Soviet Union continued its military buildup in Cuba. The U.S. estimated that as many as 3,000 Soviet troops were now stationed on the island. (In reality the number was closer to 40,000, the CIA fooled again.) Kennedy explained he was continuing to examine the situation. Republican Senators Capehart and Keating blasted the President, asserting he was fiddling with his dick while the virginal vagina of Cuba burned with Russian rape. Both Senators claimed to be in possession of data indicating the Soviets were installing offensive missiles on Cuba capable of reaching the United States. *Oh, bullshit,* thought Kennedy. But the weather on Cuba remained bad throughout early October.

Finally, on Sunday, October 14, the weather cleared like cataracts lifted from an old man's rheumy eyes and the first U-2 reconnaissance overflight in more than a week took off, crisscrossing the 800-mile-long island like a spider weaving its deadly web. The black-and-white photographs obtained from this mission rang out as boldly as a fireball in the night: they revealed hidden in the lush green Cuban countryside a total of eight ballistic missile launch pads. Although there was no firm photographic evidence of the presence of nuclear warheads, the clear assumption was that they were already in storage somewhere on the island. Or very soon would be.

President Kennedy promptly convened an executive council composed of the men (there were no women) whose judgment he most trusted both in and out of government to consider all possible American reactions. Dean Acheson, the former Secretary of State under Harry Truman, was a member of this Ex Comm (as it was soon dubbed) but Lyndon Johnson, the Vice President, was not. In time, two major options emerged from the council's deliberations. The first was an immediate (and unannounced) air strike against the missile launch sites. The other was a blockade of the island of Cuba with a simultaneous demand for the immediate dismantlement of the launch pads and a withdrawal of all offensive missiles. The Attorney General, the President's brother Robert, led the campaign in favor of this latter option. He compared an air strike on Cuba with the infamous Japanese sneak attack on Pearl Harbor, Hawaii, on December 7, 1941. Dean Acheson, for one, regarded this analogy as inappropriate and absurd and Robert Kennedy as a sophomoric clown far out of his depth. Acheson favored wiping out the missile sites at once. The more time passed, the more difficult it would become to act at all, he believed. This was the same Dean Acheson once derided by a frothing Vice President Nixon as "the red dean of the cowardly communist college of containment."

By now the latest U-2 photos showed the presence in Cuba of at least thirty-two SS-4 ballistic missiles, each with a range in excess of 500 miles; launch sites for twenty-four 1,500-mile range SS-5s (still at sea); twenty-four SAM (surface-to-air) sites, all ready to fire; forty-two IL-218 medium range bombers capable of carrying nuclear bombs.

In other words, the missiles already there could hit New Orleans, Miami, Mexico City, and/or Washington D.C. Once the SS-5 sites became operational, every major city in the continental U.S.A. could be wiped out with the lone exception of Seattle, Washington.

On the Ex Comm a consensus gradually developed in favor of the blockade to be dubbed a quarantine instead. The President agreed. On Monday, October 22, at 7:00

P.M. Eastern time he appeared before a national TV audience and in the course of a seventeen-minute address announced the imposition of the quarantine around Cuba. He called upon the Soviet Union to dismantle its launch sites and to remove all offensive forces from the island.

Fifty-six American warships were already steaming south to set up the blockade. The Pentagon under Secretary of Defense McNamara (who had favored the quarantine) ordered all U.S. military personnel worldwide to a state of DEFCON-3 alert. (DEFCON-1 is full-scale war.) (Later in the crisis the chief of the Strategic Air Command would, on his own initiative, raise the alert level to DEFCON-2, causing the Soviets much anxiety.) All military leaves were canceled. Bases were sealed up tighter than tomato juice cans. More than 200 ICBMs in silos across the Western U.S. were cocked for launching. Polaris submarines carrying 144 nuclear missiles moved right up close to the seacoasts of the USSR, sixty B-52s armed with 196 H-bombs were airborne at all times while 628 more of the bombers with 2,016 nuclear weapons aboard were dispersed to airfields around the world.

On September 24 (Tuesday), Secretary of State Dean Rusk, waking in his office, roused his undersecretary, George Ball, sleeping on the couch in his own office. "We have won a considerable victory in the night," said Rusk. "We are still alive." (The Attorney General was watching the Secretary closely at this time, concerned about his mental state. Later Rusk would decide to forgo official shelter in the event of an attack. The first thing any survivors would do after the war, he figured, was hunt up Kennedy, McNamara, Bundy, and himself and hang the lot of them from the nearest trees. Nuclear immolation would be a more dignified exit from life, he decided.

On Wednesday, October 24, a meeting of the Ex Comm was interrupted by CIA Director McCone when a messenger arrived with a sealed note. It appears, McCone announced in a voice like lightning in a fruit jar, that some of the Russian ships approaching the blockade line have gone dead in the water.

The two powers had gone eyeball to eyeball and it was the Russians who had blinked first.

(More to come, though.)

CHAPTER NINE

In which a message from outer space is described and discussed—

Richard Nixon sat stiff-backed and stiff-legged as a trout in the plush cushioned seat in the private rear coach of his campaign train, surrounded by aides milling thickly like chickens in a barnyard.

Murphy shoved his way into the circle surrounding the candidate.

An unlit cigar clenched in his fist, Nixon formed a circle in the air with his hands.

". . . last night," he was saying, "last night around 10:30. I just happened to glance up in the sky and there it was, floating there, just like the time before. A light, boys. A vast bright spherical light. This big around. A light in the sky. And then—*whoosh*—it moved. All at once. I jumped a little, I admit, and then . . . then I realized it was coming for me, dropping down, swooping like a great bird out of the sky. I thought to run. But I was frozen in place. I couldn't budge a muscle. Then it caught me, boys. The light bathed me like a shower of water. A strange powerful golden light. I felt myself being lifted in the air, carried into the ship. There were three of them on board. Creatures, yes, but much like men. Men such as ourselves except that their bodies were pure golden light. You could see right through them. Clear as day. And then one of them spoke to me."

"What did he say, Mr. Vice President?" asked the young intern, Campbell.

"Bert," said Nixon, swinging his head and looking at Murphy. "Bert, have you been able to get through to Jack Kennedy yet?"

CHAPTER TEN

In which the news of the day touches the Nixon motorcade— Barney Runyon, riding in the coal-black Cadillac limo four car lengths behind the open-topped white convertible carrying the stiffly waving, rigidly grinning, yo-yo head-bobbing Republican candidate, could not for the life of him see one thing that was going on up front. What was the fucking point, he asked himself as the Nixon-for-Governor motorcade clawed a precarious path through the throngs gathered on San Francisco's Montgomery Street, of having the press riding back here in the dust when the only thing of any even vague interest was happening up front? Runyon just hoped somebody didn't decide to shoot Nixon in the center of his fucking butt. Because if they did, nobody was going to report it in time for the bulldog edition to hit the street. It would be old news before anybody found out.

Christ, thought Runyon, for all the good this was doing he might as well have stayed home. (With Normie, he thought. With that lying, cheating, fucking, whore bitch.)

About the only thing he could actually see to report were the puzzled, bored, slack as dogshit expressions on people's faces once the motorcade passed by. Nobody looked especially dazzled at having glimpsed the real candidate in his real flesh, that was for sure.

The whole thing was running way behind schedule anyway. They hadn't even reached Sacramento till past ten and now this supposedly twelve noon event was just getting started as the chimes struck three P.M. Nixon's main trouble (among many) was that he didn't know crap about real people, what they wanted from life. By this time of the day, Runyon knew, the average working slob had only one thing on his mind and that was getting the hell out of the office and getting home to the liquor cabinet. Or, if not home, then at least a good, clean, warm, wet bar. The last thing he wanted was some clown of an ex-Vice President splaying through the streets like a dog searching for a hydrant and clogging up traffic the rest of the day.

Runyon made a soft wet kissing noise into the palm of his hand. *There goes another few thousand votes you ain't going to win, Mr. Nixon,* he thought. Not that it mattered to Runyon. Hell, he was a Democrat anyway.

He'd voted for Kennedy in '60, hadn't he? (Well . . .
hadn't he?)

As the crowd continued to swirl languidly through the
broad, deeply shaded boulevard, Runyon wondered
about his wife, about Normie, what she was up to right
this moment a thousand miles away in far off exotic Los
Angeles. He wondered if she liked to blow her new little
boyfriends or if she was still just straight up missionary
style the same as she'd always been with him. It was
something to conjecture over, that was for sure, something to picture in his head as vivid as a technicolor
movie, especially now that he had made up his mind the
first thing he was going to do when he got back home
was blow her fucking brains all over the fucking refrigerator, all gooey and sticky and wet as paste.

The man sitting next to Runyon, an asshole in a pin-
stripe suit who worked for one of the networks, had
something with a wire in it sticking out of his ear. Now
he plucked it out and took a deep breath. "Christ," he
said. "Christ, and I have to be stuck in fucking
California."

"What about it?" Runyon asked.

"That was my producer. It's just been announced
Kennedy's going on TV at four. With a big
announcement."

"Jackie's pregnant?"

"They think it's probably Cuba."

"Cuba, huh?" said Runyon. "You think old ski-nose
up there knows anything about it we don't?"

"Nixon?" said the TV man. "You're kidding. Nixon
lost."

CHAPTER ELEVEN

*In which the son of the governor, a seminary student,
enters the picture—*

The son of the Governor of California, a twenty-four-
year-old sometime seminary student dressed in black
jeans and a gray turtleneck sweater, laid down the copy
of *Franny and Zooey* he'd been reading and bent over
to answer the telephone. He was alone in the Governor's

Mansion tonight, his father and mother and sister having left right after the President's speech to catch a waiting plane for a late campaign reception in Los Angeles.

"Governor's residence," said the son.

"Yes, um, is Governor Brown there?"

"I'm sorry but the Governor's just left for Los Angeles."

"I—this is Richard Nixon."

"I know. I recognized your voice."

"But he shouldn't be going there. Not tonight."

"The reception was already scheduled. Mostly old friends. He decided it wouldn't be right not to go."

"He must be mad."

The son paused for a moment before replying. This, after all, was the man his father was running against, the man who wanted his job. "He did what he needed to do."

"Who the hell are you anyway?"

The governor's son told him who he was.

"Ah, the seminary student."

"Yes," he said, surprised at first that Nixon knew. But of course he would. You didn't go as far as Nixon in politics without learning as much as possible about everyone. Even your supposed enemies.

"Do you believe in angels?" Nixon asked.

"I—what do you mean?"

"Angels. You know, son. Creatures from heaven. The reason I ask, I've been seeing certain odd things lately. Signs. Portents. Such as in the Bible. I'm fairly certain they're from outer space, but you never really know, do you? They could be angels as well."

"I—" he hesitated. "I wouldn't know much about that."

"A pity. Goddamn it, I thought all you Catholics believed in that sort of thing. Me, I was brought up a Quaker, you know. A plain and simple faith. No adornments. No bullshit. I was brought up that way my entire life by my dear mother."

"It's not quite that simple," he said.

"Well, no. Nothing is. Take sin, for example. That's

something you Catholics and we Quakers share in common. You can't tell me sin is simple."

"I wouldn't, no."

"Well, I'd better be getting along. But I'll tell you what, son. If your father calls, I'm in San Francisco. At the Mark Hopkins. Have him get in touch with me. I need his advice."

He thought for a moment. "I could give you the number of his hotel in Los Angeles. But he might not be there until late."

"I'll be up for a time. Expecting visitors, you know. By the way, you don't have the President's number, do you? A private line where you can get through without an idiotic operator getting in the way?"

"No, I don't think so."

"I understand. Can't be too careful. Not about that sort of thing. Hell, for all you know, I might be Vaughn Meader. What with the Russians and Cuba and all . . ."

"I'll give my father your message," he said.

"Thank you, son. I thank you from the bottom of my heart."

There was a long pause.

He almost hung up.

Then Nixon said: "One other thing. This mess over Cuba. It's going to work out fine in the end. Trust me, son. I know that for a fact."

CHAPTER TWELVE

In which events take a somewhat nasty turn—

"Five hundred dollars," Runyon was saying, spitting the words like a volcano spurting fire. "Five hundred in cash or I'm going to splash your little blow job in the park across the front page of tomorrow's *Dispatch.* I can see your mommie's eyes now—bigger than a couple flying saucers. 'Nixon aide caught licking wrong dick.' How the hell do you think that's going to play over the dinner table tomorrow night?"

Murphy nodded soberly. But he should've known better. He should've spotted this one coming like a hot horse thundering down the backstretch. (Not that he was a gambler.) That bastard Runyon. Up till now it had only been access he'd demanded, information, inside dope. But now with the campaign dwindling down toward the vanishing point of ultimate defeat, he had chosen to raise the stakes.

He wanted money.

"Who do you think I am?" Murphy asked, turning his head, gazing out his hotel window at the magical golden lights of San Francisco crazily winking under a slate black sky. He looked back. "I haven't any money. I'm an unpaid volunteer."

"But your mommie's not. Or Daddy. And if you don't want to go to them, get it from somewhere else. Hell, get it from Nixon. He's loaded. We all know about the fucking Hughes loan."

"That was personal," he said automatically. It was what he always told the press. "I'll get the five hundred for you. I don't know how. Some way. But then you'd better leave me alone. You can't come back asking for more."

"Now why would I do a horrible, rotten, mean thing like that?" Runyon asked. "What kind of sleazy rat do you think I am?"

Murphy decided not to answer.

"Make it eight o'clock tomorrow morning, then," Runyon said. "After that you'll never see me again. Unless Nixon wins. Or decides to run for something else again sometime later and you're still around to wash his dirty laundry for him."

Murphy shook his head. "The banks don't even open till ten."

"All right, by noon, then." Runyon scowled. "We're supposed to be taking off for L.A. at twelve. Have the cash in my hand by the time the plane leaves the ground and everything'll be just a-okay, I guarantee."

"Why the hurry? I'm not going anywhere."

"No, but I am. I've got something to buy. A gift. For my wife."

"Flowers and candy?" Murphy said. "That doesn't sound like you, Runyon."

"Better than flowers. I'm getting her a gun."

Murphy stared at him.

But Runyon winked, turned, and headed for the door.

Murphy continued to stare after him.

Whoosh!

There was a noise like the biggest vacuum cleaner in the whole universe.

Stopping, Runyon swung his head. "For Christ's sake." He pointed at the window with a shaky hand. "Take a look out there."

But Bert Murphy had already seen it, too.

CHAPTER THIRTEEN

Good news out of D.C.—!

(More on the '62 missile crisis)

It was on Thursday, October 26, in the green, shark-infested waters north of Cuba that the U.S. Navy boarded and searched the Soviet chartered freighter, the *Marcula*.

The ship's captain, a Greek, spoke no English. (Or Russian.)

None of the boarding crew spoke Greek. (One spoke a little Russian, though, a CIA man, you can bet cheese on it.)

On board the vessel—after some confusion due to translation problems—they found sulfur, newsprint, asbestos, and about a dozen Russian-made trucks.

They were really lousy trucks, everybody in the boarding crew agreed.

The *Marcula* sailed on. (It was the first ship stopped and searched by the quarantine.)

Meanwhile back in Washington, the President of the United States, John Kennedy, and his aides on the Ex Comm were to a man (no women, remember) as depressed as a bowl of dirty dishwater.

Ships or no ships, they knew, the Soviets nevertheless showed no signs of dismantling the launch sites already established on the Red island.

War had never seemed more imminent, thought Dean Rusk.

Pressure for a military strike continued to build like a

horse dropping to its knees for easier mounting. Acheson, Bundy, Maxwell Taylor, and the Joint Chiefs thundered like rain clouds in unison: the time to strike was not only now—it was like half-past-now. The advantage was slipping away like mud through a fist.

What goddamn advantage? wondered the President bleakly. A thought kept rummaging through his mind like a mouse after cheese, something General LeMay might have said but perhaps hadn't: eight to thirteen million Americans dead. At most. (Nobody was counting Russians or Cubans.)

Just then a letter arrived from Premier Khrushchev way over in Moscow. It was a queer letter, many on the Ex Comm thought, disjointed and almost hysterical in parts. (Though obviously authentic because of that.) "Guarantee that you will never invade Cuba," Khrushchev wrote, "and everything else can be worked out."

It looked like a glimmer of pure golden light in a sea of encroaching blackness.

But before there was even time to consider this first letter, a second letter was released publicly through Radio Moscow.

"Withdraw your Jupiter intermediate range missiles from their bases in Turkey," Khrushchev wrote, "and we will do the same in Cuba."

Good Christ, thought everyone in the room, aghast with dread.

For one thing, the Jupiter was an obsolete hunk of junk that took hours to fuel and fire and had about as much chance of striking its intended target as a can of prune juice hurled blindly in the air. Its military value, even in Turkey right on the Soviet border, was zero (at best). But the Turks liked having the missiles there and you couldn't just pull them out because it would look weak and spineless and the Congress would raise a hue and stink, etc.

The Ex Comm seemed befuddled.

So it was decided to reply to Khrushchev's first letter with a big wet sincere thank you and ignore the second letter as if it did not exist, as if it were dirt in the wind.

That done, everybody went back to talking of war.

General Taylor, speaking for the Joint Chiefs, wanted to launch the invasion of the island within thirty-six hours, preferably no later than the morning of the 29th. (Estimates placed probable U.S. casualties in an invasion at between fifteen and twenty thousand, half of them on the bloody beaches at the beginning. Nobody was counting Cubans or Russians here either.) (Or what would happen if the Soviets launched one or two of their nuclear-tipped SS-4s at, say, Miami or Elgin AFB in Florida.)

It was around this time on Saturday morning that news arrived that a U-2 conducting reconnaissance over Cuba had been killed. Kennedy had said more than once that any American plane fired upon would be retaliated against instantly in kind.

But all of a sudden nobody wanted to say a word.

The invasion of the island of Cuba was set for dawn, Tuesday, October 30.

CHAPTER THIRTEEN AND ONE-HALF

The Cuban missile crisis of 1962, part 3 (how it ended)—
On Sunday morning October 28, at nine A.M. Radio Moscow broadcast Khrushchev's reply to Kennedy's response to his first letter.

He wrote: "The Soviet government, in addition to previously issued instructions on the cessation of further work at building sites for the weapons, has issued a new order on the dismantling of the weapons which you describe as 'offensive' and their crating and return to the Soviet Union."

(The Jupiters were pulled out of Turkey the following January.)

CHAPTER FOURTEEN

In which a somewhat overly serious young man ponders some chance remarks overheard at a party—
The son of the Governor of California stared deeply at the swirling cheap red wine in the paper cup he was

grasping and wondered not for the first time what the hell he was doing here.

Far across the crowded hotel ballroom his mother waved to him.

It was a victory party, a celebration, his father having this day been reelected to office over his opponent by a margin of almost 300,000 votes.

Across the room his mother waved to him again.

A tall blonde woman in a white dress with a glass of what looked like champagne clutched to her breast strode up to him. She was an attractive woman with round blue eyes and wore almost no makeup.

"You're the son, aren't you?" she asked in a voice that struck him as strangely cold and mechanical.

He nodded.

"I have a message for you."

"For me? Who from?"

"From Nixon. He said to tell you he was right all along, they were coming for him."

"He said what—?"

But the woman turned away.

He watched her leave the room, hips rolling under her dress like ships at sea.

She paused at the door. The hair on the back of her head suddenly parted.

Like a butterfly opening its wings.

Her third eye winked at him.

CHAPTER FIFTEEN

Last Press Conference—

"Now that all members of the press are so delighted that I have lost, just think how much you're going to be missing. You won't have Nixon to kick around any more, because, gentlemen, this is my last press conference . . ."

Barney Runyon of the *Dispatch,* scribbling notes, felt the weight of the gun under his right arm as heavy as a lead battleship.

CHAPTER SIXTEEN

Hung Upside Down—

Late in 1968, President-Elect Nixon entered unannounced a dimly lit art gallery on New York City's Upper East Side called the "Unidentified Flying Object." He was accompanied only by one aide, Bert Murphy, and two Secret Service men.

Nixon walked straight up to one painting hanging on the wall and stood there staring at it, not moving.

The painting depicted a bright gleam of golden light, a spherical glowing light, shining in a surrounding mass of sheer blackness.

Nixon stared and stared.

There were no other objects in the painting, no other colors.

Nixon glanced back over his shoulder at Murphy.

"Bert, tell me one thing," he said.

"Yes, sir?"

"How can they be sure it's hanging right side up?"

RANDOM ACTS
by Marc Bilgrey

Marc Bilgrey's writing credits include a situation comedy
pilot for CBS TV, *MAD* magazine, Marvel Comics, material
for comedians and a story in the anthology *Phantoms of
the Night*. He's just completed a novel.

I got the phone call at ten o'clock on a warm night in
April. Phil Roberts was dead. I felt my mouth go dry as
I listened to the news, then managed to mumble a few
words into the receiver and hang up. For a while, I stood
and stared at the floor until I was interrupted by the
sound of Linda's footsteps walking into the living room.

"Are you okay?" she asked.

"Huh?" I said, still in a daze.

"Who was that on the phone?"

"Jack Ferlin. Phil Roberts died."

"Phil? But he was only a couple of years older than
you. What did—"

"He was hit by a bus," I said, as I went into the
bedroom.

"That's horrible," said Linda, following behind me.
"Where did it happen?"

"Not far from his house, in Santa Monica," I said, as
I took my suitcase out of the closet and placed it on the
bed. "He was riding his bike. He never had a chance."
I opened the bureau and took out a couple of pairs
of underwear.

"Where are you going?"

"The funeral is the day after tomorrow." I put some
shirts and a few pairs of socks in the suitcase.

"I know how much you admired Phil," said Linda,
smoothing back her shiny black hair.

"I did," I said, as I tossed a pair of pants into the suitcase, "there aren't that many people I've kept in touch with from twenty years ago."

"I wonder what's going to happen to his show."

"How can you think about a TV show at a time like this?"

"It's a natural thought. I mean, he was the creator and it is still number one in the ratings."

"What kind of world is it that can take a guy who has everything: a hit TV show, a big house, a beautiful wife, a kid, and bam, suddenly it's all gone."

"I don't know," said Linda, kissing me softly on the cheek, "I don't know."

That night, I had trouble getting to sleep. The previous week, I had gone to see a hypnotherapist to help me with my insomnia. I had thought that I had begun to make some progress, but now sleep came slowly and with great effort.

The next morning I went to La Guardia and got on a plane. A minute after we took off, I looked out the window and watched the Empire State Building fade into the distance. Then I sat back in my seat.

I regretted that Linda hadn't come with me. I hated going to funerals alone, and I hated flying. But Linda was a sales representative at a furniture company and couldn't take the time off. My hours were a little more flexible. That's just one of the many perks of being an unemployed playwright. Come to think of it, it's the only perk.

It was an overcast day, and big fluffy clouds flew by my window. All I could think about was Phil Roberts being hit by that bus. Twenty-one years ago, Phil and I were both struggling young playwrights trying to get somewhere. Phil was the first one to actually achieve any success. His first play was mounted in a tiny basement theater downtown. On opening night, during the second act, the pipes on the ceiling started to make noises. But Phil couldn't have cared less. He was standing in the back, smiling. You'd have thought that he was watching

a production on Broadway, instead of in a dive in the
East Village.

Gradually, the productions moved uptown. Off off
Broadway became off Broadway, and then, a few years
later, Broadway. His show ran a year and after that, he
got offers from Hollywood. Then he moved to Los
Angeles.

After creating a couple of sitcoms that only made it
through half a season, Phil hit it big with his next one.
It was a situation comedy that even the critics had liked.
It had never failed to be in the number one or two spot
since debuting three seasons earlier.

Over the years, Phil and I had kept in touch by phone.
He would talk about his marriage (to a onetime soap
opera actress) and his success. And now it was all gone.

A flight attendant asked me if I wanted something to
drink. She gave me a club soda and then I stared out
the window again. Things hadn't fared as well for me,
careerwise, as they had for Phil. Over the years, only a
few of my plays had been produced. Mostly they'd been
small productions that had managed to elude any serious
attention. But making money had never been that big
an issue for me. I was happy doing the occasional play
and supplementing my income with a variety of free-
lance writing work. I liked the idea that, unlike TV, I
never had to compromise my playwriting because of the
whims of some network executive or the equivalent.

After the plane landed, I took a cab from LAX to
Bel Aire and checked into my hotel. It was small and
very elegant. Even though I knew I shouldn't be spending the money, somehow it didn't seem very important
now.

The funeral the next day was well attended. I saw a
lot of familiar faces. Not just the people I knew from
New York who'd moved there, but well-known actors
and writers. Phil had only been in L.A. for five years,
but you'd never have known it by the turnout. It looked
like half the town had come to pay their respects. Afterward I told Phil's widow, Connie, how sorry I was.

Later in the day, a bunch of the former New York
contingent and I went to a deli on Fairfax. We talked

about the old days and Phil, and then the conversation drifted to movies and to the new TV season. I had the sense from the group that they were already trying to emotionally distance themselves from Phil. Maybe, they figured, that way they wouldn't be next.

I went back to the hotel and sat on my little balcony and stared at the pool. As the sky got dark, the smog did not dissipate. At that moment, it wouldn't have mattered to me if it engulfed the whole city.

The next day, I walked alongside the beach and watched men and women laughing, singing, and roller skating. Others rode bikes or just strolled hand in hand.

That night, I went to the airport and boarded a plane back to the East Coast.

As we took off, I looked out the window, watched the lights of the city disappear into the darkness, and thought about Phil. His death had made me realize that everything could be over in a snap. And what did it all mean anyway?

I read a few magazines, then some chapters in a paperback I'd bought. I was interrupted by a burst of lightning outside. Then I must've fallen asleep. The next thing I remembered was waking up from my nap, which I thought was very unusual, since I'd never been able to sleep on a plane before.

Some time later, we landed in New York. As I got off the plane and walked into the terminal, I looked at my watch and noticed that we were forty-five minutes late. I didn't think anything of it, though I did hear a couple of people behind me comment on it.

When I walked into our apartment, Linda ran over and gave me a big kiss. We hugged for a while and I told her all about the trip.

After dinner, we talked some more, and then I went into the bedroom, got into bed, and fell asleep immediately. I was shaken awake by Linda. "What is it?" I said. "Are you okay?"

"I'm fine, I'm worried about you," she said. "You were thrashing around and crying in your sleep. You looked like you were having a nightmare."

I thought for a few seconds and then it came to me.

"I was back on the plane," I said, "and something horrible happened."

"What?" said Linda, turning on the light on her night table.

"I was in the plane and suddenly there was a burst of light and I looked out the window and I saw an object."

"What kind of object?"

"A UFO."

"Weird dream."

"There's more. The UFO came closer to the plane. It was round, just like a, well, you know, a flying saucer. It was frightening. And it was huge, much bigger than the plane."

"What happened then?"

"Well, it kept getting closer and closer, and then I felt the plane shaking."

"Like turbulence?"

"No, it seemed like it was vibrating. I saw a strange blue light outside, and then I saw a figure walking."

"Walking where?" said Linda.

"That's the strange part. Somehow the plane was now, well, inside the UFO. The engines of the plane were off, and everything was quiet. Then I got a better look at the figure walking around on the floor outside." I swallowed. "It was one of those big-headed guys with the huge black eyes."

"You mean the kind they always have drawings of on the cover of the supermarket tabloids?"

"Yeah, only there was no sign of Elvis or Bigfoot. And then you woke me up."

"That's a scary dream."

"It felt so real."

"You should try to go back to sleep," said Linda, glancing at her alarm clock.

"Yeah," I said, "I guess so."

Linda turned over and within a few seconds was snoring. I read a couple of pages in a biography I had started and then turned out the light.

The next day, after Linda went to work, I sat down at my typewriter (let others use a computer—hey, Phil wrote on legal pads and it didn't hurt him) and tried to work.

After a while, I realized that I couldn't get anything started, so I turned off my typewriter and went out to take a walk. I thought about Phil Roberts, then about the futility of it all. Did anything mean anything?

I stopped at a newsstand and bought a paper. Eventually, I went back to the apartment, ate a bowl of puffed corn cereal, and read the newspaper. On page nineteen, I came upon a tiny story that sent chills down my spine. "UFO seen over Ohio." It went on to quote witnesses who described seeing a massive, saucer-shaped object with blue rotating lights around it. The time of the sightings was between nine and ten o'clock P.M.

"It's just a coincidence," said Linda later that night, as she took the dinner dishes off the table and placed them in the sink.

"But how can you ignore the fact that the plane I was in happened to be right over that area around the time of the sightings?"

"Did *you* see anything?"

"At one point I saw lightning."

"That doesn't count."

"Well, then, how do you explain the fact that my plane was forty-five minutes late?"

"Planes are always late."

"Yeah," I said, "that's true, but when they're late, there are reasons. In this case, there weren't any. I checked with the weather bureau. There was no wind, no storms, no rain. It was one of the clearest days on record. What do you say to that?"

"I say that you should get to work on something constructive and then you wouldn't have to fill up your days with pointless activities."

"Yeah, well . . . maybe you're right."

Linda smiled at me and said, "Want to watch a movie tonight? I stopped by the video store on the way home."

That night, I woke up screaming. Linda turned on the light and put her arms around me. I was breathing heavily, and tears were streaming down my cheeks.

"It's okay," she said, "it's okay."

I looked at her and wiped my eyes.

"Don't tell me—"

"Yeah," I said. "It was the same dream again. Only this time it picked up where it left off. Remember how I told you that I saw this guy with a big head and big black eyes walking around outside the window? This time he was joined by a few other guys who looked just like him. They all wore little silver skintight suits. After milling around for a few seconds, one of them pointed his bony finger at something on the side of the plane. Then they went away for a minute, which gave me a chance to turn around and look at the other passengers on the plane. It was amazing. All of the people were staring straight ahead, frozen, like statues. Anyway, a couple of minutes later, I looked outside and saw the little guys come back again, and this time, each one of them was carrying something that looked like a weapon. And then they started walking toward the plane."

I shivered and Linda held me again. Then I said, "I think they were doing something terrible to the plane, sabotaging it somehow."

"How do you know?"

"I just felt it. They were tampering with the machinery in the plane. Who knows what they were planting in there. Maybe some kind of bomb."

"Boy, what an active imagination."

I stared at Linda, wondering how she'd take what I had to tell her, then I decided that I didn't care. "Maybe it wasn't my imagination. Maybe it wasn't a dream."

"Then what was it?"

"A memory. Maybe the aliens put everyone in some kind of a trance, except me, and I'm the only one who saw what they were doing."

"Why would you be the only one out of a whole group of passengers to witness something?"

"I was trying to figure that out. I thought that maybe the hypnosis I was under last week might have had something to do with it."

"That was for insomnia," said Linda. "Why would—"

"Maybe it made me less receptive to *their* hypnosis."

"It all sounds crazy."

"How do you account for the fact that the plane was forty-five minutes late, that people reported seeing a UFO, *and* I'm having this recurring dream?"

"I have no idea, but UFO or no UFO, I have to get up in the morning."

"Okay," I said, as I watched her turn over. A few minutes later, I managed to fall asleep. I didn't have the dream again, but I did not sleep well.

When Linda left for work, I sat at the kitchen table and stared at the refrigerator. I wondered if the plane I'd been in *had* been brought aboard a UFO. Maybe a bomb *had* been put on it. Or the plane had been tagged in the way the scientists implant tracking devices in animals for study. Or even that the plane had somehow been turned into a big lab experiment, where everyone who went aboard it became a guinea pig for the aliens. Was this all conjecture, or was there anything to it?

As I walked to the phone, it occurred to me that maybe Linda was right, maybe it *was* all crazy. Delusional even. But suppose it wasn't? Suppose that somehow I had been the only witness to some kind of horrible event that would change the world for the worse.

Suppose that the creatures I'd seen were the advance scouts for a wave of invasions that were about to happen? Shouldn't humanity be warned? I realized that even to myself, I sounded like a total wacko. What I needed was some kind of proof. I opened the phone book and pressed the number for the airline into the keypad.

A couple of hours later, a cab let me off in front of the terminal. It felt strange to be walking through the airport without going to a plane.

I had no trouble finding the Wings cocktail lounge. I was sipping a club soda at the bar, when a man in a dark blue uniform walked up to me.

"Mr. Collier?" he said tentatively.

"Captain Hayward?" I said. He nodded. I picked up

my drink, and we walked to an empty table and sat down.

"As I mentioned to you on the phone," said the captain, looking at his watch, "I don't have much time, I have a flight in half an hour."

I appreciate you meeting with me, Captain."

"Sure thing. On the phone you said you were a playwright and that you were writing a play about an airline pilot."

"That's right, I am a playwright. I've had a number of my plays produced off Broadway, but the reason I wanted to talk to you concerns something else."

"Oh," he said, arching an eyebrow. He looked like a pilot from central casting. Square jaw, high cheekbones, blond hair, blue eyes. "What's on your mind?"

"I was on your plane the day before yesterday. Flight 204 from LAX to La Guardia. I was wondering if you could tell me why we arrived in New York forty-five minutes late?"

"You wanted to meet me just to ask me that?"

"Yes, sir. According to the weather department there was no wind, no clouds, no rain. Do you have any idea what caused the delay?"

The pilot looked down at the table, then back up at me. "I don't have an answer for you. I've been flying these birds for twenty-five years, and this is the first time anything like this has ever happened to me. I asked my copilot for his opinion, and he was baffled, too. You're right, there were no logical explanations for the delay. When you eliminate weather as a factor, then you're left with pilot error or mechanical failure.

"After we landed, I double-checked everything across the board and came up negative on both counts. At this point, your guess is as good as mine."

"Weird, huh?"

"I'll say. That all you wanted to ask me?"

"That's it." The pilot stood up, and then I said, "Oh, by the way, you didn't happen to see anything odd during the trip, did you?"

"Odd, like what?"

"I don't know, just—"

"You're not one of those UFO nuts, are you?"

"No, sir, not at all."

"I haven't had much sleep in the last two days, I don't need this."

As he started to walk away, I said, "Been having nightmares, Captain?"

He turned, looked at me for a couple of seconds, then nodded quickly and walked out of the bar.

I took a sip of my drink. I was wondering what to do next when a young man in jeans and a T-shirt sat down next to me, and said, "I couldn't help overhearing that you were talking to Captain Hayward about flight 204 from L.A."

"Yeah," I said.

He had red hair and looked like he was in his late twenties. He turned around clandestinely, then stared back at me. "I'm a mechanic on the ground crew. I worked on the 727 you're talking about, and I have some questions about that flight, too."

"What kind of questions?"

"Well, for instance, how is it that the plane had hairline cracks on the fuselage before it took off for L.A. and when it got back, they were gone."

"What does that mean?"

"Just what it sounds like. I spotted them in the pre-flight walk around inspection. Hey, it's not like I didn't report it. But who listens to a grunt like me? Those things can be dangerous. The small ones might not hurt anyone, but if they spread, they can lead to multi-site damage, and then it's bad news."

"Wait a second, let me get this straight. You mean to say that there were cracks in the fuselage, and then when the plane came back, they were gone? How do you know that they didn't just fix 'em in L.A.?"

"I called. No one did a thing. Besides, there wasn't time. And not only that, but this patch-up job was smooth as silk. I've never seen work that good done that quickly. No signs of welding, not a scratch on it. There was something else, too. There were a few spots around the aircraft that had dings on them. A tiny dent here, a little corrosion there, but when I checked them out the other night, they were all gone. I can't understand it. It's as if someone went over the whole plane and remade it. I've been on the job for four and a half years, never seen anything like it."

I thanked him for talking to me, then got up and left him sitting at the table, shaking his head.

That night it was Linda who was shaking her head in the living room. "Just because the pilot didn't know what caused the delay doesn't mean it was a UFO."

"No," I said, "it doesn't. But the mechanic is harder to explain away. What I think is that the plane I was in *was* taken aboard a UFO, but it wasn't to put a bomb on it, or to plant some kind of homing device or experiment. It was to fix it. To prevent an accident that may have been about to happen."

"There's no way to prove that."

"I suppose not. Sometimes it's hard to prove a positive."

After Linda went to bed, I stayed up a while in the living room, looking out the window. You couldn't see many stars from where I was. The city lights and the pollution obscured them. As I stared at the sky, I wondered if maybe it wasn't a senseless universe we lived in after all. Maybe for every random tragedy, there was an equally random act of, for lack of a better word, goodness.

Sometime later, I went into the bedroom and got into bed. I didn't have any more dreams about planes or spaceships. But a few nights later, I had one about Phil. He was sitting on a cloud writing away on one of his legal pads, unconcerned about ratings, and he looked as he did when we'd first known one another.

The following week, I started writing a new play. It felt good to get back to work again. There was something very comforting about sitting at my desk, listening to the sounds of my old IBM Selectric purring and clattering away, like a distant train coming to take me to places I'd never been before.

IF PIGS COULD FLY
by Jack C. Haldeman II

Jack Haldeman began his writing career combining science
fiction and sports, and soon progressed into writing novels
such as *High Steel*, co-authored with Jack Dann, which ex-
amines the construction of a space station from the view of
one of the men who built it. His short fiction appears in
Alternate Celebrities, Warriors of Blood and Dream, and
Alternate Tyrants. He lives in Gainsville, Florida with his
wife, author Barbara Delaplace.

Television is in my blood.

I was born to cover news. Hard news. The harder the
story, the better I like it. Give me a crackerjack remote
crew and a fast-breaking disaster and I'll have you glued
to the tube. I'm hell on wheels with a heartrending
human interest story, squeezing every pitiful tear possible into my twenty-second slot.

Of course it hasn't actually happened yet. I've only
been in the biz ten months, and I haven't gotten all that
many assignments. But it's only a matter of time. Talent
rises to the top in my chosen profession, and talent I
got. In spades. When it happens, I'll be ready.

Television is in my blood.

Watch my dust. I'm going to be the Peter Jennings or
Walter Cronkite of my generation in a couple years. I
wasted a lot of time before I discovered my true calling.
But I imagine Einstein didn't wake up one morning in
his crib knowing he was going to be a rocket scientist
either. Talent, like a good wine or imported beer, needs
time to mature.

"Sam, run this tape over to Bubba's Real Pit Barbecue. See if they like this one any better."

"Sure thing, Earl," I said, leaning my broom against a desk. "Can I take the Cadillac?"

Earl frowned at me and shook his head. He owns the station, and what he says goes. Still, I wish they'd trust me with the Cadillac, just once.

It took a few minutes to get the old Chevy truck cranking and pointed the right way up Route 41. It looked right at home in the rural Florida countryside, just one more clapped-out pickup chugging through the pine-scrub flatland. Hell of a place to put a television station.

But I didn't mind. I was going to ride it all the way to the top.

I was in sales before I became a newsman. To be honest, I wasn't much good at it, but that doesn't bother me much anymore. Vacuum cleaners and I just didn't hit it off. Things like that happen. And I wasn't so hot at meeting the public, either, which is fairly important in the door-to-door sales profession. Some of us just aren't face-to-face people. I'm much better facing a camera and telling the public what they need to know, which is the heart and soul of the television news business.

I've had lots of life experience, which is helpful in the news biz. Before I was in sales, I drove a delivery truck for a department store. To this day, I swear it wasn't my fault. They shouldn't have built that brick wall so close to the loading dock. Just my bad luck I was carrying a load of expensive glassware, and who would have thought that the computers under the glassware were so darn delicate. They should have packed them better. And I suppose I shouldn't mention that job I had washing dogs for that vet. I wasn't there but a couple of days, and they found most of them, anyway.

I do miss Springfield, though, since my mother sent me down south to live with my uncle. Dade City is an okay town, as far as Florida goes, but nothing much ever happens here. I have to admit, though, my mother was right. A change of pace and a fresh start were just what I needed to find my true calling. I don't miss the snow, though. If it hadn't been snowing, I'd probably still be driving for that dumb old department store instead of being a television star.

To be truthful, I'm not quite a star yet, but I'm working on it.

Bubba's Real Pit Barbecue was at the intersection of 41 and 19, a prime piece of real estate shared by a Pic Quik featuring cheap beer and a run-down wood frame house that leaned a little to the right. The house was a combination ceramics studio, notary public, and fortune-telling emporium. An elderly woman was sitting on a rocker on the front porch, cracking pecans and sipping tea from a clear glass. The air was thick with the smell of wood smoke and barbecue sauce. I waved to the woman and went into Bubba's.

"This better be good," said Bubba, taking the tape from me. "I can't say that I've seen much of an increase in business since I started advertising on television."

"I've got two different ones on the tape," I said. "Either one is bound to sell a lot of ribs."

I had to admit I hoped he'd like the first one better, since I wrote the script and shot it myself. It might not be *Casablanca,* but I was proud of it. Earl let me do it because tape's about the cheapest thing there is around a television station.

It looked like Bubba could be selling a few more ribs. There were only four customers in the place, and two of them weren't eating anything, just drinking beer. He put the tape in his VCR and the large screen TV on the far wall switched from a talk show to the station's logo with a sweeping countdown starting at six.

"You'll like this one," I said. Bubba just grunted.

One of the cowboys at the bar sure liked it. He started laughing right away.

"What the hell's that?" cried Bubba.

"It's a cow," I said. Darn. Maybe I should have used a pig. Pork. The other white meat. I should have used a pig.

"Damn cow's staring right into the camera," said Bubba. "Just chewing away."

"Look at those big brown eyes," said a woman, pushing her plate of barbecue away. "How can anyone think of eating something with eyes like that?"

"What's that around that creature's neck?" asked Bubba.

"It's a bib," I said. "See, the idea is that the cow is enjoying a good meal."

"That cow is chewing its cud," said Bubba. "I never met a cannibal cow. And that bib looks like a tablecloth."

It was.

"Listen up," I said. "Don't miss the soundtrack."

"What's that?"

"It's a voice-over," I said. "That's a technical TV term."

"I mean, what's that noise?"

"It's the cow making slurping noises. You know, having a great meal and all."

"It sounds like someone throwing up," said Bubba. "Not exactly the image I want to project."

I thought it was pretty good, myself. One of the slurps matched pretty closely with the cow licking its nose, too.

The ending was my *pièce de la résistance,* my *gran finale.* I had filmed a herd of cows going across a pasture at twilight. The words BUBBA'S REAL PIT BARBE-CUE floated in the setting sun and the voice-over said in my deepest baritone, "Bubba's. Where all the best cows go."

It was a great ending, but I think they missed most of it on account of they were all laughing so hard. Everyone but Bubba, that is. He hit the pause button on the remote.

"I can't believe I have just seen that," he said.

"Not what you'd expect from a local TV station," I said proudly. "That kind of quality is usually reserved for your big budget New York productions."

"It sucked swamp water," said Bubba. "I hated it."

"I told them they should have used a pig," I said.

"Let's see what else you got."

Earl had shot the second one on location right where I was standing. It was real boring, just a bunch of people eating and drinking and playing the jukebox. Bubba loved it.

"Now that's what I like to see," he said. "People up to their elbows in grease and barbecue sauce. Good shot of the sign out front, too. Tell Earl I'll go with it."

I was feeling pretty low when I walked out to the truck. The woman was still rocking away. She waved me over and I walked up to the porch.

"How come I see you going into Bubba's, but I always see you come right back out? You don't stay long enough to eat. You in the habit of throwing back a quick afternoon beer?"

I laughed. "No, nothing like that. I sell television time."

"You sell time? What kind of a fool notion is that?" There were pecan shells all over the porch.

"Television. You've probably seen me on television."

"Don't own one. Wouldn't have one. If something important is going to happen, I'll know it. I've got the gift."

Her eyes were real dark. They kind of reminded me of the cow's eyes. It made me a little nervous.

"I . . . Well, I got to be going."

"Wait," she said sharply. I froze as she dug into a pocket of her apron. She handed me something. I figured it to be a pecan, but it wasn't. It was a small ceramic pig about the size of a jawbreaker.

"This is a pig," I said.

"You're an observant young fellow," she said. "You'll go far in television."

"But why a pig?"

She shrugged. "I made about fifty of them one day," she said. "Never sold a single one of them."

"Is it a lucky pig?" I asked.

"Beats the hell out of me. I guess it is if you want it to be."

"I *could* use some luck," I said. "I'm way overdue for my big chance."

"Oh, that'll come soon enough," she said.

"You sure about that?"

"I've got the gift," she said. "It's in the stars."

That lifted my spirits, and as I drove back to the station, I tried to figure out a way to convince Earl that we should use a pig in Bubba's next commercial.

Earl's my uncle. He came into some money a few years ago and bought the television station. It's not much of a station, but I figure everybody's got to start somewhere, even me. Peter Jennings—he's Canadian, you know—probably started someplace small, too. Someplace like Nome, maybe, doing features on walrus and killer whales. Thoughts like that sure make me appreciate Florida, which is an okay place to live, even if it's got bugs big as hubcaps.

I wasn't sure Uncle Earl would hire me right off the bat like that, but Mama said he owed her a big one, and I guess he did because he put me on the payroll right away.

Of course, nephew or not, I couldn't start right out anchoring the 6 o'clock news. Mostly I swept out the studio and ran errands. That's still part of my job, but I'm on the air now, too.

My first on-air job at the station was reading the public service announcements. Lost dogs, bake sales, things like that. It was voice-over work, against a tasteful background advertising Buddy Shaw's Funeral Home. My big break didn't come until later.

Betty's husband, Bob, got transferred to Homestead. Betty covered the City Commission meetings every other Monday night, and I took over for her. Mostly what I had to do was make sure nobody tripped over the camera's cables, but I also got to do a five-minute stand-up at the end, recapping that night's business. I learned a lot doing that, like how to think on my feet. Twice I had to make everything up because I'd fallen asleep. I just mumbled about ordinances and setbacks and zoning exceptions and no one noticed.

This is a small station in a small town, which is good for me because I'd rather be a big fish in a small pond at this point in my career. Most of the day we show old movies and reruns of sitcoms nobody remembers. We're in the shadow of Tampa, see, and they get all the good programming. But we got a captive audience of sorts, being in a rural area, and we cater to them with local news and local color. In the winter, we even cover the high school football games. The Fighting Palmetto Bugs went two and nine last year.

Still, I'll break out of here yet. I just need one big break. My time will come.

Television is in my blood.

Earl handed me the broom when I got back.

"Well?" he asked me.

"It was close, but Bubba liked yours just a little better. I think it was the sign that did it."

"The sign. People like to see their signs on television. Nothing better than a sign unless it's the owner. People just love to see themselves on the tube. Nobody else does, though. I try to discourage that particular trend. It plain doesn't work. Dogs are good, too. Throw a gratuitous dog in a commercial and you've got a sure winner. People love dogs."

"I was thinking of pigs," I said hopefully.

"You think too much," he replied.

So I swept for a bit and then took out the trash. The windows needed washing, too. There's always a lot to do in a television station.

I wish I got more airtime, but that's a common complaint in the biz. Even the big stars gripe about airtime.

Still, I don't get to do much before the camera except for the City Commission meetings. I hate to say it, but I think it's my smile.

Don't get me wrong, I have a fine smile. It's just that I can't turn it off. I get in front of a camera and the smile just comes. Nothing I can do about it, either. I could read a teleprompter report of a plane full of nuns crashing on top of an orphanage on Christmas day and grin all the way through it.

And they know it, too. I've heard them talk.

Smiling Sam, that's what they call me. *Smiling Sam.*

Don't let Sam near any hard news, they say. *He'll blow it bad. If you have to give him a story, make it soft and fuzzy.*

I'll show them. I'll show them good.

Time passes fast in a television studio. Before I knew

it, we'd put a wrap on the 6 o'clock news. I handled
the public service spot well, except for mispronouncing
"Alachua," a mistake that could happen to anyone.

Since there wasn't a City Commission meeting, I
started to get my stuff together to go home. To tell you
the truth, I wasn't in a big hurry. I live in a trailer behind
my uncle's house. It's comfortable enough, though a bit
cramped. But there's no excitement there, if you know
what I mean.

So I was watching Sara load a tape of episode nine of
My Mother the Car when Earl came up. He seemed a
little agitated.

"I hate to ask you this, Sam," he said. "But can you
work a remote tonight?"

"Can I?" Yikes. *"You bet!"*

"There's an eclipse of the moon tonight," he said.
"It'll happen at 9:07. A bunch of amateur astronomers
are going out to the airport to watch it. Go out, get
some tape, and bring it back. Sara will edit it and run it
at eleven. Think you can handle it?"

"I sure can," I said. "It'll be a feature you'll never
forget."

"That's what I'm afraid of," he said, sighing. "I
wouldn't cover it except that the Mayor's daughter is a
stargazer and he called me. Be sure you get her on
camera."

"I can handle that," I said. "Maybe I should run over
to the library and bone up on eclipses."

"Forget it, Sam. We're not talking about a team of
scientists out there. These are just ordinary people who
like to check out the stars. The moon goes behind the
Earth's shadow. It's not such a big deal except for those
who are into that kind of stuff."

"So what's my hook?"

"Hook?"

"Every feature has a hook. You know, something special to grab the audience."

"This is not a feature, Sam. Hardly anyone in the area
is going to be up to see it. But there is a hook of sorts,
a comet. It's one of those comets that come by here
every million years or so. Maybe you can get the May-

or's daughter to explain how they know it zapped by Earth so long ago there wasn't anyone around to watch it."

"Yeah. Good idea. Nice hook. I've always wondered that myself."

"Stan will run camera and sound. I've already called him in."

"I'd better get the van ready," I said. The van was cool, state-of-the-art. A shiny new Dodge with lots of goodies.

"No way I'm letting you take the van," said Earl. "Take the football."

"No, not the football."

"The football."

When Earl makes up his mind, it's made up. It was a setback, but a minor one. I was finally getting to go out into the field on my own. A remote!

Earl went on home and I loaded up the football, an old flatbed trailer with a huge fiberglass football-shaped broadcasting booth on it and enough lights hanging all over it to illuminate half the town. Florida is serious about its football, even high school night games.

I packed away the camera and made sure we had lots of tape. There's tape everywhere. We just shoot over the old stuff, so it keeps going and going.

What evidently wasn't going to be going much was Stan. His wife dropped him off, and it looked like she'd found him in a bar. It was all I could do to get him in the football. He was asleep before I pulled out of the parking lot.

The airport was actually just a grass strip and a hangar outside of town. A half dozen or so small planes were usually tied up there, some semipermanently in need of repair. Someone at the entrance had me cut the lights as I drove in. I parked the football by the side of the field.

As my eyes grew accustomed to the dark, I could make out the star folk. There were quite a few of them and a whole bunch of telescopes. I wandered over there while Stan unpacked the gear.

I'd never seen so many different kinds of telescopes and fancy binoculars in my life. Everyone was whispering, which was kind of funny, since there wasn't anybody around but us.

It was dark out there, even with the full moon. The place was dead flat, and treeless for what seemed like miles. It was a real clear night and there were about a million stars hanging up there. Someone said you could see a lot more if the moon wasn't out, which is the reason they were all out there, to catch a glimpse of the comet while the moon was being eclipsed.

The comet had some foreign-sounding name that I kept mispronouncing. I found out it was named after three amateur comet-watchers who discovered it. This was an unexpected semihook and I got to ask each of them if they'd ever discovered a comet or a new planet or anything like that. I was kind of disappointed that none of them had ever discovered anything. It would have made a great lead-in.

Stan finally managed to get everything set up after a fashion, and I did some moonlit interviews of uncertain quality considering the poor lighting. The Mayor's daughter, a kid about fifteen, explained how they determined how old the comet was. She used a lot of big words for a little kid and I didn't understand a bit of it. As near as I could figure out, they were just guessing. Hell, I do that every time I play the horses at Tampa Downs, and you can see how far that gets me.

I had people show me their fancy telescopes. That was kind of fun, even though I couldn't get it on tape. The stars were pretty dull, but Saturn was a gas. They ought to put rings around all the planets.

Eventually, the eclipse started. It was slow at first, just a little bit of darkness at the edge. Gradually, more and more of it turned dark. It looked odd, seeing a chomped-on moon. I shot enough tape of that to fill a PBS Special.

After 9 o'clock there wasn't much left. Sure enough, we could see more and more stars. Everybody had their telescopes pointed to where they calculated the comet would be.

Someone started a countdown. "Five . . . Four . . . Three . . . Two . . . One . . ." Then a cheer went up. I couldn't see a thing, so I ran over to the football and snapped on all the lights.

The field was flooded with incandescent brilliance. "I'm blind!" screamed someone as he walked into a telescope. "I can't see anything," yelled another.

People were staggering all over the place, bumping into each other and sending tripods crashing into the ground. I was the only one who could see good, since my back was to the football.

But what I saw was nothing like I'd ever seen before. A giant saucer-shaped disk was settling down in the middle of the field. My big break was touching down.

I grabbed my mike and ran toward the spaceship. "Cover me, Stan," I yelled. "Keep the camera rolling."

"I can't see a damn thing," he said.

I reached the ship just as a door slid open and a pig walked out. Well, it wasn't exactly a pig, but it looked like it might be shaped like a pig under its space suit. It walked on its hind legs, though, and I've never seen a pig do that. The alien pig looked at me and its snout quivered behind its helmet. It extended a hand in a very human gesture. I went to shake it and found my hand stuck to something hard and sticky.

As soon as our hands touched, all kinds of static started buzzing in my ears. It sounded like a radio tuned just to one side of a station. In a second it cleared up and there was a squeaky voice in my head, like the alien was projecting his thoughts or something.

"We've come here to heal you," it said. At least that's what I thought it said. It also sounded like "We've come here to *kill* you." Could have been either one.

The alien withdrew its hand, leaving the sticky mess in mine. I figured if it gave me something, I should give it something back, so I dug out that little ceramic pig and handed it over.

This seemed to upset the alien, who got all agitated and held it up so the other two aliens peering out the door could get a good look at it. Then the alien threw the pig away, got back in his spaceship and zipped away without a sound. The whole thing hadn't taken more than thirty seconds.

"Did you get that, Stan?" I called out.

"Get what? I still can't see anything."

The amateur astronomers had become a sightless and unruly mob. They didn't want to hear anything about aliens; all they knew was that the football's lights had blown their chance of a lifetime. Imaginary aliens come and go all the time, but that comet won't be back for another million years. They escorted us out by throwing clods of dirt at the football.

When I got to the main road, I called Earl on the cell phone. "You got to come to the station," I said. "I got tape that'll knock your socks off."

"Don't tell me, Jimmy Hoffa showed up for the big event, with Amelia Earhart and Judge Crater in tow."

"Better than that," I said. "I covered a flying saucer landing. I even shook hands with an alien."

"Sam, tell me this. Did anyone see this happen but you?"

"Not exactly," I said. "There were extenuating circumstances."

"With you, there always are."

"But I got the tape. Meet me at the station. This is huge. We'll be famous."

"I should never have listened to your mother," sighed Earl. "I'll meet you there, but I don't have much hope."

"You won't be sorry," I said. But Earl had already hung up.

We all arrived at the station at the same time. I rushed inside and slapped the tape in a player.

"Awful dark," said Earl.

"These are the interviews I did before the saucer landed," I said.

"There! That white thing," said Stan. "Is that the saucer?"

"That's my smile," I said. "The moonlight is reflecting off my teeth."

"Well, at least you got the Mayor's daughter," said Earl. "I can hear her, even if I can't see her. That'll make her old man happy."

I fast-forwarded the tape and then slowed it down.

"Here," I said. "It's about to start."

The screen flickered. There were a few seconds of white snow and static and then the picture came back on.

"That's a cow," said Stan. "I know a cow when I see one."

"And that cow's wearing a tablecloth," moaned Earl. "You got me out of bed for this?"

"Something must have happened to the tape," I said. "These are old commercial outtakes."

"What you've got here is nothing," said Earl. "Absolutely nothing. I'm going back to bed."

"Wait," I said. "Look here." I held out my hand.

"That looks like a pecan," Earl said dryly. We grow a lot of them around here.

"No, this is a real alien artifact. If we touch it at the same time, we'll be able to read each other's thoughts."

"I'm not sure I want to read your thoughts," said Earl. "And I know damn well you won't like mine."

"Come on, Uncle Earl. Give it a try."

"It's sticky." He looked thoughtful as he touched it. "Maybe it *is* working," he said. "I'm not picking up anything at all."

"Me neither," I said.

Things were a little rough after that. Earl fired me, and then rehired me after Mother got on his case. He won't even let me do the City Commission meetings anymore. Says he doesn't want me anywhere near anything that's going out over the air. The local astronomy club has a bounty on my head.

The only good thing to come out of this mess is that I can talk to pigs.

That thought transmitter thing the alien left only seems to work between me and pigs. Unfortunately, pigs don't have a lot to say.

But me, I've taken to watching the skies. There's a story up there, a big story. And when it happens, I'll be ready to cover it. I was born to news.

Television is in my blood.

KITE PEOPLE
by Gary A. Braunbeck

Gary A. Braunbeck has sold over sixty short stories to various mystery, suspense, science fiction, fantasy, and horror markets. His first collection, *Things Left Behind,* was released in early 1997. He has been a full-time writer since 1992, and lives in Columbus, Ohio.

> "No testimony is sufficient to establish a miracle, unless . . . its falsehood would be more miraculous than the fact which it endeavors to establish."
> —David Hume, *Of Miracles*

Later, many would claim the kites were drawn toward the spot—not those flying them, mind you, for all but one of the colorful objects in the sky over Dell Memorial Park in Cedar Hill that late summer were attached to no earthbound strings—but the kites *themselves;* people spoke of them as they would any other sentient being ("Look at the red box one! It's showing off for the Smiling Lady.") and, in truth, several of those who came to gather, to watch and ponder (many from very far away), began to think of the kites as their friends, as family: Elderly ones, a breath away from succumbing to the sad cynicism of age, found renewed wonder in the sight and began to pick out individual favorites whom they greeted verbally upon their arrival ("Hello, Blue Boy!"); children, both those cherished and those unloved, smiled and laughed at the adults who stood gawking, because they now had proof of magic's existence and no one would ever be able to say to them again, "Stop pretending, show some sense," because what occurred in

178

the skies over the park that late summer made no sense, none whatsoever, and it was *great!* So there.

Later, after the phenomenon had been studied, after all the data had been assembled, analyzed, interpreted, and debated, Professor Edward Ridgway, head of the Physics Department at Ohio State University, whose recent experiments in the field of bioacoustics were raising quite a few eyebrows and even more snickers behind his back, *that* Edward Ridgway would make a fool out of himself on local television when, during a Sunday morning news program, he offered the following explanation: "It's very simple, actually. The Vedic religious tradition teaches its followers about something it calls the 'vibration metaphor': throw a pebble in a pond, and the vibrations ripple outward in concentric circles; strike a bell, and it vibrates in waves of sound; meditate on a thought, and it will echo through the realm of the collective unconscious. Now, if one were to theoretically apply the vibration metaphor to some recent discoveries about the susceptibility of brain wave patterns to nonphysical stimuli, then it might be possible to employ a blended and sequenced series of binaural sound pulses to induce a frequency-following response in the brain, creating a ripple effect that could alter EEG wave patterns and generate expanded states of consciousness. Given those conditions, resting-state alpha activity would be suppressed and replaced by synchronous slow-wave activity in the median of the central cortex. If one were to then increase the amplitude and frequency of the sound impulses, the resting-state alpha and slow-wave activity could be induced to operate simultaneously, accompanied by temporal gamma brain wave activity, enabling an individual to perceive nonphysical energies outside the confines of the physical-law belief system; not only that, but the individual would perceive these nonphysical phenomena as constituting his or her whole field of awareness—not unlike a waking dream."

"So," said the interviewer, "what you're saying, if I understood all of that correctly, is that these reported 'voices' are nothing more than auditory hallucinations?"

"Yes. Somehow, one of those people in the park has

found the materials to generate an audioencephalographic interferometric effect to stimulate alternate brain wave patterns in those nearby, inducing a transcendent-state experience—what you've characteristically oversimplified as 'auditory hallucinations.'"

"Then how do you explain the reports of those people who live hundreds, in some cases thousands, of miles away who came there *after* hearing the voices? All of them had family members who were killed in the—"

"I'm well aware of the circumstances of the case, thank you."

"Fine. Then please explain."

Viewers watching the program that morning were treated to a rare sight: Edward Ridgway clearing his throat, blinking his eyes, then adjusting his tie as he whispered, "I have no idea."

But all this happened later.

After Miriam Spencer met Donald Lucas.

Before anyone knew They were watching, listening, waiting.

One late-summer afternoon, under a blue, cloudless sky, in the park of miracles.

Miriam Spencer was walking along the small cobblestone path that ran alongside the east side of the park. She had a small portable radio attached to her belt and headphones covering her ears, but the radio was no longer playing because the batteries had died. Not that she noticed.

Miriam was beginning her second year of widowhood that day. The sound of the radio had been nothing more to her than pretty static, intended to overpower the incessant, droning noise of loneliness in her mind, echoed second after second by the chasm in her heart.

She was walking slowly and took no notice of the fifty-five-year-old retarded man standing ten yards away, facing southeast.

She did not see the look of bliss on his face as he stared upward at his star-shaped kite.

And she did not see the kite turn in her direction as she passed by.

The kite was constructed of stripwood, fretwork nails, plywood, and unbleached greaseproof paper; two frames, one diamond-shaped, the other a simple cross attached to opposing mitre joints, formed the eight corners of the star, while a trio of balancing cups attached to the three highest corners by bracing strings created up-currents of air, giving further lift to its delicate, slender form. Each set of corners were decorated in a different color of tinfoil—red, blue, bright green, gold—which, when reflecting the sunlight, turned the star into a flying prism, made all the grander by the unbelievably bright square of thin, silver, twisted metal in its center.

Light from the silver centerpiece glittered downward in waves, bounced off the upward inclination of the lowest wing-corner at the angle of positive dihedral, and transformed into another sort of wave before it came into contact with the young widow who did not know she was being watched.

Miriam was jarred out her numbed thoughts when the dead radio suddenly came on.

"Honey? It's me. L-listen, I, uh . . . I don't know if you'll get all of this . . . there's a lot of static, but . . . something's happened to the plane and we're going down. The pilot says we've got about two minutes . . . he's aiming for the foam they laid out on the runway . . . oh God, Miriam, I love you so much, and I wanted to let you know that if . . . if we don't . . . if anything should happen to us, I wanted to let you know that Katie and I both love you more than anything in the world. Katie's asleep next to me—that damned cough syrup Mom gave her had codeine in it—and she's all strapped in and I've got my arm around her, but I don't want to wake her up. I don't want her to know what's . . . what's happening. I hope to God she'll wake up after we've landed and we can all have a good laugh about this later, but I don't think that's gonna happen, honey, I think we're never going to see you again and I'm scared because she's so small and I'll never get to feel you near me again and . . . Jesus, what's *that?* . . ."

Flight 418, en route from Florida to Columbus. 287 passengers. Developed engine trouble over Indianapolis and was turning around in the stormy weather for an emergency landing when something—a bolt of lightning was the official explanation—blew off three-quarters of the port wing. The pilot issued a distress call (most of which was never made public), informing the control tower that the tumble rate suggested enough of the starboard wing was left to provide the surface area needed to keep the terminal velocity a little lower than maximum.

"Can you give us an ETA?" asked the tower.

"One-minute forty, two minutes tops."

"Crews are out there spraying now."

By the time the plane hit the foam-drenched runway, the remaining engines were fully aflame, the tail section was splintering away, and most of the crew were already dead. The plane exploded on impact, scattering debris in a twelve-mile radius. There were no survivors.

It had taken Flight 418 exactly one minute and fifty-two seconds to crash. Somewhere in the midst of those last, terrible one hundred and twelve seconds Bill Spencer, who, along with his four-year-old daughter Katie, was returning home from visiting his parents in Florida, grabbed the cellular phone next to his seat and called his wife to say good-bye. Miriam, who'd never gotten along with Bill's mother and so decided not to join her husband and little girl on their visit, had left the house to drive to the Columbus airport only a few seconds before the phone rang and the answering machine clicked on, but what she found on the tape when she returned home late the next day, after hours of gut-searing anxiety, tears, questions, official announcements, and the final, horrible confirmation, was this: ". . . oney? . . . s'me . . . minutes . . . oh God . . . you so much . . . Katie . . . thing in the. . . asleep . . . Mom . . . arm . . . her up . . . have a good . . . later . . . so small . . . you near . . . *that?*"

For months afterward Miriam played that message over and over again, listening intensely to every wave of static, every break in the noise, every ghost of an inflection, trying to figure out, to piece together, some semblance of what her husband had been trying to tell her.

And now, one year later to the day, under a clear sky, alone and shuddering, Miriam Spencer heard for the first time her husband's final words to her.

Her legs gave out and she began to fall, but the retarded man she had taken no notice of caught her before she hit the ground.

"It was a accident," he said to her. "They pulled up the curtain too soon, and the plane was right there. There wasn't nothing they could do."

Gulping in breath, trying to ignore the stares of the other people in the park, Miriam looked up into Donald Lucas' round, chubby, aged face, and whispered, "Did you hear him?"

"Uh-huh. I didn't know who it was, but then they told me it was for you."

"Who? Who told you?"

Donald smiled, looking upward. "The Kite People."

Miriam followed Donald's gaze with her own and saw not only his exquisite star-kite, but a stringless red box-kite, three glider kites, several small fish-kites, several colorful, complex butterfly-kites, and a few rounded-head tonking kites as well.

Flying themselves.

Though there was very little wind, the kites hovered, majestic, around Donald's star. They almost looked as if they were breathing.

"See?" said Donald, pointing toward them and laughing. "They're coming. They said they was going to figure out a way to do it so's no one would get hurt, and they're coming."

"The Kite People?" asked Miriam.

"Yeah," said Donald, nodding his head. "I used to just call 'em spacemen, but they told me their real name . . . it sorta sounded like, uh . . ." He shrugged. "I don't remember so good, so now I just call 'em the Kite People on account that's what they most look like to me."

"But how did you—" She froze, her eyes widening. "Shhh. Do you hear it?" A smile began to form on her face. "Do you hear him? It's . . . my God, it's *Bill again!*"

"Is he still on the plane with Katie?" asked Donald.

Miriam turned her left ear toward the kite. "No. No, he . . . he's somewhere else."

"Real close, huh?"

"Yes. And—oh, I can hear Katie."

"She's singing, ain't she?" whispered Donald.

"Yes."

" 'Camptown Races'?"

"She always liked the 'do-dah, do-dah' part."

"Thas' a funny part. I like that song, too."

"But—" She looked around frantically. "Wait. I can . . . I can hear *myself,* too."

"Is there like a . . . is there the music from a merry-go-round somewhere?"

"Yes! Oh, my God. . . it's the amusement park at Buckeye Lake! We were . . . we were going to go there after they got back from Florida. Katie wanted to see the Wild West Show they performed there. She always got a big kick out of the singing and dancing cowboys."

"Sounds like you're having a good time," said Donald, swaying along with the music of the calliope.

"They sound so close."

"Other side of the curtain," said Donald.

". . . yes . . ."

Donald helped Miriam to her feet and led her out to where he'd been standing, then, making sure she faced southeast, handed her the string to his kite. She took it, and stared at the bright silver center of the star.

The wind whispered ancient secrets as her face became a mask of bliss.

AMBASSADOR TO THE PROMISED LAND

by Dean Wesley Smith

Dean Wesley Smith is an editor and writer whose works appear in *Journeys to the Twilight Zone, Phobias, The Book of Kings,* and *Wizard Fantastic,* among other places. He has also published several novels, including *Laying the Music to Rest.* He lives in Oregon with his wife, writer and editor Kristine Kathryn Rusch.

This Christmas Eve I met an alien, or maybe a ghost, and saw the promised land. Sort of like a bad Dickens nightmare, only it happened for real, right in the front formal dining room of my neighbors, Dotty and Harvey Jones.

My wife, Amelia, Amy for short, thinks the entire ghost/alien incident can be clearly explained. Now understand that Amy always says that, and more times than not, she's right. Her parents conceived her while on a vacation to the South Pacific, so they named her after Amelia Earhart, thinking that maybe she might be the reincarnation of the famous flyer. This start in life made Amy the most practical, down-to-earth woman I have ever met. She also hated to fly.

On the way back from the Emergency Room Amy said my alien/ghost incident was a combination of too much eggnog and the knock on the head I got when I looked up Dotty Jones' skirt while reaching for my napkin under the table at the annual Christmas Eve neighborhood dinner.

I didn't argue with her. But just for the record, it was

before I hit my head, *while* I was reaching for my napkin and *after* looking up Dotty's skirt, that I had the ghost/alien incident. However, Amy was right about the egg-nog. I had drunk even more this year than the year before.

In my defense, I hadn't actually been *trying* to look up Dotty's skirt, even though her skirt was the shortest red thing I had ever seen, and ex-dancer Dotty most surely was worth looking at. Granted I had been staring across the table at her all during dinner as her husband Harvey talked and talked and talked about his car deal-ership. Besides the eggnog, ham, and sweet yams, she was the only interesting thing happening. Pam and How-ard McDonnell from two houses down hadn't said two words since dinner started, and Walter and Wendy Clark, who had the house on the other side of mine, looked as bored as I felt.

During most of dinner Dotty had been smiling back at me when Amy wasn't looking, laughing at any word I managed to get in edgewise in her husband's mono-logue. But I never once thought about dropping my nap-kin so I could look up her skirt.

To be honest, the idea just never crossed my mind.

No, I dropped my napkin like anyone might drop one at a Christmas Eve neighborhood dinner. I was reaching for a second helping of ham and the red cloth thing just slipped off my lap. It happens. It has happened to me before. Even once in a really fancy restaurant I dropped one. No big deal.

I did the normal thing required in good social settings such as Dotty and Harvey's formal dining room. I scooted my chair back slightly, and went under the fes-tive holiday tablecloth to retrieve the napkin.

There, I came face-to-face, or make that face-to-legs, with Dotty's lower half. She had legs that, from my per-spective of head-under-the-tablecloth, clearly belonged in *Playboy* or *Cosmopolitan*. Now I'm a normal, red-blooded American male, and any normal red-blooded American male would hesitate when faced with a vision as clear and pure as those legs.

And I did.

I hesitated.

And hesitated.

And hesitated.

There was no time passage for me under that table. I had left this plane of existence and gone on, drifting in a timeless place that existed only under that holiday table, in that close space between me and those legs. I had no name, no reason, no pride.

It was like getting drunk back in high school.

Or the time Linda, my first girlfriend, let me slip my hand under her bra.

Or the time in college when I took mushrooms and ended up staring intently for hours at the design on a bathroom wallpaper.

This was like all those times, only more so. Now, at age forty, I no longer did drugs. I had a great job in city hall, a wife of fourteen years, two kids in junior high, and a three bedroom house in a subdivision. I hadn't had a mind-altering experience in a long, *long* time.

Too damn long.

So I hesitated.

I forgot who I was, where I was, why I was even living. I doubt I even took a breath. I doubt I would have been able to take a breath.

But there was no doubt I had totally forgotten about my napkin.

Then two things happened that changed the entire experience.

First, Dotty uncrossed her legs.

Now, from the perspective of my mind-altered state, this took about six wonderful and glorious years of slow motion. It was a pure cinematic moment.

My cameralike gaze followed the line of her ankle.

The line of her calf.

The shape of her knee.

And then beyond.

Beyond to a place I should *never* have gone. A place I had no intention of ever going. But I went because I was faced with the challenge.

And when challenged, any red-blooded American male will step up and face his challenger.

She uncrossed her legs, so I looked.

And I saw the promised land.

The gates of heaven stared me in the face.

I heard the "Hallelujah Chorus."

Dotty wasn't wearing underwear.

Now, I swear, Dotty showing me the promised land broke the illusion. I came back to real time, the last bite of ham choking in my throat. Seeing such a sight, under normal circumstances, would have sent me out from under the tablecloth, back into my chair with a red face and a giant desire to sprint for home.

But normal circumstances were not to be. There was this *second thing* that happened.

At that moment an alien, or ghost, or whatever he was, decided to make a trip into my reality, or to my planet, right there under the table with me, while I faced the promised land and a new religion, all on Christmas Eve.

The alien/ghost guy stood about sixteen inches high, his bald head barely coming up to Dotty's right knee. He was naked as the day he was born, tinted pure white like any ghost on television, and I could see right through him like a clear plastic shower curtain.

Now again an event such as a short, naked, see-through white guy appearing under a table would have sent me back into my chair, and then maybe right down the street to a local bar to try to drown the memory.

But I couldn't move. Not a muscle below my shoulders. I fought and fought for all of ten seconds, but I just couldn't budge or even feel the rest of my body.

My mind screamed "Practical Joke!" as I panicked, fighting to move.

But after another long ten seconds of panic, a little voice in my head said, "Calm down. This is not normal."

Sometimes little voices can be so damn smart. But I calmed down anyway, and without once looking at the little ghost/alien man, or the promised land, (avoidance is a good thing sometimes) I looked around under the table.

From what I could tell from my position (bent over double, head under the tablecloth) no one around me was moving either. Harvey's constant talking had suddenly stopped. In fact all sound had stopped from everywhere the moment the little guy appeared. I had never heard it this quiet in this neighborhood in the ten years Amy and I had lived next door. I could actually hear my own breathing.

Amy's legs beside me were not moving, still crossed. But that was nothing unusual. She could sit like that for hours and never uncross her legs. I swore she had no blood flow at times.

Harvey's right leg was frozen in mid tap. Wendy's legs were crossed and also frozen in position, her brown pant leg riding up above her sock enough to show me she hadn't shaved her legs in a few weeks, a piece of information I didn't really want to know.

And Dotty's legs were being held in the open position, leaving just about exactly *nothing* about the promised land to my imagination.

The short, white, naked, see-through guy did a full turn surveying his surroundings as I stared at him. He looked like a normal male, except for being very short, as pure white as a ghost, and transparent. Maybe he was a ghost. Maybe he was a ghost Dotty and Harvey had been hiding. Knowing them, anything was possible.

Or maybe he was an angel who made a break from heaven when Dotty opened her legs and showed me the pearly gates. But if that was the case, why wasn't he making fast time away from her? I sure wanted to at that moment.

Maybe this was a bad movie and he was my conscience? Maybe he was here to punish me for looking up Dotty's skirt?

There was just no way of telling. Somehow I managed to keep the panic down to a dull roar in my head.

The little guy stopped looking around, then said something in a high, Mickey Mouse–like voice in a language that I might have guessed to be Latin, if Latin wasn't a dead language.

With that he got a little less glowing white, and a little more solid, as if he'd been fine-tuned a bit. I could see through him still, but not as clearly.

He again said something in the strange language into the air, then made a nodding motion to himself. Then he turned to face me.

Surprise. I managed not to panic completely again, but I swear my stomach had left my body. Up until that moment I wasn't sure he even realized that the head part of me wasn't as frozen in place as the rest of the body parts he could see. Obviously he did.

He looked me right in the eye and asked in a high, squeaky voice, in English. "Human?"

He actually wanted an answer.

Now I had never been asked a question before while in full-blown panic. It was just another first among many this Christmas Eve.

I took a deep breath, then managed to reply. "I think so. But at this moment I wouldn't put money on it." My voice sounded very weird in the complete silence of the world under the table.

He nodded, turned, and said some more quick Latin-like mouse-words into the air, then faced me again. "Greetings. We are pleased."

"Hello to you, too," I said, sort of getting miffed. Panic had always turned almost immediately to anger for me, and this time was no exception. "Now that we have that out of the way," I said, "would you mind telling me what's happening? And who you are? And what you're doing under Harvey's and Dotty's formal dining room table?"

That got him confused, which was just damn fine with me. If I was confused, he was going to be confused right along with me.

He turned back to look into the air, said a few more quick words in his strange Latin, then faced me again. "Too fast," he said slowly. "Computers cannot translate."

Wonderful. The little white guy had computers. I should have expected as much. This had to be a prank by some computer nerd somewhere. Maybe the Wilson kid from down the block. He was always doing this sort of thing. I'd just play along until it ended. I nodded as best I could.

"Un-der-stand," I said.

The little guy listened for a moment to the thin air, then smiled, showing me a mouthful of sharp, pointed teeth. "Good."

"Who are you?" I asked. I'd have pointed at him, but my arms were no longer in use.

After he listened for a moment, he said, "I am friendly. Who are you?"

"I am confused," I said, and with that the little white translucent guy smiled real big and nodded happily.

Now that we were formally introduced, I wanted some answers. "Where are you from?" I asked while he was still nodding.

After the customary pause to check the air beside him, he said, "Spattcha. I am from Spattcha."

Okay, that made sense to me. I could tell we were getting someplace now. I wasn't sure exactly where, but if it got me out from under this table, it would be a good place. I glanced at the promised land over the guy's shoulder, then asked, "Where is Spattcha?"

"Cannot see it from here," he said.

"To be honest," I said, "I'm seeing a lot more under this table than I ever expected to see, so you might be surprised." Somewhere, no doubt, some computer nerd was laughing himself silly. But my little voice didn't believe what I was thinking about this being a joke. My little voice said I should be taking this translucent guy seriously, since he could freeze bodies and make all sound go away. But taking a sixteen-inch white, translucent, naked man under a dining room table seriously was damn hard.

The short guy looked puzzled as he listened to thin air, then glanced around at his location. Now granted, his location must have looked damn strange to him. It looked damn strange to me, and I knew what I was looking at. Eight pairs of legs under the tablecloth, plus one head and a naked short guy. Weird by any measurement.

The short guy pointed at Amy's legs. "Human?"

"All but four days a month," I said.

That seemed to confuse the little guy even more, so

he turned and pointed at Dotty's legs. Only he actually pointed at the promised land. "Human?"

"No," I said. "Fantasy, mixed with divorce, unemployment, and a drunken death." Of course as I said all that I was looking at where he was pointing. What red-blooded American male wouldn't?

He listened to the thin air, then shook his head. "Our language computer is having problem."

"I can understand that," I said.

He listened, then frowned.

I was getting nowhere fast. And at that point I wanted to be moving anywhere that wasn't under Dotty's formal dining room table. "I have a simple question?" I said slowly.

After a moment he said, "I will answer question."

"Why is nothing moving around me?"

The short guy waited for a moment, then smiled like a contestant on a game show who could give the right answer to a question. "I am projection through space/time. Other humans still move, only very slowly. Time pass slowly here."

"And I can see and talk to you because . . . ?"

The little guy consulted with the thin air for almost a full three seconds, then said, "you are inside my time/space influence. It was a good happening, to talk to a human. We only planned to look around."

He glanced at the air again, then turned to face me fully. "Little time left. I must do the event."

"Event?" I said, wishing like hell I could stand up straight and run. Or even feel my body enough to know that someday I might again stand up straight.

The little translucent guy nodded. "Event. I proud. I bring humans welcome."

He stepped forward and stared me right in the eye, smiling, his sharp teeth looking damn dangerous, even though I could see through them.

I didn't say anything, because, to be honest, I had no idea what to say. And again the panic had gotten my brain locked down tight.

After a moment he looked confused, looked off into thin air for a consult with his thin air friends, then turned back to face me. "Did you not understand?" he said slowly. "I bring welcome. My people. Your people."

Suddenly I understood. The little guy wanted me to represent my country and all the rest of the world and the entire damn human race, while bent over double, head under a holiday tablecloth, staring up my hostess' skirt.

It would be a challenge, but I was up for it.

"Welcome from all of us humans," I said.

He smiled real big as soon as his computer translated.

"Our people," he said. "We be friends someday."

"You will be returning?" I asked. Suddenly the thought of this little guy popping in and out all the time had me more frightened than I wanted to think about.

"Return," he said. "Need vast power. Right conditions. Your planet must circle your sun two hundred and eleven times first."

I hope I didn't show the relief I felt. "We will be waiting," I said.

The little guy flickered from pale white to bright white like an old television set going bad. "Must go now," he said. "Much information to study before next time."

"Don't stay up too late," I said.

The little guy frowned, then flickered and was gone.

Suddenly Harvey was talking again.

And Dotty was still moving those legs apart.

And I could feel my body again.

Then the worst thing possible happened. Amy, my wife in the real world above the table, tapped me on the back to see if I was all right.

Now I had just seen an alien, or a ghost, or whatever he was. And come face-to-face with the promised land. My panic was still way too close to the surface and I didn't need Amy tapping me on the back right at that moment.

But she did. A simple, solid little tap.

But my reaction wasn't so simple. It was as if she had punched the "on" switch and every muscle in my body decided to move at once.

Now, even though I didn't, it must be remembered I

was face-to-face with Dotty's legs at this point, bent over in my chair, tablecloth over my head.

So when Amy tapped me and every muscle in my body suddenly fired, I came up straight, the back of my head smashing into the underside of the formal dining table.

Dishes scattered, ham was tossed into the air, and people yelled.

But it wasn't over yet. Intense pain made my entire body jerk, sending my chair smashing backward into a glass corner table that held a big ugly plant.

I went down like a log, flat onto Harvey's and Dotty's green shag. Now granted, right at that moment I suppose I could have said I saw God, too. God would have been a nice addition to the evening I was having. But instead I'm fairly certain that all I saw was a bunch of swirling blue and purple and red lights clouding my vision. I doubt very much if those lights were God. More likely they were just revenge for me looking in on His promised land.

The next thing I remember I came to, still on the floor, but someone had dragged me out beside the table and turned me face up.

The light was beyond bright, and my head felt hollow and empty with someone ringing a loud bell inside it.

Amy was crouched beside me, holding a cloth to the back of my head and looking worried. Harvey was swearing about how I broke his glass table, and Dotty stood over me, smiling, her long legs showing the way directly up into the dark, where I knew only trouble waited.

Luckily for me the Emergency Room was slow on Christmas Eve and we got out in just under two hours.

On the way home I tried to tell Amy about the alien without telling about the promised land part. I even told her about the moment where I had represented the entire human race. After all, shouldn't she be proud of me? I had been the first human to ever talk to an alien. In two hundred and eleven years the world would know the truth when the aliens returned and I would be famous.

But being the down-to-earth Amelia Earhart name-sake that I married, Amy just laughed, as if she were seeing right through me like I had seen through the little guy under the table.

After pulling into our driveway and parking, she patted me on the leg and suggested that I not tell anyone about my adventure with my alien friend. Then she laughed again and told me that a bad headache and hallucinations were what I deserved for drinking too much eggnog and trying to look up Dotty's skirt.

Even though the lump on my head hurt something awful at that moment, I was smart enough to keep my mouth shut. Probably the only smart thing I had done all night.

BLACK OPS
by Barbara Delaplace

Some of Barbara Delaplace's more than thirty short fiction pieces appear in *Deals with the Devil, Christmas Bestiary,* and *Horse Fantastic.* She has been nominated twice for the John W. Campbell Award, and lives in Florida with her husband, Jack Haldeman.

The Men in Black made him nervous. Maybe this scheme wasn't such a hot idea after all.

Not that Charles Grauer had anything against secrecy. In his line of work, discretion and nondisclosure agreements were the order of the day. After all, if you were making a documentary purporting to reveal the actual location where Noah's Ark came to rest ("Was it the top of Mount Shasta?") or what *really* happened to Aimee Semple MacPherson ("Was it just a simple romantic tryst? Or was there a more sinister explanation to the mysterious disappearance of this modern American prophetess?"), the last thing you wanted was a leak of the actual program contents before it aired. Program directors paid big bucks for the rights to a network exclusive premiere.

But these guys . . . they were *serious.*

It had all seemed like such a great idea at the time. He'd been cruising the net, always a fertile source for program ideas. There were conspiracy-minded webheads spouting enough wacky theories to keep any filmmaker interested in earning a fast buck busy for a lifetime given the current obsession with UFOs, ghosts, cattle mutilations, and government cover-ups.

The light bulb had clicked on for him when he read a cynical message posted in one of the myriad UFO news groups: "The government's behind all the fakes."

That was when he'd gotten his brilliant idea (or so he had thought, he now reflected sourly). Grauer phoned a reporter he knew, an old friend currently working for an infamous national tabloid. Like any good reporter, the newsman had contacts in a lot of unlikely places, and was able to set up an appointment for him.

And look where it had led him: a threatening gray monolith of a building straight out of a paranoid's fantasy about the FBI. Phone calls by a guard at a gated entrance. ID badges. An escorted walk with an unsmiling young man in a black suit, to an anonymous room where he was left alone to note the ominous "click" of the lock as the door closed. For someone who preferred operating in the far more fluid world of film production with its frequent departures from reality, this was all too discouragingly regimented and straitlaced.

A few minutes passed, then the door opened and three men entered the room. They were dressed, like his escort, in black suits and white shirts, and wore dark glasses. (The sunglasses seemed unnecessary, since the room had no windows.) Grauer didn't know if they were the Men in Black referred to so often by UFO believers—menacing characters thought to be government agents who frequently showed up shortly after a sighting, seizing physical evidence and intimidating witnesses into silence—but he was prepared to accept them as good enough until the real thing came along.

The interview did not start well.

"We've been doing a little checking up on you, Mr. Grauer," said the lead Man in Black. "You have a rather unsavory reputation." The other two men stared unsmilingly at Grauer.

He shifted slightly in his chair. "I don't know what you mean."

"Oh, I think you do, Mr. Grauer. Quite aside from your current activity of producing documentaries of questionable content on topics like the Shroud of Turin and the Face on Mars, there's your earlier work on less respectable subjects. The films you made for Hot Nights Productions, for instance . . ." The man's voice trailed away, suggesting further, unspoken knowledge.

Grauer shifted again. *Damn, they really must have done some digging if they'd found out about Hot Nights.* Why, he hadn't even been filming under the name Charles Grauer then. He began to think that all the rumors he'd heard about the Men in Black were true.

"So, Mr. Grauer. What was this project of yours that you wanted to see us about?"

Feeling at a distinct disadvantage, Grauer cleared his throat. "Well, as you know, I make television documentaries for a living on a variety of speculative subjects. Naturally, in the course of my research I come across all sorts of people with all sorts of theories." He paused.

"Go on, Mr. Grauer."

"Yes, well, in the course of my researches on UFOs, I've come across rather frequent suggestions that the government, in some form, is trying to suppress knowledge about sightings."

"What has that got to do with us?"

Grauer wasn't sure, but he thought all three men were focusing on him even more intently than before. "Well, what if a documentary were made that proved that the government was covering up the first actual landing by an alien race?"

"And?"

Grauer was getting rattled. This wasn't going at all the way he had planned it. These guys weren't taking the bait. "Only it turns out that the documentary is a fake. It's actually an attempt to discredit the government. The government is an innocent victim of a scam run by a cunning antigovernment militia." He sensed increasing interest on the part of his audience. "Instead of the government conspiring against its own citizens, it turns out that bunch of militants are conspiring against the government."

"Interesting idea. Please continue."

Grauer began to regain his confidence as he spoke. *Just like selling a story to a roomful of execs,* he thought. "See, it all depends on getting good media coverage. First the P.R. buildup. 'Did aliens land on Earth for the first time earlier this year?' 'Why is the government hiding the most significant event in human history?' Stories in all the newspapers about the shocking revelations that yes, extraterrestrials *have* actually been on Earth. Can you imagine the newspapers and TV? They'll be going crazy. Then the film airs on network television. Even more media frenzy, as it shows the alien craft landing and the ship's occupants emerging from the ship. And we have an actor playing the role of the courageous cameraman who secretly made a copy of this historic footage. Naturally it's not a very *good* copy—things are a little grainy and out of focus. The 'cameraman' says he came forward to reveal the truth after it became obvious that the government wasn't going to reveal what happened.''

Grauer paused for breath, lost in the excitement of pitching his story. "The news stories in the next few days after the show airs are sensational. The feeding frenzy builds to a height. And then—the actor playing the cameraman steps forward. 'It's all a fake,' he says. 'I'm just an actor. I was hired by the Citizens' Militia to play a role in this film. They just want to foment distrust in the government.' Suddenly the government is an innocent victim of a plot by one of those scary militias. Dynamite P.R.!" Grauer clapped his hands together.

The room was silent, and suddenly he remembered where he was. He looked at the Men in Black. Their leader exchanged glances with each of the others in turn, then looked back at Grauer.

"All right, Mr. Grauer. It's an intriguing idea. What is it you want from us?"

"It costs money to make a film like this, even a one-hour TV documentary with lots of narrative fill. Especially when you need aliens and a UFO landing. Special effects don't come cheap."

"But you'll make a fortune selling the television rights. Both here and abroad, correct?"

Damn, they knew the business better than he'd expected. He should have been expecting that. "You're absolutely right. But I need production money to make the film itself. Actors have to be paid. Makeup and effects technicians have to be hired. And if you're as thorough as I think you are, you know that my bank accounts just don't have that kind of money. Whereas you guys could probably fund me out of your petty cash."

The Man in Black smiled at that. "Candor never hurts, Mr. Grauer. How much do you need?

"Two hundred thousand dollars will cover it. Some friends in the business owe me favors."

"I'd think that would more than cover it. However, it may be worth it to us to have some of these groups silenced for a time. I'll discuss it with my colleagues. Whatever decision we reach, I do hope your friends are good at keeping secrets, Mr. Grauer, or things could become . . . awkward," said the leader with heavy significance.

"Hey, you know my work. My crews are used to keeping their mouths shut. Besides, most of them will think it's the usual stuff about UFOs and government cover-ups. The only ones who'll know there's more to it will be the actor playing the cameraman and my own crew. People I've worked with for years. You can count on their silence."

"Good. And I'm sure we can count on *yours*."

With them knowing about those bachelor party films he'd made? "You certainly can."

"Good. Because we'll be keeping an eye on you. You'll be hearing from us."

The three men stood up and left the room, leaving him alone. But not for long. His escort reappeared and led him back through the maze of corridors to the entrance. There the man left him without so much as a "take it easy."

Grauer blinked as the tall gate slid shut behind him. He wondered what sort of impression he'd made.

Evidently a favorable one. Exactly one week later, a package arrived in the mail. It was stuffed with cash— two hundred thousand dollars' worth.

There was no return address.

"But, Chuck," said Roger Oldshaw, "I don't get it. If we've already collected the cash for this little scam, why are we making a movie at all? Why don't we just split with the bread right now?"

Grauer sighed. Rog was a good cameraman, and he knew how to keep his mouth shut, but sometimes he was a little slow to appreciate the big picture. "For starters, my dear Roger, it would be wrong. We've been paid to make a documentary, and make it we will."

Oldshaw snorted in derision. "Come on, Chuck, this is *me* you're talking to, your partner for fifteen years in doubtful filmmaking. Tell me another fairy tale."

"In the second place, that government spook I talked to said they'd be watching. So we've at least got to go through the motions of making a flick. That means pre-production, hiring the crew, and all that. And besides, if we want the networks to pay us for a film, we'd jolly well better *have* a film to show them, right?"

"Chuck, I know all about the bucks we can get from the networks." Oldshaw continued to look unconvinced.

"Okay, look: We've been saying for years that all we've wanted is one big score, so we can get out of this racket, right?"

"Right."

"So I've figured out a way to milk this one for all it's worth." Grauer looked pleased with himself. "We're going to be making the same documentary for two different sets of people."

Oldshaw looked dumbfounded. "Let me get this straight. We're going to make a fake film of the first landing by E.T.s, which is aired and then deliberately revealed *as* a fake? Who else is going to want a fake documentary?"

"The organization I'm going to visit next. They're dying for us to make this film."

"They are?" Oldshaw sounded skeptical.

"They are. They just don't know it yet." Grauer reached for the telephone.

The Network for Scientific Study of UFOs was one of the most serious and high-minded of the organizations devoted to flying saucers. It was also one of the most prosperous, the main reason Grauer had decided to approach it.

The network maintained a suite of offices downtown. Grauer found them as different from the office of the three Men in Black as it was possible to be. The color scheme was an attractive combination of dove gray and peach. The furniture was birch. Here and there were hung abstracts in soothing cool colors. The entire effect was one of relaxed yet businesslike welcome.

That may have been the atmosphere. His reception by the organization's secretary, Derek Lowrey, was another matter.

"I'm not interested in your proposition, Mr. Grauer." Lowrey leaned back in his office chair.

"But imagine the possibilities," wheedled Grauer. "A one-hour documentary, broadcast by one of the major television networks, on the fine work done by the Network for Scientific Study of UFOs in their continuing search for the truth. UFOs are incredibly popular right now. I'd have no problems selling debut broadcast rights in a minute. Think of the exposure it would give your group."

"I'm still not interested."

"Why not?"

"Because you're a fraud."

Grauer smiled easily at Lowrey. "Why, I could take insult at your remarks, Mr. Lowrey."

Lowrey did not return the smile. "I intend that you should. You're a fake. I know all about those films of yours. All hype and no solid content. Outrageous claims backed up by a few facts. NSSUFO has more than enough problems with frauds."

"Mr. Lowrey, I admit to the hype." Grauer continued to smile. "Unlike you, I'm not solely in the science business, I'm also in show business. And my documentaries have to be entertaining as well as informative, or I can't sell them."

"There's a difference between informative entertainment and outright fraud."

"Indeed there is. And as you yourself just admitted, my films *do* contain some facts—"

"Some very thin facts."

"But facts nonetheless."

"A fine distinction when dealing with a one-hour program consisting mostly of wild speculation."

Grauer kept his smile in place with some effort. "There are, as you noted, a variety of speculative answers, supplied by qualified experts that take those facts you mention into account. Nonetheless, to label my work as fraudulent is bordering on the defamatory—"

"Mr. Grauer, I can see I'll have to be blunt. Your reputation is so questionable that even having you here in my office is likely to cause inquiries by some of the more skittish members of NSSUFO. Many of us have all too vivid memories of the Santelli film and the damage it caused."

"The Santelli film was a fake. I think we can all agree on that."

"Whether or not it was genuine or fake is beside the point. The fact that it was called into question so quickly after such widespread initial exposure was what did the damage. Because it was fresh in everyone's mind, the questions raised were considered hot news by the media. It received enormous exposure. Those of us trying to put UFO research on a serious scientific footing were portrayed as unwitting dupes of a fast-buck filmmaker, fools eager to accept anything that might bolster our theories." Lowrey's face darkened. "Now very few reporters are willing to treat us as sober, responsible researchers. They see us as woo-woos. And just when we were beginning to make progress in serious exploration of the idea that UFOs were a genuine extraterrestrial phenomenon. That film set us back twenty—no, thirty years."

Grauer smiled sympathetically. "I can appreciate your situation. Why, the whole military-industrial complex couldn't have done a better job of discrediting the scientific study of UFOs if it had set the entire CIA to coming up with schemes."

Lowrey smiled thinly. "I'd have to agree with you there, sir. In fact, a few of the more wild-eyed members of the UFO community have speculated that is indeed what happened. That the whole situation of the film, its worldwide broadcast, and the sudden appearance of experts questioning its accuracy, all in the full glare of the media—all of that was orchestrated to compromise the entire UFO movement. It's gained quite a following among the conspiracy-minded members of the community." Lowrey paused, then said half to himself, "Sometimes I wonder myself if they don't have something there. There's no doubt that *some* force has been at work, thwarting many of our most significant discoveries and impairing their potential impact."

Sensing the opening he needed, Grauer leaned forward slightly in his chair. "What sort of problems have you had?"

"Vital photographs and negatives vanishing from our offices. Witnesses recanting on their depositions, or vanishing altogether." Lowrey smiled sourly at Grauer. "I'm sure you're all too familiar with the symptoms—as I recall, they play an important part in the speculations in many of your films."

Ignoring the dig, Grauer said sympathetically, "It certainly is awfully coincidental that all those factors came into play at once. Have you had any hint that there was anything more than coincidence involved?"

"Oh, it's the Men in Black, all right," said Lowrey, grim-faced. "We've got pictures. After the first disappearance—some excellent videotape of a scout ship—we immediately put in a security system, including cameras. There's no doubt it was a group of total professionals making the break-ins."

"That must be extremely frustrating for you," said Grauer sincerely.

Lowrey unbent further. "You have no idea, Mr. Grauer. Several times we've had evidence that we were ready to take public. Incontrovertible evidence: clear photos, solidly respectable witnesses ready to back them up, even—" here Lowrey dropped his voice, "—even fragments from a ship that crashed in Area 51." He slammed the desk with his fist. "And *every* single time, the evidence has vanished."

"That's appalling! And by our own government, too.

I can see why you're so frustrated," said Grauer. "And I can see why you wouldn't be ready to go public just yet."

"Yes. You understand our situation. Without the physical evidence, we really can't go with witnesses alone, no matter how sincere they are. We'd be written off as just another bunch of UFO nuts."

"Mr. Lowrey, this situation is intolerable."

"I agree with you. But what can we do? There's no one to take our case *to*. The Men in Black don't even exist, as far as most people, including most of the government, are concerned. Just another fevered imagining by one of those weirdo conspiracy groups." He clenched his fist. "I *wish* there was some way we could do to them what they've done to us. Discredit *them* for a change."

"Hmm . . . maybe there is," said Grauer.

"What do you mean?"

"Well, the film I'm proposing would be a sort of reverse sting. You'd come out looking like the victims of a scam operation designed to discredit you."

"But we *are* victims!" exclaimed Lowrey.

"Exactly—and this would show it."

"That would be *great*," Lowrey exulted. "Making *them* look bad instead of us."

"But you have to understand, this wouldn't be the documentary that reveals 'The Truth About UFOs.' This film would be the one that exonerates your reputation."

Lowrey's expression sobered again. "A documentary you, no doubt, would be delighted to make for us, Mr. Grauer?"

Grauer made himself look abashed. "Well, yes. I'm hoping you'll let me do the first film as well. You see, I'd like to rehabilitate my reputation, too. As you pointed out earlier, it's deplorable, and I thought . . ." He dropped his gaze and studied his hands for a moment. Then he looked up and squared his shoulders. "I want to get out of this sleazy documentary business and start doing some serious films. This exposé of the government could be my ticket."

Lowrey's expression changed to one of compassion.

"Why don't you tell me what your idea is? We'll see if we can't work together."

Perfect, thought Grauer. Once they thought of themselves as part of the team, they were hooked. "We could make a film which showed the landing of the first alien spaceship on Earth. We'd see the aliens emerging and greeting Earth officials."

Lowrey frowned. "But that's the sort of thing we've been *trying* to get solid evidence for, so that the average citizen knows that the aliens are here."

Grauer smiled. "But this is where we set up the sting. We'll make the landing sequences grainy and fuzzily focused. We won't have any identifiable officials—no recognizable faces, no name tags or serial numbers. The media will start speculating that this is just another one of those Charles Grauer Productions, nothing to be taken seriously. Right?"

"Right," Lowrey answered, uncertainly.

"And *that's* when we hit them with the sting," Grauer said triumphantly. "Just when the derision reaches its peak. We'll have an actor step forward, claiming he was the cameraman who supplied the footage, and that the whole thing was an intentional fraud set up by the government to discredit your organization. That your group had been singled out because you were accumulating serious physical evidence, getting too close to the truth. And when some official government spokesman issues a denial—"

"—nobody'll believe it because they'll assume the government's just trying to cover up their wrongdoing!" finished Lowrey. "I love it!"

"Even better, you can back it all up with your security photos of the break-ins you've already had," Grauer said. "Your position will be unassailable."

"By golly, Mr. Grauer, I think your scheme is brilliant," gushed Lowrey.

"There's just one problem, Mr. Lowrey." Lowrey's face fell. Grauer noted this gleefully. He'd lured another fish! *Now to set the hook.*

"Nothing serious, I hope?"

"Lack of start-up money is only serious when you

don't have it. Effects are expensive: alien makeup, the ship, and so on. Unfortunately, I can't hire actors and technicians on a promise of future payment. They have to be paid in full by the end of filming. And then there's post production costs. Of course, I'll recoup my costs when I sell the documentary to TV, and I'll be able to repay my loans immediately after that. But in the meantime . . ." He paused meaningfully, and mentally held his breath. Would Lowrey pick up the ball?

Lowrey frowned. "I don't see how NSSUFO can make you even a temporary loan, Mr. Grauer. If it ever came to light, then it would be obvious the film was not actually made by the government."

"You're quite right about that," Grauer said smoothly. "But if there's some sort of executive officers' discretionary fund? To be repaid as soon as the documentary airs . . ." By which time, Grauer profoundly hoped, he and Rog would be out of the country.

"Hmm," said Lowrey. "That might be possible. As it happens, we *do* have a sizable discretionary fund . . . perhaps something in 'Travel' . . ."

The details were quickly concluded to both parties' mutual satisfaction.

"*Where* did you say this location was?" Grauer sounded disgruntled as the van Oldshaw was driving bounced its way down the rutted dirt road. Their vehicle was the leader of a line of cars, trucks, and vans containing the rest of the crew and equipment.

"On the back forty of a rancher I know."

"Must be the *back* back forty. I'll bet we've driven fifty miles since we left the city."

Oldshaw glanced at him. "From what you've told me, the more privacy we've got, the better. It'd be darned embarrassing to have someone announce that a flying saucer just like the one in our film landed in Jimmy Rivera's pasture a few months before the program aired."

Grauer sighed. "You're right, Rog. Sorry. I'm just a little short on sleep. I hate night shoots."

"Me, too. We're getting too old for this business,

Chuck. You're right—let's pull this one off and head for the Bahamas."

"Deal. I just hope my spine will last for the duration of this ride."

"My spine joins your spine in that fond hope."

The van continued to jolt down the road.

"Chuck, I think we're about set," said Manny, the assistant director. "The ramp's lights are all working perfectly."

"Finally." Grauer studied the floodlit corner of the pasture, where the mock-up of the entrance ramp of an imaginary interstellar spacecraft was artfully located between a couple of huge oak trees. Made of lightweight materials, it loomed above the masked and costumed actors standing next to it. Careful positioning of the camera would show only the ramp, not the missing spacecraft to which it was supposedly attached. "Thanks, Manny. Let's try for one take."

Manny grinned. He'd worked with Grauer before, and knew the phrase was his mantra. Sometimes they actually did get it in one take, too.

"Okay, everybody!" Grauer shouted. "Let's get started! Kill the floods!"

The area darkened, lit only by the lights lining each side of the ramp.

"Quiet, everyone, please!" The buzz of conversation quickly died down.

But there wasn't complete silence. Instead, there was a deep, throbbing vibration almost too low to hear. Grauer turned to Oldshaw in irritation. "I thought you said this was a remote location. That sounds like machinery of some sort."

"It *is* deserted, Chuck. There's nothing within forty acres of here but the occasional Holstein."

"So who's running the generator?" Grauer asked. The throbbing made his teeth ache.

"Beats me. I suppose it could be—" Oldshaw stopped, his attention distracted by the shouting of the actors by the ramp. They were pointing toward him, over his head. The two men turned and looked up.

"My God."

Looming overhead was the source of the sound: a vast flattened disk of—metal? Ceramic? Unmistakably of intelligent, nonhuman construction, with portals and creases in its surface, with mysterious arrays of instrumentation, glittering with lights set in incomprehensible patterns.

Grauer stared upward, drop-jawed in astonishment. *All those years of will-o'-the-wisp pursuit,* he thought, *and here it is in all its enormous reality.* Lowrey and his ilk were right, after all. Maybe not in the details, but in the basic reality of alien visitors to Earth.

"I don't believe it," whispered Oldshaw, his words barely audible above the throbbing of whatever it was the craft used for propulsion.

"Believe it, Rog," he breathed. *I wonder if we're the first to see this?* he thought. *If we hadn't needed such a remote location for filming—!*

"Rog, quick! Start filming!" Oldshaw didn't respond at first. Grauer grabbed him by the shoulder. "Rog! FILM!" he shouted in the cameraman's ear. Oldshaw seemed to shake himself, then came to his senses and lunged for his camera. Grauer snatched up the handheld camcorder he used to line up test shots and began recording as the ship continued to glide overhead and across the pasture.

Together, they shot the footage they knew would make them the most famous filmmakers in the history of mankind.

Derek Lowrey flicked the switch and the lights flickered back on in the tiny screening room. "I'm supposed to be impressed by this film of yours, Mr. Grauer?" he asked acidly.

"But—you don't understand. This is the *real thing!* My cameraman and I, my crew, my actors—we all saw the ship!"

"Really, Mr. Grauer, you must think I'm a real patsy. I've seen better UFO footage faked by teenaged boys."

Grauer was astounded. Couldn't this idiot see the difference between genuine footage and fakery? "Here I am, bringing you actual photographic proof of the first appearance of a genuine UFO, and all you can tell me is that you've seen better fakes?''

"You really set me up, didn't you? That was a wonderful tale you spun for me, about how shocking it was that our evidence kept disappearing, and how we could run a sting on the government. I should have realized what you were really up to all along: you just wanted to scam NSSUFO with some bogus footage of your own.''

Grauer blushed, but continued to protest. *"This is the real thing! I swear it is!"*

"Of course it is—as though I'm supposed to believe you after all the lies you've told. I just wish there was some way for me to get our money back. But of course you'd planned for that, too. I can't possibly go to the police without explaining that I was planning to be part of a scheme to defraud the public myself.''

"But—"

Lowrey grew angrier as he realized all the ramifications of the situation. "I'm going to have to tell the board of directors about this and tender my resignation. I'll be extremely lucky if they don't press charges. You bastard!'' His voice rose to a shout. "You've ruined me! Get out of my office!''

Grauer got.

He didn't go looking for the Men in Black. They came for him.

"I'm very disappointed in you, Mr. Grauer. We expected a documentary film, not twenty minutes of poorly focused footage.''

"But you don't understand," Grauer said, with an awful feeling of déjà vu. "This is actual film of an actual UFO that my crew and I actually saw.''

"But that's not what we made a deal for, is it, Mr. Grauer? We expected a film that could be used to discredit one of the major groups in the antigovernment militia movement. But this—'' the Man in Black tapped the film canister "—this won't discredit anyone. Except perhaps your own reputation as a professional who's mastered the technical aspects of his craft. I realize we agreed the footage of the aliens' landing would be grainy and out of focus, but this is footage of an object that could be just about anything."

"I've already explained, it must have been something, some energy field the UFO was emitting that caused that graininess."

"That proved very convenient for the UFO, didn't it?"

"I can't help it that that's how it turned out," Grauer said wearily.

"Yes, that's what the photographer at Roswell claimed, too. Of course, no one ever heard from him again." The Man in Black stood up. "I wouldn't plan on making any more documentaries if I were you. I suspect you'll find the market for Charles Grauer Productions has dried up." And before Grauer could respond, he left the room. After the door clicked shut, he realized the Man in Black had taken the canister of film with him.

But I've still got the negatives, he thought. *And the video footage.* There would be one final Charles Grauer Production. *This* time there'd by plenty of UFO footage to back up his witnesses. *This* documentary would be the blockbuster, the one he'd been waiting all his life to make.

It wasn't until he returned to his own office that he discovered it had been broken into in his absence. And that the negatives and videotape were gone.

The Men in Black were always thorough.

ABSOLUTION

by Paul Dellinger

Paul Dellinger is a longtime reporter for the Roanoke (Va.) *Times,* which is the only place where he's worked with computers (the newspaper was upgrading from manual to electric typewriters when he started there). He still manages to crank out an occasional high-tech science fiction story, despite being cyber-impaired. Other stories by him appear in *Wheel of Fortune, The Williamson Effect* and *Future Net.*

Kasey couldn't help wondering how everything could seem so normal in the little late-night restaurant when the rest of the world had been turned upside down barely four months ago. "I'm looking for Father McDermott," she told the buxom hostess who seemed about to burst out of her micro-mini.

"Oh, sure, honey. He's right back here. Walk this way," the hostess said. Watching the sway of the curvy young woman's hips, Kasey found herself thinking: *Not on my best day.* She followed more sedately to the corner booth where Mac was sitting. One look at him erased all levity from her thoughts.

Father Edward McDermott's clerical collar was loose, his dark hair mussed, and his five o'clock shadow more obvious than usual in contrast to the pallor of his face. He started to stand up at Kasey's approach, caught himself—not the first time his concepts of chivalry and feminism gridlocked—and slumped back onto the worn vinyl seat.

The hostess became a waitress, brought a Diet Pepsi for Kasey and refilled Mac's coffee before she wiggled away. Kasey could hear Mac's cup rattle against his saucer as he picked it up.

"So," Kasey said, "what's a nice girl like me doing in a place like this at such—pardon the expression, Mac—an ungodly hour?"

Mac closed his eyes and put his fingers to his temples. She noticed the redness of his eyes when he opened them again.

"I'm sorry, Kasey. I have no right to involve you. I don't know what I was thinking—"

"Okay, let's pretend we've gone through all that, and I've done the what-are-friends-for number. You phoned, I'm here. Now, what's going on?"

Still he hesitated, and that really worried her. She had known Mac only four months, but she had thought him totally unflappable. She had seen him calmly disarm a man who, in a still-unexplained burst of sadness, had been threatening to shoot himself. He had handled mean drunks and officious civic leaders opposing a spouse abuse shelter in their neighborhood with the same calm aplomb. She had first seen him in the daily crowd that surrounded "the lost acre," as some reporter had dubbed it—as good a name as any for where something had swooshed down with a blinding light into the outskirts of this low-rent bedroom community in northern Ohio. Luckily, none of the three houses that it squashed had been occupied at the time.

The lost acre had been there ever since, impenetrable, visible only as a shifting dome-shaped grayness, but Kasey had to admit that it did revive the old neighborhood. Military people, researchers, UFOologists, end-of-the-world nuts, reporters, and curiosity seekers descended on it like ants to a picnic.

It drew Katherine Callahan—or Kasey, as her small circle of friends called her—like a magnet. As a child, she had devoured books like John Wyndham's *The Midwich Cuckoos* despite her school librarian's best efforts to steer her toward stories more "suitable" for little girls. Likewise, her mother would be horrified when little Katherine monopolized the old-movie cable channels for titles like "Village of the Damned," among others.

"Why, it hasn't even been colorized," her mother protested. "It can't be worthwhile for a child to watch."

But occasionally her father would side with her (he liked vintage movies, too) and this had been one time her mother did not overrule them. Kasey still remembered her excitement when, only minutes into that particular film, she realized it was based on Wyndham's novel. The opening sequence, involving an English village sealed off from the outside by something generated by a grounded UFO, was merely incidental to the plot but recalling it still delivered a thrill of recognition. That had been her first bond with Mac, when she interviewed him for one of her feature stories. It turned out he had fond remembrances of many of the same books, movies, and other memories that she had.

She had never completely forgiven her mother for throwing out all the books, tapes, and magazines she had collected over the years. "They were cluttering up your room," Kasey's mother explained when she came home from college one Christmas. "I knew you'd outgrown them, dear." Kasey managed to hide her sense of outrage and a loss of trust she never completely regained. The damage was done; there was no point in both of them being upset.

Nor was it all bad, now that she looked back at it. Such possessions would have tied her down, she realized, to some place where she could keep them. With their loss, she could either spend years restocking or avoid collecting such baggage altogether, and being emotionally tied to its fate.

As she saw it, she had been truly liberated. After college, she had moved about the country—indeed, the world—accumulating experiences rather than things. Her mother, right up to her dying day, worried that Kasey's lifestyle would keep her from finding some nice young man and settling down. Well, maybe it had.

Of course, if Kasey had been less of a free spirit and opted for marriage and children, she could hardly have come here to the scene of the lost acre so readily. When she heard the first news broadcasts of it, she felt reverberations from that old movie which had so imprinted her as a child. Part of Kasey's peripatetic lifestyle had included jobs on various newspapers and one stint at a TV station, all of which she used to wangle a for-the-duration news service assignment here. It paid a small stipend for an occasional feature—no mean accomplishment, since the acre did absolutely nothing but sit there—and to keep her around as an early warning system in case something finally did happen.

Kasey felt that she earned her salary, such as it was—enough to live on, and at times she had lived on less. Her stories ranged from interviews with scientists studying the lost acre to human interest pieces on some of the others it had brought here—like Mac. The church needed to be where people were, he had said, and right now there were an awful lot of them here.

"Are you sure you didn't come to exorcise it, Father?" Kasey had joked, but with the knowledge that there was an element among the particularly devout that thought of this enigma as the work of the devil.

"You're thinking of Max von Sydow," he smiled, unoffended. "Or was it Richard Burton?" And Kasey suppressed a giggle of delight at having found another old-movie buff.

Soon they were laughing heartily at exchanges that nobody around them understood. In the next half hour, she learned such things about him as how he got the only "A" on his philosophy final in seminary (the exam had consisted of a one-word question—"Why?"—and Mac had given a one-word answer: "Because!") and she was telling how she once acquired the nickname of "Deanna Jones" during a summer on an archaeological dig in Egypt. Some of the other volunteers had been classic-film buffs, too.

She realized that she had picked that particular anecdote to impress him. There seemed little future in it, since priests were not exactly the best prospects for marriage or even an affair, certain popular literature notwithstanding. Maybe, she chided herself, it was the same kind of challenge so many girls she'd known in her teens had found in imagining themselves seducing Mr. Spock.

Despite a childhood of Sunday School classes imposed by her mother, Kasey remained basically irreligious. But even she could see how Mac's mission congregation filled a need among a segment of those living here now, and the article she wrote about him reflected that. Mac had his beliefs, but he and Kasey soon became comfortable enough with one another for cheerful argument on religion and innumerable other topics.

That was why Mac's reticence now was alarming. Kasey forced herself to sip her soft drink, waiting for him to speak again.

"It's hard to see myself confessing to you, Kasey," he said, attempting a smile that didn't quite come off. "But I badly need another viewpoint, and from someone I can be sure would never talk about it."

She assumed he meant that as a compliment. Since it also happened to be true, she accepted it.

"Kasey," he said, averting his red-rimmed eyes, "I very nearly murdered a young woman tonight."

His cup was shaking so badly that he put it down. He placed both of his big, powerful hands flat on the table.

"That's not possible," she said quietly.

"But it happened. I was walking around the perimeter of the lost acre. I know, I know—nobody's supposed to go there at night because nobody knows even now what it might do, but I've found it seems to attract the most troubled people at those hours. In the past few months, I've talked at least four potential suiciders out of there. You remember one of them, you wrote about it. Once they're back at the mission or anywhere else but there, they seem to recover . . ."

"Four?" Kasey was surprised.

"I thought it was about to be five tonight. You know how the perimeter always seemed fogged in, almost like the gloom is boiling off that vast gray egg or whatever you want to call it. I couldn't find her at first, but I could hear her crying, so very softly, as though just to herself."

"Who was she?"

"I'd never seen her before. I can't really describe her that well even now. Tall, long dark hair, rather pale, tears streaming down her face . . . I can't remember!"

"What was she wearing?" Kasey persisted, hoping a different approach might help.

Mac hesitated. "I'm not sure about that either. Some sort of white gownlike thing, I believe. Once I spotted her, I went to her and asked what was wrong. She had extremely large, dark eyes, and they seemed to reflect all the sadness in the world, Kasey. I tell you, my heart went out to her. And then I—I . . ."

Kasey waited, afraid that anything she might say now would bottle up his words.

"I put my fingers around her neck, and began to squeeze. She just kept looking at me. She didn't struggle or try to escape. I'd have killed her if the policeman hadn't come along."

Mac grabbed his cup and gulped down the rest of the coffee.

"He came out of the mist and of course saw what was happening. He knocked my arms away, and demanded to know what I thought I was doing. Then he started to say something to her. . . .

"His lips suddenly went back against his teeth. He took out his revolver, very slowly, and pointed it at her. She just stood there, looking at us out of those sad eyes, and he cocked the thing. I snapped out of it in time to push his arm down. The gun went off, but it only hit the sidewalk. The policeman stood there staring down at it, as though he couldn't believe what he'd tried to do. The woman slipped away—and so did I! I was afraid to stay, afraid I'd find myself following and attacking her again. I can't go back while she's there, but she needs someone's help."

"How do you know she's still in the perimeter?"

Mac lowered his voice even more. "I saw where she went, Kasey. She went inside!"

As a child, Kasey had a secret place she would visit on an occasional Saturday or whenever school homework allowed a free afternoon. Actually, it wasn't all that secret; it was more that nobody else cared to make the climb to the ugly little shock of trees over the opening of the railroad tunnel below her home. But when a train would come thundering out of the tunnel beneath Kasey's hidden perch, the whole earth seemed to shake and steam surrounded her, isolating her from everything. She could imagine herself on a strange planet, in the grip of some gigantic sorcerer, or anywhere else that her mind cared to take her.

That was long ago. But she had a tinge of the same feeling now, as she prowled along the edge of the lost acre.

She had come directly here from the restaurant where she left Mac. She saw no reason to mention to him that she'd paid a few nocturnal visits here, too, and knew what he meant by its oppressiveness, but she had attributed that to the absence of the daytime crowds. Her forays never uncovered any secrets of the lost acre—but she'd never had Mac's specific directions before.

It seemed even more difficult for Mac to admit the sexual arousal that had accompanied his attack on the woman than to speak of the attack itself. Mac, she knew, didn't think of his calling as magically purging his biological urgings, but the possibility that they were accompanied by an unsuspected streak of necrophilia left him shaken. And yet, he had reasoned, the policeman had been affected, too. Whatever caused it must be external. That was when he'd thought of her, he told Kasey. If there was a sexual basis to the men's reaction, then another woman might be impervious to it.

It made a strange kind of sense. She hoped he was right.

The sameness of the houses in this old company town—the identical tin roofs, tiny porches and window shapes—was depressing enough to Kasey without the gloom of the lost acre. Of course, the authorities had evacuated the homes within several blocks of it after it had sprung up. And the town's beefed-up police force tried to keep people out of the area altogether after dark. It occurred to Kasey to wonder, for the first time, why there was such insistence on that. Did the authorities know something she didn't?

One thing they couldn't know was the path she was following now, or they'd have acted on it themselves. Part of a smashed house lay just outside that gray obscurity, its broken pieces of wood seeming to lean against emptiness. Kasey slipped under one of the beams and crept toward the grayness.

That was another thing she'd managed to do, despite police efforts to keep people away from the edges. Twice before, when she'd slipped by them and tried to penetrate it, she found exactly what government volunteers said they encountered—not a sudden invisible barrier, not the rigid forcefield of her science-fictional stories, but a cloying thickness that quickly became impassable. They had found it just as impossible to push or fire solid objects into it beyond a certain point.

But this time was different. Mac had been right.

The mist concealed everything around her—Kasey could barely see her own dark tennis shoes at the bottom of her slacks—but she continued moving forward, one careful step at a time, far beyond the point she'd gone in her earlier attempts. The only sound was the soft scrape of rubble under her feet. She noticed a faint tangy odor that she couldn't identify.

It occurred to her that she was being very foolish. Suppose she walked across the lost acre and came up against the barrier on the other side—and then couldn't relocate the path by which she'd entered? Shouldn't she go back while she could, and tell someone about this pathway so it could be properly investigated?

But she kept moving. It was Mac who had discovered this entry point, and it was for him that she was following it now. Mac had hoped Kasey could bring the woman back out, and hadn't really thought beyond that point.

Kasey had.

That woman didn't stumble in here blindly. Not the way Mac described her movements. She knew precisely where she was going, which could only mean she had come from inside. When Mac started thinking more clearly, he would realize that, too.

Kasey didn't wait that long. If something should happen to her, Mac would still be available to point the way in to others—but she was here now. Nobody could take that from her.

A muted sound reached her ears, and she strained to hear it. As she continued walking, it began taking on the characteristics of a faint, soft sobbing. . . .

Kasey froze. Until now, it had all been nice and theoretical—but she was not alone in here! This was no imaginary adventure above the railroad tunnel back home. Again she had second thoughts about what she was doing.

But she didn't turn around. She moved toward the sound with her hands slightly in front of her. The mist hid the landscape inside the acre, but the crying seemed closer.

A whitish form loomed up before her with startling suddenness. Kasey stifled a scream. Well, what had she expected? Mac had been right about everything else. But what was she supposed to say to this apparition, now that she'd found it?

The figure had its back to Kasey, but it did seem female in form. Its shoulders moved in unison with the soft crying and, taking a deep breath and swallowing, Kasey reached out to turn it around.

It felt human enough, too, but its face—the face seemed vague, at first glance, as though Kasey was having trouble focusing on it. Then it became almost familiar, though she couldn't have explained how.

All she knew was that she hated it.

She felt her throat tighten with anger, and her fingers clench into fists. The figure didn't move, even when Kasey raised her fists to strike. She read in the face a sense of unutterable sadness, and acceptance of whatever was to happen.

Unlike Mac and the policeman, Kasey had some warning of how she might react when she met the mysterious figure and she had tried to steel herself against it. She turned her face away and squeezed her eyes shut. It helped a little. She lowered her arms, which had been poised to strike out, imposing her will on them despite a convulsive resistance by her own muscles. What was it about that face?

It never occurred to Kasey that she was in any danger by blinding herself to whatever the other being might do. She knew with an absolute certainty that, if there was danger from anyone, it was from herself. She had encountered a few people during her life that she disliked, but never had there been such a feeling of malice as she experienced now. It was instinctive, overpowering, pouring into her from the very center of her being. . . .

It was her mother!

Intellectually, Kasey knew better. She remembered the nursing home where her mother had spent her final months—the combined odors of disinfectant and urine that pervaded the little room where her mother lay wasting away, day after day, criticizing Kasey's lifestyle and other perceived shortcomings to the last. The visits could never have been pleasant, considering her mother's deteriorating condition, but having to listen again and again to those judgments made them all but intolerable. There were times then Kasey found herself wishing, involuntarily, that her mother could just go ahead and die, and let her get on with her own life. . . .

"Oh, God, no!" Kasey had never admitted that to herself, not in so many words. This apparition standing before her was somehow drawing it all to the forefront of her mind, she realized. This thing that so resembled her mother—it was to blame. Again her hands came up. . . .

Again, she fought them down.

She strained to call up the good memories—how proud both her parents had been when she came home with her grade school spelling bee trophy, the birthday gift from her mother of the computer program with which Kasey learned to type, the extra jobs her mother had taken to pay her college tuition . . . but her mind kept dredging up other remembrances: her mother making fun of the stories Kasey had tried to write as a child, her insistence that Kasey accept a date to the senior prom with a well-to-do but insufferable snob when Kasey wanted to go with a boy who had been her partner in a science fair project. . . .

Kasey shook her head, trying to clear it of the conflicting recollections. They were beside the point, she told herself; this was not her mother, no matter how it might look. And, as she clamped that piece of certainty into her mind, the figure changed. It broke up into five globes of pulsing golden light, hanging in the air before her roughly where the head, shoulders and midsection of her mother had been. Then they seemed to coalesce into an immense face of sorts, a benevolent visage reminding Kasey of a scene from yet another movie, *The Wizard of Oz*. What seemed to be eyes stared at her, full of pain, and a silent wail of misery echoed in her mind. She knew, as certainly as if she'd heard the words, that it had wanted her to end that misery—but dimly, almost drowned out by that soundless shriek, was a growing glimmer of something that felt like hope to her.

The Oz-like being desperately wanted—needed—something from her. But what?

In the next hour, Kasey whirled through the most intense experiences of her life. She viewed at least a dozen worlds—she lost count after that—and observed the life-forms on each one. It was as if she were a child again, huddled in her secret place and letting her imagination range across space and time. . . .

Only now she had guides, or a guide. She was never sure whether the intelligence she faced was five separate entities or a composite creature. She continued to think of it (him? her? them?) as Oz, since that seemed closest to the memory it had plucked from her mind for this manifestation—just as, before, it had dredged up images better left dormant, trying to provoke her fury as punishment for its great sin.

Only gradually did she come to understand what that sin had been.

It—they—had indeed come from space, as others had before them, to gaze upon Earth and its endless, teeming varieties of life. Perhaps some of the flying saucer hysteria once in vogue had some foundation in reality, after all. The visitors knew of no other world such as this, not in any of the vastness of the galaxy through which they ranged. The feeling Kasey picked up from them was one of awe—almost of worship.

Herbert George, she thought, *how far off base you were with those tentacled invaders that you dreamed up and we've echoed in so many ways since.*

They showed her, in their minds (or mind), some of those other worlds they knew. Kasey had no way to tell whether any were planets or moons of her own solar system, but—remembering all the photographs every schoolchild had seen from the Mariners, Voyagers, and other space probes—some could well have been.

But it was no wonder those probes had detected no life on those seemingly barren landscapes. It was so tenuous, so frighteningly rare. . . .

Not in quality, but quantity. Kasey witnessed with closed eyes the lonely beings who, by comparison with her kind, left scarcely a mark on the vastness of their environments. She understood that they must be products of longer, less robust but more selective evolutionary processes. Even the archaeologists she had once accompanied to Egypt would have been hard-pressed to find evidence of them on those alien surfaces, no matter how long they scraped and dug.

It took a while, but Kasey finally understood what the Oz-creature was trying to make her grasp. Earth was the exception, the uncultivated jungle world, where life proliferated without boundaries. In a universe where each small existence was a precious gift to all the rest, the rich anarchy of plants, animals, viruses, and so much more beckoned as something the outsiders had to see for themselves—a world so achingly full of life, but of death, too. That repelled yet fascinated them. They seemed able to handle the concept of all those deaths, so long as they could remain distant and detached.

But, in this instance, they had not been able to do that. . . .

"Eleven houseflies . . . two mice . . . three dozen or so ants . . . flowers, a yard full of weeds and grass. . . .

Mac was staring across the restaurant table at her. It seemed as if he had not moved the whole time she was gone—a time that, to Kasey, seemed almost forever.

"Those were what they showed me," she said. "Mac, they even knew how many individual blades of grass their accident wiped out."

"And you think I can save their lives, but . . . only by giving up my own? The only life I know?"

"I can't explain it any better," Kasey said. "Their guilt—what they think of as guilt—is all that holds them here. Now that they've corrected whatever went wrong with their vehicle, they'd be off like a shot if they could be made to believe that our world had forgiven them. It would be instantaneous, that was clear. I couldn't make them understand that we would need time to get clear before everything under that mistlike dome takes off from our world."

"But surely," Mac said, "if they hold life as precious as they told you, they wouldn't want to isolate one of us from our own kind."

"Showed me, not told me. I only got impressions from them—images, not words. I do think I understood correctly, though."

Mac looked around the restaurant, empty now except for the hostess, one waitress, and two sleepy-looking men occupying a table by the front window where dawn was just lightening the sky. He looked to Kasey like a desperate man seeking an escape.

"This is crazy," he said. "We're sitting here talking about aliens from space waiting down the street."

"If we wanted their lives in retribution, Mac, they were willing. They still are. They even tried to force us—you, me, that policeman. It seems as though they'd prefer it to the kind of lingering death they're suffering through now."

"You really believe just being on our world is killing them?" Mac asked, for about the fifth time.

She nodded. "All the life on our world—it's too much for them. It's like a diabetic overdosing on sugar. They empathize with every living creature, every insect—I almost think every germ. They hear all our thoughts, and whatever passes for thought processes in grass and leaves and fish." She shook her head, aware of how she sounded. "That's how they probed below our conscious levels for images that would provoke the rage they thought they deserved," she said.

"Maybe I'm the one that deserves punishment. If I have an inclination of the sort they brought out of me, subconscious or not." He closed his eyes, and Kasey again noticed the new lines of strain on his face. That strength of his which she had taken for granted seemed to be faltering.

"Stop it, Mac. It's what you do that counts, not what you think. Anyway, you wanted the truth, didn't you?" she couldn't help adding.

Mac opened his eyes and glared at her. "Yeah." After a pause, he added: "You overcame whatever it was they threw at you, didn't you, Kasey?"

"I don't want to talk about it," she said, the sudden weariness in her voice surprising her. "Anyway, all that's beside the point. The question is do we help them or not?"

"Why must all the burden fall on me?" he asked angrily. "Why didn't you just tell them the rest of the world could absorb the loss of those bugs and plants they're so worried about?"

"My God, Mac, don't you think I tried? They didn't believe me. Sure, they looked into my mind, and I hope they saw that I was sincere, but I only represented me. Don't you see? You honestly believe that you represent the creator of us all. . . ."

" 'Represent' isn't the word I'd choose."

"Mac, I don't know that even your beliefs would be enough to convince them. I just know it's the only way I can see. And I'm even more sure that their time is running out. The fact that they came out from behind their barrier as they did shows that."

"Kasey, I don't want to leave my world! If I knew I could do it and then leave before they blasted off or whatever it is they do . . . but to live out my life alone among nonhuman creatures. . . ."

"You wouldn't be alone, Mac."

It took a minute for him to understand what she meant. "You'd go back into the acre, with me?"

"I never planned anything else."

The bitterness that had been in his voice was suddenly gone. "Kasey, I'd never ask that of you."

"Mac, don't misunderstand. I want to go with them! I want to see those other worlds they gave me glimpses of. I think it's what I've wanted all my life. If I could have freed them of their guilt and they'd zipped off with me, I wouldn't be laying all this on you now."

"My God, Kasey, you're . . ." She waited, wondering if he was going to call her magnificent or insane. Instead, he gave a simple nod. "All right. We'll try it. I don't know that my faith will be strong enough to convince them either, but we'll find out. . . ."

He was in the process of sliding his chair back to rise when it happend.

The sun came up like thunder. Its glow bathed the entire room in brightness. Kasey could still see afterimages of the two men staggering back from the window, even with her eyes squeezed shut. She could hear the waitress' hysterical screaming: "Not again, please, not again! Why didn't I leave this town after the first time? Oh, my God, we're all gonna die. . . ."

Almost blindly, Kasey made her way to the door, bumping into tables and overturning chairs. She flung it open in time to hear a kind of whooshing sound, as the light shot upward toward the brightening skies like an uncaged bird, and then was gone.

"Wait," she whispered in the sudden stillness. "Wait for me. . . ."

She could still see a few stars not yet obscured by the natural dawn. And then she saw more—not from her own vantage point on the chilly street outside the restaurant, but from another point of view entirely.

She was seeing the inside of their ship, its window showing the Earth dwindling behind it as it roared into space. . . .

And she realized that the visitors had known of Mac's decision the instant he made it, that distance was no barrier to their ability to receive thoughts. Or, obviously, to send them.

Kasey couldn't suppress a shout of glee. She would never be Earthbound again.

TAKE ME TO YOUR LEADER

by Jody Lynn Nye

Jody Lynn Nye lists her main career activity as "spoiling cats." She lives near Chicago with two of the above and her husband, SF author and editor Bill Fawcett. Among Jody's novels are the *Mythology 101* series, *Taylor's Ark, Medicine Show,* and four collaborations with Anne McCaffrey: *Crisis on Doona, The Death of Sleep, The Ship Who Won,* and *Treaty at Doona.* Her latest works include *The Magic Touch, The Ship Errant,* and an anthology, *Don't Forget Your Spacesuit, Dear!*

Peggy Ross settled one hip on the arm of the chair beside Shalimar's carpeted pedestal, and put the dish down in front of the cat.

"Fresh tuna, sweetheart," she cooed. "Mama found nice steaks on sale at Wright's. All mashed up, just for you."

The white chinchilla Persian opened her eyes from the squat-in-the-sun squint and looked at the dish, pretending disdain at its contents. Peggy felt a surge of affection for the cat.

"Oh, come on," she said, pushing the dish a little closer and shaking it. "You love tuna. Taste it. For Mama."

The cat stretched out her neck and nibbled a little of the food. Suddenly, she lurched to her feet, hunched over the plate, and began to wolf the fish with gusto. Peggy watched her fondly, reaching out occasionally to stroke the long fur. She adored it when Shalimar enjoyed a treat.

The cat finished eating and went back to her nap. She spent her days on specially made perches that were adjustable and movable so she could have the best sun at the best times of day, no matter what the season. Peggy Ross liked to make certain that her cat had the best of all things. Sometimes, her husband Ralph joked that he was afraid he came a distant second to Shalimar in Peggy's heart. Peggy always laughed at that.

Peggy scooted back just a little so the bright sun wasn't gleaming straight in her eyes. They lived in the Bascomb Building, at 135 stories the tallest residential building in the world. Above their apartment were a weather station and half a dozen television transmitters, but the engineers didn't live there. She did.

She stood up to admire the view. The Bascomb was the most exclusive building in the city, and this was one of the most exclusive apartments in it. There were only four penthouses, each of which wrapped halfway around two sides of the narrow top of the building so the wide glass outer walls commanded a splendid panorama of the city. Peggy thought her apartment, which looked south and west, was the nicest. She felt lordly, in a ladylike way. If anyone could see into the window just then, they'd behold an elegantly tall woman with aristocratic features wearing a jade silk lounging suit. Queen of the city. Peggy laughed at her own imagination and leaned over to give Shalimar a pat. The cat's fur was so soft. Shalimar murmured in her sleep.

"You're such a beauty," Peggy crooned. Without opening her eyes, Shalimar purred.

Peggy squinted out into the afternoon sun. She could see tiny, moving glints rising and falling in the distance: jets taking off and landing from the city airport which lay almost due west of the Bascomb. She knew they came and went all day long, but they were almost invisible except at dawn and dusk, when the horizontal rays of the sun picked out the shiny metal fuselages. The bright specks were dyed with an orange glow now.

One dot of light coming in from the north caught her attention. Instead of following the others on an inclined plane leading to the distant runways, it stayed on a level

with her windows, and appeared to grow larger. Peggy
thought it was coming straight toward her. She gawked.
Oh, no, it was probably a helicopter, carrying either a
traffic reporter or some bigwig who didn't want to fight
the traffic on the ground.

But the small craft didn't divert toward the downtown
area. It kept zooming closer, homing in on the Bascomb.
Peggy felt a moment of panic. Should she call someone,
and report an impending crash?

The dot came closer and closer. Oddly, it seemed to
slow down outside her window, and hung in the air next
to the building, almost touching it. Peggy rose from the
arm of the chair and sidled over to see better. She
blinked.

She was looking at a flying saucer. No doubt about it.
But such a thing couldn't be *real*. Perhaps a producer
was filming a sci-fi movie in the city, using the Bascomb
as a setting, without telling anyone in the building. *How
silly of them,* Peggy thought, chidingly. Why, a movie
company could have all the extras they wanted, if they'd
only ask. Plenty of people would volunteer, just for the
fun of it. She would. Peggy confessed to a secret fond-
ness for that kind of movie, the hokier the better. That
was it. She was looking at a prop spaceship. It was odd
that she couldn't see the crane or the helicopter that was
holding it up. It might be quite high in the sky, to stay
out of the way of the camera. Wherever that was. Trying
to stay behind her curtains, she peered upward. She
didn't want to spoil the shot and make them take it over.

The little silver ship was very well made. It resembled
a straw sun hat, with lights around the band. As she
studied it in admiration, a door on the side nearest the
building slid open, and three little beings climbed out
onto the brim of the "hat." They were clad in suits that
looked like jointed white enamel, except for the helmets,
which were clear in the front and black enamel in the
back. She got a slight shock when they turned toward
her, even though they couldn't see her. The faces
weren't human. In shape they resembled ocelots or jackals—sort of a cross between canine and feline, but with
intelligence in the round brown eyes. The gloved hands

only had three fingers and a thumb apiece. The booted feet were round, like pegs or hooves.

They couldn't be actual people. They were much too small. This was terrific, Peggy thought, settling down with one hip on the back of an armchair. She was watching special effects in action.

Suddenly, the small beings turned toward her window. Afraid she had been spotted, she scooted to the left, and pulled a fold of curtain in front of her. To her shock, the beings walked right through the window, into her living room.

They had to be some kind of holographic projection. But no, the round feet made marks in the brushed nap of the carpet. No special effect could do that. They were *real.* Peggy stared in horror as they walked toward her. She backed away fearfully, wondering how she could defend herself against creatures who could pass through glass.

To her dismay, they kept going past her, toward Shalimar. The cat had awoken, and was eyeing the visitors without concern, but Peggy was frantic.

"No! Stay away from my baby!" she cried. She jumped to get between the aliens and her cat. The three beings brushed her aside, very gently but firmly, but so quickly she never understood how it happened. They kept going toward the pedestal near the corner. Peggy watched them for a moment, then staggered back toward the telephone. She picked up the receiver and dialed with shaking hands.

"Ralph?" she asked, in a voice that squeaked when her husband answered, "you'd better come home. Spacemen just landed in our apartment, and they just presented their credentials to our cat."

Ralph shouted something in her ear, but she barely heard him as she set the receiver down. She was watching the visitors. The little, white-suited creatures were gathered around Shalimar's cushion-covered platform. They didn't seem to be hurting the cat, but they were preventing Peggy from getting close. It worried her. She wanted to snatch Shalimar up in her arms and cuddle her, not for the cat's comfort, but for her own.

"She's just a cat, you know," Peggy called to them. They didn't pay any attention to her. From pouches slung on their shoulders, they produced small bronze squares, which they offered to Shalimar. The cat sniffed them, even rubbed the corner of her mouth against one of them. That seemed to please the little beings. They talked among themselves in low, musical voices. One of them, elected spokesman by the others, made an elaborate gesture with one hand, and started to speak to the cat. Shalimar regarded them blankly. When she got bored, she looked up at Peggy, and meowed. As one, the aliens turned to look at her.

They weren't scary looking, like the monsters in Saturday afternoon movies. They looked, however inhuman, like people. She was conscious of the absurdity of her position. What did you say to aliens?"

"Um, she's my cat," Peggy began. "Look. Cat." She moved away from the end table, and the visitors went on guard. Were they armed? They didn't reach for any weapons, but Peggy's heart was pounding in terror. "Look." She edged over to the mantelpiece and showed them her collection of cat statues and mugs, all presents from her friends and relatives. "Cat. See?" She pointed to a narrow tapestry that hung beside the fireplace that depicted cats at play.

Enlightenment seemed to dawn on their little muzzles. They looked at Shalimar, who had put a paw down on one of the bronze plaques and was rubbing her jaw against it, and turned to Peggy. They retrieved the other two plaques and brought them to her.

The aliens only came up to her thigh. She had to reach down to accept the offerings, and wondered if they were radioactive.

"Um, thank you."

Peggy was conscious of the hopeful and expectant expressions on the little visitors' faces as she scanned the bronze squares.

Both plaques were identical. Etched into the surface of the metal were two images approximately the same height. Peggy recognized the shapes as being the aliens before her, but without their suits on. There were minor differences between the drawings, so she figured out they were meant to show two genders. She was faintly embarrassed to be looking at pictures of naked aliens. Beside one of the figures was a small circle with a tiny figure crouched inside.

"Oh, it's an egg!" Peggy said, with a surprised laugh. "Well, *we* have babies." She looked around until she spotted what she wanted. On her coffee table was a folding picture frame with facing portraits of her daughter and son. Both children were away at college. She wished they had been here with her now. With their love of weird movies and TV shows, they'd have handled an interplanetary diplomatic situation like old pros.

"My children," she said, holding her hand about waist-high. It was higher than the aliens' heads. so they probably didn't understand what she meant. "Wait a moment."

She bent beside her bookshelf, and went through the family photo albums until she came across that one embarrassing picture Ralph had taken of her when she had been pregnant with their daughter. She held out the photo to the aliens, and patted her belly.

"See?" she said. "We don't lay eggs. I mean, we keep the babies inside us. I mean, women do."

The aliens gabbled at one another, and looked back meaningfully at Shalimar, watching them cautiously from the window.

"Oh, she's not my child," Peggy said, addressing the round brown eyes. "She's my pet. Pet. I didn't give birth to her." She showed them the cat collectibles again, handing them a couple of the figurines to look at. The three passed the cast-resin tabby, the china Persian, and the carved ebony Abyssinian among themselves, then solemnly handed them back to her.

The spokesalien reached into his white pouch and came out with a small, oddly shaped device. It held it out to Peggy. She started to reach for it, but the creature snatched it away. Frightened, she jumped up and backed away.

"Don't hurt me," she said, keeping her hands up. She started to move toward Shalimar. Ralph ought to be home soon. If she could grab the cat and lock herself in the bedroom—but no, they could go through walls. What could she do?

The aliens, alarmed at her reaction, went into a huddle, and gabbled among themselves. They broke, then the leader held the device up at one of its companions. She heard a pinging sound. Slowly, the leader turned the device around and showed her the back. The flat glass plate held an image of the second alien.

"A camera?" she said. Her knees all but collapsed under her in relief. "Oh, yes, please. Photograph anything you want!" She gestured around the apartment. The aliens scooted happily past her, their devices pinging as they collected images of her apartment. Thank goodness the cleaning woman had come today, she thought. All the aliens converged on Shalimar, who swiveled her ears curiously this way and that as the devices pinged at her.

"Peggy?" Ralph scrambled in at the door of the living room. His eyes were wild, and his thin gray hair was askew. "Are you all right? Where are the . . ." He caught sight of the visitors. His mouth kept moving, but his voice died away to a whisper.

"It's all right, they're friendly," was all Peggy had time to say before a crowd of men in dark suits and dark glasses burst into the apartment. They all had guns drawn, and she let out a little squawk of protest.

"FBI, ma'am," said the largest man, flashing a billfold. Peggy glimpsed something flat and gold for a fraction of a second before he clapped it shut and put it back in his breast pocket. "Special Agent in Charge Lewis. Have they harmed you in any way?"

"No," Peggy said. "They've been very nice, and . . ."

"Get back, ma'am," said Agent Lewis, gesturing with his pistol. "You, too, sir." Peggy and Ralph flattened themselves against the wall next to the fireplace.

"My God, how'd they get in here?" one of the agents exclaimed, staring at the three visitors.

"There's a spaceship outside the window," Peggy said

helpfully. She leaned forward to point, and one of the agents pushed her back.

"Don't interfere, ma'am," said the agent. "This is a matter of national security." Three of the men hurried over to look out the window, and she saw their mouths drop open.

"Take 'em, boys," Lewis said. The agents tried to round up the little aliens, who stared at them with impassive looks on their cheetah faces. Just before a man touched one of the visitors, the little alien shimmered out of existence and reappeared behind him.

"What the . . . ?" he exclaimed. He spun around, bent over, and made a two-armed grab for his quarry. The visitor looked as bored as Shalimar as he shifted again, this time reappearing behind the cat's perch.

"You know, you haven't asked them yet," Peggy said, to the astonished faces of the agents. She was amazed herself at how calm and reasonable she sounded. She promised herself a nervous breakdown later. She didn't know what bothered her more, having aliens invade her living room, or having the FBI burst in. Peggy waved to get the spokesalien's attention.

"Go-with-them," she said, very carefully keeping her tone upbeat, as if she were talking to a toddler. She made scooping motions with her hands, and pointed at Agent Lewis. "Go with him. All right?"

The aliens chittered and jabbered among themselves, then formed a wedge with the leader at the front and the other two side by side behind. They marched over to Agent Lewis and looked up at him. Lewis stared from them to Peggy.

"They're really friendly," Peggy said. "All you have to do is show them what you want." Special Agent Lewis frowned at her, but he didn't hesitate any longer. He pointed toward the door. The three aliens blinked at him. They came over to Peggy, and crouched down, bending their knees and elbows outward as they ducked their heads. Then they went to Shalimar, and made even deeper obeisance to her. The cat crossed one forepaw over the other and narrowed her eyes at them.

"What is all that?" Ralph whispered to Peggy.

"Tell you later," she whispered back.

Lewis came over to herd the trio away from the cat, and led them toward the door. The rest of the agents fell in behind, sidearms at the ready. "By the way, where are you taking them?" Peggy called.

"You're done now, ma'am," Lewis said, over his shoulder. "Thank you for your assistance. Please don't discuss this with anyone at all. It is a matter of national security."

"But . . ." Peggy began.

"It's a very serious matter, ma'am." Lewis took off his glasses, revealing ice-cold blue eyes. Peggy immediately regretted cooperating with him.

The door boomed shut behind them. Ralph plumped down on the couch without really seeing it, and Peggy went to gather up Shalimar for a long-delayed hug. The cat nestled into her arms and let out a throaty purr.

"Oh, Ralph," Peggy said, feeling forlorn. "They were so nice!"

"Aliens?" Ralph asked blankly. "Nice?"

"Yes," she said, staring at him over the cat's head. He wasn't really hearing her, but he hadn't had time to get used to the little visitors as she had. "Now I'm going to worry about them. What's going to happen to them in the hands of people like that?" She shuddered, and felt as if she might burst into tears. That promised nervous breakdown was on its way. Shalimar nudged at her chin, and Peggy automatically started to scratch under the cat's ear.

Ralph sprang to his feet. "I'll call somebody," he said. "We donated plenty to the President's reelection campaign. Somebody owes us. I'll just go up the ladder until I find him."

Peggy hardly left the apartment for months for fear of missing a mention of her aliens on any of the news programs. She thought about the aliens daily. Her friends complained that she was preoccupied and withdrawn, and tactfully left open opportunities for her to share her worries with them. Peggy couldn't tell her concerns to anyone but Ralph, hampered as she was by the orders of that cold-hearted FBI agent and her own fear that her friends would think she was crazy. Well, she had no proof that they had even been there—nothing, that was, except the little plaque in Shalimar's basket. The silver saucer had vanished from outside her window just after the aliens had left with the government agents. Since then, she'd heard nothing.

"But we know they were here, don't we, precious?" she said to Shalimar. The cat just blinked her eyes and purred knowingly.

Ralph had pulled every string he could reach to get word. Once he'd gotten over the shock of finding aliens in his living room, he had been delighted, even thrilled, and asked Peggy for every detail, all over again. They called a high-ranking agent they knew in the local FBI office, but he couldn't help them. The subject had become "need to know only." No one who had been in on the pickup was talking. Even the *National Inquirer* was silent. Peggy was dying to call someone and ask, but it would start a train of inquiry that would lead the mean-looking Mr. Lewis right back to her. But she was still worried. She found herself looking out the window, hoping for a sight of the spaceship.

Overhead, she heard the ubiquitous sound of the traffic choppers. One of them got obnoxiously loud, and she turned the television volume up to drown it out. She heard a key in the lock, and Ralph's voice.

"Honey, are you here?" he cried. She ran to meet him. Ralph looked as excited as a schoolboy.

"Are they all right?" Peggy demanded, not even waiting for him to take off his jacket. "Oh!" she said, as she noticed a fresh-faced man in his thirties standing behind him.

"Peg, you remember Scott Papodopolous?" Ralph said, gesturing him forward.

"Of course. You're the White House chief of staff now, aren't you?" Peggy asked, offering her hand.

"Yes, ma'am," Scott said, smiling. He had very white teeth.

"Right," Ralph said. "He has a favor to ask you."

"Me?" Peggy asked. "Is this about you-know-who?"

Ralph laughed. "You can talk about the visitors with him. He not only knows who they are, he's seen them."

Peggy turned to the young man. "How are they? Are they alive? The government didn't do, you know, what they did to ET, did they?" Laughing, Ralph threw himself onto the couch and put his hands behind his head.

"Honey, you didn't have anything to worry about. Somebody who can go through walls isn't going to stick around for someone to dissect him," Ralph pointed out.

"No, indeed," Scott said. "NASA ran those little guys through every kind of test you can imagine, blood, tissue, stress, endurance, and they got through them all just fine. They have got blood, by the way. It's green. They'd do anything the testers wanted, as long as someone showed them what they wanted to do. Very obliging. Those little guys are pretty strong, got the Little Green Men's version of the Right Stuff."

"At least one of them was female," Peggy said defensively.

"How did you know that?" Ralph asked in amazement. Peggy borrowed the bronze plaque from Shalimar and showed it to them. Scott looked at it, and gawked. "You'd better not let anyone know you kept that," he said. He put it back out of sight under a cushion in the cat basket. Shalimar turned over and settled her furry tail across the place where it was hidden.

"How will anyone know?" Peggy said, watching him curiously. "I'll never see them again. Need to know, right? National security."

"I'm getting to that," Scott said, scratching the cat between her ears. "We have every major linguistics researcher in the country working on their language, but they haven't gotten very far yet. All they've figured out is that the visitors are peaceful. They're here as ambassadors."

"I could have told them that," Peggy said, impatiently. "I'm so glad they're safe."

"Better than safe. The President asked to meet them! The Secret Service brought the visitors to the White House and tried to explain to them in sign language that the President is the most important man in the world, but they don't buy it. The linguists get the idea that the aliens think the White House is too low to be important, if you know what I mean. The highest spot in Washington is the Monument. That may be why they came here in the first place. High place, high people. Maybe it's like that on their planet."

"Yes," Peggy said, with perfect understanding. "And so?"

"And so," Ralph continued, "the aliens showed the President your picture and Shalimar's. The President introduced them to his cat, and they went over and bowed down to it. The visitors seem to feel that showing respect for our deities will please us. Scotty thinks they think cats are our gods. They figured if the President had a cat, he was a decent, religious man. In a way, they're right thinking cats are sacred, considering what I spend on that animal."

"Oh, Ralph," Peggy chided him. "Well?"

"Well," Scott said. "After that, they got downright friendly with the President, but they still weren't convinced that he's in charge. They think you are." Peggy's mouth dropped open. He grinned at her expression of shock. "Well, you live in the highest place on the planet. That seems to have impressed them."

"So, what do they need from us?" Peggy asked, astonished.

"We want you to go to Washington," Scott said. "You and your cat."

"Us? Why?"

Scott raised his eyebrows and his hands. "So you and Shalimar can fix things up for him with the aliens. In the interest of national security. He can't go on CNN and say that aliens have landed, but they won't negotiate with him because he lives too close to the ground. In exchange, you have a standing invitation to stay at the White House, any time you like. What do you say?"

"Well, if our country needs us, of course we'll come," Peggy said, looking at Shalimar. "She has a travel cage. When?"

"Now," Scott said, promptly. "That's our helicopter

on the roof. We'll take it to the airport. My plane is waiting. Will you come? The President will be very grateful."

"Of course we'll come," Peggy said, elated. "I'll be thrilled to see them again, both the President *and* the visitors."

She could hardly say a word during the helicopter ride. Shalimar's travel cage was bundled up in quilts to protect her sensitive ears from the noise. The short trip to Washington in an official government jet left her speechless with awe. Ralph sat beside her, holding the hand that wasn't holding Shalimar's coop.

They transferred to another helicopter that dropped them off on the White House lawn. The President met them with a strong handshake and his trademarked smile.

"Glad you could come, Peggy."

"I'm happy to help, Mr. President," she said, shifting the heavy carrier on her hip.

Behind him, surrounded by Secret Service agents and armed servicemen, were Peggy's three alien visitors. Their brown eyes brightened when they saw her, and they began to jabber. Inside her coop, Shalimar heard familiar voices, and let out a chirrup. Peggy put the coop down and took the cat out into her arms. At once, the aliens broke away from their guards and came to surround the two of them, talking and bowing. She crouched down among them. It was funny. She'd only seen them once, when they'd scared the stuffing out of her, yet she felt responsible for them.

"I'm so glad to see all of you." Their chatter sounded fond, too, as if they were greeting an old friend. They made many soft comments that had Shalimar purring like an engine.

Scott whispered in Peggy's ear. "If you could take care of that situation right now?"

"Of course!" Peggy said. Beckoning the aliens over the President, she pointed at him. "You know me. I came from the place high up. Do you understand? This man is the leader of my country. The *most important* man." She held her free hand as high over her head as she could reach. "See? Him. High up." An inspiration hit her. She turned to the President and made the knees-out bow the little aliens had made to her. It was awkward and undignified, and she hoped no one had a camera. "He's the big boss. Get it?"

It seemed they did. They gathered around the President with their little cameras pinging away, chattering in their own language. The linguists moved in to surround them, and the small aliens were lost from view. Peggy, holding Shalimar in her arms, moved back out of the way, escorted by Ralph and a triumphant Scott.

Hundreds of newsmen crowded the White House lawn as the President made a momentous presentation to the world. The small aliens stood on a high platform beside the raft of microphones so they could be seen all the way at the back of the mob. More news vans arrived, and men in dark suits and dark glasses patrolled the lawn with dogs.

"We are most honored to welcome these visitors from another world," the President said, holding up his hands for silence. "We are honored that they have chosen this nation to begin their acquaintance with this world, and I hasten to assure our fellow nations of Earth that they will have equal access to our visitors and any information we glean about them.

"We hope that our relationship will be peaceful, leading us toward a future where we will walk among our neighbors from the stars. I want to thank everyone who has been responsible for helping to make this happen."

Standing amid the crowd of White House aides, Ralph nudged Peggy in the side. She cuddled Shalimar close and gave her a kiss on the top of her head. Shalimar, wary of the Secret Service dogs, crouched low in Peggy's arms.

"It seems that we already have much in common with our visitors," the president continued, giving his big smile to the news cameras. "It appears that they like cats, and any species who admires cats is all right with me."

Hearing the word "cats," Shalimar perked up and let out a trill.

"Shh, precious!" Peggy bent her head over her pet. She stroked the soft neck and looked down lovingly into the cat's lazy green eyes. "He can have all the headlines. But we both know who's really the most important being in the world, don't we?"

THE SEEPAGE FACTOR
by John DeChancie

John DeChancie has written more than twenty novels in the science fiction, fantasy, and horror fields, including the acclaimed *Castle* series, the most recent of which, *Bride of the Castle,* was published in 1994. He has also written dozens of short stories and nonfiction articles, appearing in such magazines, as *The Magazine of Fantasy and Science Fiction, Penthouse,* and many anthologies. In addition to his writing, John enjoys traveling and composing and playing classical music.

"Halt! Who goes there?"

In answer, a voice came out of the official-looking black limousine that had rumbled down the dusty desert road and pulled up to the gate.

"The President of the United States!"

"Huh?"

"You heard right, kid. He's in the car. Now, open up that gate and let us through."

"Hold it!" came another voice, one the guard instantly recognized. "Let me out."

"But, sir—"

"I'm going in alone, on foot."

"Sir, you can't do that."

"I can't do what?"

The limo's back door opened and out stepped a figure quite familiar. It was the President of the United States.

But the guard had orders.

The President stepped up to the gatehouse.

"Now, son, are you going to let me through? You know who I am."

"Sir, I can't. I have no orders about your coming here today."

"I know. Your superiors have pulled every trick to stall me. But it's time for this crazy secrecy to end. I'm pulling a surprise inspection of this installation, and no one is going to stop me. I am the Commander in Chief of the Armed Services of this country."

"Uh . . . yes, sir."

"Now, lift that gate and let me through. No one else is going in but me."

The Secret Service man who had followed the President out of the car protested, "Mr. President, you know that by law we must not let you out of our sight."

"Jerry," the President said, turning his head, "back off. This situation is without precedent. If there is some deep, dark secret in there that has to be kept, I don't want it to spread any farther than it has to. It stops with me. Understand?"

Jerry nodded. "Yes, sir. But keep in radio contact, please?"

The President held up his miniature walkie-talkie. "All the way. I'll keep a channel open."

Jerry wasn't satisfied. He shook his head worriedly. "But, sir, the *risk*."

"Jerry, if I can't trust the United States military to honor its Commander in Chief, who can I trust?"

"I suppose. But, sir, listen. I'll just—"

"Jerry, I have to do this myself."

Jerry nodded reluctantly. "Yes, Mr. President."

"I'll be okay." The President patted the dark suited Secret Serviceman's shoulder, then turned to the young gatekeeper. "Okay, son, lift her up. Tell your base commander I'm here, and ask him to meet me at that building right over there. That looks like an interesting place to start."

The guard was frantically punching numbers into his telephone.

"Mr. President!"

It was General Bradford J. Matson, Chairman of the Joint Chiefs of Staff, with an incongruously nonchalant smile. Returning the smile in spite of himself, the President shook his hand.

"This sun is a killer," the President said. "Why the heck do you guys always put secret bases smack in the middle of the desert?"

The Chairman's smile turned to an impish grin. "Because it's hot and sticky and miserable, and no one lives here."

The President's grin faded. "So you knew I was coming."

"Sure. I barely beat you here. Wish you hadn't, Mr. President. I tried to tell you that it was a matter best left undisturbed. That it had absolutely no bearing on national security."

"How could it not? How could the stuff I suspect is here not be a national security concern? Brad, tell me the truth, now. Is what I think is here really here?"

Brad shrugged noncommittally.

"Brad, please. This is insane. Isn't one of you guys—whoever you are, you guys in this . . . this CABAL that's kept the secret so long—isn't one of you guys ever going to break and let the damned President of the United States in on the biggest thing since the discovery of fire? In the campaign I swore I'd be the first president to get to the bottom of this business. And I'm keeping my pledge. Brad, I order you to answer me. Yes or no?"

Brad's nod was barely perceptible. A deep reluctance seemed to heave out of him. "Yes."

"You mean, the whole crazy story is true. The crashed saucer, the dead occupants—?"

"Not dead."

The President's jaw dropped. "You mean . . . you've got *live* ones here?"

"One. One live one."

The President rolled his eyes in disbelief. "Jesus have mercy. I can't . . . I just can't . . . Christ! All this time. How the hell did you do it? *Why* the hell did you do it?"

"Mr. President—"

"It's an outrage. To've kept the American people in the dark all this time, misleading them, bamboozling them. It's an absolutely outrageous usurpation of power, a shameful conspiracy. I mean, to do such a conniving—"

"Mr. President! Please. Once you know, you will understand."

The President threw up his hands and began to pace in an angry circle. "I'll understand? What the hell will I understand? You guys are nuts! You must be, trying to get away with a tawdry little charade like this. Did you think you could do it forever? Didn't you know that sooner or later someone would get into office who had the stones, who had the guts—"

"Do you know me?" Brad asked with pointed suddenness.

The President halted and turned to face him, looking suddenly deflated. "I've known you since we went to military school together. We've been friends for years. Of course I know you. Which only makes it more mystifying that you could take part in a plot to deceive me."

Matson straightened. "Mr. President."

The President took a deep breath. "Yes, General Matson?"

"If you know me," Brad went on, "then you know that my reason for not telling you has to be absolutely valid."

The President thought about it. Then he nodded. "I guess I do know that. But I can't possibly imagine why."

"It's time you found out," General Matson said. "No use trying to put it off any longer. Why haven't we told sitting presidents? Because it's simpler. If the President can credibly deny any knowledge, that makes the Big Lie all the more believable. And we need the Big Lie. Believe me, we need it. Just step into this building with me."

The President spoke into his walkie-talkie. "I'm going in now." Then to Brad: "But didn't Ike know?"

"Eisenhower knew. Truman knew before him. But Ike was the real architect of the conspiracy. He set it up. He instructed the cabal, as you call it—we call it the Investigating Committee—to refrain from telling any sitting president unless absolutely necessary. It never became necessary until you got a bee in your campaign bonnet. You backed us up against a wall. So here you are. And here we are."

They had entered the low concrete building and come to a set of elevator doors.

"Of course, the installation is deep underground," Brad said.

"How many are you?"

"The Investigating Committee? About a dozen people at the top. Perhaps one hundred lower-echelon workers and technicians."

"That few? But even at that, how the hell do you keep up the secrecy?"

"Those who are told are screened very carefully. The real reason, though, is that once any normal, rational person finds out, he or she instantly understands why the secret must be kept at all costs. That's how we've kept up this charade through almost three generations."

"Unbelievable."

"It is, a bit," admitted Brad with a smile. "But it's seeped out despite our best efforts."

"You mean, all this saucer business that's been brewing lately?"

"Sure. And it's not just lately. Remember the early days of the UFO flap? The space critter movies, the monster flicks?"

"In the fifties. Sure. I ate that stuff up as a kid."

"So did we all. That was an early manifestation of what we call the Seepage Factor. Somehow, this secret of ours has leaked into the popular consciousness by some process that is still completely obscure to us."

"Somebody's been talking."

Brad shook his head. "I don't think so. As I said, it's a mysterious process. Some kind of cultural osmosis." Brad shrugged. "Something."

"But it's all true. Isn't it? Everything the UFO nuts have been saying. It's all true."

Brad was still shaking his head. "Not exactly."

"Not exactly?"

"Not quite. They got it mostly right. But they don't know the biggest secret of all."

"Dear Lord. There's more?"

"Yes. It's how we know nobody's been deliberately leaking information, because we never hear evidence of anyone on the outside knowing the most crucial aspect of all this. Here we are, Mr. President."

"What crucial aspect?"

Brad Matson made no reply.

The elevator doors opened onto a circular hallway. Directly across the hall stood another set of doors, huge steel doors, quite formidable. A guard armed with an M-16 stood by.

On General Matson's signal, the guard turned and threw a switch. The big metal doors parted silently, giving access to another circular hallway, concentric with the first.

The general and the President went through two more sets of doors before arriving at a capacious concrete cavern at the center of which sat a metal dome, an enclosure of some sort, its side perforated with a row of windows.

"I'm getting a little scared," the President said. "All this security, those big doors."

"The security was designed in the early fifties, when no one could really assess the risk factors."

"And were these measures justified?"

"No, not really. It's very safe here."

"Then why keep up with all this?"

Brad shrugged. "You know the military. When in doubt, do it like it's always been done."

They walked across the huge concrete floor toward the dome.

"My God, Brad, what the hell do you have penned up here? Come on, the suspense is killing me."

Matson and the President drew up to the windows on the dome structure. The general pointed inside. "There it is."

"Jesus Christ!" The President's face blanched, and his eyes bulged almost comically.

There, on a strange lozenge-shaped bed inside the circular enclosure, lay an alien creature pretty much in line with the current media image. Skin a bloodless gray; heart-shaped head with huge almond eyes, shiny and reflective; a suggestion of a nose and mouth; diminutive humanoid body; tiny hands and feet. The body was dressed in a tight-fitting black suit with boots to match. There was something unreal about it. A movie in three dimensions. A cartoon come to life. It couldn't be real; yet there it was.

"I can't believe it!" the President almost shouted. "It's true. It's *all true!*"

Brad only nodded solemnly. "I still have trouble getting my brain around it. First time, my reaction was the same."

"This is fantastic," the President said after composing himself. "This is the biggest thing since . . . well, hell, there's nothing to compare it to. And you guys have kept it under wraps for . . . Christ, how long has it been?"

"Since the late 1940's," Brad said. "It's been a masterpiece of secrecy."

"Those eyes," the President said, shaking his head. "Spooky. Can it see us?"

"Oh, yes. It can see us. This isn't one-way glass."

The President turned his head sharply. "It isn't?"

"You, there," came a voice. That small slit of a mouth hadn't moved, but somehow the President knew it was the alien speaking.

The alien rose from the bed and came to the window. It did a strange thing. It took off its "eyes" to reveal a second pair underneath: the real ones. These were spherical and looked like an owl's.

"Jesus," the President said softly.

"Should have warned you," Brad said. "Those reflective coverings aren't part of its eye structure. Apparently it's hypersensitive to particulate matter in our atmosphere. And our sunlight gives it trouble. So it wears those things. Kind of like high-tech sunglasses. They're made of some organic material, we think; and we think it bonds with the creature's flesh in some way. So . . . well, you figure it out."

"I don't know which set of eyes creeps me out more," the President said.

"You," the alien said. Its mouth had barely moved, but the sound, coming through a speaker somewhere, had definitely originated from the alien.

"I sense you are in authority. I have been telling your underlings that they are soon to die. You might as well hear it directly. Your world is doomed. Even as we speak, a mighty armada of warships is on its way from your moon to crush this planet. Our race is all but divine, our command of the physical sciences unsurpassed. Tongues of plasma will leap from our ships to burn your cities to ashes. Bombs and missiles will reduce to rubble what remains. Your kind will be driven into the wilderness to exist like animals, and then we will hunt you down until the last of you is exterminated."

The creature slapped its "sunglasses" back on with a curious clicking sound.

Chilled to the very core of his being, the President could not bring himself to speak.

The alien went on, "For years we have drawn our plans against you. Operating from bases on the far side of your moon and from remote locations around your solar system, we have infiltrated the highest levels of your governments. We control the secret levers of power. We can subvert from within any organized resistance. You cannot win. We shall conquer. We shall have this planet of yours for our own. Nothing you can do will avert this fate."

"Christ," the President said. He whirled on General Matson. "This is like some damned movie. This is mind-boggling. Brad, what can we do?"

General Matson was smiling oddly. "They're telepathic, you know. Play back the tape of his speech and it sounds like babble. Yet when it speaks, you understand. We haven't quite figured out the process yet. He is speaking English, somewhere among those hisses and grunts. But if it weren't for the telepathy—"

"Brad, for Christ's sake, don't you hear what it's saying?"

"Yes, Mr. President, I hear. A mighty armada is approaching."

The President swallowed brassy-tasting bile. "Well?"

General Matson's mouth acquired a scornful curve. "There ain't any armada."

"Jesus, Brad, how do you know?"

"Because, Mr. President, we have eyes in the sky. If a task force of alien spaceships was threatening Earth, we would know. There isn't anything approaching Earth. There isn't a single anomalous thing out in space that we can see, much less a fleet of spaceships."

"Then the damned thing is lying?"

Brad shrugged. "Mr. President, there's something you must understand. This creature has been making these same threats for the last fifty years. None of what it's saying has ever panned out. There aren't any bases on the far side of the moon. We've been to the moon, and there's nothing, absolutely nothing there."

The President exhaled. "Then, there's no immediate cause for alarm?"

"There never has been. Ask it to tell you of their other bases throughout our solar system. On the moons of Jupiter, on Titan, Saturn's moon, or on Mercury. It says there are military installations all over the solar system. Ask it about these huge warships. It'll tell you they're bigger than some asteroids and have black holes as energy sources. Ask it. It'll tell you. It'll talk for hours and hours."

"And none of it's true?" the President asked breathlessly.

"We've sent out probes to the planets, we've watched the heavens for decades. Not just the government. Every night all around the world, tens of thousands of amateur astronomers search the heavens for signs of movement. Any movement against the backdrop of stars. Sometimes they find things. Usually, it turns out to be a comet. Since the date this being crashed his space vehicle on this planet, no one around the world has spotted a single suspiciously extrasolar thing out there. No one. Nothing."

"Then there is no invasion."

Brad shrugged. "We've been waiting for it for years. At first, the Investigating Committee took the creature at its word. Shock waves of alarm went through the defense establishment. You might even blame some of the Cold War—both sides; who knows what the Russians got wind of—on the fear this creature generated with its tirade. He hasn't changed it in years. That little speech he gave—I've heard it thousands of times. It never varies, never changes with current events. Of course, it doesn't know what's been going on. We've told it nothing. It doesn't know that we've been on the moon."

"But we haven't been on the far side of the moon," the President said. "Have we?"

Brad chuckled. "Maybe you're forgetting? We've seen the far side, mapped it, radar-imaged it, computer-imaged it. Nothing there, Mr. President. Nothing there that shouldn't be there. Nothing on any of the moons of the other planets, the ones we've managed to get to. Nothing on Mars, despite the flap over the Martian 'Face.' That's Seepage. The Face, indeed." The general chuckled again. "It's uncanny how the media seems to have an antenna that picks this stuff up out of the ether."

"But I still don't get it," the President said. "There it stands. That's an alien creature. You said it crashed its ship here. Anything left of that?"

"Scraps," Brad said. "Not much. Nothing we've ever been able to piece back together. For all we know, that 'ship' might have been merely a capsule, a lifeboat or something. It had no propulsion system that we could discern."

"Yet this critter's standing in front of us, Brad. It exists."

"Sure it does. But we don't know where it comes from, or why it's here, or how it got here."

"Haven't you been talking to it all these years?"

Brad shook his head sharply. "You can't talk to it. It keeps reciting that jeremiad you heard, prophesying doom. Our scientists have tried for decades to get something of substance out of it. It simply launches into its spiel every time, tirelessly repeating it over and over. I've learned to tune it out, really."

"This is . . ." The President regarded the creature with a look of profoundest perplexity. "I can't understand any of this."

The walkie-talkie blurted, *"Mr. President?"*

"I'm fine," the President said into the instrument.

"You are doomed," the creature stated flatly. Then it

turned away from the window and went back to the bed, where it lay down again, to stare at the curved ceiling.

A faint light of comprehension glimmered in the President's eyes. "You mean . . .?"

Brad nodded, grinning bleakly. "Totally insane. That's what we concluded long ago. Whether it's the result of a disease process or injuries from the crash, we don't know."

"Haven't you examined the thing, done tests on its physical makeup?"

"Over and over. It's DNA structure isn't that much different from ours in principle. The scientists say that's very interesting, and indicates a lot about evolutionary processes on other planets. But, frankly, nothing the scientists have come up with is at all startling in any way. It's of interest only to biochemists. And not all that interesting, either, so they tell me. To date, this creature has given us nothing but conundrums."

"I can't get over it. There it is, a creature from another world. Crazy as a bedbug."

"That's about the size of it. You see, now, don't you?"

The President nodded ruefully. "Panic. Utter panic would result if you'd let the media in here. They'd smear the critter's spiel all over the airwaves."

"Who wouldn't have believed it, back then—or now, for that matter? Who could guess that what it's saying is pure delusional raving? Not many. Only us few. And we didn't cop to that for years. Years and years. We sweated. A good thing we took on this burden. The world would never have survived it."

The President walked away from the window, taking Brad in tow. "But listen, isn't there a chance it's telling the truth? Aren't distances between stars vast? Couldn't the armada be on its way here? Maybe these critters are long-lived."

"Oh, we think they are," Brad said. "This one hasn't aged one iota since it arrived. Very long-lived, probably. But if the armada is on its way, why would this individual be warning us so far in advance? Why does it keep parroting that speech about bases on the moon? Why the fixation on a seemingly preset line of rhetoric? Why the paranoiac flight of ideas? Mr. President, after you spend some time with this creature, you know intuitively that it's deeply psychotic. It has very little sense of reality. Granted, we know nothing of its psychological makeup. We don't know what 'insanity' means in a creature of this sort. But intuitively, you can sense its lack of rationality. This is a pathological individual."

"The ships are coming."

The creature was back at the window. The President wheeled around to look at it.

"The ships are coming, and you are doomed. From your own moon, they come. They will fill your skies with their bulk. They will blot out the sun. They will flatten your cities—"

The President grunted. "Seepage."

"What do the psychologists call its tone of voice? 'Flat affect?' It's almost as if it doesn't believe itself."

"No, it's never been passionate or demonstrative. It doesn't seem to have real emotion. It's . . . it's sick. It's not well. And it keeps raving on, year after year."

The President flopped his hands over helplessly in a gesture of despair. Here, for anyone who could gain access to this place, was a glimpse into the deepest mysteries of the universe. But to look was not to comprehend. It was simply Mystery, dark and impenetrable. A select few of the country's top scientists had spent decades trying to crack the problem. Even if the President of the United States ordered up a new investigation, even if efforts were redoubled, what were the chances that a solution would be found? And what about the increased risk of the secret getting out? A leak would be disastrous. He could see, now, why the conspiracy had been absolutely necessary. No, there was nothing to be done. Nothing at all. The President heaved a deep sigh, and out of him came every hope of understanding.

He turned his back and walked away.

The yellow-red afternoon sun declined over a line of mesas in the distance. Otherwise, the bleak landscape offered for viewing only an occasional Joshua tree or clump of sagebrush as miles of bare dirt rolled by.

The President of the United States sat staring out the window. He hadn't said a word since he'd come out of the installation and gotten back into the limo.

In a forced jovial tone, Jerry ventured, "Mr. President, I get the feeling that we'll never know what's in that secret base. Am I right, sir?"

The President turned his head, a wryness barely curling the corners of his mouth.

"What secret base are you talking about, Jerry?"

THE ALLURE OF BONE AND ICE

by Linda P. Baker

Linda Baker is the author of the novel *The Irda*. Her short fiction also appears in *New Amazons* and *Dragonlance: The Dragons of Krynn*. She and her husband, Larry, live in Mobile, Alabama.

From sound came silence and from light, sudden darkness. Black as pitch, with not even a touch of gray to mark the end of the tunnel.

The bright, white light, when it came, was for a moment as blazing as the sun. A hot circle of lustrous silver, painfully skewering the back of Patrick's eyes. As always, it calmed him, thrilled him, and he breathed deeply, taking in the scents of rubber and nylon.

Around him, there was the whisper of breaths, just like his, sucked deep into lungs then let out again, slowly, quietly. The hush before the battle.

More lights joined the first, hot white, warm gold, glowing purple. The bright spots of color circled, turned, twisted, threatened to become something recognizable, then just as quickly danced away again. Stabilized into hot, steady circles of light.

The quiet was broken. Booming, raucous noise. Then the voice, so loud it vibrated inside his skull, echoed off the walls. "Welcome to the dungeon!" Thousands of voices raised in protest, in approbation.

Patrick's teammates surged forward, eager to step into the tunnel, the long taped ends of their hockey sticks held aloft in the air.

"Is she here tonight?" An elbow jabbed playfully into Patrick's ribs, a stick tapped his helmet, as Matt hissed the question over the noise.

Patrick, jostled in the crunch of bodies waiting at the end of the darkened tunnel, had no time to answer before another voice joined in. "She? Did you say *she?* Patrick's got a girlfriend?"

"Not a girlfriend. A good luck charm," Matt supplied.

"A charm?" Larry shoved forward, past the two of them and peered into the darkness of the auditorium, as if he could see past the dancing lights.

Patrick shot Matt a murderous look, but the smaller man just grinned at him, showing a black gap where his front teeth should have been.

Larry turned back. "So . . . Is she here?"

"She who?" Another of the big defensemen shoved forward and mimed peering into the darkness. "One of Patrick's aliens?"

"It was only bright lights," Patrick protested. "I never said it was an alien."

Before Craig could respond, the announcer started calling out the names of the starting lineup, and Patrick was shoved forward with the rest of his linemates. He was the third to step forward into the swirling lights. Into a cacophony of music and screaming fans and razor-thin blades on ice, all echoing back at him from the dome overhead.

The moment his skates touched the ice, he knew she was in the stands. He could feel it in the way his feet shot out of the tunnel, carrying him into the spotlight, sure and fast and smooth. He circled the half of the rink that was designated his team's, his legs warming to the motion of skating. The ice was smooth as silk, as glass. He didn't even feel the little bumps and cuts that were part of the surface.

As his teammates took their places on the ice or the bench, and the national anthem was sung, he looked for her. He scanned the tiers of seats stepping away up to the ceiling of the auditorium. She was never in the same place from one game to the next, but he knew she was there. The ice never felt as smooth when she wasn't.

He started at one end and scanned slowly until he found her, midway up in the opposing team's end. She was easy to spot. She was wearing white. She always wore white. White cap, white sweater, white pants. Glowing in the darkened arena.

As the whistle blew to start the game, and the crowd screamed in anticipation, Larry skated past him. "Is she here?"

Patrick nodded, glanced at the stands again, just checking, and waited for the gibe. He knew it was coming, knew he should never have mentioned her to Matt. But none came. Instead, Larry touched the team logo on his shoulder, grinned as he slipped his mouthpiece over his teeth and mumbled around it, "For luck."

Patrick couldn't help but grin back. He slipped blue, molded plastic over his own teeth, worked it with his tongue until it seated properly. The taste of rubber filled his mouth, the puck dropped and he skated.

There was nothing he loved so much as the game. On a good night, it was almost as good as sex. Almost. There was something delicious and primal about slamming an opponent into the boards.

Sometimes, he wondered whether his teammates analyzed their love of the ice. Did they think about the crash of the hit, the glass vibrating in its metal slots, the whoosh as air left a rival's lungs, as his body was squashed? He didn't think they did, and he didn't feel comfortable asking.

But now . . . Right now, even he didn't stop to question his elation. It was enough that he was everywhere the puck was, working both sides of the ice with equal ferocity. The thirty pounds of pads floated on his body as if they were nothing. The ice was like glass and the puck was wherever he wanted it to be. He knew what was going on behind him, beside him, across the rink. He skated as if he couldn't fall, couldn't fail.

And when it was over, and they had beaten their opponents by a record-breaking 11-3, he knew he'd played the game of his life.

The horn sounded to signal the end of the game, and his teammates converged on the goalie at the end of the huge oval, pounding each other on the back and whacking each other with their sticks.

Patrick hung back, looking for her among the milling crowd in the stands, but he couldn't see her. He never did, after a game started or after it ended. So he skated into the thick of the celebration and allowed himself to be whisked off the ice, to showers and more congratulations.

The night was warm, unnaturally so to Patrick. He was Canadian born, raised in Quebec, and despite two seasons in the south, he was not used to warm November nights. He was not quite sure he would ever be, but it was something he could bear.

For the chance to play professional hockey, there was much he would bear. Even living in the heart of the southern United States, where he stuck his hand out the patio door every morning to gauge what to wear, where his new friends wore shorts and played tag football on Christmas day. Back home, had he ventured out in December, the only part of him visible through layers of coat and hat and scarf would be his blue eyes.

But he was adjusting. He would adjust to anything to feel the way he felt tonight.

He sucked the rich, humid Alabama air into his lungs, brought his elbows up, and swung his arms back in a wide arc. There was a sore spot in the middle of his back, another the size of his fist above his right elbow. And his thighs had that warm, mushy feeling of being worked beyond the point of exhaustion. It felt fantastic.

"Great game, Patrick!" A stranger punched him lightly on the shoulder as he walked past. He was a young man, wearing a white, home game jersey, and he had his arm around the shoulders of a woman wearing a purple, away game jersey. The woman smiled back at him, bright green eyes in a rounded, rosy face.

Another group swept past him, three adults and a gaggle of children clutching miniature souvenir hockey sticks in their fists. "That's Patrick," one of the little girls told another in an awed whisper.

Patrick smiled at her and waved. Fans. Another thing to which he was adjusting. Perhaps if his English was

better . . . So often, in the midst of a crowd, English—
which he had learned in school but rarely used—spoken
in slow Southern drawl left him feeling totally alone. He
wound up nodding and signing grubby little hockey
sticks and smiling until his jaws ached without knowing
what he was smiling about.

But tonight . . . he could smile all night. He used the
back entrance to the hotel and edged into his seat in the
dining area just as the most of the others were starting
their dessert.

He gulped his food, skipped the dessert and joined his
teammates in the lobby where a roomful of after game
supporters were milling around, waiting to collect
autographs.

He waded into the thickest of the crowd and began.
Smiling, nodding, signing. Patrick Packaen, #19. Over
and over.

Gradually he realized there were very few of the comments he wasn't understanding. They were mostly of the
"great game" variety, but it was amazing, the way the
melodious Southern voices seemed suddenly to be
speaking a language as natural to him as his own French.
The transition was as smooth as stepping onto the ice.

He glanced up, the fat, black pen in his fingers forgotten, and she was there. Across the room, standing in a
crowd around one of the goalies.

White sweater glowing in the darkened room. Dark,
very dark hair. White skin. She was looking at Nicky,
head in profile. There was a man beside her, holding out
a program book to Nicky, and Patrick couldn't tell
whether she was with him or not. The thought that she
might be caused a flush of totally irrational irritation.
He didn't even know her.

The kid whose stick he was holding tugged on his
pants imperiously, and Patrick apologized and finished
his autograph.

"Sorry," he mumbled and went on to the next one.
When he looked up again, she was gone. It suddenly
seemed that everyone was speaking a vaguely foreign
language again. And wasn't that a silly thought, that the

mere presence of another person could make him hear better!

Still he looked for her in the crowd. Even after it thinned and was mostly friends of the players and friends of friends, he couldn't find her.

"Hey, come on, Patrick!" Matt grabbed one arm and Larry the other. "Come up and have a beer with us."

He rode to the seventeenth floor crammed into an elevator with five of his teammates and twice as many fans. They all seemed to be talking and laughing at once. Over their unintelligible voices, he could hear the creaking of the elevator cables.

He mumbled a prayer in French that they hadn't over-filled the elevator, and the woman who was crushed up against his ribs grinned at him. He didn't quite under-stand what she said, but the meaning of it wasn't impor-tant anyway. She was small and blonde and her eyes were even bluer than his own.

He was just dredging up the courage to ask her name when the elevator doors swooshed open, spilling the mass of bodies into the short hall that led to the bar. She stayed in step with him until they reached the dou-ble doors, and the smoky, beer smell of the bar wafted over them. After that, he had no idea where she went.

"Ça porte bonheur," he muttered under his breath. *Good luck.* She was standing across the room, staring out the floor-to-ceiling windows that overlooked the en-tire downtown area of the city. In the middle of a crowd, but still, somehow, alone.

"Hey-y-y, is that her?"

Larry crowded him several steps across the room be-fore Patrick could dig in his heels and refuse to move. He nodded and resisted the insistent grip Larry had on his arm.

"Hey, come on, man. Let's go meet her!"

His feet seemed frozen to the floor. Patrick shook his head, disentangling his forearm from Larry's fingers. *"Non. Non. Ça porte malheur."* At Larry's puzzled look, he realized he'd reverted to his native French, and he struggled to bring the right words to his tongue. "Not good. Bad. Bad luck. It would be bad luck."

Larry gave him a crooked smile, revealing even white dentures. "Not for me, bud."

Patrick hung back as Larry worked his way through the crowd, went up behind the woman and started talking to her. Bad luck or not, he couldn't stay where he was. His feet, which had formerly been so insistent on staying put, now edged him closer. Around a table, through a group of young women surrounding Nick, until he was standing at the glass, too, only a few feet from Larry and the woman.

She was younger than he'd thought, but still probably a couple of years older than his twenty-five years. Tall and curvy and beautiful, almost untouchably so. Strangely beautiful, as if her face had been put together out of separate pieces. As if someone had taken pictures of beautiful women and chosen features from them, a nose from one, eyes from another, chin from another, and plunked them all together on this woman's face. All beautiful features, but strangely not quite knit together.

He was staring, and he only realized it when he saw that both she and Larry had stopped talking and were staring back at him. He grinned and jerked his gaze away, felt heat creeping up from underneath his collar.

"Patrick." Larry reached out and grabbed him by his collar. "Meet Karisa."

He obviously mangled the name badly, because she repeated it for Patrick, and it came out more like Karacea. A strange name, fitting for so strange a face. Almost French, but not quite.

He nodded shyly and allowed Larry to drag him closer. "I told Karisa about your close encounter. She says she's seen them, too," Larry explained, pointing at the sky, barely visible through the heavy condensation on the window.

Patrick glanced at her again, then at Larry. His teammate raised and lowered his eyebrows at him, grinning widely.

"I never said I saw a UFO," Patrick protested.

"I'll leave you two to get acquainted," Larry said with exaggerated, uncharacteristic politeness. He wiggled his eyebrows again, and as he slipped past, whispered, "This one'd be better off with Nickle. That boy just ain't right, and neither is she!"

Patrick looked after his teammate, then back at Karacea.

She was smiling at him as if she'd heard Larry and thought it funny rather than offensive. "Your friend doesn't believe in aliens."

"It was just bright lights. Probably a helicopter." Patrick cleared a spot on the fogged over window and peered down at the street. It was still busy, crawling with cars heading toward the freeway, their lights reflected in the glass of the buildings. Far off in the distance, he could see the lights from Battleship Park, the place where all the old ships and planes were displayed.

"Do you?" Karacea moved a little closer. Her hair was jet black, shinier than his, long and ropy.

He shifted a little closer, too, inhaled. She gave off no scent! He expected perfume or shampoo or soap, but there was nothing in his nostrils except the smoke from a nearby cigarette. He was so surprised she had to repeat her question before it registered. "Do I what?"

"Believe in aliens?"

"No. Do you?"

She smiled brilliantly, exposing bright white teeth. "Of course. Don't you think it would be sad if we were the only ones in the universe?"

He shrugged. "I suppose."

She stood there, the top of her head barely reaching his shoulder, face tilted back so she could look up at him. It seemed she was waiting for him to continue.

"You bring me luck!" he blurted suddenly, and instantly felt like a fool.

"I do? How?"

He could feel his neck turning red again. "At the games . . . I skate better when you're there." The red climbed all the way to the roots of his hair. Now he'd compounded his error by telling her he'd been watching her. Next he'd be telling her he could hear better when she was in the room.

"You knew I was there? But, of course, you would know me. Just as I knew you."

Her voice had started out with a delighted pitch to it, then switched over to puzzlement, then back to delight. It was like a musical instrument, and he had heard the rise and fall of it, but he didn't quite comprehend the music. "Eh-h?" He leaned closer to her, thinking as he always did, that if he got closer, he would understand better.

"Listen—" She laid a hand on his arm. "Would you like to—? Well, it's so noisy in here." She indicated the bar, growing more crowded by the moment, with a quick gesture of her head. "We could go for a walk."

He could feel the warmth of her fingers all the way through his jacket. His body, tired and bruised from combat, stirred to life. He nodded, wordlessly, and trapped her fingers between his forearm and ribs as he turned.

Through the crowded bar, the hallway, into the elevator, she left her hand tucked beneath his arm. Once there, she extricated it and put it to better use. She moved her hands across his shoulders, his biceps, more as if she were exploring than caressing. "What a wonderful world, to have such creatures in it," she said softly. Her fingers slipped over his chest, moved down to his ribs as if she were carefully counting every one. "You're so hard."

Words like that, he had no difficulty understanding. "There's more," he invited, moving her back against the wall, his hands reaching greedily to see if she was as soft as he was hard.

She tilted her head back as if inviting his kiss, but when his lips touched hers, she jumped. Her fingers flexed at his waist. A startled gasp escaped into his mouth. She permitted the contact and slowly pressed back, but without moving her lips.

Then the elevator doors were whooshing open, and he backed away. She slipped out, through the crowd waiting to get on, leaving him behind.

He pushed past the outstretched adult hands containing programs and pens, but he couldn't bear to bypass the kids. By the time he'd signed all the programs and T-shirts and banners, Karacea was nowhere in sight.

He hurried out to the street, thinking she might be

waiting outside, but the parking lot was full of empty cars and shadows. There was no one moving on the sidewalk in either direction.

He stood on the edge of the sidewalk and bounced up and down on his toes, feeling the grab and stretch in his calves. Where could she have gone so fast? There was no car driving away slowly, no sound of an engine warming in the parking lot.

A light rain had fallen while he was inside, coating the black asphalt with a shiny layer of moisture, reflecting the pinkish glow of the streetlights.

He glanced up. The rain had cleared the mist from the sky and, even with the light pollution, he could see the stars, bright pinpricks against the night sky.

As he watched, the brightest speck seemed to twinkle faster, brighter. It grew from a pinhead to a spot the size of a dime. To a quarter! It looked like the lights he had seen last month when he'd gone to the Island with a group of friends, except those dancing lights had seemed strangely familiar and comforting. Those dancing lights had moved across the sky, not downward!

Whatever it was was falling. Falling fast. Falling right toward him. He took a step back. Another. It was still coming, too bright to be anything but a star. And it was going to fall right on top of him. Right into the parking lot.

He took two running steps backward, toward the hotel entrance, still unable to take his eyes from the plummeting object. Bright white light, streaking straight toward him.

His heels caught on the high relief edge of the grass. Like a skater on a breakaway caught on the receiving end of a stick, he sat down, hard. His teeth clicked together. His hands caught at the wet grass, scrabbled for purchase.

He scrambled back, feet pumping, butt scooting across the grass, until his head hit the brick wall of the building. Still his feet kept moving and he pushed, climbing the wall with his shoulders and hands.

And the star kept coming! Falling toward him!

The bricks with their glue of concrete scraped his

palms, snagged at his jacket, but he pushed until he was standing, back against the hotel. *Run!* his mind commanded. *Run!* The muscles in his thighs bunched, lifted. His knee came up. His foot came up, but it all seemed in slow motion. Like running in dream, like running in molasses.

He sidestepped and stepped again, back still pressed into the wall, but there was nowhere to go. The star was upon him! He hunched, curling his shoulders, arms coming up to protect his belly, the way he would ward off a heavy check against the boards. He squinted against the explosion he knew would be next, but it never came.

The white light swooped toward him, bleaching the color out of the ground in a fifty-foot circle, and instead of crashing, whooshed up and away in a graceful loop.

Where the light had touched him, at temple, shoulder, hip, and thigh, his skin tingled. The thing swooped at him again, coating him in light that was cool and smooth and crackled like cellophane on his flesh.

Fear knotted the muscles in his stomach. He crouched tighter, assuming an almost fetal position. The brick wall was rough against his face.

The light zoomed away, looping high up over the parking lot. He could see nothing inside of it, just a shape-shifting rainbow of light. He unwound his tall body, took a step toward the door.

The thing dipped toward him again. Sparks flew outward in a half sphere where the light hit the brick wall in front of his face. Chips of mortar and red brick stung the backs of his hands. The light backed away, flung itself at the wall again.

It was herding him back, away from the door. It wanted him out in the open.

Suddenly, as suddenly as the light had been there, she was there. Karacea. Dark hair flying as she ran across the grass.

The shower of brick and sparks ceased. He came up, fists clenched, ready to fight, but she was between him and the light, protecting him from it. Touching it. Her hand outstretched, melting in the brightness.

Where her arm met the light, it disappeared. She looked like some terrible, white Statue of Liberty with the stump of one arm raised.

He gasped. He was a brave man to the point of foolhardiness. No one cowed him on the ice, not a better skater, not a bigger skater, not a fiercer skater. No one cowed him *off* the ice. But this . . . This was something he did not know. His mind didn't even quite comprehend it. He saw with his eyes. The image skittered down the pathways to his brain, but his brain rejected it. Stars didn't come down from the sky to attack. Women didn't melt into them.

Too much to drink. He backed away slowly, wiping the sweat from his face. Trying to wipe some sanity in. He couldn't remember drinking that much, but drunk was an explanation he could comprehend. He backed away faster.

Before he'd gone ten feet, Karacea turned back to him, detaching herself from the light. First her arm, then her slender, white wrist reappeared. Then finally her hand, whole and undamaged. The light twinkled and bulged behind her, faded, slowly slipping away.

She smiled as if she understood how odd he felt. "It's all right. They are not here for you. It is only an urging . . . to me. They grow impatient." She searched the sky as if she would pick out the falling star, shining in the sky.

"Impatient?" Some semblance of sanity was beginning to return. He could hear his own breathing, as harsh as if he'd just skated wind sprints around the rink. Feel the pounding of his heart, threatening to burst from his chest. "For what?"

"For me to complete my mission. They think I'm taking too long. It's just that . . . I want to be sure you're ready. And I've so enjoyed watching you. Seeing your . . . ice game."

"Hockey," he corrected automatically.

She nodded and held out her hand. "Perhaps they are right. Perhaps you are ready."

"Ready for what?"

"To go with me. To go home."

He stared at the hand she was extending. Long, slender fingers. Beautiful white skin. The hand which had melted.

Patrick ran like something was pursuing him.

When he got to his car, folded his long legs inside, had slammed and locked the door, he risked a glance back over his shoulder. The parking lot was empty. In the pinkish glow of the streetlights, there were only light poles, dangling their globes from extended arms, and the few cars, reflected in the wet pavement.

There was only him and the strangled sound of harsh, frightened breathing. Careful to check the lock before he closed his eyes, he leaned his forehead on the steering wheel until his breathing slowed, until the fear had let go of his shoulders.

Patrick woke to the loud, insistent ring of his alarm, his brain as fuzzy as a tongue after an all-night beer party. He was lying on his back on his bed, on top of the comforter. He was alone, still wearing all the clothes he'd worn to dinner. Still wearing his shoes.

He struggled for a moment with his thoughts, like wrestling wet pasta, and dimly remembered stumbling through the dark apartment, falling back onto the bed, exhausted and drunk. No, not drunk. He'd only had a couple of beers. Something else . . .

He couldn't think with the alarm ringing and ringing and ringing, and he slammed his fist down on top of the clock radio. The snooze button clicked under the weight of his hand, but the ringing continued. Loud. Demanding. Like a telephone.

He struggled up on his elbows. It *was* a phone ringing. His phone. He slumped back down and dragged the receiver to his ear. "Hello?"

"Pac, where the hell are you? Larry's voice hissed in his ear. His tone was pissed and worried and whispering. "Coach is yelling his head off."

"Oh, shit, what time is it?" He rolled, squinting to see the red letters on the front of his alarm clock, but he didn't really need to see them to know he was late for practice.

In the background, behind Larry's voice, he could hear the rattle of hockey sticks, the hiss of the propane torch the equipment manager used to repair the aluminum sticks. That meant Larry was crouched behind the manager's worktable, out of sight of the coach, with the phone line stretched across the floor.

Patrick swung his legs off the bed, rolled to a sitting position. His head really didn't feel that bad. He was just a little groggy, a lot better off than he had been in the past after too much drinking.

But you didn't have too much . . . that niggling little voice said at the back of his head. He tilted his head back, squeezing it toward his shoulders, hoping to stifle the voice, because something told him looking at other possibilities for the night's events was much worse than drinking too much before a practice day.

"—better get over here fast!" Larry was hissing in his ear, in almost the same tone as the torch in the background, something about practice and having to do wind sprints around the ice.

Patrick cupped the phone between his ear and shoulder and used the heel of his hand to scrub at his forehead. His hand came away gritty, as if his skin was covered with flakes of concrete. With dawning horror, with dawning remembrance, he stared at his palm.

"Pac, are you there? Hey!"

Don't think about it. Just move. He shook the memories away. Crazy dreams. Too much to drink. "I'm on my way," he growled into the phone and shoved himself off the bed, galvanized.

He was dressed, at the rink, redressed in his pads and warm-up jersey and on the ice in record time. The ice welcomed him, clean and smooth from a recent resurfacing.

"Packaen!" the coach bellowed the moment he saw him. "Give me twenty laps around the rink!"

Patrick grinned. The coach in drill sergeant mode, that was something he understood. He stretched quickly, efficiently, and set out around the edge. The cool wind, caressing his face as he moved faster and faster, circling his teammates, cleared his head. His feet, moving without conscious guidance, gliding across ice smooth as glass, calmed him.

As he skated, he tried to remember exactly what the woman had said last night. Something about going home? Something about him knowing her? His frown came back. He didn't believe in any of that junk. Bright lights in the sky. Hands disappearing.

Then the coach was yelling again, calling him into the drill, and he had no more time to think.

The coach was pissed. Pissed at him for being late. Pissed at Jace for missing the net on his scoring runs. Pissed at Larry for missing the puck at the blue line. Pissed at Swan for missing his blocks. Pissed at both goalies for missing their saves.

He worked them harder than he'd ever worked them before. He made them repeat and repeat their patterns, their drills. And when Patrick's ankles were beginning to tremble with exhaustion, wobbling like a kid new to the ice, the coach put them back into warm-up drills. Then more wind sprints around the ice.

By the time he let them go, Patrick was too exhausted to even shower. He just stood under the hot water and let it sluice over him.

The locker room was too quiet as he dressed. The others were as exhausted as he, too tired to jeer and toss towels across the room and slam their lockers as they normally did. He dragged his sweater on over his head and left his wet hair to dry as it would. It would have taken too much effort to lift his arms and comb it.

Larry punched him on the shoulder as he left. "Wanta go for a beer?"

Patrick shuddered and waved him off. All he could manage was to grunt a good-bye. It was already dark by the time he was outside. Practice had lasted even longer than he realized.

He glanced up once and felt a pang of fear at all the stars visible in the inky sky. But they all stayed in place, and he trudged back toward his car with his head down, shoulders slumped.

There was more chill in the air than there had been yesterday, and as he struggled to wiggle his fingers past the flaps on his jacket pockets, he almost ran head-on into Karacea.

She was standing in the middle of the sidewalk, smiling her brilliant smile, and he was absolutely sure she had not been there a moment before.

He froze, fingers curling into fists half in half out of his pockets. Adrenaline and arousal surged through him with a strength he would not have thought his tired body could manage.

She was there, smiling at him. Not a drunken dream. A real woman, soft and warm and smelling of nothing. Images of the night before flashed through his mind, of her body against his.

But if she was real . . . His gaze darted upward, and it was there. The falling star. Bright speck the size of his fist, hovering just above the roofline of the rink.

He turned to run, mind already working feverishly. What was safest? Back toward the rink? Into the bushes? Stupid thought! A light that could crack bricks wouldn't be stopped by bushes. But could it find him inside?

"Patrick. Please don't go." Her voice was like light, clear and silvery, as velvety as the glow from a yellow bulb.

He turned back to her, reluctantly, almost as if he didn't have control over his own feet.

Her palm was up, defenseless, held out to him like a mother coaxing a frightened child to safety. "I'm sorry. They didn't mean to frighten you. I didn't mean to frighten you. They only wanted me to complete my mission. But they don't understand. We've never met someone who didn't know."

The words didn't make sense. He shook his head. "Know what? I don't . . ." Then he realized. She was talking about the light. A light, a bright, white, dancing light—a *they?*

His anger blossomed, filling up the space the confusion had left. "Listen, I don't know what you're talking about!" he said hoarsely. "And I don't think I want to know."

"You have to know." Her hand was still extended to him.

But the way she said it, almost reluctantly, didn't make him eager to hear. "Why?"

"Because I've been sent for you. And I can't stay any longer. It's not safe."

"Sent for me?" His voice squeaked on the last note, the way it had when he was a boy. Suddenly, he started to laugh. She was a nut. Since he'd been in college, his teammates had told stories of fans who were nuts. Finally, he had one of his own.

She smiled at his laughter.

Despite his mirth, he couldn't help but notice how really beautiful she was. Even if the features of her face didn't quite seem to fit together. The adrenaline that had been powering him was seeping away, and he was suddenly very tired again. "Maybe you could come for me some other time, okay? I'm really too tired for it tonight."

He relaxed his fingers, thrust them fully into his pockets and hunched up his shoulders against the cold. He skirted wide around her and went past.

She turned with him as he passed.

He saw the movement out of the corner of his eye. Then another movement from the other side. The white light screamed in at him, moving so fast it was only a blur. He backpedaled, the way he had in the parking lot the night before. And just as he had then, he fell back, onto his bottom. Scrambled away to keep the light from touching him.

He remembered it on his legs, crackling and creepy, reaching through his clothes to his skin.

He twisted on the cold ground, away from the dancing light. Anything to keep it from touching him again.

Suddenly, she was there, kneeling beside him. Her fingers on his shoulder were as insubstantial as air, but strong enough to stop his frantic struggling, to hold him in place. "It's all right. It's all right. It won't hurt you. You're one of us."

"What? What? One of what?" He looked around

frantically, for help, for escape. There was no one in sight. The street was empty and dark.

"It won't hurt you," she repeated firmly. To illustrate, she held up her hand to the light. It settled toward her. Just as it had the night before, the brightness touched her fingers and swallowed them. Settled farther down until it had devoured her palm, her wrist.

The ground was cool and damp beneath his fingers, and he gripped double handfuls of the wet grass as he gulped in lungfuls of air. Striving for calm. For sanity. "What is it?"

"I told you. One of us."

"Us? As in we? Me? This is a joke, right? Larry put you up to this?" The last was as much a plea as a question.

The light drew away, leaving her hand whole again.

Yeah, sure. His teammates had set this up. A crazy woman with a hand-eating light. How did he explain that? Was he crazy, too?

"Please." She touched him again, lightly. "Let me explain. I will tell you how you've come to be here. I will show you your true form."

He nodded slowly, ready to hear anything which might explain this away. Surely at some point Larry would jump out of the bushes, screaming with laughter. "My true form?"

"Your parents taught you this form to protect you. Because you were just a baby when their ship crashed on this planet."

She ran her hand down his body, but her touch no longer had the power to distract him with tingles. He shifted, uncomfortable, not trusting her.

"When their ship crashed . . . ?" His voice cracked, but he wasn't sure whether it was fear or laughter that caused it.

"Have you heard of Roswell, New Mexico?"

"Yeah. That place where the spaceship was supposed to have crashed." He shifted, wanting very much to get up, knowing he could not. "Yeah, everybody with a TV's heard of that. It turned out to be a joke. A weather balloon or something."

"It was the crash of a Gaearen reclamation ship. Two of the crew were killed. Three escaped. Your parents and you. They assumed human form, taught you human form, assimilated themselves into the world around them."

"Wait a minute! That Roswell thing, it happened in the 50s!"

"1947, by earth time."

At last, the chink he'd been waiting for. "I'm only twenty-five years old!"

"We age more slowly than humans, even when in human form. 2.231 years to one of theirs. Have you never noticed how young your parents appear? To raise you as a human, they would have moved many times on this planet, to disguise the slowness of your growth."

Patrick started, the skyline around him going black as he remembered a childhood that did at times seem confused. There had always been oddities. A frequent sense of déjà vu all through school, of having already read certain books, of already knowing certain lessons. And hadn't he always remembered two tenth birthday parties—one in a big, rambling wood house, one at the seashore?

How many times had he seen an expression that seemed almost sad pass between his parents when he was confused about something that had happened only years before? He'd always thought they were upset by his bad memory. "Why didn't they tell me?" he whispered. He wasn't even aware he'd spoken, that he'd *accepted*, until she answered.

"Because you were so young, your parents allowed your memories to slip away. They could not trust that one so young would not slip and reveal himself. They did not know how long it would be before help came."

He grasped double handfuls of the grass on either side of him, as if he needed to anchor himself to the earth. "And my parents, where are they? Now?"

She pointed at the sky, at the stars which no longer looked like stars, but like small floating balls of light. "Home, in the main ship. Waiting for you."

It was crazy. But it wasn't. Because he knew now why

the dancing lights on the Island hadn't frightened him.
He remembered. Because they looked so much like the
lights he'd seen outside his bedroom window when he
was a child. When they'd lived far north in Canada, far
out in the woods. Warm balls of light playing gleefully,
dancing across the sparkling snow.

"I don't . . . I don't know . . ."

She smiled and touched him lightly on the leg. "That's
why I'm here. To take you home."

"I don't suppose they have ice hockey there?" He
glanced at the rink. There was a sudden hollow pain at
the base of his throat.

"No." She stroked his leg lightly.

A white-hot, searing pain lanced down his thigh into
his knee. He cried out and tried to jerk loose, but she
held him firmly. In just a fraction of a second, the pain
was gone, and so was the world around him.

He opened his mouth to scream and no sound came
out. All he could hear was a high-pitched whine, like
wind whipping past his ears at gale force.

His mind told him he was jerking and twisting, trying
to wrench free, but he couldn't feel his body. Everything,
his hearing, his sight, his voice, was gone! Only one sensation remained and it wasn't true. It told him he was
weightless and skinless. It told him he had no boundaries
but those he defined for himself. No muscles, no hair.
No bones.

She had clawed her way up his body, prized open the
top of his skull with red hot pincers and was spilling all
that he was out into the sky. His essence was bright,
white light. Radiance streaming out of his brain like
water under pressure. Dissipating as the luminescence
which was Patrick spread out into the air.

He gasped, choking for lack of air, for lack of lungs
to breath it. He cried out as he felt the awareness that
was his self scattering, coming apart, dissipating like a
fluffy cloud before a breeze. He was spread so thin
across the sky that he wasn't visible. He was invisible
and blind and deaf and dying.

Karacea pulled him back.

Awareness came slamming back into his body with

such force, such frenzy, he heard his muscles snap, his joints pop. The ankle he'd broken last season screamed in agony, the bone bent to the breaking point.

He welcomed the pain as he felt his soul, a waterfall of light, roar back into his physical self. The force slammed him to the ground. He fell backward, body twitching like a crazed string puppet. His head bounced off the wet ground and he rolled to his knees, retching and coughing and gasping.

He hung there, blades of grass swimming before his eyes, so long his arms began to ache. He rolled, without grace, and pulled himself to a sitting position, drawing thick night air into his lungs. He could taste it, sliding down the back of his throat, redolent with the scent of the nearby mills, and it tasted like the finest whiskey.

He was flesh and bone again. He clasped his lower legs, his knees, his thighs. Good solid muscle that could do what he demanded of it. He cupped his hands in his crotch, to reassure himself he was still a man. Ran his fingers over his face. Good, solid covering of skin, that held him all in one place. All in one piece.

He stretched his fingers, worked the bad ankle, coaxing twinges of pain from it, just to prove to himself that he still had bones.

Karacea reached out and caught his fingers.

He flinched away from her, muscles prepared for flight, for war. He would kill her, if he had to, but he would not allow her to subject him to that again.

She didn't try. She simply held his hand in her own, turning it, examining it, pressing the flesh of his hand as if to feel the bones inside. When she looked up at him, her eyes were full of unshed tears. "I'm sorry," she whispered, still clutching his hand.

"You live like that?" he rasped. His throat was sore and dry, but at least he could feel it.

"It's not that way! It's not that way for us. I don't understand . . ." She turned his hand, examining his scarred knuckles by touch. She examined her own, smooth and soft by comparison, then returned to his. "I thought you were ready."

She released his hand and held her own up to the

light, flexed her long, slender fingers. "Or maybe I do understand. This body is very beguiling. I had not realized how beguiling. Perhaps you need more time."

He sat for a long time, working his fingers into the grass, past the wet blades, down into the cool dirt beneath. She, too, was silent, so quiet he couldn't hear her breathing. Perhaps she didn't breath. But she must, because she was like him, and he breathed. He breathed and he cried and he had bones which would break and skin which would bleed.

And a mind which would go around and around in circles until he was lost. It was crazy. Too crazy. What he had seen was undeniable, accepting that he was still sane, and yet . . . He couldn't quite get his mind to wrap around it. He only knew he wasn't going anywhere without a fight. "I don't need more time."

She shrugged, a movement eerily wrong on her slender shoulders. "I misjudged. I did not realize how much being human could mean. We will start over. I will be more gentle."

"You can take twenty years—" he began, but she motioned instantly, abruptly, for silence.

She glanced up at the sky.

Patrick's gaze followed, but the bright ball of light was nowhere to be seen. He was glad. He didn't want to see anymore hand-eating.

Karacea leaned close to him, her breath soft on his face. "We will start over. I will give you time. Go slower, so that you can learn. My mission is to take you home."

Her eyes were shining like new pennies, bright with anticipation.

He mimed a laugh he didn't feel because of the weird, sloshy feeling in his stomach. "Home is my apartment, and I can find my own way." And he held out a hand to her that was flesh and bone. That had never melted into a ball of white light.

The fake fog puffed down the tunnel, blown by two small fans. Through the dark passageway, he could see the spotlights—purple, gold, and white—dancing on the ice.

It was going to be a good night. He could feel it. In the electric energy of the crowd, in the restrained eagerness of his linemates, in the way his bones sat inside his flesh.

The announcer started calling out the names of the starting lineup. His own name was among them, and he stepped forward. He was the third to step forward into the swirling lights.

The moment his skates touched the ice, Patrick knew Karacea was in the stands.

FIRST CONTACT INC.

by Julie E. Czerneda

Julie E. Czerneda is a Canadian science fiction writer whose first novel, *A Thousand Words for Stranger,* will be published this year by DAW Books. Formerly a researcher in animal communication, Julie has also written nonfiction, from biology texts to the use of science fiction to develop literacy. She currently lives at the edge of a forest with her family, enjoying rocketry and canoeing whenever there's time.

First Contact Custom Simulation PC91-Base Borden
© First Contact Inc. Licensed for military use only.

Humanity's big moment. And a moment was how long it lasted.

They'd run. Lt. Courtland—the Ironman himself—had been the first to break, flinging from him the state-of-the-art translator they'd brought to this meeting place with such care, his boots driving deep into the mud with each stride so that he lurched from side to side in an agonizing effort to put distance between himself and It.

Lt. Desroches had hesitated a second longer, staring into the writhing mass of filaments as if somehow this would help her find a point of correspondence, a suggestion of a face. Then she shuddered and whirled to follow Courtland.

Lt. Smith, the one who'd barely made the final cut for this mission, the one considered the weakest link, remained the longest. This had more to do with his complete conviction that his legs wouldn't obey him than any desire to stay within reach of that thing. *His paralysis left him with the alien's first tentative reach in his direction.*

*   *   *

"So I tell the Colonel: You pick the partner; we just do the music."

Nance's pale eyes gleamed through her ragged fringe of bangs. "And what did he say to that?" Her fingers continued to search for a disk among the piles of Post-it-coated pages layered on her desk. The keyboard balanced on her lap shifted with every movement as though trying to save itself from falling to the floor and being lost among even more piles of journals and clippings. For a company listed among the top five software producers, the office of its CEO and resident genius looked a great deal more like a newsroom from the early fifties than the site of executive splendor.

Henry Fergus, graphics whiz and sales rep, when he wasn't fussing over hardware, dropped his voice into a fair imitation of Colonel Dunwithy's growl. "Your so-called music sent three of my best officers into therapy! Why should I pay for that?"

"To which you said . . ."

Henry flopped into the swivel chair that doubled as a printer stand on the odd occasions when they needed hard copy. "You know what I said." Two fingers tugged a folded check from his pocket. "You pay for it, because it worked."

Nance, Dr. Nancy Vzcinza to those who were not her friends, pushed her hair out of her eyes for a moment. "Henry. Driving people crazy is *not* what we do here."

"No?"

"No. They do that all by themselves." She found the disk she was after and dropped it into the drive, fingers now jabbing at keys. Henry glanced around in vain for the mouse. She'd lost it again, he bet, or was using it as a foot pedal. "We just . . ." tap, tap, ". . . illustrate . . ." tap, tap, tap, ". . . the circumstances." Tap.

He kicked off his shoes, thinking nostalgically of the days not long ago when he'd made all his sales calls in sandals. Even better, when most of his business contacts had been over the vidphone. He'd really loved putting on that shirt, tie, and jacket over his bike shorts. Pants and dress shoes. The cost of success.

"So what's up?"

She looked up from the screen as though startled to still find him there. Henry was used to that. He blanked out the world himself when there was a glitch to track down. "Last minute upgrade for the new theme park in Australia."

He whistled. "Way to make those bucks. We can retire soon." Which was a joke. Nance had no clearer concept of how much the company—and they—were worth these days than he did. There were people on the next floor who kept track; annoying people in suits who drove better cars than he did and who routinely forgot to tell new staff that he and Nance paid their salaries. That always messed up the lunch-hour softball games.

And retire? Just when they could at last actually own the best systems for themselves? Just when they could do what they loved doing all day long? Being paid for it was, was—

"Convenient."

"Pardon?"

Nance looked innocent. "Convenient that the park wants this particular upgrade. I've been wanting to play with it a bit more."

Henry winced. Nance's idea of playing usually involved roping him and anyone else still breathing into the VR chamber at ungodly hours. "What did you have in mind?" he sighed, slipping down into a more comfortable slouch—interested despite the likely unpleasant consequence to his own workload.

First Contact Custom Simulation DC101-Smithers © First Contact Inc. Licensed for home experience only.

Dark red blood settled into the star-shaped cracks in the windshield, forming a network of pleasing regularity. Mildred Smithers, grandmother of three and leading voice in the Real Goldies Choir, shut off the still-racing engine of her car with a satisfied nod. "Gotcha again, you bastard," she said primly, glancing around as if to reassure herself that this descent into rough language had been safely unnoticed. But she was alone, of course.

She pushed up her bifocals to better see the face of her

watch. Not bad. Shaved at least a minute off her response time. Practice makes perfect, as she always reminded her good-for-nothing son-in-law. For a moment she considered the lifeless form draped over what was left of the hood of her car. Pity you couldn't buy the same experience a little closer to home, she thought. Then again, the whole point of the exercise was to be ready to act—something she knew full well her family would depend on her to do. "When you get here," she promised the tentacled being her driving skill had shattered into two equal halves, "Mildred Smithers will be ready."

The next morning, Henry poked his head into Nance's office. Nothing appeared to have changed, unless you counted the accumulation of dead leaves under the plant cowering on the windowsill. "How's the Aussie upgrade?"

There was an incoherent grumble from behind the monitor. He used his knuckles to sound a drumroll on the door frame. "Made a coffee run."

Half a face showed, the one eye looking wistful. "Bagels?"

"With blueberry cream cheese."

The eye blinked slowly. "I hope Meaghan appreciates you."

Henry, unable to find a clear surface for his offering, chose the most stable pile of paper and set the tray down with care. "She appreciates me. It's the rest of my family that has doubts."

Nance popped the lid from one of the coffees, blew away the steam, and took a huge swallow, looking as though the caffeine was heading straight to her bloodstream. Henry was convinced her mouth had an asbestos lining. "So how's the sim?" he persisted. "Mustafa said you've been on it all night."

She gave him a condescending look over a mouthful of cheese-drifted bagel. "How would he know? Mustafa's idea of getting in early is anytime after the traffic's died down on the freeway." Another gulp of coffee. "It's weird."

His eyes went to the wall unit behind Nance's chair,

loaded with dusty jars of pickled insects and mollusks, interspersed with museum-quality replica skulls of various mammals, and tied bundles of bird feet. Fortunately, the cleaning staff had insisted the eyeball collection go home, despite Nance's protests about the importance of biological reality to her simulations. "Weird how?"

Nance stood up, stretching with a twisting motion that made audible cracks. "They keep adding to the specs." She handed him a set of faxes clipped together with a clothespin Santa her niece had made last year. Nance kept everything.

"Bit late for this many changes. Park opens the day after tomorrow." Henry started leafing through the pages. Each contained one minor requested change. There must have been about twenty, sent at roughly equal intervals over the past day and night. "You've told them modifications on the fly like these are extra, I hope."

Head half inside a sweater, Nance muttered darkly, "I told them to stop it after the first two. I hate being interrupted. But they wouldn't." She pushed her head out and glared fiercely at Henry. "Not to mention that what they're asking for is silly."

"Silly." Henry looked more closely at the top page and read aloud, "The pupil of each eye must be an unreflective black, not luminous orange." The next page, "Four appendages in total, mobile at a sequence of six joints." He tried not to grin. "They are being quite specific. Someone's had a nightmare lately."

Nance dropped back into her seat. "I'll give them nightmares."

First Contact Custom Simulation PC225-Fernandez © First Contact Inc. Licensed for home experience only.

He wasn't sure what had disturbed his sleep. It was an older building; pipes and joists had a tendency to be musical in changing weather. But that wasn't it this time.

Juan sat up, trying to listen more carefully. There. A scraping sound. From outside. He yawned and lay back down. The old elm out front was wide enough to kiss the bricks with an east wind. He'd remind the super about having it trimmed at the next tenants' meeting.

Snick. Skitter, skitter.

That wasn't the tree! Juan had his feet on the cold floor this time, hand racing for the light by his bed. Sounded like a cockroach convention. He hit the switch and found himself facing what he'd never even dreamed of. . . .

Equally startled, his visitor scampered from the now-open patio doors to the top of his bureau in a ripple of reflective scales.

For a seeming eternity, the only sound was a sigh of wind through the doors and Juan's heart hammering in his ears. Then the creature shivered, a motion that made the plates covering its gaunt body touch together with a faint bell-like tinkle. It had eyes, two large and one smaller, centered on a triangular head. Around its neck was a wreath made of autumn leaves.

Juan reached slowly for the phone at his bedside. When he brought it to his ear, there was a soft voice already speaking to him. The creature tilted its head and settled more comfortably on the bureau.

"Juan Fernandez," whispered the soft voice. "I have chosen you to contact first of all of your kind. Your music has touched even the stars. Play for me and let there be peace between us."

Numbly, his eyes never leaving his visitor, Juan put down the phone and reached for the saxophone on its stand beside his bed. He'd always known he'd make it big one day—not necessarily this big—but big.

"What's the original design base?"

"Standard PC30, peaceful contact following initial suspicion, overtones of economic congruence of mutual benefit. Nothing flashy." Nance sent the fifteenth paper airplane of the hour soaring overhead. "Not until they started this last minute nonsense."

Henry caught it before it hit his ear and unfolded the paper to read the request. "Strands of keratin 30 cm long to be attached behind each auditory organ?"

Nance raised her eyebrow. "We are definitely dealing with someone who knows their biology—if not how to stay within a budget. Hair, Henry. They want me to put hair on its head."

There was no place left to hide, Roger decided grimly, his bike sucking fumes as it coasted off the deserted highway. He could stand and fight here and now—or die without ever seeing the face of his enemy. Funny, he hadn't imagined death would come as a cliché.

Had it only been yesterday? The aliens had been so well prepared, their technology so superior. The only wonder was that crumbs of humanity like himself still existed on the planet. A crumb. What a joke on the world that he had lasted hours after the rest were obliterated.

There was a whistle in the distance, the sound piercing and ominous as though it could summon hell's demons to chase him. And weren't they, despite their appearance of being only machines? He'd watched the trackers demolish a city block of apartments—an economical way of dealing with the vermin inside. He'd known better than to hide in the subways, too, having witnessed yet another set of machines burrowing into the streets, somehow fully aware of every crack that still harbored humankind. Roger no longer remembered how he escaped. There were too many other images in the way.

Another whistle, this time an answer from the direction he'd vaguely hoped might be away from Them. Roger considered his surroundings: the once-blue sky smudged by the smoke from the city, the highway boiled away in places where cars had been targets, the landscape pitted and ruined overnight. He reached into the saddlebag of his bike and pulled out the gun he knew was there. Would he have the courage to end it for himself this time? Or would he have to wait for the mercy of the aliens to make it stop?

"Good morning, fellow geniuses!" The door flew open as if propelled by a hurricane. "Have you started celebrating without me?"

Mustafa, a man who rarely smiled before noon and then required an excuse to make the effort, was beaming from ear to ear. Henry and Nance traded knowing glances. "Cracked the blackjack table?" Nance asked.

"Much better," Mustafa announced. He pointed one pudgy finger at them and shook it. "You didn't check your mail again. When are you going—"

Henry cut short what promised to be the usual diatribe about corporate responsibilities and other nonsense that had invaded their lives since home simulation machines had become the rage—with First Contact Inc. already poised for success with its custom VRs. "Tell us what we need to know, oh, keeper of the secret."

"Guess who's opening the Aussie theme park."

Nance scowled, which widened Mustafa's smile even farther. "Am I supposed to care?" she growled. "Some rock star or other."

Henry tsk-tsked. "You never think about sales. So who, Mustafa? Must be a good one to make you drool."

"The President."

Nance's head came around from its hiding place behind her monitor. Henry swallowed hard and managed what he hoped was a nonchalant, "Pardon?" that cracked partway through the middle. He tried again. "Which President?"

Mustafa positively glowed. *The* President. You know. The first one to win a majority from every country."

"President Polemski. *He's* going to open the park."

"Gets better, compadres. The Pres is apparently a fan of your work, Nance. He's going to be the first person to try your latest and greatest First Contact sim."

Henry and Nance dived for the pile of pages in the wastebasket, Henry winning by an arm's length. "No wonder you couldn't track down the source with the Aussies," he gasped, trying to smooth the abused paper into order. "These must be straight from his office."

"Whoa, there," Nance interjected uneasily. "That's a pretty big guess, Henry."

He shook his head, holding up the pages. "What time exactly did the President's office announce this?"

Mustafa looked from one to the other of his bosses,

his satisfied look fading into puzzled concern as he saw the expressions on their faces. "At the nine A.M. press conference yesterday. I e'd you guys when I found out. Why?"

Nance took the sheaf of faxes-turned-airplanes from Henry. She found the first one. It was dated yesterday, 9:30 A.M. Their eyes met. "I think I'd better input every one of these after all."

Henry nodded slowly. "And I think we'd better have a look before it goes out."

First Contact Custom Simulation PC 30mod352a-Australia's Down Under Theme Park Corporation © First Contact Inc. Licensed for public on-location viewing only. Test run.

Until today, he'd enjoyed flying; sympathetic but unable to understand why so many of his aides became white-knuckled with every air pocket. This flight was different. He wasn't sure whether his new-found anxiety stemmed from being the only living thing on board or his destination. Likely both. He turned from the window and switched on the recorded briefing from his aides for the third time. The familiar voices were reassuring, edged though they were with unfamiliar tension.

The arrangements had been made using numerical expressions that both sides understood. There was some negotiation required regarding the location of that critical first meeting. The home world was not as wet as that of the guest. And beauty was important. The meeting would be carried live on both planets. A good first impression would do wonders for the ultimate response from the public.

Yet, despite concern and some honest fear of the unknown, there was goodwill. There was a sense of inevitability, too—that events would unfold regardless of the careful planning of governments. All that remained was the moment when strangers met.

He'd studied the pictures, but nothing truly prepared one for such an encounter. Aides had informed him of what they understood to be appropriate alien protocol.

No weapons, at least none in sight, was a reassuring common factor. Gifts might be misconstrued at this earliest point; who knew what values they shared or didn't? What to wear—best to err on the side of formality; no one liked to be slighted. And much of what transpired was meant purely for the viewers. His people had definite expectations of him, if not of the one he met.

They'd chosen a beach on an isolated, uninhabited island, large enough for automated transports to land. He set the controls as the techs had instructed in order to set up the transmission and recording equipment. Each, visitor and host, had a designated half of the landmass for their preparations. The island was blessed with a central lagoon lovely by any standard. Its beach was the designated meeting site. It could be reached by either representative in a short walk.

He drew in a last deep breath of the salt-scented air, took one last look at the technology that was his only link to his own kind, and prepared to make history.

"Stop." Henry hit the kill switch on the simulation and looked at Nance and Mustafa. "This is ordinary. It's dull. Some nice work on the scenery, but face it. First Contact Inc. makes its money on custom sims real enough to make you wet your drawers. Any one of our competitors could do better than this."

Nance stopped him just by raising her eyebrows. "We haven't reached the climax, Henry. And that's where most of the changes were made. Shall we?"

Henry muttered something to himself, but restarted the sim.

First Contact Custom Simulation PC 30mod352a-Australia's Down Under Theme Park Corporation © First Contact Inc. Licensed for public on-location viewing only. Test run.

He drew in a last deep breath of the salt-scented air, took one last look at the technology that was his only link to his own kind, and prepared to make history.

The walk was too short. World leader or not, there

*was something inherently terrifying about this meeting,
something that threatened his very grasp upon reality. Before panic could truly overwhelm his intentions, it was
too late. There was the Other.*

*The Other was strangeness given life. The body shape
was roughly cylindrical, with appendages located with
reasonable symmetry. Clothing covered many of the
important details, but he knew from his aides that the
appendages had a remarkable range of movement. The
body was topped by a short stalk that in turn supported
a round cranial mass. Keratin strands attached behind
each auditory organ tossed in the wind.*

*Some sort of exudate coated the rest of the cranial
mass. It glistened in the warm sun and the Other used
one appendage to spread the exudate over the keratin
strands in what looked to be a reflex. Just in case, he
mimicked the gesture as best he could. The openings on
the front portion of the cranial mass changed position
almost at once. Startled, he moved back a bit. The Other
spread its appendages in what seemed a peaceful gesture.*

*His people were watching. He gathered himself, then
moved forward slowly. The Other echoed his movement
until they were close enough to touch. He held out his—*

"Stop!" This time it was Nance's decision.

"Holy Mother of Mainframes," Henry breathed, not
surprised to feel himself shaking. "We just made contact
with the President." The other two looked just as
shocked, then Nance began to chuckle, a deep throaty
sound so contagious Henry found himself laughing suddenly, too.

"I don't see what's funny," Mustafa said, his complexion as pale as it could get.

Nance popped the sim's cartridge out of the player
and held it up reverently. "Don't you get it? These last
changes didn't come from the Australians."

"Of course not, they came from the President. But
why would Polemski want to meet—himself?" The
words came more and more slowly. Mustafa's eyes
glazed over and he sat down on the floor. "Oh, my."

Henry nodded, not too sure on his feet either. He

took the cartridge from Nance and stared at it. "Looks like we have a new customer for First Contact Inc."

Nance's expression was the same one she'd had when they'd delivered the quad photon storage system for her computer—a combination of worship and glee. "I'd better make sure this gets sent out immediately. The customer may want to run it a few times to get it right."

They all glanced up at the ceiling. "Shouldn't we tell someone?" Mustafa whispered.

Nance held out her hand and Henry dropped the cartridge into it. "Well, if you can think of someone who'd believe us, I'll give it a shot." She paused and swept her bangs out of her eyes. "You realize we're all out of a job in two days. First Contact Inc. will be definitely redundant once it really happens."

Henry thought happily of shorts and sandals. "I've been telling you we should be doing more historicals. And westerns. I've always wanted to do westerns."

"Westerns," Nance grumbled, leading the way out of the VR chamber. "Pirates, maybe."

As they went down the corridor, Mustafa's voice trailed behind. "What about the new guys? They already like our stuff."

PALINDROMIC

by Peter Crowther

Since the World and British Fantasy Award-nominated *Narrow Houses* (1992), Peter Crowther has edited or co-edited eight more anthologies, continued to produce reviews and interviews for a variety of publications on both sides of the Atlantic, sold some fifty of his own short stories, and completed *Escardy Gap,* a collaborative novel with James Lovegrove published in September 1996. A solo novel, a short story collection, two more anthologies and *Escardy Gap II* are all currently underway.

It was on the third day after the aliens arrived that we made the fateful discovery which placed the future of the entire planet in our hands. That discovery was that they hadn't arrived yet.

There were three of us went over to the vacant lot alongside Sycamore . . . that's me, Derby—like the hat—McLeod, plus my good friend and local genius Jimmy-James Bannister and Ed Brewster, Forest Plains' very own bad boy . . . except there was nothing bad about Ed. Not really.

We went up into that giant tumbleweed cloud thing that served as some kind of interstellar flivver—it had been at the aliens' invitation, or so we thought: our subsequent discovery called that particular fact into some considerable dispute—purely to get a look at whatever this one alien was doing. Jimmy reckoned—and he was right, as it turned out—he was keeping tabs on what was going on and recording everything in some kind of "book."

Not that he—if the alien *was* a "he": we never did find out—was writing the way you or I would write, because he wasn't. We didn't even know if he was writing at all until later that night, when Jimmy-James had taken a long look in that foam-book of theirs.

Not that this book was like any other book you ever saw. It wasn't. Just like the ship that brought them to Forest Plains wasn't like any other ship you ever saw, not in *Earth Vs The Flying Saucers* or even on *Twilight Zone*—both of which were what you might call "current" back then. And the aliens themselves weren't like any kind of alien you ever saw in the dime comic books or even dreamed about . . . not even after maybe eating warmed-over, two-day-old pizza last thing at night on top of a gutful of Michelob and three or four plates of Ma Chetton's cheese surprises, the small pieces of toasted cheese flapjack that Ma used to serve up when we were holding the monthly Forest Plains Pool Knockout Competition.

It was during one of those special nights, with the moon hanging over the desert like a crazy jack o'lantern and the heat making your shirt stick to your back and underarms, that the whole thing actually got itself started. That was the night that creatures from outer space arrived in Forest Plains. Then again, it wasn't.

But I'm getting way ahead of myself here. . . .

So maybe that's the best place to start the story, that night.

It was a Monday, the last one in November, at about nine o'clock. The year was 1964.

Ma Chetton was sweeping the few remaining cheese surprises from her last visit to the kitchen down onto a plate of freshly-made cookies, their steam rising up into the smoky atmosphere of her husband Bill's Pool Emporium over on Sycamore, when the place shook like Jell-O and the strains of The Trashmen's *Surfin' Bird,* which had been playing on Bill's pride-and-joy Wurlitzer, faded into a wave of what sounded like static. Only thing was we'd never heard of a jukebox suffering from static before. Then the lights went out, and the machine just ground itself to a stop.

Jerry Bucher was about to take a shot—six-ball off of two cushions into the far corner as I recall . . . all the other pockets being covered by Ed Brewster's stripes: funny how you remember details like that—and he stood up ramrod tall like someone had just dropped a firecracker or something crawly down the back of his shorts.

"What the hell was that?" Jerry asked nobody in particular, switching the half-chewed matchstick from one side of his mouth to the other while he glanced around to put the blame on somebody for almost fouling up his shot. Jerry was never what you might call a calm player and he was an even worse loser.

Ed Brewster was crouched over, his shoulders hunched up, watching the dust drifting down from the rafters and settling on the pool table, his girlfriend Estelle's arms clamped around his waist.

Ma was standing frozen behind the counter, empty plate in her hand, staring at the lights shining through the windows. "Felt like some kind of earthquake," she ventured.

Bill Chetton's head was visible through the hatch into the kitchen, his mouth hanging open and eyes as wide as dinner plates. "Everyone okay?"

I leaned my pool cue against the table and walked across to the windows. By rights, it should have been dark outside but it was bright as a nightime ball game, like someone was shining car headlights straight at the windows, and when I took a look along the street I saw sand and stuff blowing toward us from the vacant lot opposite.

"Some kind of power failure is what it is," Estelle announced, her voice sounding even higher and squeaker than usual and not at all reassuring.

Leaning against the table in front of the window, my face pressed up against the glass, I saw that the cause of that power failure was not something simple and straightforward like power lines being down between Forest Plains and Bellingham, some thirty-five miles away. It was something far more complicated.

Settling down onto the empty lot across the street was something that resembled a cross between a gigantic metal canister and an equally gigantic vegetable, its sides billowing in and out.

"Is it a helicopter?" old Fred Wishingham asked from alongside me, his voice soft and nervous. Fred had ambled over from the booth he occupied every night of the year and was standing on the other side of the table staring out into the night. "Can't be a plane," he said, "so it must be some kind of helicopter." There sounded like a good deal of wishful thinking in that last statement.

But wishful thinking or not, the thing descending on the spare ground across the street didn't look like any helicopter I'd ever seen—not that I'd seen many, mind you—and I told Fred as much.

"It's some kind of goddam hot air balloon," Ed Brewster said, crouching down so's he could get a better look at the top of the thing—it was tall, there was no denying that.

"Looks more like some kind of furry cloud," Abel Bodeen muttered to himself. I figured he was speaking so softly because he didn't feel like making that observation widely known because it sounded a mite foolish. And it did, right enough. The truth of the matter was that the thing *did* look like a furry cloud . . . or maybe a giant lettuce or the head of a cauliflower, with lights flashing on and off deep inside it.

Pretty soon we were all gathered around the window watching, nobody saying anything else as the thing settled down on the ground.

Within a minute or two, the poolroom lights came back on and the shaking stopped. "You going out to see what it is?" Fred asked. Nobody responded. "I guess *some* body should go out there to see what it is," he said.

Right on cue, the screen door squeaked behind us and we saw the familiar figure of Jimmy-James Bannister step out onto the sidewalk. He glanced back at the window at us all and gave a shrug. Then he started across the street.

"Hope that damn fool knows what he's doing." Ed Brewster was a past master at putting everyone's thoughts into words.

The truth of the matter was Jimmy-James knew a whole lot of things that none of the rest of us had any

idea at all about. And anything he didn't know about
he just kept on at until he did. Jimmy-James—born
James Ronald Garrison Bannister (he'd made his first
name into a double to go partways to satisfying his father and partways to keep the mickey-taking down to
an acceptable minimum)—was the resident big brain of
Forest Plains. Still only twenty-two years old—same age
as me, at the time—he was finishing up his Master's
course over at Princeton, studying languages and applied math.

Jimmy-James could do long division problems in his
head and cuss in fourteen languages which, along with
the fact that he could drink anyone else in town—including Ed—under the table, made him a pretty popular
member of any group gathering . . . particularly one
where any amount of liquor or even just beer was to be
consumed. He was home for Thanksgiving, taking the
week off, and there's a lot of folks owes him a debt of
gratitude for that fact.

Anyway, there went Jimmy-James, large as life and
twice as bold—though some might say "stupid"—walking across the street, his hands thrust deep into his trou-
ser pockets and his head held high, proud and fearless.
There were a couple of muted gasps from somewhere
behind me and then the sound of shuffling as folks tried
to get closer to the window to get a good look. After
all, we'd all seen from the *War Of The Worlds* movie
what happened to people who got a little too close to
these objects . . . and we'd all pretty much decided that
the thing across the street was about as likely to have
come from anyplace on Earth as it was to have flown
up to us from Vince and Molly Waldon's general store
down the street. Nobody actually came right out and
said it was from another planet, but we all knew that it
was. But why it was here was another matter, though
we weren't in any great rush to find out the answer to
that question. None of us except Jimmy-James Bannister, that is.

"Go call the Sheriff," Ma Chetton whispered.

I could hear Bill Chetton pressing the receiver and
saying *Hello? Hello?* like his life depended on it. It

didn't come as any surprise when Bill announced to the
hushed room that the line seemed like it was dead. Then
the jukebox kicked in again with a loud and raucous *A
papapapapapa* . . . the needle somehow having returned
to the start of the Trashmen's hit record.

The street outside seemed like it was holding its
breath in much the same way as the folks looking out
of the window were holding their breath . . . both it and
us waiting to see what was going to happen.

What happened was both awesome and kind of an
anticlimax.

Just as Jimmy-James reached the sidewalk across the
street, the sides of the giant vegetable balloon canister
from another world dropped down and became a kind
of shiny skirt reaching all the way to the ground. No
sooner had that happened than a whole group of smaller
vegetable things—smaller but still twice the size of
Jimmy-James . . . and, at almost six-four, JJ is not a
small man—came sliding down the platform onto terra
firma . . . and into the heart of Forest Plains.

We could hear their caterwauling from where we
were, even over the drone of The Trashmen telling anyone who would listen that *the Bird was the Word* . . .
and, as we watched, we saw the vegetable shapes come
to a halt on the sidewalk right in front of Jimmy-James
where they kind of spun around and then gathered
around him in a tight circle. Then all but one of them
moved back a few feet and then the last one moved
back, too.

At this point, Jimmy-James turned around and waved
to us. "Come on out," he yelled.

"You think it's safe?" Ed Brewster asked.

I shrugged. "Doesn't seem to be they mean any
harm," Ma Chetton said softly, the wonder in her voice
as plain as the streaks of gray coloring the hair around
her ears and temples.

"They come all the way from wherever it is they come
from, seems to me that if they'd had a mind to do us
any harm they'd have done it by now," said Old Fred
Wishingham. "That said, mind you," he added, "I'm not

about to go charging out there until we see what it is they *have* come for."

"Maybe they haven't come for nothing at all," Estelle suggested.

Somebody murmured that such an unlikely scenario could be the case, but they weren't having any of it. That was the way folks were in Forest Plains in those days—the way folks were all over this country, in fact. Nobody (with the possible exception of Ed Brewster, and even he only did it for fun) wanted to make anyone look or feel a damned fool and hurt their feelings if they could get away without doing so. With Estelle it could be difficult. Estelle had turned making herself look a damned fool into something approaching an art form.

"You mean, like they're exploring . . . something like that?" Abel Bodeen said to help her out a mite.

"Yeah," Estelle agreed dreamily, "exploring."

"Well, I'm going out," Ma said. And without so much as a second glance or a pause to allow someone to talk her out of it, she rested the empty plate on the countertop and strode over to the door. A minute or so later she was walking across the street. It seemed like the things had sensed she was going to come out because they'd moved across the street like to greet her, swiveling around at the last minute—just as Ma came to a stop—and ringing her just the way they had done with Jimmy-James.

They seemed harmless enough, but I felt like we should have the law in on the situation. "Phone still out, Bill?" I shouted. He lifted the receiver and tried again, then nodded and returned it to the cradle.

"Okay, Ed," I said, "let's me and you scoot out the back and run over to the Sheriff's office."

Ed said okay, after thinking about that for a second or two, and then the two of us slipped behind the counter and into Bill's and Ma's kitchen, then out of the back door and into the yard, past the trashcans toward the fence . . . and then I heard someone calling.

"What was that?" I whispered across to Ed.

Ed had stopped dead in his tracks on the other side of the fence. He was staring ahead of him. When I got to the fence, I looked in the direction Ed was looking, and there they were. Three of them. Right in front of us, wailing. I'll never forget that sound . . . like the wind in the desert, lost and aimless.

The door we'd just come out of opened up again behind us and Fred Wishingham's voice shouted, "Hold it right where you . . ." and then trailed off when Fred saw the things. "I was just going to tell you that some of those things had just turned around and headed over to where you'd be appearing . . . and, well, you already saw that." Fred had lowered his voice like he'd just been caught shooting craps in church.

Ed nodded, and I told Fred to get back inside.

As I heard the lock click on the door, I whispered to Ed. "You think maybe they can read our minds?"

Ed shrugged.

The things were about ten, maybe twelve feet high and seemed to float above the ground on a circular frilled platform. I say "floated" because they didn't leave any marks as they moved along, not even in the soft dirt of the alleyway that ran behind Bill's and Ma's store.

The platform was about a foot deep and, above that, the thing's body kind of tapered up like a glass stem until it reached another frilly overhang—like a mushroom's head—at the top. Halfway between the two platforms a collar of tendrils or thin wings—like the gossamer veils of a jellyfish—stuck out from the stem a foot or so and then dropped down limply about three feet. These seemed to twitch and twirl of their own accord, no matter whether a wind was blowing or not, and it didn't take me too long to figure out these were what passed for arms and hands on the things' own world.

I looked up at the first creature's top section, trying to see if there were any kind of airholes or eyes but there was nothing, although the texture of the skin covering was kind of opaque or translucent . . . see-through, for want of a better phrase, and I could see things moving around in there, shifting and reforming. Where the noise they made came out, I couldn't tell. And we never did find out.

We watched as the creatures moved closer. Suddenly,

the one at the front turned around real fast and the
hand-arm things fluttered outward, like a sheet settling
on a bed, and, just for a moment, they touched my shoulder. There was something akin to affection there. At the
time, I thought I was maybe imagining it . . . maybe
reading the creature's thought-waves or something, but
I was later to discover that there was, if not an outright
affection, then at least a feeling of familiarity on the
creature's part.

This confrontation lasted only a few seconds, a minute
at the most, and then the creatures moved back away
from us in the direction of the Sheriff's office, the wing
things outstretched toward us as they went.

"What did you make of that?" Ed Brewster said, his
voice a little croaky and hoarse.

"I have absolutely no idea at all," I said.

I kept watching because one of the creatures intrigued
me more than the others. This one carried what seemed
to be some kind of foam box, thick with piled-up layers
of what looked like cotton candy. All the time we'd been
"meeting" with the leader—we supposed the thing that
had touched me *was* the leader—this other creature was
removing small pieces of foam which it seemed to absorb
into its tendrils. It was still doing it as the three of them
moved down the alleyway. Just as they reached the back
of the Sheriff's office, the leader put down its wings,
turned around and, leaving the other two behind, moved
up onto the sidewalk and out of sight.

I turned at the sound of hurried footsteps behind me
and saw Jimmy-James running along the alleyway, his
face beaming a wide smile. Ma Chetton was following
him, her head still turned in the direction of the street
to see if any of the creatures were following *her*.

"What about *that!*" JJ said. Then, "What *about* that!"

I nodded; when I turned to look at Ed, he was nodding, too. There didn't seem much else to do.

"Did they say anything?" Jimmy-James asked. "Did
they say where they've come from?"

"Nope," I said. "Not a word. Just that mournful wailing. Gives me the creeps . . . sounds like a coyote."

"Or a baby teething," Ma said breathlessly.

"Same here," said JJ. "I tried them with everything I know . . . English, French, German, Spanish, Russian . . . quite a few more. And I tried out a couple of hybrids, too."

"Like standing in the United Nations," Ma Chetton muttered testily, her breath rasping. "Or hanging atop the Tower of Babel come Doomsday."

"What the hell are hybrids?" Ed Brewster asked.

"Mixtures of two or three languages," JJ explained. "In the old days, that was the way most folks communicated . . . I mean before any one single language or dialect had gained enough of a footing to be commonplace. And I tried them with all kinds of signs and stuff, but they didn't seem to know what I was doing. I thought maybe they would have known all about our language by listening to our radio waves out there in outer space. But it was no-go. I can't figure out how they communicate with each other at all," he said. "Unless it's that wailing noise or maybe through that thing that one of them's carrying around."

"You mean the box thing? The thing that looks like a pile of cotton candy?"

JJ nodded. "He's messing with that thing all the time, changing it even as I'm trying to talk to them."

"Yeah," I agreed, "but did you notice he's taking things *out* instead of adding to what's already in there."

"I'd noticed that," JJ said. "I was wondering if that stuff is absorbed into him and enables him to communicate to the others. Like a translator."

I shrugged. It was all too much for me.

Ed glanced around to make sure none of those creatures had sneaked up on him and said, "We figure they can read our minds."

"Really?" said JJ. "How's that?"

"Well," Ed said, matter-of-factly, "they knew we were coming out here into the alleyway."

JJ frowned and glanced at me before returning his full attention to Ed.

Ed gave a characteristic shrug. "Why else would they come on down here from the street if they didn't know we were coming out?"

While JJ mulled that over, I said, "What do you figure they want, JJ?"

The back door to the poolroom opened and Abel Bodeen peered out. "Is there any of those things out there?"

"Nope, they've gone down to see the Sheriff," I said.

Abel pulled a face and gave a wry smile. "That should please Benjamin no end," he said with a chuckle.

The fact was that the creatures *did* please Sheriff Ben Travers, as it turned out. Or they didn't *dis*please him anyway. The truth of the matter was that the aliens didn't do anything to upset or irritate anyone. In fact, they didn't do anything at all.

"Why the hell did they come, Derby?" Abel Bodeen asked me a couple of days after they'd . . . after we'd first seen them.

"Beats me," I said.

We were sitting out on the old straight-backed chairs Molly Waldon had left out in front of her and Vince's general store, watching the creatures wander around the town, just as they had been doing all the time. But I was watching a little more intently than I had done at first. The folks around town had become used to the aliens after two full days and nobody seemed to care much *what* they were there for. So it's probably fair to say that people hadn't picked up that the attitude of the creatures was changing. It wasn't changing by much, but it *was* changing.

"You've noticed, haven't you?"

I shielded my eyes from the glare of the late afternoon November sunshine and looked across at Jimmy-James. "Noticed what?"

He looked across at two of the creatures gliding along the other side of the street. "They're slowing down."

I followed his gaze and, sure enough, the creatures did seem to be slower than they had been at first. But it was more than that. They seemed to be more cautious. I mentioned this to JJ and Abel, and to Ed and Estelle who were leaning on what remained of an old hitching rail at the edge of the sidewalk.

Ed snorted. "That don't make no sense at all," he

said. "Why would they be cautious now, when they've been here two goddam days."

"Ed, watch your mouth," Estelle whined in her high-pitched voice.

"He's right," agreed Jimmy-James.

"Who?" Ed asked. "Me or him?"

"Both of you." JJ got to his feet and strode across to the post behind Ed and leaned. "They *are* getting slower and they do seem to be more . . . more careful," he said, choosing his words. "And, no, it doesn't make any sense for them to be more careful the longer they're here."

"Nothing for them to be nervous about, that's for sure," Abel said. "They've got us wrapped up neat as a Christmas gift."

The aliens had effectively cut off the town. There were no phone lines and the roads were . . . well, they were impassable. It was Doc Maynard had seen it first, trying to get his old Ford Fairlane out to check on Sally Iaccoca's father, over toward Bellingham. Frank Iaccoca had taken a bad fall—cracked a couple of ribs, Doc said—and Doc had him trussed up like Boris Karloff in the old *Mummy* movie.

The car had cut out three miles out of Forest Plains and there was nothing Doc could do to get it going again. So he'd come back into town for help, without even taking a look under the hood, and Abel, Johnny Deveraux, and me had gone out there to give him some help. Johnny, who works at Phil Masham's garage, had taken some tools and a spare battery in case it was something simple he could fix out on the road. Doc Maynard was not renowned for looking after his automobile.

When we got out there, Johnny tried the ignition, and it was dead. But when he made to move around to the front of the car to open the hood, he suddenly started floundering and dropped the battery. That's when we found the barrier.

A "force field" is what Jimmy-James called it.

Everything looked completely normal up ahead in front of Doc Maynard's Fairlane, but there was no way for us to get to it. It felt like cloth but not porous. JJ said it was an invisible synthetic membrane—whatever *that* was—and he reckoned the creatures had set it up around the town to protect their spaceship. Sure enough, the same barrier traveled all the way around town . . . or so we figured. We tried different points on farm tracks and woodland paths and each one came to a complete halt.

Like it or not, we were caught like fish in a bowl. But that didn't seem to matter . . . at least not until JJ took a look in the creatures' "book."

"There he goes, if it is a 'he,' " said Jimmy-James, pointing to the creature with the box of cotton candy. The funny thing was that the box now looked to have a lot less of the stuff in it than it had done at first. The first time we'd seen it, the thing had looked to be almost full.

"The other thing," said JJ in a soft voice that made you think he was realizing what he was about to say at exactly the same time as he said it, "is they seem not to be touching people with those . . . those veil things."

"Yeah," I agreed. "I guess that was what I meant about them being more cautious. Part of it, anyway."

Ed snorted. "Maybe it's a case of the more they see of us the less they like."

Estelle rubbed Ed Brewster's oiled hair and puckered up her mouth. "I'm sure they like what they see of you, honey," she trilled without changing the shape of her mouth. "Anyone would." It sounded as though Estelle was talking to a newborn babe sitting in a stroller. Ed must've thought so, too, because he told her to can it while he readjusted his quiff.

"We need to get a look in that box thing," JJ said.

"How are we going to do that?" I asked. "And what good is it going to do us anyway? Just looks like a load of gunk to me."

JJ stepped away from the rail and out onto the street. "That's just it," he shouted over his shoulder as he strode across to the creature with the box. "None of us has seen what's in there, not up close."

We watched the confrontation.

Jimmy-James stopped right in front of the creature and it turned around. Almost immediately, the little veil-arms wafted out as though blown by a breeze and settled on JJ's shoulders, the wailing sound rising a pitch or two in the process. Then it started to back away, its arms still blowing free.

JJ shouted over to me to come on along. Ed Brewster stood up and moved alongside me. "I'm coming, too," he said.

"Now you be careful what you're doing, Ed, honey," Estelle warbled.

"I will, Estelle, I will," Ed said, with maybe just a hint of a sigh. And the two of us walked onto the street to join JJ. Which was how we got into the creatures' spaceship.

The alien with the book kept on backing away from the three of us and we just kept on walking after it. Eventually, we reached the ship, where we discovered two more of the creatures standing by the ramp.

The creatures then backed on up into the ship. We kept on following.

A few minutes later the three of us were standing amidst a whole array of what looked to be lumps of foam, all of various sizes, piled up on or stuck against other lumps. Some of the lumps were circular—cylindrical, JJ said—and others looked like tears of modeling clay thumbed into place by a gigantic hand without design or reason.

Up inside the ship, the things' wing-arms were fluttering faster and more frequently than ever . . . and the alien that we reckoned to be recording the whole visit was mightily busy, removing small pieces of foam with the tendrils and absorbing them. When I glanced inside the box, I saw there was hardly anything in it.

Over to one side of the crowded room a wide lamp thing stood by itself. Standing beneath the lamp, two aliens were seemingly absorbed in another of the boxes, their wing-arm fluttering like a leaf caught in a draft This particular box was completely full, a collection of multi colored shapes and lumps and pieces, all pressed into each other or standing alone.

"We need to get a look at that," JJ whispered to Ed and me.

"Leave it to me," Ed Brewster said. He walked across

to the box and lifted it with both hands. "Okay if I borrow this for a while, ol' buddy?" he said, waving the box in front of the two creatures.

The things didn't seem to do anything as Ed stepped back and moved back alongside us, although their arms were fluttering faster than ever. Then, suddenly, the little arm-wings dropped limp and the two creatures turned around. As they did this, the creature standing in front of the other two in the center of the room waved its arms, and then it, too, spun around.

"Let's get out of here," Jimmy-James said. "I'm starting to get a bad feeling about this."

As we ran down the platform leading back onto Sycamore Street, I asked Jimmy-James what he'd meant by that last remark. But he just shook his head.

"It's too fantastic to even think about," was all he'd say. "Just let me take a look at the box, and then maybe I'll be able to get an idea."

We hightailed it back to Jack and Edna Bannister's house down on Beech Avenue and, while me and Ed drank cup after cup of JJ's mom's strong coffee, JJ himself pored over the contents of the alien box. It was almost three in the morning when a wild-eyed Jimmy-James rushed into the lounge and slammed the box onto the table. Ed was asleep, curled up like a baby on the sofa, and I was reading the *TV Guide*.

"I have to look at the other box," he said. "Now!"

Ed smacked his lips together loudly and shuffled around on the sofa.

I looked up from a feature on *Gilligan's Island* and was immediately surprised to see how much Jimmy-James resembled that hapless shipwreck survivor. "What's up?"

JJ shook his head and ran his hands through his hair. I noticed straightaway that they were shaking. "A lot, maybe . . . maybe nothing. I don't know."

"You want to—"

"I've been through all of the usual coding techniques," JJ said, ticking off on his outstretched fingers. "I've applied the Patagonian Principle of repeated shapes, color motifs, spacing. . . . I've run the Spectromic

Law of shading relationships and the old Inca constructional communication dynamics . . ."

I held up a hand and waved for him to stop. "Whoa,
boy . . . what the hell are you talking about?"

JJ crouched down in front of me and looked up into
my eyes. "It makes sense," he said. "I've made it
work . . . made the patterns fit."

"You *understand* it?" I glanced across at the box of
jumbled shapes. *"That?"*

JJ nodded emphatically. "Yes!" he said. Then, "No!
Oh, God, I don't know. That's why I need to check.
And I need to do it tonight. Tomorrow may be too late."

"I still don't know what you're—"

The resident genius of Forest Plains placed a hand on
my knee. "No time," he said. "No time to talk. It has
to be *now.*"

I studied his face for a few seconds and saw the look
in his eyes: there was an urgent need there, sure . . . but
there was something else, too. It was fear. Jimmy-James
Bannister looked as scared as any man could be. "Okay,
let's go do it."

He stood up and looked at Ed. "What about him?"

"He'll be fine. We expecting any trouble in there?"

"I don't think so."

"Okay. Let's go."

And we went.

The ship was silent and dark. JJ borrowed his old
man's flashlight and the two of us crept up that platform
and into the depths of the creatures' rocketship. The
place was deserted, which was just as well. It didn't take
too long before JJ found the second box—the one the
creature had been using all the time—and he scooped it
into his arms and rushed out of the ship.

We were back in the house almost as soon as we had
left. The whole thing had taken less than ten minutes.

I watched as JJ sat in front of the new box—now
containing but a few lumps and dollops of that clay-
stuff—wringing his hands and muttering to himself. I
couldn't stand it anymore and I grabbed hold of JJ and
shook him until I could hear his teeth clattering. "What

the hell *is* it, JJ? Why don't you tell me, for God's sake?"

He seemed to come to his senses then, and he quieted down. Then he said softly, "It's the aliens."

"What about them?" I said.

"They're . . ." He seemed to trying hard to find the right words. "They're palindromic."

"They're *what?*"

"They run backward . . . their time is different to ours."

"Their time is *different* to ours? Like *how* different?"

"It moves in a different direction . . . backward instead of forward—except to them it *is* forward. But to us it's—" JJ waved his arms around like he was about to take off. "Well, it's bass-ackwards is what it is."

"What the hell is all the goddamn noise about?" Ed said, turning over on the sofa. He reached for his pack of Luckies and shook one into the corner of his mouth, lighting it with a match.

I didn't know what to say and looked across at Jimmy-James. "Maybe you'd better tell him—*us!*"

JJ sat down at the table next to the two boxes, one full and one almost empty. He smiled and said calmly, "It's this way.

"I've broken the basics of their language. It wasn't really too difficult once I'd eliminated the obvious no-go areas." He pointed to the almost empty box. "This is the 'book' they're using now . . . the one that's recording everything that happens *here* . . . here on Earth."

"Looks like a mound of clay to me," Ed said, blowing smoke across the table and shuffling one edge of the box away from him.

"That's because you're you," JJ said impatiently, "because you're from Earth. To them, it's the equivalent of a diary . . . a ship's log, if you like."

Ed settled back on the sofa. "Okay. What's it say?"

"It starts at the very moment they opened the doors. It says they found a group of creatures standing outside watching them disembark . . . get out. These creatures, their record says, held instruments . . . they thought at first the things might be gifts."

I frowned. "When was that? I never held no instrument."

JJ leaned forward. "That's just it. You didn't. It didn't happen. At least it didn't happen yet." He lifted the box onto his knee and pointed at the shapes inside. "See, it's all arranged in a linear fashion, with each piece linking to others, building across the box in waves and doubling back to the other side. It's like layers of pasta furled over on itself. But see the way that it's arranged . . . you can pull pieces out of place and the gap stays. It's an intricate constructional form of basic communication. I say 'basic' because I've only been able to pick up the very basic fundamentals. There's much much more to it . . . but I don't have the time to work it out. Not now, anyway."

Ed tapped his cigarette ash onto the carpet and rubbed it in with his free hand. *"Why* don't you have the time? What's the panic?"

"The panic is that the record goes on to say how surprised they all were to find creatures—"

"Not half as surprised as we were to see them!" I said.

JJ carried on without comment. "It goes on to say how they came out and stood in front of us and nobody—none of *us*—moved or did anything. We just stood there. Then we all moved away and went to some structures. They walked around and looked at the outside of these structures and then went back into their ship. They were concerned that they had somehow created the situation by their ship's power."

"Huh?"

JJ waved for Ed to keep quite and continued.

"Listen. Then it says that, after some early investigations—they say that much more research has to be carried out—after these early investigations, we came on board the ship and borrowed their log."

"Yeah, well, we've got the log," I said. "For what good it's doing us."

"But none of that other stuff happened," JJ said. "This stuff in here . . ." He pointed at the individual pieces of clay . . . lifted one end of the carefully interwoven sheet of linked pieces and tiny constructions.

"This only amounts to less than one single day. The creatures have been here almost three days now. There's no mention of all the other things that have happened. And bear this in mind . . . the stuff in here is what's *left,* as far as we're concerned."

I figured someone had to ask so it might as well be me. "How do you mean 'what's left'?"

"I mean, we've been watching the creature remove stuff from this box all the time he's been here, right?" I nodded and saw Ed Brewster do the same. *"And,"* JJ continued, emphasizing the word, "What we have here, *now*—and which represents what's left in the box after he's been removing the clay stuff for almost three days— is a record of when they first *arrived.* The creature has been removing the stuff from the *top*—I've watched him . . . so have you, Derby; you, too, Ed—and leaving the stuff at the bottom completely intact. And that stuff records them *arriving."*

Ed and I sat silently, watching Jimmy-James. I didn't have the first idea of what to say and I was sure Ed didn't either. JJ must have sensed it because he started speaking again without giving us much of a chance to comment.

"Derby, the creatures . . . have you noticed how they seem always to be turned away from you when you go up to speak to them?"

We'd already figured that the clear part of the mushroom tops more or less worked as the things' faces. And it was true, now that Jimmy-James mentioned it, that the things always had that part of themselves turned away whenever you went up to them.

"That's because at the moment you start trying to communicate with them, they've actually just finished trying to do the same with you."

"That sounds like horseshit," Ed said. "Not even Perry Mason could convict somebody on that evidence."

"And have you noticed how they keep facing you when they move away? That's because, in their time frame, they're *approaching* you."

Some of it was beginning to make some kind of sense to me, and JJ noticed that.

"And we've all commented on how their attitude to us is changing," he said. "You said they seemed to be getting slower . . . more cautious."

"That I did," I remembered.

"Well, they're getting more cautious because where they are now is they've just *arrived*. Where they were when we first saw them was in their third or fourth day around us. They were *used* to us then . . . they're not now."

"Okay, okay, I hear what you say, JJ," I said. "Maybe the creatures' time does move in reverse, if that's what you're saying. I don't understand it, but then I don't understand a lot of things. The thing that puzzles me is why you're getting so hot under the collar about this. Everything's going to go okay: we saw them 'arrive'—which you say is when they left—and nothing happened in the meantime. All we have to worry about is our future which is their past . . . and they've come through that okay, haven't—"

I saw JJ's face screw up like he'd just sucked on a lemon. He reached over and pulled the full box across to the edge of the table, held up another of those interlaced jigsaw puzzles of multicolored clay pieces. "This is the previous diary," he said, "the one before the one they started after they had arrived.

"You remember I said there was an entry in the current ship's log about the creatures being concerned that they had somehow created the situation they found when they arrived?" We both nodded. "Well, that situation is explained in a little more detail in the previous record." At this point, Jimmy-James sat back on his chair and seemed to draw in his breath.

"Okay: the log says that they were following the course taken by an earlier ship—one that had disappeared a long time ago—when they experienced some kind of terrible space storm the like of which had never previously been recorded. For a time, it was touch and go that they would survive, though survive they did. But when the storm subsided, they were nowhere that they recognized. After a few of their time periods—which, based on the limited information in the new book, I

would put at quarter days . . . give or take an hour—
there was a sudden blinding flash of light and huge explosion. When they checked their instruments, they discovered that the ship was about to impact upon a planet
which had apparently appeared out of nothingness."

Ed looked confused. "So this explosion went off *before* they hit the planet?"

JJ nodded.

"I don't get it," Ed said.

I said to let Jimmy-James finish.

"There hadn't been any planet there at all until then,"
JJ said. "Then, there it was. And that planet was Earth.

"They narrowly averted the collision," JJ went on,
"and settled onto the planet's surface. After checking
atmospheric conditions they prepared to go outside. The
log finished with them wondering what they'll find
there."

While JJ had been talking I'd been holding my breath
without even realizing it. I let it out with a huge sigh.
"Are you sure?"

The owner of the best mind in town shook his head
sadly.

"But you *think* you're right."

"I think I'm right, yes."

"And they found us, right?"

"Right, Ed," JJ said. "They found us." He waited.

I thought over everything I had heard and knew there
was something there that should bother me . . . but I
couldn't for the life of me figure out what it was. Then
it hit me. "The blinding flash," I said. "If before that
blinding flash there was nothing and after it there was
the Earth . . . then, if the creatures' time *does* move
backward, and their version of their arrival is—or *will*
be—our version of their departure, that means the aliens
will destroy the planet when they leave."

JJ was nodding. "That's the way I figure it, too," he
said.

I looked across at Ed and he looked across at me.
"What are we going to do?" I asked JJ.

JJ shrugged. "We have to stop them leaving . . . in
terms of our *own* time progression."

"But, in their terms, that would be to stop them *arriving* . . . and they're already here."

"Yes, that's true. In just the same way, if we do something to stop them—and I see only one course, they've arrived already as far as we're concerned. What we do is prevent their departure in our terms."

Ed Brewster shook his head and pushed himself off the sofa onto the floor. "Jesus Christ, I'm getting a goddam headache here," he said. "Their arrival is our departure . . . their departure is our arrival . . . but if they don't do this, how could they do that . . . and as for *palindoodad* . . ." He stood up and rubbed his hands through his hair. "This all sounds like something off *Howdy Doody*. What does it all mean? How can we play about with time like that? How can *any*body play about with time like that?"

"I think it may have been the space storm," JJ said. "I think, maybe, their time normally progresses in exactly the same way as our own . . . although Albert Einstein said we shouldn't allow ourselves to be railroaded about time being a one-way linear progre—"

"Jesus, Jimmy-James!!" Ed shouted, and JJ winced . . . glancing up toward his parents' bedroom while we all waited for sounds of people moving around to see what all the noise was about. "Jesus," Ed continued in a hoarse whisper, "I can't keep up with all of this stuff. Just keep it simple."

"Okay," JJ said. "I figure one of two things: either the aliens always move backward in time or they don't.

"If we go for the first option, then we have to ask how they found their way into our universe."

"The space storm?" I suggested.

"I think so," said JJ. "If we go for the second option—that they *don't* normally travel backward in time—then we have to ask what might have caused the change." He looked across at me again and gave a small smile.

I nodded. "The space storm."

"Kee-rect! So either way, the storm did the deed. But whatever the cause, the fact remains that they're here and we have to prevent whatever it was that caused the explosion."

We sat for a minute or so considering that. I didn't like the sound of what I'd heard but I liked the sound of the silence that followed even less. I looked at Ed. He didn't seem too happy either. "So how do we do that, JJ?" I said.

JJ shrugged. "We have to kill them . . . kill them *all,*" he said. He pulled across the almost empty box that we all reckoned was the aliens' current ship's log and lifted up the few lacelike constructions of interwoven clay pieces. "And we have to do it *tonight.*"

I don't remember the actual rounding up of people that night. And I don't recall listening to JJ telling his story again and again. But tell it he did, and the people got rounded up. There was me, Sheriff Ben, Ed, Abel, Jerry, and Jimmy-James Bannister himself. We walked silently out to the spaceship and weren't at all surprised to see faint wisps of steam coming out from the sides or that the platform was up for the first time since . . . well, the first time since three days ago. As we waited alongside the dusty ground of the vacant lot across from Bill's and Ma's poolroom, I heard JJ call out my name.

"Derby . . ."

I turned around and he held up his rifle, then nodded to the others standing there on Sycamore Street, all of them carrying the same kind of thing. "Instruments," he said.

By then it was too late. The bets were placed.

As soon as they appeared we started firing. We moved forward as one mass, vigilantes, firing and clearing, firing and clearing. The creatures never knew what hit them. They just folded up and fell to the ground, some inside the ship and others onto Sycamore Street. When they were down, Sheriff Ben went up to each one and put a couple of bullets into its head from his handgun.

We continued into the ship and finished the job.

There were sixteen of them. We combed the ship from top to bottom like men in a fever, a destructive killing frenzy, pulling out pieces of foam and throwing them out into the street . . . in much the same way as you might rip out the wires in the back of a radio to stop it

from playing dance band music. God, but we were
scared.

When the sun came up, we put the aliens back on the
ship and doused the whole thing in gasoline. Then we
put a match to it. It burned quietly, as we might have
expected of any vehicle operated by such gentle creatures. It burned for two whole days and nights. When it
had finished, we loaded the remains onto Vince Waldon's flatbed truck and took them out to Darien Lake.
The barrier—or "force field" as JJ called it—had gone.
Things were more or less back to normal. For a time.

It turned out that JJ found more of those ship's logs
that night, when the rest of us were tearing and destroying. Turned out that he sneaked them off the ship and
kept them safe until he could get back for them. I didn't
find that out right away.

He came round to my house about a week later.

"Derby, we have to talk," he said.

"What about?"

"The aliens."

"Oh, for crissakes, I—" I was going to tell him that I
couldn't stand to talk about those creatures anymore,
couldn't stand to think about what we'd done to them.
But his face looked so in need of conversation that I
stopped short. "What about the aliens?" I said.

That was when Jimmy-James told me he'd taken the
old diaries from inside the ship.

Walking along Sycamore, he said, "Have you ever
thought about what we did?"

I groaned.

"No, not about us shooting the aliens . . . about how
we changed their past?" Someone had left a soda bottle
lying on the sidewalk and JJ kicked it gently into the
gutter. The clatter it made somehow set off a dog barking, and I tried to place the sound but couldn't. It did
sound right, though, that mixture of a lonely dog barking
and the night and talking about the aliens . . . like it all
belonged together. "I mean," JJ went on, "we changed
our future—which is okay: anyone can do that—but we
actually changed things that, as far as they were con-

cerned, had already *happened.* Did you think about that?"

"Nope." We walked in silence for a minute or so, then I said, "Did *you?*"

"A little—at first. Then, when I'd read the diaries, I thought about it a lot." He stopped and turned to me. "You know the big diary, the full box? The one that ended with details of the explosion?"

I didn't say anything but I knew what he was talking about.

"I went into more of the details about the missing ship . . . the one that had disappeared? The last message they received from this other ship was at these same coordinates."

"So?"

He shrugged. "The message said they'd been moving along when they suddenly noticed a planet that wasn't there before."

"Do I want to hear this?"

"I think the Earth is destined for destruction. The aliens were fulfilling some kind of cosmic plan."

"JJ, you're starting to lose me."

"Yeah, I'm starting to lose *me,*" he said with a short laugh. But there was no humor there. "This other ship— the first one, the one that the diary talks about—I've calculated that it's about forty years in their past. Or in our *future.*"

I grabbed a hold of his arm and spun him around. "You mean there are more of those things coming?"

JJ nodded. "In about forty years, give or take. And they're going to be going through this section of the universe and BOOM! . . ." He clapped his hands loudly. "'Hey, Captain,'" JJ said in an accent that sounded vaguely foreign, "'there's a planet over there!' And there's no kewpie doll for guessing the name of that planet."

"So, if they're moving backward, too . . . then that means they'll destroy us." The dog barked again somewhere over to our right.

"Yep. But if the aliens we just killed were going to do the job, how could the others have done it, too?"

"Another planet?"

JJ shook his head. "The coordinates seemed quite specific . . . as far as I could make out in the time I had. That's another problem right there. I can't go back and double-check."

"Why's that?"

"The diaries are gone. They liquefied . . . turned into mulch."

"All of it?"

"Every bit. But it *was* Earth they were talking about. I'd bet my life on it . . . hell, I'd even bet *yours*."

That was when I fully realized just how much of a friend Jimmy-James Bannister truly was. He placed a greater value on my life than on his own.

"Which means, of course," JJ said, "that we were destined to stop the aliens the way we did."

"We were *meant* to do it?"

"Looks that way to me." He glanced at me and must have seen me relax a little. "That make you feel better?"

"A little."

"Me, too."

"What is it? What is it that's causing the destruction?"

"Hey, if I knew *that* . . . Way I figure it, they're maybe warping across space somehow—kind of like matter transference. The magazines have been talking about that kind of thing for years: they call them black funnels or something.

"But maybe they're also warping across time progressions, too," he said, "maybe without even realizing they're *doing* it. Then, as soon as they appear into our dimension or plane, one that operates on a different time progression . . . it's like a chemical reaction and . . ."

I clapped my hands. "I know," I said. "BOOM!"

"Right."

"So what do we do?"

"Right now? Nothing. Right now, the balance has been restored. But the paradox will be repeated . . . around 2003, 2004." He smiled at me. "Give or take."

We went on walking and talking, but that's about all I can remember of that night.

The next day, or maybe the one after, we told Ed Brewster. And we made ourselves a pact.

We couldn't bring ourselves to tell anyone about what had happened. Who would believe us? Where was the proof? A few boxes of slime? Forget it. And if we showed them the blackened stuff at the bottom of Darien Lake . . . well, it was just a heap of blackened stuff at the bottom of a lake.

But there was another reason we didn't want to tell anyone outside of Forest Plains about what we'd done. Just like nobody else in town wanted to tell anyone. We were ashamed.

So we made a pact. We'd keep our eyes peeled—keep watching the skies, as the newspaperman said in *The Thing* movie . . . and when something happens, we'll know what to do.

What really gets to me—still, after all this time—is not just that there's a bunch of aliens somewhere out there, maybe heading on a disaster course with Earth . . . but that, back on their own planet or dimension, there's *another* bunch of creatures listening to their messages. And *that* bunch we killed on the streets of Forest Plains almost forty years ago.

> "What seest thou else
> In the dark backward and abysm of time?
> —William Shakespeare, *The Tempest*

Science Fiction Anthologies

☐ **FUTURE NET**   UE2723—$5.99
 Martin H. Greenberg & Larry Segriff, editors

From a chat room romance gone awry . . . to an alien monitoring the Net as an
advance scout for interstellar invasion . . . to a grief-stricken man given the
chance to access life after death . . . here are sixteen original tales that you
must read before you venture online again, stories from such top visionaries as
Gregory Benford, Josepha Sherman, Mickey Zucker Reichert, Daniel Ransom,
Jody Lynn Nye, and Jane Lindskold.

☐ **FUTURE EARTHS: UNDER SOUTH AMERICAN SKIES**
 Mike Resnick & Gardner Dozois, editors   UE2581—$4.99

From a plane crash that lands its passengers in a survival situation completely
alien to anything they've ever experienced, to a close encounter of the insect
kind, to a woman who has journeyed unimaginably far from home—here are
stories from the rich culture of South America, with its mysteriously vanished
ancient civilizations and magnificent artifacts, its modern-day contrasts between
sophisticated city dwellers and impoverished villagers.

☐ **SPACE OPERA**   UE2714—$5.99
 Anne McCaffrey & Elizabeth Anne Scarborough, Editors

Welcome to an interstellar concert beyond your wildest imagining, as you rocket
to distant worlds in twenty original tales powered by the music of the galaxies
written by such modern-day maestros as Gene Wolfe, Peter Beagle, Anne
McCaffrey, Alan Dean Foster, Marion Zimmer Bradley, Elizabeth Ann Scarborough, and Charles de Lint.

☐ **SHERLOCK HOLMES IN ORBIT**   UE2636—$5.50
 Mike Resnick & Martin H. Greenberg, editors
 Authorized by Dame Jean Conan Doyle

Not even time can defeat the master sleuth in this intriguing anthology about
the most famous detective in the annals of literature. From confrontations with
Fu Manchu and Moriarity, to a commission Holmes undertakes for a vampire,
here are 26 new stories all of which remain true to the spirit and personality of
Sir Arthur Conan Doyle's most enduring creation.

Welcome to DAW's Gallery of Ghoulish Delights!

☐ **DRACULA: PRINCE OF DARKNESS**
 Martin H. Greenberg, editor
A blood-draining collection of all-original Dracula stories. From Dracula's traditional stalking grounds to the heart of modern-day cities, the Prince of Darkness casts his spell over his prey in a private blood drive from which there is no escape!
UE2531—$4.99

☐ **THE TIME OF THE VAMPIRES**
May 1996
 P.N. Elrod & Martin H. Greenberg, editors
From a vampire blessed by Christ to the truth about the notorious Oscar Wilde to a tale of vampirism and the Bow Street Runners, here are 18 original tales of vampires from Tanya Huff, P.N. Elrod, Lois Tilton, and others.
UE2693—$5.50

☐ **WEREWOLVES**
 Martin H. Greenberg, editor
Here is a brand-new anthology of original stories about the third member of the classic horror cinema triumvirate—the werewolf, a shapeshifter who prowls the darkness, the beast within humankind unleashed to prey upon its own.
UE2654—$5.50

☐ **WHITE HOUSE HORRORS**
 Martin H. Greenberg, editor
The White House has seen many extraordinary events unforld within its well-guarded walls. Sixteen top writers such as Brian Hodge, Grant Masterton, Bill Crider, Billie Sue Mosiman, and Edward Lee relate of some of the more unforgettable.
UE2659—$5.99

☐ **MISKATONIC UNIVERSITY**
 Martin H. Greenberg & Robert Weinberg, editors
Miskatonic U is a unique institution, made famous by the master of the horrific, H.P. Lovecraft. Thirteen original stories will introduce you to the dark side of education, and prove once and for all that a little arcane knowledge can be a very dangerous thing, especially in the little Yankee college town of Arkham.
UE2722—$5.99

Buy them at your local bookstore or use this convenient coupon for ordering.

PENGUIN USA   P.O. Box 999—Dep. #17109, Bergenfield, New Jersey 07621

Please send me the DAW BOOKS I have checked above, for which I am enclosing
$_____ (please add $2.00 to cover postage and handling). Send check or money order (no cash or C.O.D.'s) or charge by Mastercard or VISA (with a $15.00 minimum). Prices and numbers are subject to change without notice.

Card #_____ Exp. Date _____
Signature_____
Name_____
Address_____
City _____ State _____ Zip Code _____

For faster service when ordering by credit card call **1-800-253-6476**

Allow a minimum of 4-6 weeks for delivery. This offer is subject to change without notice.

Don't Miss These Exciting DAW Anthologies

SWORD AND SORCERESS
Marion Zimmer Bradley, editor
☐ Book XIV   UE2741—$5.99

OTHER ORIGINAL ANTHOLOGIES
Mercedes Lackey, editor
☐ SWORD OF ICE: And Other Tales of Valdemar   UE2720—$5.99

Martin H. Greenberg, editor
☐ CELEBRITY VAMPIRES   UE2667—$4.99
☐ VAMPIRE DETECTIVES   UE2626—$4.99
☐ WEREWOLVES   UE2654—$5.50
☐ WHITE HOUSE HORRORS   UE2659—$5.99
☐ ELF FANTASTIC   UE2736—$5.99

Martin H. Greenberg & Lawrence Schimel, editors
☐ TAROT FANTASTIC   UE2729—$5.99
☐ THE FORTUNE TELLER   UE2748—$5.99

Mike Resnick & Martin Greenberg, editors
☐ RETURN OF THE DINOSAURS   UE2753—$5.99
☐ SHERLOCK HOLMES IN ORBIT   UE2636—$5.50

Richard Gilliam & Martin H. Greenberg, editors
☐ PHANTOMS OF THE NIGHT   UE2696—$5.99

Norman Partridge & Martin H. Greenberg, editors
☐ IT CAME FROM THE DRIVE-IN   UE2680—$5.50

Attention:

DAW Collectors

Many readers of DAW Books have written requesting information on early titles and book numbers to assist in the collection of DAW editions since the first of our titles appeared in April 1972.

We have prepared a list of all DAW titles, giving their authors, titles, reissue information, sequence numbers, original and current order numbers, and ISBN numbers.

If you would like a copy of this list, please write to the address below and enclose a check or money order for two dollars or the equivalent amount in stamps to cover the handling and postage costs. Never send cash through the mail.

DAW Books, Inc.
Dept. C
375 Hudson Street
New York, NY 10014-3658